SECONDHAND SUNSETS

Kittleson's writing style fosters instant empathy as her quiet heroine, Addie, struggles through daily living in Iowa during WW2. Readers are introduced to Addie through patriotism, friendship, and self-realization. "I've spent my whole life in fear instead of living each day," highlights Addie's growth in overcoming an emotionally abusive husband. Highest recommendation.

Carolyn Cobb

Kittleson deftly writes strong female characters facing heartbreaking tragedies. *Until Then* features two: Marian, caught in the Blitz, and Dorothy, a surgical nurse whose work with the 11th Evacuation Hospital has taken her to North Africa, through Sicily and into France. Their stories intertwine in a narrative that touches then heals the soul. Highly, highly recommended!

Literary Soirée

In Times Like These clearly portrays the difficulties for women during WW2. First, there are the challenges of raising food, preserving it, making money stretch, wisely using ration cards and just plain living in fear of the war. But then the overlay of Addie's controlling husband made me instantly empathize with the main character. His verbally abusive and cold treatment of Addie unfortunately is not just a problem from another era. God's provision for her was intriguing. The value of faith, friendship and compassion are evident in this book. I personally enjoyed the food tips and recipes, as well as vivid descriptions of farm life. This may be my favorite book by Gail Kittleson. It is the first in the series, *Women of the Heartland*. Be sure to read the books in order.

Cleo Lampos, co-author of
The Food that Held the World Together
A World War 2 Holiday Scrapbook

Also by Gail Kittleson

Women of the Heartland Series
With Each New Dawn
A Purpose True
All for the Cause
Until Then
&
Kiss Me Once Again
a Women of the Heartland story

and

In This Together
Catching Up With Daylight

Secondhand *Sunsets*

a novel of the Mogollon Rim

GAIL KITTLESON

WordCrafts

Secondhand Sunsets
Copyright © 2021
Gail Kittleson

ISBN: 978-1-952474-54-5

Cover concept and design by Mike Parker.

Published by WordCrafts Press
Cody, Wyoming 82414
www.wordcrafts.net

Dedication

To M, who first introduced us to Mogollon Rim Country.

The 1846 Albert Speyer Expedition to Mexico included Dr. Adolph Wislizenus, whose report, *A Memoir of a Tour to Northern Mexico* (Washington, Tippin and Streeter, 1846), was also published by the 30th Congress, First Session as Senate Misc. Doc. No. 26. Previously, Dr. Wislizenus had toured the Northwest and published *A Journey to the Rocky Mountains*. He prophesied the long-range effect of expansion into the wilderness:

"…the few fierce tribes who may have maintained themselves until that time in the mountains, may offer some resistance to the progress of the waves, but the swelling flood will rise higher and higher, till at last they are buried beneath it. The buffalo and the antelope will be buried too. But for all that there will be no smoking of the pipe of peace; for the new generation with the virtues of civilization will bring also its vices. It will ransack the bowels of the mountains to bring to light the most precious of all metals, which when brought to light will arouse strife and envy and all ignoble passions, and the sons of civilization will be no happier than their red brethren who have perished." (pg. 160)

Along with the "red brethren" who perished during this great move westward, many white wayfarers lost their lives as well. Almost one in ten who embarked with a cry of "Westward, ho!" died before the end of the journey.

But this era also created the perfect opportunity to reinvent oneself. One might alter one's name, origin, even one's allegiance. Like a desert chameleon, a man could present himself in various forms. In this complicated web of deception, he might even thrive.

After the Civil War, desire for land, gold lust, or a passion for adventure drew tens of thousands of fortune-seekers west. Others devised their own wily methods of raising easy money. They followed their unique set of rules, and used whatever and whomever they could to enrich themselves.

Chapter One

Poplar Bluff, Missouri—Late April 1863

This spring afternoon brought a wistful mix of expectation and melancholy. In Mama's big backyard garden, the marigold seeds Abigail Ferguson planted three weeks ago now peeked through the soil. Ah, the promise in these fledglings!

Bending over a row of carrot seedlings that would soon need thinning, Abby took in the lush Missouri landscape spreading past the wagon path behind their property. Beyond a field of sweet hay a mass of honeysuckle bushes, redbud, dogwood, and hawthorn trees inundated the riverbank. A month ago, so many lacy white blossoms attended that stretch, it looked as though an untimely snow had fallen.

But today, variegated greens splashed with gold hinted that one day, autumn would frost the countryside. Along the Black River, the waterwheel at Hank Jenkins' sawmill created a steady backdrop to the thud of logs dropped off by landowners intent on earning some cash. This fresh enterprise rose of a sudden, thanks to the new railroad boring its way through the iron ore fields north of Poplar Bluff.

In Papa's store, word had it they would call the railroad the *Iron Mountain and Southern.* Concerning this, Abby had her own ideas—why not the *Zephyr* or the *Streaking Flame*—something a little more exciting?

A sudden whirlwind taunted her skirt, stretching the fabric's black crepe covering tighter against her knees. With soil-caked fingers, she brushed the ugly wrinkled stuff as she knelt to pull a few weeds—what matter if her dress got a little dirtier before washday? With her schooling nearly at an end, she would soon work in the store every day, and each time new bolts of yard goods arrived, Mama relished first choice.

From the arbor, Aunt Susan's voice rose and fell with Mama's. "Early string bean crop this year—if the rains hold right, of course —no guarantees in this life, especially with this ghastly war... But you and Loyal keep each other in balance, a lovely thing to observe, dear sister..."

"Yes, I had all but given up hope, but then Loyal came to town, full of wit and dreams. And now, as soon as the war ends, he plans to—"

The wind stole Mama's last words, but Abby finished her sentence for her. "—expand the store, and work on a library."

Keep each other in balance—a perfect description of Mama and Papa. Rising from the backyard soil, she swayed a bit. Little wonder she felt dizzy by times these days, bereft of her beloved Elwood in this fast-changing world.

A verdant tomato leaf lent its fragrance to air tinged by offerings from the McClatchey's cow next door. Bunches of small, dark green tomatoes hanging thick on these vines would soon begin to color, first the faintest pink, then redder and redder, like the sunsets she cherished. One day, deep ruby globes would greet her on these vines, ready for the picking.

So it was—change all around. The war, however, rendered these alterations more abrupt and cruel. Recently, word of nine Union ironclads sailing into Charleston Harbor reached the telegraph office. Of course, the news immediately generated talk inside Ferguson's Store, where Abby had helped Papa last Saturday.

"The Confederate batteries badly damaged the ironclads. Those Rebs forced our sailors to withdraw, and we thought our Navy so stalwart, with those new monitors fashioned after the original."

When the first newspapers had arrived with more details of the debacle, talk rose to a fever pitch. "Such preparations our sailors made, and the tide and visibility proved auspicious. But those monitors move too slowly. When the tide turned, Rear Admiral Du Pont was forced to suspend the operation."

"Indeed. We were unable to penetrate even the Rebels' first defense."

"Yes, and they left one vessel near to sinking, the others damaged as well. One of our sailors perished, with twenty-one wounded. At least all of the captains agreed 'twas no use to continue the battle anew in the morning."

Papa summarized the discussion. "I had hoped we would occupy the harbor with ease, but alas, such a battle. I fear there will be a passel more before this conflict finds resolution."

Here in the garden, the tale swirled in Abby's memory—how long could this horrid war last? Then a late afternoon breeze brought a whiff of dogwood, returning her thoughts to her one all-consuming focus… dear, beloved Elwood.

Poplar Bluff bustled like a mama hen gathering her chicks at the first sign of danger. On the south end of Main Street, clinks and clanks pinpointed where Aloysius Smart struggled to settle a new pump into the stubborn clay loam after digging himself and his hired man into a sweat. The huge mound of red-yellow sand and gravelly clay they unearthed already reached building size.

On this clear June morning, Abby paused after filling her pail at the well behind the general store. For a moment, the crunch of shovels halted while Mr. Smart and his help paused to wipe their foreheads. In the brief serenity, low-lying swamplands to the south and east beckoned.

At the same time, from miles north of town, the *click-click* of rugged railroad workers' picks resonated. How they thought to bore through that impenetrable iron ore piqued her curiosity.

On her way to the back entrance, an elderly man called old Duff rehashed the scene she had witnessed with her own eyes less than a month earlier. Seemed as though folks tended toward either the past or the future these days, and old Duff favored the past.

"Yeeess, sir. General Marmaduke's men swept right through here on the way up t' Cape Girardeau. Headed in from Arkysaw fer pervisions fer his men, half of 'em with no mount."

He spat into dry clay. "But Gen'l McNeill put 'im down, that's what. Learnt 'is lesson, ol' Marmaduke did. 'Tain't likely he'll be raidin' these parts no more."

Avoiding the wizened sages gathered around him in the shade of a tall poplar, Abby slipped up the wooden stairs. She only had to close her eyes to see Marmaduke's long-cut hair bouncing against his collar as he rode through town in his fancy uniform.

Extra gray hairs sprouted from Mama's scalp that day, gospel truth. At least Marshal Tibbets and his local minions had managed to protect Poplar Bluff from looting, which was more than many other small towns around here could boast.

But now, up Main Street to Virgil G. Riggin's blacksmith shop and down the other way to Doc's house, the only brick one for miles, no one would know this small habitation had experienced such a threat. And before that, there had been even more—Abby's breath caught in her throat at the recollection.

Morning haze still rose from the Current, Black, and St. Francis rivers that met here on an old Indian trail. Low-lying humidity lent a peaceful aura to the town's layout, but visions of Confederate raiders ranging the outlying hills still remained vivid.

Ever since the battle at New Madrid that snatched three young Poplar Bluff men from this world in the spring of '62, Abby kept an eye on the front door of Ferguson's General Store, as Papa instructed. "Be always at the ready, child. Flee out the back if necessary, and run to the church. Your mother and I will search for you there."

For the moment all was well, but last night, her second story bedroom window revealed Union campfires twinkling like fireflies on the outlying hills. Bound farther south, the troops camped here temporarily, but their presence still produced a shiver.

She set to dusting the shelves, her perennial responsibility. Half an hour later, Papa gestured for her to follow him outdoors. "Help me position the Founder's Day banner, daughter—this should take only a minute." Of course, Loyal Ferguson would be the first to decorate for the upcoming festivities.

Below the wide front planks, two Union soldiers dismounted. Abby dipped her head as Papa climbed the side ladder to the roof. "Go right in, gentleman. I shall return soon."

Papa's hammer blows from on high dissolved in a sea of speculation by some dawdlers leaning against the storefront. He crossed to the other side of the roof, and Abby, stationed in the dusty street, motioned her directions with her hand.

"Up a bit more. Now to your left a couple of inches."

Then, from the far end of Main Street, a sudden dust whorl rose higher than Poplar Bluff's church steeple. That could only mean one thing.

"Hurry, Papa—the stage." Mr. Ferguson climbed down the ladder as Abby preceded him up the steps. The self-proclaimed vigilantes ogled her, and one spewed a stream of tobacco juice into the folds of her skirt. Though Papa urged forbearance, she marched straight up to the leader.

"You did that on purpose, Hollis Brum!"

Hollis turned his back to face his so-called local warriors. "Them Rebs wolf down California gold and Kansas Territ'ry, too—think they own the world. Quantrill's Raiders ran wild, but Ol' Brains showed 'em who was boss."

"Major Gen'l Halleck?"

"Yep—brung order and made us proud at Shiloh. We's th' militia, ready n' aimin', if'n they think t' come back." Rousing hurrahs launched an even stronger tirade, but Abby stamped her foot.

"Local militia, my foot! *Made us proud at Shiloh*—don't you know 23,000 men perished there?"

Hollis spewed more tobacco juice as she scurried inside. Behind the counter, a wet rag made quick work of the stain on her skirt. Her black crepe sleeve rustled against a tattered wall poster with a painting of Old Glory and praise for Missourians already mustered with the Third or Sixth Cavalry.

In the store's shadowy recesses, a good-looking Union captain studied a worn *St. Louis Dispatch* while his sergeant eyed the shovels. His clipped mustache lent the slender captain an Eastern air, but the sergeant's rawboned features hinted at farm country origins.

At another *hurrah* from the would-be gallants on the stoop, Abby muttered a promise to her feather duster. "Watch your back, Hollis Brum. I know a girl who could take you down." Inspired by the poster, a plan took shape in her mind.

The captain's voice carried over a row of new Callahan frock coats. "Says here a Sergeant Bascom riled an Apache hornet's nest in Arizona Territory last winter, and actually met Chief Cochise. After this war, shall we proceed south to do some Indian fighting, sergeant?"

His comrade chuckled low and deep, like the rush of water at a turn in the river. "We have enough on our hands, sir. How many shovels do we need?"

The captain shelved the newspaper. "Six ought to do." He dropped an elbow on the thick oak counter and cupped his chin. His handsome profile brought to mind—no, Abby would not allow the thought.

"May I help you?" She drew herself to her full height.

"Ma'am, I hear tell federal officers warrant a discount today."

"June nineteenth, sir? When did you receive this notification?"

His affable blue eyes twinkled, but just then, some shovels crashed to the floor, and the big sergeant nearly propelled headlong over the counter. Taking note of his massive farmer hands, Abby leaped back.

His earthy scent filtered to her—wood smoke, horseflesh, and worn wool. As he righted himself, his violent flush ignited a twinge of sympathy.

The captain doffed his cap and added a handful of chocolate creams to his purchases. "Captain Whitaker and Sergeant Tolzmann at your service."

"A pleasure to meet you, gentlemen." Abby weighed the candy and figured the bill. "That will be five dollars even."

"At this rate, the Army will go broke. Tell this lovely young lass how we await our paychecks, sergeant." The soldier fixed his eyes on his boots, so the captain addressed Abby again. "Last paid in January of '63. Do you call this treatment just?"

"President Lincoln surely has his reasons."

He steered the conversation elsewhere. "Sergeant, I deem these fine dimples and upturned nose the prettiest in the state."

The tall soldier fidgeted, so Abby took up the banter. "Only in Missouri? What about parts north?"

"Surely no Iowa belle holds a candle to this southern beauty? What think you, sergeant?"

A crooked smile jagged below the sergeant's pained dark eyes. *Men of few words make the best suitors*—where had she heard that?

The captain plunked down some coins. "Here you go, and a nickel for a pretty ribbon to highlight your chocolate eyes."

"Sir, there is no need—"

"Please accept this token for the privilege of gazing upon the finer species."

Pocketing the coin, Abby removed the ragged poster from the wall and thrust it toward him with her best smile. "Sir, a favor, if you please. That noisy ruffian outside talks a good war, but perhaps you might remind him of his patriotic duty?"

"Happy to do so—the Union always needs to muster fresh troops."

Leaving his partner front and center, he shouldered a couple of shovels. "Bid this young lady *adieu*, Sergeant Tolzmann."

The soldier finally found his voice. "Good day." He touched his cap and pivoted so fast his boots squeaked.

Most soldiers entered Ferguson's store with decorum. Others stared at her with such brazen looks that Abby fetched Papa from his meat cutting, but none had revealed this sincere a shyness. She crossed to the window.

"I hope Papa's right about the fight moving south. We already paid dearly at New Madrid." Dry black crepe crushed between her fingers, matching her sigh. There, she had finally named the site of Elwood's demise, even if only to these tall shelves.

"Oh, Elwood, by now we would be married and on our way out West." Her whisper circled in ever-present dust motes, while through the window, Hollis fidgeted under the captain's sharp surveillance.

A mongrel meandered by as the sergeant secured their shovels to his saddle. At a pitiful whine audible even inside, he squatted to pet the scraggly animal. Abby drew nearer the window as sunshine highlighted the big fellow's smile.

"Why, I believe I might..." She dragged a wooden stool to the window and set to work as the duo rode away. Half an hour later, she still bent over her sketchpad.

"Hello?"

Immersed in her task, she had failed to notice the door open.

"Why, you're sketching!" Lizzy, her dearest friend, leaned over her shoulder. "I passed this fellow on that sharp curve east of town, riding abreast an officer toward the Union camp."

"You recognize him?"

Lizzy lifted the pad. "A perfect likeness." She did a little jig. "This must mean my old friend has returned."

"Perhaps. I do feel more spirited today—you will never believe what I did to that Brum fellow."

After Lizzy left, the likeness Abby had created stared up at her. This bashful soldier would likely never pass through again. *Adieu*, after all, meant farewell forever. This war tossed people around like dry leaves, and fate might soon steal his life, too.

"Abigail Belinda Ferguson, must your work never end?"

Abby looked up from snapping green beans.

"Oh, Aunt Susan, I hoped you would stop by."

"This time of day makes me languish, dear. Sometimes when afternoon wanes, I drift into melancholy."

"Now Sister, have a glass of lemonade and be your bright, cheery self again." Abby's mother descended with a tray, so Abby gave her aching fingers a rest.

"I would be mortified if anyone else saw me like this."

"Everyone needs someone, Auntie. Sunset still brings me Elwood's image. I wish I could forget, but the sun was setting when he first spoke to me of our future."

"As years pass, those memories become our treasures, child."

"Pondering the plans we made only makes me sad, like seeing those rotting pears in the side yard. Every year the wasps infest them and turn their sweetness sour."

Mama's pursed lips filled Abby with regret, so she softened her outburst. "You know patience has never been my strength."

"Nor mine." Aunt Susan patted her forearm. "But sometimes, patience is all life leaves us, along with the memory of our plans."

"Well spoken, Sister, and you have borne your burdens with a noble spirit. Now come inside and help me in the kitchen."

The last pile of string beans diminished as children's voices drifted from the riverside. Shadows slithered the shed's length, and in spite of Abby's morning determination to think on pleasant things, heat welled behind her eyes.

Leaving the bean basket on the grass, she paced the yard. Only a few years ago, she and Elwood had capered along the Black River's shore like those youngsters. Without a care in the world, they frolicked with Lizzy and other friends. So many joys they shared—simple times, like discovering a painted lady in his mother's yard.

The leaves had died back in June, but early in July, one day she and Elwood came upon a stalk two and a half feet high, right where he had cut the grass two days before. Mrs. Partridge called these surprise lilies—a perfect name. Elwood tried to fit a giant blossom, pink with a white throat, behind Abby's ear. How they giggled at his attempt.

Then one autumn night he hid in the bushes near the back porch, preparing to sing *Open thy lattice, Love, listen to me...*

After supper when she emptied the dirty dishwater, Abby had no idea he lurked there until he yelped and jumped out, soaked to the skin. He sang to her anyway. Dear, dear Elwood. This recollection brought such a mix of laughter and misery, she pounded her fists on the clapboard shed.

"Oh, why did you have to go off to New Madrid? By now, we might be expecting our first child—how I despise this vile war!"

Across an expanse of prairie grass came the familiar sound of the store's back door. That meant Papa would soon appear on the wagon path. He always washed at the back pump and left his apron to soak in the shed before entering the house. His day had begun extra early, cutting steaks and roasts from the beef he butchered yesterday.

He worked so hard—mustn't let him find her in such a state. In the shadow of the shed, Abby wiped her eyes and took herself in hand.

"Enough lamenting, Abigail Belinda. Open your eyes to all the goodness around you, like Aunt Susan."

Papa found her composed, but quiet, and they walked together across the yard. Yes, so much good all around her. But a stifling sensation below her collarbone testified otherwise.

Chapter Two

One hot July morning when Abby entered the store, Papa stood talking with a Union soldier. Only snitches of their conversation wafted, a word or two about cattle. Something about the big fellow seemed familiar. When someone summoned Papa from the back room, she took his place behind the counter.

"Did you need anything?"

The sergeant eyed the glass candy case. "Umm—two of those chocolate creams."

He gripped the counter with such large fingers; could this be that jocular captain's comrade she had sketched in June?

"Anything else?"

"Mmm—some rope."

"How much would you like?"

"Ah—ten feet?" He lowered his eyes. "Maybe twelve."

"One minute, please." She stepped into the back room and returned with his order. "Forty-five cents, please."

He dug in his pocket, and once again, his muscular hands stood out. She waited, and finally, his warm brown eyes found hers. As they did, his cheeks flushed.

"You came in here before, for some shovels."

His lips opened without a reply.

"Will your unit be traveling to Mississippi now?"

"Ma'am, I..."

"Forgive me. You may not be at liberty to say."

"At liberty—no. Yes—Mississippi." The bashful sergeant's

forehead resembled hickory grain before sanding, full of dips and variations. Instead of dallying, he clutched his purchases and backed toward the door.

Despite his obvious strength—those muscles could surely lift heavy bales of hay—he seemed far too timid to wage war. But his unit was headed to Vicksburg, where everyone predicted a fierce battle would ensue.

"God go with you."

He fled with such haste, she doubted he heard her at all.

"I hear raspberries abound near the creek." Mama eased a bundle of fresh herbs onto her drying rack. "Would you mind picking some for supper, Abby?"

"Do you need anything else?"

"More plantain and comfrey for ointments, as always. Thank you, dear."

The ever-present laughter of children drew her to the spot. Papa called these young ones the future of Poplar Bluff.

Not much later, when her pail hung half full on her arm, the sharp tang of crushed thyme and mint wafted—Granny Ferguson must be about. In a few minutes, the old woman's humped shoulders appeared beneath a gray wool scarf.

Granny set down her pail and smoothed Abby's hair with a crooked forefinger. "Locks that sparkle like the sun, and gold within dark eyes doth run."

She carried on while Abby emptied her harvest into a flour sack bag and continued picking. Finally Granny set to work, too, but her prophecies continued.

"The future flows Mississippi dark, the life on which you ere embark."

Mama often warned, "Never encourage Granny," so Abby steeled herself.

"This day glows like strained cider, but rain cometh on the morrow. Aye, the gloom of wartime sorrow."

"But the Union has won steady victories, Granny, one far to the east and at Vicksburg. Don't you remember the news coming on July fourth? We control the Mississippi all the way to New Orleans now, and have cut off the rebels' supply lines. Texas troops can no longer travel east, nor can California's gold. Some declare the war will soon be over."

"Yet more sadness for thee, I fain would tell." The glitter in Granny's eyes twisted Abby's stomach.

Granny grasped her elbow and stared into her eyes. "She travels far, and darkness assails. Yet light shines, a love so true, and justice prevails." Having said her piece, Granny focused on her picking.

"I have enough for now, Granny. Shall I walk you home?"

"No, child. I've more to do. A thinking mind and a ready heart, grow you strong and full of art."

The back door screeched, sending a sharp vinegar smell through the store. "Abby?"

"Yes, Papa."

"New pickle barrel from St. Louis. This war brings both suffering and opportunity." With much scraping, he rolled the barrel into place and stood back to wipe his dripping forehead.

"And some shysters turn this chaos into opportunities." A distinct draft of lavender announced Mama's entrance through the front door. "Like that cattle man."

"Now, Mrs. Ferguson." Papa raised his brows.

"Loyal, I cannot trust that fellow."

"McHale keeps his word and provides good beef. Judge not, lest—"

"I only use the discernment the good Lord gave me. Something about Ray McHale sets wrong with me, I tell you."

"Ah. Remember that newspaper report about General Grant after the Rebs stymied the Union at Shiloh? One reporter has it out for him and described him drunk on the eve of battle. But after his Vicksburg victory, folks believe he was misaligned."

"I fail to see what that has to do with McHale." Mama turned to Abby. "Go on home, dear, if you like. You will attend tonight's lecture, won't you?"

The flyer hanging beside the counter had heralded this speaker for weeks.

Popular orator, Horatio Culver, on
The Railroad and its Promise.
Rolla, Missouri - August 29, 1863
Poplar Bluff - September 1.
Raise funds for the Union—
Neglect not to do your part.

She had been excited to go, but taking a walk to the river sounded better right now. "I planned to, but if I can help out—"

Papa spoke up. "Ray usually brings my orders right on time, so I must move ice tonight. But as your mother says, you should get out in society."

"Oh, *pfft*. I like helping with the ice blocks."

"If need be, I can help your father, dear."

Mr. Ferguson drew his wife close and addressed Abby. "Elizabeth will be there?"

"Yes, and Annabelle."

Mrs. Ferguson's eyes brightened. "Put off your mourning crepe, then. Wear your new *tabinet* frock. You agree, don't you, Loyal?"

"As always, dear." He faked a startle when Mama jabbed him in the ribs. "Enjoy yourself, Abby, and regale us later."

He stretched over the counter to kiss her forehead, and Mama flashed her brightest smile. On the way home, Abby pondered the special blessing Mama had given her after Elwood asked for her hand. "Finding a kindred soul means so much. You and Elwood enjoy that special bond."

She shook off the memory. "No. I must re-channel my thoughts." But the prospect of living here in Poplar Bluff for the rest of her life dulled in comparison to the wild dreams she and Elwood shared. As it was, she would become like Aunt Susan, always with that wistful, faraway look in her eyes.

Donning her new frock brought a certain comfort. She pinched her cheeks and studied her face in the oval mirror—grief had made her cheekbones sharper. She made haste as the hall clock shooed her toward the park.

Near the lecture site, Lizzy hailed her. "Finally—no more mourning weeds. Oh, look, Annabelle wore something cheerful, too. Mama says the boys would want us to continue on with our lives."

But on the far side of the growing crowd, Elwood's mother still wore her black crepe. Abby pulled Lizzy to some nearby seats, where Annabelle joined them with Abby's copy of *Oliver Twist* in hand.

"Thank you for lending this to me—in case the speaker waxes long, we might be glad I brought it." They took seats, and Annabelle went on. "Mother read Mr. Dickens' tale right along with me, and she debates Mr. Fagin with Father.

"She calls Fagin a miserly, vile, hideous character, but Father, who has been listening in, follows the Universalists. They believe a divine spark exists in every person, you know."

"But he preaches Baptist?" Always one to speak her mind, Lizzy jumped in.

"Yes, though Grandmother was an Anabaptist and Grandfather a Moravian who studied back in Boston. Our family dates back to John Adams, and Father's uncle founded a university in St. Louis—"

Annabelle shrugged. "Anyway, Father believes that even Mr. Fagin can be redeemed, but Mother parts ways with him on that point. You should see her bristle when Father sets aside his *Universalist Companion* and chimes in.

"'Jonathan! You would grant salvation to a scoundrel who organizes innocent London street urchins into a thievery ring? This villain makes his living off the backs of orphans and instructs them in deviltry?'"

"'Ah, but does not Mr. Fagin show some kindness to little Oliver? We dare not discount his solicitous attitude when he sends the boy out with the—'"

Lizzie poked Annabelle in the ribs. "Shhhhh!"

Poplar Bluff's mayor took the platform. "Friends, I should like to present our evening's speaker, Mr. Horatio Culver, whose expertise lies with progress. And with every hammer blow coming from the north, progress had indeed come upon us."

A diminutive man with a handlebar mustache, Mr. Culver obviously hailed from other parts. He soon turned eloquent about the inevitable tide of change sweeping the country. "Mark my words, good citizens of the West, 'twon't be long before a machine will carry our voices to the Atlantic coast."

A listener murmured, "If voices were meant to travel, t'would be ordained."

"Railroads will one day connect your fair village with the Pacific. Your location, so close to the great Mississippi, assures future prosperity. Our great cities back East require lumber from your forests, and the iron ore beneath your soil for their factories."

A murmur ran through the crowd.

"As sure as tulip poplar trees beautify your distinguished bluff, as sure as the auspicious Hernando de Soto passed through this fine area, your future beckons bright."

He teetered back on his heels. "Friends, heed this advice from R. W. Emerson. 'accept the place divine Providence has found for you—the connection of events.' And remember the words of Doctor Samuel Johnson, 'To improve the golden moment of opportunity, and catch the good that is within our reach, is the great art of life.'"

Applause swelled as the mayor reclaimed the stage. "Ladies and gentlemen, it pleases me now—"

"Fire! Every able-bodied man to Main Street."

In the bedlam, Abby lost Elizabeth and turned toward home. Smoke eddied above a bucket brigade, and a high wail pierced the night. "Mercy, the store is on fire!"

Chills cascaded her shoulders. Halfway there, someone reeking of manure and liquor collided with her. "Might be best t'—" She had heard that voice somewhere, hadn't she? But rushing ahead, she warded off the ungainly fellow.

A few feet away, a blazing timber sizzled to the earth, and nearby, three men manned a hose. "Make way for the pump!"

Marshal Tibbets directed folks. "Back off, now. Allow the men to work."

Highlighted by the conflagration, the tall roof of Abby's home beckoned, and the familiar creak of the back stairs calmed her. Day in and day out, this familiar sound marked their comings and goings.

But eerie reflections cast a glow over the kitchen. Smoke billowed through the open window over the new-fangled pump Papa had installed to lighten Mama's workload.

"I do believe folks make deliveries just to see our pump, Loyal." Mama might have been here right now, making supper, but the kitchen stood empty.

A lump bigger than the whole of Butler County choked Abby. "Please, help me find—" Through the dining room and parlor, acrid gray air burned her eyes. Then the front door swung open, and in the hallway, she ran into with Aunt Susan.

"My dear sweet girl."

A sickening odor preceded heavy boot steps from the back of the house. "Don' know what happened—Ferg'son tried t' save his wife, but they's both dead now."

"Oh, no, no! This cannot be!"

Abby collapsed in Aunt Susan's heady lavender aura.

"I never knew Loyal to smoke. They had plenty of time to get

out, and he built the store with three exits, for just such a time."
Marshal Tibbits pursed his lips. "Did your father have an enemy
that you know of?"

"Papa?"

Aunt Susan's hand steadied Abby. "Oh, I simply cannot believe—"

Papa never met anyone but what he found common ground.
But now, he and Mama had both been snatched from this world
in an instant. How could this be true?

Aunt Susan moved into the downstairs bedroom, found some
black crepe and began stitching over Abby's dresses. Again. Time
stood still, even though autumn swept into winter.

Dismal days ran into weeks. Abby swept and dusted, beat the
rugs over the clothesline and washed down the walls as Mama
always did. Under Aunt Susan's tutelage, she also attempted to
increase her sewing skills.

"Keeping busy does the soul good." Aunt Susan purred her phi-
losophy over a plate of fried chicken, turnips, and garden peas.

"Yes," Abby replied. But her voice sounded peculiar, and something lodged in her throat. As long as she followed Aunt Susan's
instructions and answered when she needed to, life floated along.
But she faded to her room when visitors called, and left the house
only for church on Sunday.

Week after week, the service swept around her like a maelstrom.
Often, she imagined herself up in the balcony, looking down
upon the faithful. What good were all these fine sentiments?
And the hymns—who could *trust and obey* through this hideous,
warped journey?

What fickle cruelty had paired her with Elwood so perfectly, but
then snatched him away? Now, dear Mama and Papa had joined
him. What could possibly be left for her in this vale of tears?

Somehow, cold December passed, then January and February.
Finally spring enlivened the countryside, and Abby helped Aunt

Susan plant a garden. Soon, early melon vines meandered on the plot's sandy side.

But one humid day in July, the marshal reappeared. This time, he investigated yet another death—Aunt Susan's.

From the dried pea rows, Abby recognized his gait. Stacking worthless vines on the burn pile kept her occupied, but behind her eyes, tears burned like flames.

Tending the garden distanced her from all-too frequent visitors laden with fresh baked goods she could never eat. They offered woeful embraces and murmured in her ear. This time, Aunt Susan could not help bear the burden.

Yesterday's funeral replayed, sniffles and communal sobs backing Preacher Fox's remarks. "Such mysteries try us beyond the telling. Our sister Susan Edith Carmichael joins her family all too soon, but leaves us with memories of a blessed life."

Abby stamped her foot on the dried up garden plot. If only she could run down to the river, away from the townsfolk's prying eyes. Aunt Susan always said that memories amounted to gifts, but the sound of those harsh grains falling on her coffin still echoed.

Less than twenty-four hours ago, the gravedigger leaned an arm on his spade, creating an odd mix of shade and sunshine over brittle cemetery grass. In the dissonance of soil on pinewood, Abby's legs gave way. Someone led her to a bench, and Lizzy's mother crushed her close.

"Oh, how I wish Elizabeth had not gone to help my cousin with her newborn. Would you like to come out to the farm for a while?" Tears rolled off her chin like early morning dew, but Abby could only wrench her soaked hankie.

After an endless mourning line paid their respects, a slipshod figure emerged out of nowhere. His shabby dress struck a poignant note as he turned his hat in his hands.

"Miss, if y' need anythin', jest..."

What was this fellow's name? His retiring demeanor riled up a peculiar sensation, something besides the numbness that stalked her. Last winter, he had stopped by now and then, with uncanny knowledge of what Papa would want to do with his property. When decisions loomed, he arrived at just the right time, but Aunt Susan doubted his intentions.

"We must recollect your Mama's concerns, Abby. That man troubles me, too."

Now, the marshal stepped over a gangly tomato vine and broke into Abby's mired thoughts. "I hate to bother you at such a time, but something is amiss here."

His clear blue eyes bespoke a man of the law—single minded and intent.

"Sam Stone checked Susan's buggy right before the accident." The marshal held out a wooden wheel rod sawed neatly into two pieces. "You can see someone hacked it almost through. Must've been just before your aunt came out of her house, and it broke when she reached a certain speed."

He rubbed a haggard brow. "The question is, who would do such a thing?"

A bitter frost penetrated Abby's heart. How could anyone hurt Aunt Susan, whose faith had carried her through the impossible winter?

"Just like your pa, she had no enemies." Marshal Tibbits clenched and unclenched his fist. "I shall ferret out the culprit, believe me."

With the back of her hand, Abby wiped away insistent tears, and the Marshal handed her his kerchief. "Let me know if you think of anything."

As she watched his progress down the alley, a wheedling inner voice taunted her. *Whose faith will you borrow now?* Absently, she continued her work until daylight faded. Then she shunted the squeaky porch swing into motion.

Some time later, a shuffle caused her to look up. Under a flaming western sky too beautiful for this awful day, someone fidgeted on the bottom stairs. A frumpy man, his slouched hat looked familiar. Then she recalled Papa using his name: Ray McHale, his beef supplier.

From the honeysuckle bushes south of the house, a mourning dove issued its sad song. Ray proceeded to the top step.

"Goin' out west come spring."

An untimely pronouncement, but Abby no longer trusted her perceptions.

"Kin help y' with your Aunt's property 'fore I leave."

Sunset caught the end of his wide nose and rendered the stubble on his chin a spiky forest. He seemed not to mind her stillness or the swing's steady creak.

He said no more, and long after his steps faded, the swing continued to sway. Papa trusted Ray enough to invite him to supper, but Mama's misgivings rang in her ears.

"Such a coarse man, Loyal, and he has shifty eyes."

Tonight, though, Ray had looked directly at her, and there was something else. His presence brought an odd sense of comfort.

If he were suspect, Marshal Tibbets would have warned her. Meanwhile, cleaning out Aunt Susan's house loomed. How could she bear the task alone?

With Ray's guidance, the store property had sold for a fair price. Though a year had passed, a faint smoky odor still drifted from that direction, or did she imagine it? As if the twilight could somehow reproduce the rambling building, Abby twisted against the worn wooden slats.

Yes, if only Ferguson's Store could stand once more. Then Papa would walk home from work, Mama would sing over her herbal concoctions, and life would begin again.

Chapter Three

Mid-September wind prevailed over Poplar Grove's rough-hewn cemetery stones. On Elwood's grave, a single late rosebud marked Abby's devotion, but her thoughts tumbled down an endless dark tunnel. A rainy channel traced the words on Mama and Papa's gravestone before dripping onto mucky clay.

For the hundredth time, she ruminated on the sentiment Elder Drury had chiseled there.

> *A kindlier pair n'er was known*
> *Who now to heavn'ly rest hath gone.*

Elder refused to take any money. "Loyal Ferguson give me credit when I oughtn't to have none. A fine man, truth be told, and gone too soon."

Aunt Susan deserved some writing on her stone, too, but Abby was hard put to decide what. Words jumbled in her mind when she attempted to put them on paper.

> *Bereft of spouse and offspring dear,*
> *Yet friend to children far and near.*

That would summarize her life, perhaps. How many neighborhood children had knocked at the door in the last weeks, hoping she would proffer a plate of fresh-baked cookies in Aunt Susan's stead?

After some time, the thick forsythia branches rustled behind her.

Probably Granny Ferguson, out for her evening constitutional—she would have a gloomy word, but what did it matter? What more harm could she possibly foretell?

But a different voice sang out. "Why Abby—it has been much too long. I—I felt uncertain..." Lizzy's tentative tone made Abby cringe.

"Have you... Are you all right? I have been away so long helping Mama's cousin—"

"What does she hear of her husband?"

"He—he came home in August, missing his right leg."

"Oh my." Abby withdrew her fingers as a mockingbird cooed a haunting tune.

"You sound so—different." Something squeezed Abby's chest until she thought her heart would stop. "Everyone expects me to find my poise again, but I am so—"

"Lonely." A gust of wind buffeted Lizzy's shawl. "I know. Ever since Obed Parcher toted back the bodies—Your Elwood, my Andrew, and Annabelle's brother, all taken at once..."

But now, my entire family is gone, too.

Realizing her error, Lizzy sucked in her breath. Abby shrank from the piteous look she could no longer tolerate.

"The new stereoscope pictures Mama ordered arrived yesterday. Do come over for dinner tomorrow night, and we can sketch together, like old times?"

"Thank you, but I think not." *Surely you would rather spend the evening with Jeremy Whidby, your new widower friend, and his three children.*

Lizzy clung to her hankie. "Oh, Abby, I wish I could help—"

"No one can. My sins have found me out." Spoken aloud, her newfound belief rang harsh.

"Your sins?"

"Hasty of heart, prone to presumption, enraptured with adventure—Mama once listed my shortcomings. Oh, and always impatient."

"We all have our shortcomings, but..." At last, understanding settled Lizzy's puzzled brow. "Surely you don't mean the church picnic? That was Elwood's idea."

"I shamed Mama and Papa that day, and Elwood's parents scolded him. After all, the whole town went looking for us."

"How could you have known you would have to wait out a storm, or—"

"It would look as though we had forsaken faithfulness and trust? Mama was right—I have always yearned for adventure, and impatience has ruled me."

"She was fearful, Abby. She only spoke out of worry."

"Perhaps but she was right, and I have received my just reward."

"Oh, Abby! You know the Scriptures; 'The Lord doth not willingly afflict the sons of men.'"

"Who afflicts me then; Granny Ferguson's fiendish imps?"

Lizzy recoiled. "Such terrible things have happened, yet you mustn't blame the Almighty—or yourself."

An icy wall encompassed Abby, as real as the cold granite markers. She stood like stone as Lizzy implored her, "This pain will pass, and you will find someone—"

"Find someone?" Abby's shriek resounded. "You must be daft to think anyone would ever want someone so cursed."

"You have suffered far too much—"

Though Abby longed to run into her friend's arms, ice stiffened her spine. She turned away, into the frigid wind.

"I will always be here, my friend." They stood in silence, so close, but worlds apart. Finally, Lizzy retreated.

Abby wanted to trail her and shout, "Forgive me, please. I will come to dinner after all." But the words wallowed in her throat.

One last time, Lizzy turned and called. "Abby, please?" The wind dashed the sun behind a cloud. Finally, she picked her way to Andrew's grave and a few minutes later, hurried toward her buggy.

The wind whistled a tart lament as Lizzy clucked to the horse. No doubt, she would immerse herself in Jeremy and his family— the right thing to do.

"But for me, no right thing remains." Callous tombstones received Abby's whisper. A cardinal landed on Aunt Susan's grave and chirruped as if all were right with the world.

The family plot still held room for one more—what difference if she died tomorrow? She had become like Granny, with evil portents writhing in her head.

The wind bade Abby clutch her cloak, and her shudder brought a certain satisfaction. Better to feel the cold than nothing at all.

In November, Lizzy married Jeremy in a private ceremony and moved to his farm. When Abby heard the news from an older lady who refused to stop bringing her baked goods, she barely reacted. But later, staring up at the ceiling of her room, she recalled she and Lizzy had planned to witness each other's marriage vows.

Foolish children.

That was before the war snatched away their dreams.

The clock struck midnight, and she rolled over. All of their cherished plans had come to naught, and now the future stretched ahead like an endless road leading nowhere. If only she could find a way to extinguish these memories.

At least everyone except that one relentless woman and Pastor Fox had ceased calling. They meant well, but she dreaded the visits—Pastor Fox's well-intended quotes crackled paper-thin in the drafty parlor.

But earlier this evening, a knock had sounded, and seeing Ray through the narrow vestibule window, Abby had slipped onto the porch. His eyes, like faded bachelor's buttons, hinted at exploits.

"After the war, the Army'll head to Arizona Territory on account a' the mines. California Column's already fightin' Apaches down thataway." Even his pockmarks perked up when he mentioned the new territory.

"Tell me about that place."

"Dry and hot, but a tall pine forest follows a long high ridge."

He traced a stubby finger on the railing. "They call it the Rim. They's deer and elk everywhere, grass higher'n my waist—made fer cattle."

His lips turned in as if he held something back. After he left, the image of Arizona Territory remained. Towering pine trees, wild animals, lush meadows... With moonlight dancing through the curtains, the faraway land cast its spell.

Two visits later, after Abby had deeded Aunt Susan's house to a young family, Ray stopped in again. Though warnings still flickered like distant fireflies, she asked him into the parlor.

"Thet Rim's two thousand feet high. Pines so tall you have to stretch your neck. Canyons, roarin' creeks, red rocks n' drippin' springs like nothin''round these parts."

"Are there towns?"

He snorted. "S'not a citified place."

"The sunsets must be beautiful."

"Cain't see 'em. A mountain they call Strawberry stands in the way."

A mountain hiding the sunset? The only place Abby had imagined without a sunset was the ugly heart of London, where Oliver Twist plied his pickpocket trade. Along narrow streets shrouded in mist and hemmed by ugly buildings, the difference between dawn and twilight might be lost.

"Them troops'll corral the Injuns. I aim to be ready for 'em." Ray's chin jutted, and for a fleeting moment, his determination reminded Abby of Elwood, bound to seek his fortune.

Now, hours later, Ray's earthy scent persisted—perspiration, beef on the hoof, and a perennial tang to his breath. Like a profound passage in a good book, his dream enlivened Abby. For the first time since Aunt Susan's death, she took up *Oliver Twist* from her bedside table and started reading again.

The filthy byways of London and Oliver's fate at the hands of unscrupulous rogues transported her across the ocean, perhaps as far as Arizona Territory lay to the west. Entering into this character's misery came naturally.

"More snow's comin'."

Even in the shelter of the porch, the late November weather chilled Abby. The whole world took on an overcast shade. Though she opened the door, Ray barely came inside. His leathery face peeked above his dirty collar, and his nose shown red in the lamplight.

"Changed m' mind. Leavin' tomorra. If y' got a hankerin', y' kin come along."

The downward lines of his mouth barely altered, and gray encroached on the blue of his eyes. When she said nothing, he shuffled his feet.

"Kin stop at th' first Justice 'long the way."

Her visions of a lovely church wedding died long ago, and she never thought to ask why the Justice here in Butler County would not do. Here stood Ray, as real as the storm that would soon shut her inside. Every other man she knew was off fighting—even Hollis had joined up.

Lizzy's calculation that she would find someone tasted like dust in Abby's mouth. Who could she possibly find?

This far-off Arizona Territory—even the name possessed a certain lilt. Ray cocked his head, revealing a balding spot. Yes, he was older, but by now, perhaps even Mama would have come to accept his good points.

During Pastor Fox's last visit, his talk of *a future and a hope* carved a painful niche in Abby's soul. The pain had loosed her tongue.

"What do you mean, a future? Every marriageable man has joined the fighting, or is too wary of my loss. An evil spell has come upon me—I am tainted."

"My dear, no wickedness on earth can stand against—" Pastor Fox paused. "Whatever befalls us, our Lord promises never to forsake His own. Your parents and Aunt Susan believed that to their dying day."

"And what became of them?"

"They have passed safely through heaven's gates, Miss Abigail. These years have brought you much sorrow, but I can see your loved ones even now, urging you to take up their faith. The psalmist says, 'no evil shall befall you—'"

"Stop!" Her cry reverberated up the empty stairway.

Pastor Fox cleared his throat. "As you wish, but I will continue to pray for you." He let himself out. When the doorknob turned, she shattered a teacup against the wall and collapsed on the floor.

"Evil *has* befallen me!" Melancholy tightened its grasp. "Nothing for it but to accept my fate." The high wainscoting echoed her words. *No hope... no hope.*

Something went askew in her mind, she knew. Her patience a fragile thread, she distanced herself more from the townsfolk, going out only at night. If someone knocked, she pretended to be gone.

But now, Ray stood before her. He reached into his pocket and handed her a small cloth bag bearing a crisp scent. Peppermints—not soothing like lavender drops, but enervating. Mama swore by peppermint tea for certain bodily ailments.

A single smooth candy tingled on her tongue, like the choice Ray offered. Why pass another year pining for what could never be?

The walls shrank around her "I could start packing—"

"Only room fer one trunk."

"A trunk. Yes. Fine."

He slipped away, leaving her with the cold click of the lock. Upstairs in the wide hallway, Abby folded her life into two feet by four, visualizing freedom from the haunting odor of the fire and pitying glances cast her way. Might as well leave her sketching pencils here, along with most everything else.

Even as she set them aside, a feeble memory emanated.

Today we shall work with your new colored pencils, dear, and at dinnertime, you may show Papa. No need to hurry—color takes more time. Do you see how the green in these leaves shows hope?

And these faint streaks of yellow purvey a sense of cheer. Grey backs the green, for they contain the same elements, but grey's softness high-lights the glory of the green...

Such a bittersweet recollection—for a moment, it seemed Mama might step out of her bedroom. But by meager lamplight, the sketches of Abby's youth brought only more heaviness.

Finally, she pulled herself up from the hallway floor. No room for these childhood relics. A new life beckoned with adventures far away from this hazy little town.

An hour later, the trunk held linens and soap, Mama's dinner platter, four cotton frocks, and the Sunday shoes Mama had given her. Keeping time with the grandfather clock Mama's people had brought across the ocean, Abby surveyed the house.

Each breath echoed as though she wandered through a mausoleum. Nothing called out to her. Even the mahogany bedsteads carried an unreal quality—without Mama and Papa, everything forfeited its meaning. She slumped into Mama's bedside chair.

Too weary to utter the *whys* that littered her heart, she basked in Mama's essence, for her lavender still clung to this cushioned seat. Each morning, she had brushed and braided her hair here before facing the day.

The clock chimed midnight as Abby meandered downstairs to the small alcove off the dining room that served as Papa's study. Smoothing her fingers along his solid walnut desk, she touched a book's spine. In spite of the shadows, she knew its title: *Les Miserables*. She had overheard the town lawyer discussing it with Papa one day.

"Could you place an order for Victor Hugo's new book? I have read the translated pamphlets from a publisher out east, but to have the whole volume would be a treasure. My uncle in the Carolinas, an avid slaveholder, has become devoted to Hugo in spite of his abolitionist leanings—says the Southern Literary Messenger calls this work 'the Bible in the fictitious literature of the Nineteenth Century.'"

"His correspondence still reaches you?"

"Somehow, the mail finds its way, even through enemy lines. You will place my order, then?"

"Assuredly, and only ten percent down. If ever a man were beset by misfortune, it is Jean Valjean."

"Still, he persevered through all his troubles, as do we all. What a boost for our troops in harm's way to read of his struggles."

"Yes, and word has it that soldiers for both the North and South agree on one thing—Mr. Hugo's story touches a deep chord."

Holding the volume to her nose brought a faint tinge of lye soap—with all the work of running a store, butchering and all, no one washed his hands more often than Papa. Abby toted the book to her trunk and settled it next to *Oliver Twist*.

In the dull hour before dawn, Mama's black leather Bible also caught her eye. She half turned away, but something about it drew her—Mama spent so many hours reading this book. Under the softness of her dresses, Abby tucked it in. One day, perhaps, she would tell her children that their grandparents once held these volumes.

In nose-biting pre-dawn cold, Ray's rap sounded. Out front waited a new wagon. Abby buttoned her wool coat and bonnet, doubled Papa's traveling blanket over her arm with her parasol, and crossed the threshold for the last time. Ray hoisted her trunk as she clambered into the buckboard.

He was no gentleman—no surprise to that. Through hushed streets, past Annabelle's house, the silent empty clapboard church, and beyond the new train depot, memories flitted one by one. With each, her heaviness lifted, and out in the countryside west of town, each squeaky turn of the wheels breathed hope.

West. Heading west. Put the past behind you. Start over.

Terrain wreathed in darkness rolled by as Ray managed the team, and the cold bore down into Abby's very bones. At least, the faintest hint of light mastered the horizon. One minute 'twas full dark and the next full light. Some time later, in ample sunshine, Ray stopped beside a creek to water the mules.

"Fifteen miles a'ready. Up ahead lies Doniphan." Abby relieved herself in the bushes and when she rejoined him, he glared. "No dawdlin', hear?"

Outside the county courthouse in Doniphan, a poster proclaimed,

WANTED: young, skinny, wiry fellows
not over eighteen, must be expert riders,
willing to risk death daily.
Orphans preferred. Wages: $25 per week
Apply Pony Express Stables
St. Joseph, MO

Inside the brick building, a disheveled judge slid his glasses past the bump on his nose. He asked no questions before duly pronouncing them man and wife. But after Ray paid him, he wanted to talk.

"Followin' the Current?"

Ray said nothing.

"Headed far?"

Turning his back, Ray hustled Abby out, his heels clicking on the boardwalk. Back on the jostling wagon seat, a fog immersed her. Not an endearing word from him, nor even a kindly touch of his hand.

Her husband.

In rhythm with the creaking wheels, words circled through her mind like poetry—*Now we are wed...* no longer alone... *heading west.*

Across the Arkansas border into Indian Territory, they camped beside a gurgling stream where she stretched her weary limbs. How good to touch the earth again! After a supper of bacon and beans, she washed the plates and took a short walk. Sitting on a rock, she unfastened her shoe buttons to soak her feet.

When Ray sneaked up beside her, she startled. "Water's too

cold fer thet. No sick woman travels w' me." His tone struck like a slap, and Granny's singsong screech echoed, *Rash the bed you make, harsh the road you take.*

A flagrant cardinal piped beside the creek as Abby washed up the best she could, and for a fleeting moment, Lizzy's face appeared in the water. That day in the cemetery seemed years ago, but her words reverberated like thunder.

God is not punishing you.

Slapping freezing water over her face, Abby whispered, "You are mistaken, Lizzy. Whatever I get, I deserve."

For the next week, Ray ignored her. When she slid across the seat on sharp inclines, he elbowed her away. But one shivery night, he crawled into the wagon smelling of whiskey. So different from how she imagined marriage with Elwood, but thankful for the extra warmth and the feel of another human so close, she ignored his heavy breath.

Other than that, nothing changed. Day followed day, until one afternoon, they stopped near a hollow tree. Bees swarmed there, so Ray climbed up and pulled out a honey stash. What a difference the sweetness made in their meals.

This dip in the land also harbored wasps, so Abby stayed near the fire that evening as sunset turned late afternoon shadows into burnished glory. Pencil in hand, head buried in a small record book, Ray ignored the spectacle, but the quiet beauty braced her for one more day. Then, without thinking, she asked a question.

"Do you know why only bees make honey, Ray?"

His scowl shriveled her desire for conversation. "How'd I know? Shoulda left y' in Missouri." His surly tone issued an unspoken warning, so she retreated to the wagon.

He kept silence until one afternoon when he gestured west. "Crossed outta Injun Terri'try yesterday."

Why hadn't he told her at the time? No matter—these windswept plains offered nothing new, anyway. She stifled her curiosity about the rest of the trip. Better to juggle her questions than abide his scowl.

Poplar Bluff's raised wooden walks and pleasant porches, pretty dresses and mirrors—the world of her youth—melted into forgotten fantasy. Their camps and the endless trail formed a predictable routine enveloped by blowing dust.

Morning and night, the milk cow Abby secretly christened Babe twitched its ears when she whispered, "I'm as strong as any of the boys, able to abide whatever comes." Her teacher, Miss Minnie, said that about her years ago—odd it would come to her now. But she grasped onto the sentiment. Here was a chance to prove her strength.

She cooked whatever Ray shot—hares, 'possum, wild geese, even doves. Beside the fire at night, he gnawed the bones and nursed the flask he kept in his pocket. Days coalesced like thin morning gruel.

Shredded by branches and thorns, the crepe ripped from Abby's skirt created a scarecrow effect. One evening, she knelt in the wagon to open her trunk, but Ray throttled her shoulder.

"No need fer fancifyin' out here."

Right. Of course.

On his hankering nights, her bones scraped rough boards in spite of the quilts. Yet through the tarp opening, moonlight winked a clandestine message. In spite of newfound pain, the glint of the next day's sunrise wafted a promise—*"catch the good that is within our reach..."*

Perhaps traveling irritated Ray, since he was used to living alone. One day, they would arrive at his property in beautiful Arizona Territory, and under that landmark he called the Rim, she would bear him a child. Surely then, he would change.

On a hazy afternoon a few days later, he visited a settlement for supplies. "Tell anybody what comes, I went up t' Kansas t' kill me some Rebs."

Against the treeless horizon, phantoms visited Abby. She would have welcomed anyone to speak with, even Preacher Fox. Long hours later, Ray appeared, reeking of whiskey and sweat.

Another night, she woke freezing in dense darkness. The fire had died. Was that a piano tinkling in the distance? Over the side of the wagon, Abby felt Babe's warmth. Finally, Ray straggled in, starlight exposing the ruby tip of his nose.

The next week, without warning, Babe's legs buckled.

"Drain 'er quick. May's well git all we kin outta her."

The milking brought revulsion and hot tears. How she would miss this reliable friend! Ray swore as he butchered her and hung her salted quarters from the wagon. Mile after high country mile, Babe's remains swished the wagon sides. Back and forth, back and forth—*no return. No return.*

Suddenly the plains plunged into a canyon boasting intricate escarpments, and the urge to sketch made Abby's fingers itch. Why had she left her pencils behind? But they veered north anyway, and time dragged until late one afternoon, singing drifted from a spatter of wagons near a river.

People singing—was she imagining the harmony? Abby's heart quickened, but Ray's eyes pierced her. "Them's crazy folk. Got more'n one wife."

A spindly-legged wayfarer stood near a campfire, his phrases drifting like mist. Out of Ray's sight, Abby bent her ear from the shelter of a thorny hedge.

"Soon, we will join the Sante Fe route, following stalwart men like Boone, Bridger, and Carson. We know our destination, and *what doth the Lord require of us but to do justice, to love mercy, and to walk humbly with our God?*"

Even glimpsing the women's bonnets and homespun dresses brought comfort. These folks could not be all bad.

But Ray grasped her arm with a harsh twist. "Git in the wagon. Now!"

He urged the mules ahead while her hopes plummeted—he knew how much the singing meant to her. He could read her mind. Dusk bathed the sinking sun, but still he drove on.

Later, he snored beside a hasty fire as the stranger's words circled like prairie hawks. *Justice, mercy, thy God*—these Sunday morning phrases fell over her. Years ago, sitting beside Mama and Papa, *justice* and *mercy* still made sense. Her cherished quilt offered scant succor, and a starless night confirmed it would be a long time before she spied another woman.

Chapter Four

Ray wiped porridge from his tangled beard. "Rough goin' ahead. New Mexico Territ'ry."

The day proved his forecast, and gathering buffalo chips near a half-cave in some rocks rosy with sundown, stiffness plagued Abby. Then she nearly stumbled over a man. He let out a croak, and she startled back against a boulder with her heart in her ears.

"Got anythin' fer a wayfarer?"

Ray turned friendly when she led the emaciated stranger to him. "Have some coffee."

The drifter gripped a proffered tin cup and guzzled as if he had never tasted coffee. In the firelight, Ray's eyes transformed to sizzling azure. The beans and bacon he gave the stranger enlivened the fellow's face.

"From these parts?"

"Up Kansas way. Met th' Reverend what shot Old Brown's son up thar."

"John Brown's son—at Osawatomie?"

"Know 'im?"

"No, but I heard."

"Confederates took my cows. Sent my fambly to Nebraska—Crondite's th' name—or they'da kilt 'em." The man's weak tone scraped like a rusty bucket. "Scouted fer the Union, but Quantrill's Missouri Bushwhackers started burnin' towns. A man cain't stand up to that. What side'r you?"

"Neither ain't worth dyin' fer."

The visitor's cough echoed off a rock face.

"What y' doin' down here?"

"Met a old prospector, tol' me whar t' look. Said them Spaniards hid treasure 'roun here."

"Find any gold?"

"Some."

"Here, have a drink."

Ray snarled in Abby's direction. "Git t' bed." She grabbed some jerky, and in her wagon niche, puzzled over their visitor until the stars wooed her to sleep.

At dawn, she fed the fire and boiled coffee. But over the coffee's rich aroma, vileness rode the air.

The putrid odor only increased. High above, a wide-winged vulture circled. As light wobbled over the horizon, Abby circled the campsite. Not far away, gooseflesh came over her at a shape crumpled at the foot of a boulder. A little closer, growing daylight revealed the man from last night.

Matted blood on his head pooled thick with flies. She touched his shoulder, but he gave no response. Heart a-thump, she raced back to shake Ray. "Mr. Crondite has fallen."

"Nah—he's dead." Ray's red-streaked eyes rolled.

"How do you know?"

"Forgit 'im." He fell back on his pallet near the fire. Abby strained the way they had come for a glimpse of those folks from yesterday, but only a vast stretch of desert met her eyes.

Finally Ray woke, downed his coffee, and hitched the mules. She drowned the fire and tiptoed around the wagon. *Love mercy.*

"Git in."

"Shouldn't we bury him?"

"Forgit 'im, I said." Ray raised a fist.

Bluffs taller than Doniphan's courthouse towered in the distance as phrases whorled through her mind. *"Do justice. Love mercy."*

Mr. Crondite's skeletal image stayed with her as melancholy sucked her down. Morning lapsed into afternoon, afternoon into evening. By now, those vultures and wild jackals had surely picked his pitiful bones.

When the sky reflected orange and red, Ray left without even building a fire, so Abby made one. Then she wrapped in her quilt. As day's colors wilted into twilight, the wind's eerie wail absorbed her sobs.

Sand peppered the wagon at a rude wooden signpost for Taos, Chimayo, and Santa Fe. They made camp, and after supper Ray vanished. The persistent throb in Abby's temple for several days now pounded across the back of her head.

This morning her legs felt like railroad ties when Ray yelled at her to hurry, but she managed to tumble into the back. Hours later, a snow-peaked mountain range hovered southward when she opened her eyes. She yearned to reach a burning finger to those freezing slopes.

Finally, the wagon halted. Voices strained, but she could no longer lift her head.

"H'ain't th' White Mountains. This here's the Sangre de Christo range."

"Got a fevered woman slowin' me down—been bad luck all the way."

"Head on down t' Chimayo, they got hot peppers fer fevers."

Ray cursed before starting the mules again. *Lost. Bad luck.* But overwhelming sickness inundated Abby's questions.

Darkness and light merged in the endless grind of wheels on garrulous rock. In the trail's normal cadence, cooking and washing the dishes had made things bearable. But now, she could claim only this fine, thin air.

"Mount Baldy... Fever you say? Get blankets... fetch the priest."

Later, flames lighted the wagon canvas, and drums pulsed somewhere. At one point, coal-colored eyes peered at Abby over the wagon side, but she dozed again as pain exploded in her head.

"Leave her here with us for the winter."

"Practically dead anyways."

Black eyes appeared again. Water slipped down her parched throat, and then a scrabbly white man's face came into view.

"Come spring, I meander t' Chief Hashkeedasillaa's people, not so fer from Green Valley. Kin bring her 'long when th' gama grass gets knee-high."

The conversation faded. Being jostled from the wagon barely roused Abby. Someone smeared her chest with a smelly salve, but she hardly noticed.

"Bear grease mixed with native plants—this will help you."

She had no idea who spoke, but waves of agony stilled all curiosity. Ice coursed her spine, yet her skin burned.

When she next woke, smoke curled above her, and someone bathed her face. Later, a woman adrift in pine tar and sage forced stinging liquid down her throat. Then a man in black hovered near and dipped his finger in a small pot.

He touched a gritty mixture to her forehead and intoned, "Santo... tierra—Chimayo." He swept two upraised fingers in a cross, bowed his head, and smoothed her shoulder. "*La paz y la curación.*"

An ancient woman swayed nearby. Someone whispered, "*Padre* prays peace and healing."

Days and nights passed. During the day, a child often sat beside her on the earth. One day, he pulled at her arm until she sat up. Sky blended with earth in a mad swirl, and she wretched.

Another day, her surroundings came into focus—women grinding corn and drying hides. A squaw brought her porridge. Later, the same woman held flat bread to Abby's lips, still warm, and nothing ever tasted so good. Another day, the squaw and the boy coaxed her to her feet.

Before the world began to whirl, she shuffled a few inches. Exhausted, she slept until they urged her to rise. Mornings and evenings melded. The priest came and prayed over her again.

"*La paz y la curación.*"

Then one day, a change occurred, like shadows shifting at sunrise.

Suddenly she understood some of the women's speech, as though listening all this time had made a difference.

That evening, the sun departed with such a flourish, Abby wept as the horizon burnished with golden tangerine glory.

See how the red remains stronger near the horizon, daughter, and the deep yellow hues stay aloft? This is the moment you want to capture... ah, yes, that's it. Dab a little more of that deep gold a bit higher on the paper.

The squaw noticed her tears and called to the lad, who planted himself near. "*Puesta del sol.* Day go sleep."

Hours later inside a tepee, those magical hues remained strong, along with the child's words. *Puesta del sol*—even now the sunset touched her. Earlier Mama's voice had sounded so clear, so true.

In the morning, she felt strong enough to join the women grinding. Day after day, she sat with them and mastered their method of kneading and pounding. Phrases from the Indian tongue swept through her now, even when she slept. Gradually, she understood where she was—these mountains were named for the blood of Christ.

But one afternoon, a visitor with rotten teeth and a tobacco-stained beard hunched near the women's circle. His voice reminded her of Hollis Blum.

"Y' alright, Missus?"

His beard hopped up and down when he spoke. His brash tone set Abby's pulse racing, but her tongue recoiled.

"I be takin' y' on down t' yer man now; hear?"

The edge of command in his voice bade her swallow her rising objections. She had thought to stay here forever.

While the trapper spoke with some men, the child handed her a packet. One of the women lifted her head with the barest hint of a smile. Then the stranger smelling of animal hides and ashes drew her toward his mule. No chance to thank these people for saving her life as she landed like so much firewood on a bony mule.

The trapper straddled his mount and yelled, "Git up thar."

From her perch, Abby could only watch those kind souls vanish from sight. The scrappy mule ride pushed against her bones, and her spirit sank.

That night, a Spanish woman—bent nearly in half—led her to a pallet in an adobe enclosure. Long after everything quieted, Abby lay listening to others breathing. Finally, she rose and stole toward a faint light.

Moonlight revealed *1816* carved into a small building's foundation, and its heavy wooden door swung open to roughhewn pews. The long narrow enclosure centered a candlelit altar fashioned from dark wood. To the left, a polished Madonna gazed over the scene. The orderly benches touched a chord and revived Abby's power of speech.

"What would Mama think? I never dreamed..." Silence and melting wax soothed her, though Mama's strong opinion wafted.

We are Protestants. Catholic people believe very differently from us.

For a moment, Papa hovered near. "But dear, do you not think the Creator fashioned us all?"

"Our memories are a gift."

Maybe Aunt Susan had been right after all—at least these memories still existed of those now passed into eternity. Such a line they made through Abby's mind, like locals parading down Poplar Bluff's main street on the Fourth of July.

The chapel's serenity soothed her. *Sangre de Cristo.* Back on her pallet, sleep came at last.

An impossible week ensued, nights so cold her guide tucked an extra animal hide around her at the fireside. But each morning, brilliance painted the east, and by noon, she shed her shawl. One day, it occurred to her that her green calico dress had become white.

Now and again, the trapper stopped. "Checkin' m' traps." He left her a fire with water and some jerky. "Bellows here makes good comp'ny. Injuns recollect 'im, too."

The mule pawed rocky soil and snuffled an impassioned bawl.

"You want your master, don't you?" Her voice still sounded foreign in her ears. Through long hours, she imagined Indian braves skulking up from one side or another, but none came. At twilight, the trapper returned, and in the morning they started out again. Eventually the snow proved too deep for the mules, as though they slogged through mashed potatoes.

"Hafta go 'round now. Takes longer, but we'll git there soon enough."

A week later, in warmer country, only the highest peaks still showed white. The mules crisscrossed a massive canyon alive with an unfamiliar plant rising as tall as the oaks back home.

"That tall cactus—what do they call it?"

"Them's saguaros. Feast yer eyes fer a spell, h'aint none where yer goin'."

Where was she going? She felt no need to know. For now, the ever-changing landscape held her interest.

Interspersed with the saguaros' grey-green shapes, misshapen parodies of dried, woody fiber twisted into grotesque forms. Something had eaten them away.

"What happened to those?"

"Too many wood rats diggin' tunnels. Done played out th' cactus."

That night beside the fire, the trapper confided, "Most calls me Cactus Joe. Who y' be?"

At first, she could think of no reply. Finally, the sign above the store in Poplar Bluff came to her—*Ferguson*. She mouthed the name, and with it came another.

"Abby Ferguson. Abigail Belinda Ferguson."

Cactus Joe lit into a story about a Ferguson he met years ago. "Ever been t' Colorady?"

She shook her head.

"Thet Ferg'son lived yonder—had 'im a fambly. I s'pect three daughters. Tol' me 'bout that Oatman gal what got taken by Injuns, her n' her sister. Injuns kilt the ma n' pa down in Arizona terr'tory. You heard a her?"

"I cannot recall."

"Waal, her sister died after some time, n' she got traded to another tribe. Injuns do thet, y'know. Anyways, they branded her on th' chin, like they do with their own gals."

Though the tale was far from pleasant, Abby fell asleep listening and wakened the next morning still beside the fire. Cactus Joe had kept it burning all night and greeted her with hot coffee.

"H'ain't fer now, gal. H'aint fer a'tall."

After an impossible descent, the mules rustled through grass up to their backs.

"This here they call th' Tonto Basin." Cactus Joe made camp near some natives and exchanged pelts for venison. They traded dried corn for tobacco, and Abby sought out the women. Serenity settled over her in the luxury of staying at a campsite for more than one night.

Gorgeous sunrises hailed each new morning, and equally outrageous sunsets put each day to sleep. These Indians seemed friendly, and one night she asked about that Oatman girl.

"You said they branded her?"

"Yep. Put their mark right on her chin so's ever'body'd know she b'longed."

These squaws, so much like the ones who had nursed her, seemed unlikely to allow such a thing. Little by little, Abby spent more time pounding with them, but after about a week, a wagon approached across the wide western meadow.

Cactus Joe studied its progress. When the mules came within hearing distance, he sang out to the driver.

A short, bull-nosed man pulled up the team and stalked over, his eyes a foamy grey. He gave Abby a quick glance and pulled Cactus Joe by the arm.

Shivers coursed her backbone. *Ray.* Until now, she had kept him at a distance, like a bad dream.

A distance away, the two men's voices rose. At last, the trapper straggled to his mules as Ray returned to survey her up and down. "Waal, looks like yer alive." He slapped the side of the wagon, but Abby only stared.

"Git on up here, then. Ain't got all day."

When they curved north across a grassy plain, Cactus Joe stood shading his eyes. Once again, no time for a farewell. But words rang a chorus through Abby's mind as she caught a final glimpse.

Mercy. Kindness. Whatever lay beyond, he had shown her mercy and reminded her that kindness still existed, even out in this lonely wilderness.

Into the same Pinon pines that straggled across New Mexico territory, Ray urged the mules. But fear clutched at Abby. He had left her with the Indians to die—why would he want her now?

Upward, ever upward, the steep trail led. After three days, as if by magic, pines taller than she ever imagined towered above spectacular red boulders. To the north, a long lazy ridge stretched east and west as far as she could see.

Ray caught her staring. "Thet's the Rim."

After another hardscrabble day, her head began to clear. Midafternoon, Ray unhitched the mules at a rivulet where treetops staggered a treacherous path leading downward. A massive crow flashed blue-black feathers, its raucous, throaty call proclaiming the trespassers. When it flapped away, a jury hidden in the trees followed suit.

Ray mounted a mule. "Climb on. Gotta get some meat on y', woman—got work t' do." He hauled her up behind him like a potato sack. Then the path, so steep and winding she clung to him, demanded all of her attention.

Strewn with roots and rocks and barred by red-barked branches, the trail promised anything but ease. The mule balked, so Ray cursed and reached for his strap. The animal understood. Finally Ray pulled on the reins and pointed almost directly below.

Sunlight glinted on something down there. Weary as she was, a thrill ran through Abby. Perhaps this grueling journey had come to an end. For some reason, her name came to her again.

Abby—Abigail Belinda Ferguson McHale.

After a long swig from his flask, Ray let forth a sigh. His heavy breath dusted her cheek as all trace of blue leached from his eyes. "Nobody's 'roun here, nobody a'tall. We go farther down, n' this here Rim keeps ever'body out."

Chapter Five

The heady pink reflection against the Rim's eastern side nearly made up for missing Poplar Bluff's sunsets. Moments later, peach transposed with violet in a vivid shadow that enlivened the Rim's hulk.

Maybe if she baked bread tomorrow, Ray would be pleased. In all this time, she had spoiled not even one batch. Learning the squaw's ways had helped, but nothing she did satisfied him. She pressed her thumbs into the nape of her neck and waited.

Use your ingenuity, Abby Belinda. This spring, Mama's instructions had begun to emerge in her thoughts, akin to the first crocuses rousing from an unforgiving winter.

Things take time... a watched pot never boils...

Ray's trips across the Rim had become more frequent, but caused little change in her daily tasks. During his absences, many unanswered questions returned. *Why don't wasps make honey? What makes the red stay low in a sunset? What happens when a wayfarer reaches the top of the Rim? Does he see hills ahead, or a flat mesa?*

Sometimes when Ray toted butter, cream, and wild brown honey over the Rim, he headed back several days later with a couple of hens to add to their collection. But on every single trip, a few more head of cattle trailed him. The columns in his notebook represented those long-horned creatures, the shade of dun horses and always bony.

"How many cattle do you have now?"

Ray cocked his head. "Forty-three steers n' six cows ready to calve." Scarred pine floorboards lifted their futile complaint as he rocked. "Injun agent pays forty cents a pound fer butter, n' good for cream, too."

"How far away is he?"

"Half a day from the top."

"How would you keep butter and cream cool for so long?"

Ray squinted. "Line crates with hemp, cover 'em with straw—"

"You would need a wagon?"

"Ain't no concern 'a yours."

Deep russet gradually threaded with smoky purple before merging behind Strawberry Mountain.

"Whatcha watchin' fer all th' time?"

Putting her thoughts into words came hard. "The way… I like how all the evening shades blend into one."

He spat over the porch side. "If I'd knowed y's so given t' dreamin'—" His glower deepened, so she looked skyward again.

Where Strawberry Mountain met the Rim, an indentation formed. If one were to head that way, perhaps the climbing would go easier. The hair on the back of Abby's neck rose. Without looking, she knew Ray still stared at her.

In the morning, sunshine would find the western slope and inch by inch, chase the shadows down the valley. Such a turnaround— instead of rising in the East, light descended down the Rim's western side until full day. In late afternoon, nature swabbed extra charcoal into each niche and cranny, igniting her desire to create the likeness on paper. But all too soon, evening came.

Besides, she had no pencils, not to mention paper. Oh, how carefully she would fill even one page of Ray's notebook—if she dared.

Forty cents a pound for butter—double the price in Papa's store. More churning awaited her in the morning, but at least the wooden paddle's steady beat would free her thoughts to roam.

Silence reigned, except for the cicadas' hum in gangly Manzanita bushes. Then a shrill howl agitated a nagging hunger—a coyote from across the Rim. Abby edged across the floor and leaned into

Ray's leg as an elk call shrilled to fever pitch. Another bull took up the cry.

"Them elks obey their mates." Ray spat again.

A desperate guttural rasping followed more elk bugles, and a turkey vulture passed over. Something about the heavy bird's ungainly flight lightened Abby's heart. "Those vultures always swoop west."

Ray's lips sealed to a stark line.

"I can't help but wonder what lies over there. Don't you ever?"

He snapped his book shut. "They's sickness at a place called Wickenburg. Nothin' diff'rent. Live oak n' hackberry. Dry land."

All this he uttered with his eyes on his notebook. She rolled to her knees—if only he would look at her.

As full dark fell, his heels hit the floor. He shoved her down and her head hit the floor. "Shoulda left y' in Missouri."

"I only want to…"

A second later, the empty rocker bobbed back and forth. Manure assaulted her senses, and pain seared her scalp. Over her, Ray's fist crushed a golden tangle.

"You—you pulled out my hair!"

Single strands drifted from his thick fingers. Renegade floorboards creaked as he turned. Abby lowered her face and braced for another blow.

His leather boot toes pleated into deep crevasses as a *whoosh* grazed her forehead, but then he backed off and leaped down the steps. His boots crunched on rock thirty-seven times. The barn hinges squeaked, and then came a *slam*.

Sharp needles pierced the tender skin behind Abby's ear. After some time, she became aware of the pine wind caressing her cheeks like Papa's gentle touch. What did these reliable pine friends whisper?

No one will come. Lying here will do no good. Dizzy and faint, she stumbled up and steadied herself on the rocker.

Another elk call issued, forlorn and desperate. Then a turkey vulture's unmistakable *chut chut* quickened her. The great bird lunged close, though Ray swore they never flew after dark.

Against a lazy moon, its updraft cooled her forearm before the creature careened upward toward Strawberry Mountain. In its wake, something nestled in Abby's palm. She poked the velvety softness safe into her apron pocket and touched her scalp. The copper smell of blood oozed on her fingertips.

"Make a cold compress—" Even her whisper trembled. "Mama would give me some of her wound drops." She took a step toward the cabin door. "He has never hurt me like this. Oh, if only I could bear him a child."

In the darkness, Granny's toothless visage prophesied. *More sorrow... travel far, where darkness assails...*

"No—no—go away!"

If Mama were here, her holy words would thwart this evil omen. But Abby could only stumble to the bed and cling to her quilt.

Chapter Six

"Must be the Fort McDowell ambulance." Martin ducked his head as an inescapable dust cloud enveloped them. He summoned his men. "Water break."

Soldiers dipped into wooden water barrels stationed near the road. Captain Whitaker waved Martin over, a veil of red dust masking his clipped mustache.

"When we finish this confounded job, perhaps we can serve as housemen for this new Major Lewiston and his wife."

"He brought her out here?"

"Yes, and some other officer's daughter, too. If women can live at McDowell, they think, why not at Camp Reno?"

"Without—" Wheels crashed against granite, and the mule driver's high-pitched cussing blotted out the rest.

"Only sluggards stoop to cussing, children. The Lord gave us thousands of phrases and a brain to use them." Mama's strong opinion always surfaced at such times.

Amidst more profanity, one straining mule perked at the name "Missy." A serpentine whip sailed as the team conquered the taunting grade.

"Sir, I heard the drivers give each mule a woman's name."

"Indeed." Captain Whitaker groaned. "Clearly, General Crook never mastered the word *impassable.*"

Now came a soldier roosted on a great thorough brace wagon seat, inciting four lively mules. Some fool had rolled up the murky canvas top, revealing splashes of pale pink and lavender.

The unnatural tints startled Martin. Captain Whitaker saluted, so he followed suit, and a young woman under a bright calico bonnet gave her fan an extra flap. Heat razed Martin's face, though he knew she aimed her gesture at his superior.

The ambulance gave way to a gigantic blue army wagon piled with boxes and camp equipage. Against tents and ponchos rolled into a corner huddled several camp laundresses, copper-skinned Spanish women with glistening black hair. Young children curled around them like beagle puppies shrouded in dust.

"Pfwhhaaa." The Captain's clay mustache flaked onto his uniform as the second wagon topped the rise.

"Sergeant, that young lady in silk would make you a fine bride."

"A sluggish old farmer like me?"

"Ah, you think too lowly of yourself. Recall that lovely girl back in Missouri—Ferguson's Store, wasn't it? I noted her interest in you."

The Captain hurried off, leaving his comment to niggle at Martin's deep conviction that he was unsuited to marriage. After Papa died, he and his brothers tackled far too much farm work to think about anything else. Then came the war and now the cavalry.

But he did recollect that girl in Missouri—in the mercantile in Poplar Bluff. Ever since he accompanied a contingent of soldiers northward after Vicksburg, she had roused his curiosity. He still wondered about her fate, for when they rode through Poplar Bluff in the dead of night, they noted that the store had burned to the ground.

On the porch next door, someone rocked in a swing—a distinct *creak, creak, creak*. Was it the storekeeper's daughter?

Regardless, his destiny included no fair-eyed bride. He had passed through that season of life and emerged unwed.

Martin turned to his crew. "Go at it, men." Picks clashed against rock—it still amazed him when troops obeyed his orders.

An hour passed and after another water break, the men lapsed into resigned silence, hands molded to axe handles and picks. Dulled by the profound afternoon heat, supper and sleep became their highest hope.

Private Harris, an Iowa giant, helped Martin shove broken boulders to the side. He lifted rocks the size of a pot-bellied stove, yet maintained a good-natured grin.

"Between California and Council Bluffs, I hear men are building a railroad, Private. Would you rather be doing that?"

"Work is work. I'd as soon do this as anything."

When Captain Whitaker crested the hill again, Martin met him. "Everything all right, Sir?"

"Colonel Masters has summoned us to his tent tonight."

"Me?"

"You. Who knows what awaits us?"

Back in camp, Martin washed up and devoured his meal, and as he finished, Captain Whitaker sidled by with a grim smile. "Ho... beef and beans. A change from our regular fare, eh?"

"If you say so."

"It was beans and beef last night. A man has to find variety wherever he can."

After supper, Captain Whitaker appeared at his tent. "Someone as important as Masters must not be kept waiting."

His tone evidenced disrespect, but Martin maintained deference to their commander. After all, Colonel Masters had survived the war, too.

A few tents away, the colonel waved them in and after the usual greetings, plunged in. "Every week, more cattle disappear from the government herd in the Tonto Basin, just under General Crook's Rim." He reached for a thick roll of maps. "We must rout the rustlers; make them a public example."

Captain Whitaker helped him flatten the maps over a wooden table.

Since the Colonel was touchy about his height, Martin cramped his shoulders. But Captain Whitaker squared his and stood a full head above the Colonel's sparse topknot.

"One of the cowhands may have connections with outlaws who

wager that with three thousand head, a few at a time will go unnoticed. Your job, men, is to ferret out the culprits."

"How many troops shall we take?"

"Choose two good scouts, ah... except Harris and Wilson, who are needed elsewhere. Sergeant Tolzmann, word has it you are a natural at reconnaissance."

Better to let such comments slide.

Colonel Masters circled a flat area surrounded on three sides by the Mogollon Rim and bordering the East Verde River on the south. "No use wasting time here. Indian burial grounds, our scouts say."

"Any other specifics?"

"You might inquire of the cowhands." Colonel Masters pursed his lips. "Certain men have no scruples—surely you find this true, Captain?"

"That is the world's way."

"And upright men must bring such scoundrels to justice." The Colonel drummed the table. "I expect a complete report—depart on Monday next. Dismissed."

Some distance away, Captain Whitaker led the way down a ravine. "What do you think, Martin?" Since they had served together for so long, Captain Whitaker sometimes waived protocol.

"Seems we have ourselves a job."

"You know all about cattle, right?"

"As much as any Iowa farm boy."

"That's all there is to know."

A quarter moon rose and evening birdcalls hushed. Martin kept hoping to hear something akin to those back home, perhaps a turtledove.

"As a sheriff's son, I bring to this task considerable intuition."

"Is that why the Colonel chose you?"

"He knows nothing of my upbringing and thinks you ignorant, despite his cheap compliment. But he knows I can write stunning reports to impress Washington. Even an inept officer can be made to look good on paper."

Martin stretched his shoulders, suddenly recalling his last hot bath, thanks to Captain Whitaker. What he wouldn't give for one right now.

"Colonel Masters desires me out of the way for a while—Major Lewiston is one of his old war cronies." Overhead, one lone star made its appearance.

"Sir, why do you think the Colonel rejected Harris and Wilson?"

Captain Whitaker took his time, long enough for a coyote to yap and receive an answer from a distance.

"True scouts would *find* the thieves, but Masters hopes we get lost, or worse."

"Sir?"

"Yes, indeed. If we find nothing, he can claim he tried. If we return with valuable information, he gleans all possible glory. But if one of his Indian scouts rides into camp with our hides draped over a horse, he can say he even forfeited two good men in the effort to secure justice."

At rare hoof beats from the east, Abby shooed away her hens and grappled with the screechy coop door. Ray's fierce look kept her from asking questions of the last stranger who rode through, and that evening, she had hovered on the dark porch to eke out the men's campfire talk.

"Hell-fire renegades ... ended up in the calaboose, by Betsy. We was armed with a passel a' firearms—best battle I ever fit."

With this guest so close, she felt even lonelier than before. Now, weeks had passed, and this steady *garumph-garumph* neared the yard. The hens broke out in wild cackling. Goose flesh scampered the length of Abby's arms. Startled pullets scattered like buckshot as she thrust the pin through the latch.

She listened again—unbelievable, but unmistakable—someone was coming.

"Better make some coffee." She washed at the tank, dropped

her chore shoes by the steps, and raced inside. Groping behind the mending pile for her clean shoes, she touched some paper instead—what could that be? But she dashed her curiosity and circled her fingers until she touched her black shoes with their delicate side buttons.

Still hidden by dense growth along the trail, the horses slowed. Hammer blows echoed from the pasture—Ray's pounding and sawing would mute this arrival, and the barn blocked his view.

Visitors all to herself.

"Whoa, now."

Pulse roaring in her ears, Abby sprang onto the porch.

"Ho there, Missus." A deep baritone belied a tall man's wiry frame.

He helped a plump woman wriggle from her horse. Abby could barely maintain her composure. The stranger dusted off her skirt, the color of dark red maple leaves. Her face bore a smile like sunlight.

"I declare—someone does still live down here." The woman extended her hands. "Elda Mae and Fred Allen, your neighbors. You must be Ray McHale's wife?"

The woman's lavender scent, so like that of Mama and Aunt Susan, rendered Abby faint.

"Yes." She remembered her manners. "Please call me Abby. Do come in for cake and coffee."

"Ma'am." Fred shook her hand, surveyed the yard, and fingered his hat.

"My husband is clearing beyond the pasture today."

"Well, then. We shall whet our whistles, and you can look things over out here, Fred." Elda Mae smoothed dimpled fingers over his shirtsleeve. "Coffee sounds wonderful, doesn't it, dear?"

The scrape of chairs and the dust on Fred's collar assured Abby she was not dreaming. She warmed the coffee and filled cups as Elda Mae set down her hat and seated herself. Fred tapped his foot, so Abby pulled up a crate.

"Sorry, we have no extra chairs, and only honey for your coffee."

"We take ours straight." Fred settled on the crate with somber aplomb, but the sparkle in Elda Mae's green eyes enticed Abby.

"This cake tastes delicious. What is that spice?"

"My Grandmother Carmichael's recipe. I experimented with an herb growing in the yard—I might add a pinch more leaven next time."

"Oh, I am so delighted to meet someone else who uses our native plants."

Outside, the pine wind stirred. Abby allowed for polite silence before asking the question thrumming inside her. "Where do you live?"

Fred flung his hand toward the window. "Up that way, probably a country mile."

A sob caught in her throat.

"I often stay home when Fred fetches supplies in Green Valley, but this time we met a man who speaks of homesteading on Pine Creek. Just think, some day, we might have more neighbors."

"Pine Creek?"

Fred's thin cheeks turned pale. With a searching look at his wife, he offered, "That would be the water running through your property."

The creek had a name? These folks must think her dim-witted.

"Would you like more coffee, Mr. Allen?"

"No, thank you." He flicked his bony thumb and finger. "Have you heard that the army brought Texas cattle here for the Indians to hunt like buffalo? The government, that is." He rubbed his palms with a *swish, swish.*

"In Green Valley, we met a man who lost a good part of his arm to snakebite. He almost died, but an army doctor performed surgery." Ray would call Fred's diction "citified," but Abby devoured every word. "My hat is off to the physicians who tend the ill and injured in these parts. What a task!"

"Fred, Abby and I need some woman talk. Maybe you can find Ray."

"Oh, no!" Abby slapped her fingers to her lips. "That is... ah, he would rather not be disturbed."

Elda Mae repositioned her weight, sending forth another lavender draught. "Well then, maybe you can spot that phantom turkey vulture, Fred. I imagine he visits here, too."

"Yes, indeed. Thank you kindly for the cake, ma'am." Fred shuffled outside, and through the open window, his shadow lengthened toward the skimpy corn patch. Wide brown suspenders pitched his trousers into tents, like a garden specter Mama created every spring to frighten away voracious crows.

"No supper for me tonight, Miss Abby." Elda Mae's countenance crinkled into pleasant folds. "I am so pleased to know another woman lives nearby!"

Another woman... close by.

Scarcely able to pose her next inquiry, Abby asked, "How far are we from your place?"

Her visitor patted her lips with her hankie. "Why, child, I assumed you..." She fingered a small jar of wildflowers. "Did you pick these?"

"I keep some inside even in fall—Mama always did."

"So many varieties here. I have even found some that puts me in mind of the pincushion flowers back east." Elda Mae peered out the window, highlighting gray hairs throughout her thick black locks.

"Fred has a nervous disposition. When he cannot bear sitting still, he drags the roadbed to the Rim, to ease access. We heard in Green Valley that the overland stage might alter its route this way, and General Crook may build a road over the top. I do hope so. Fred's work requires quiet, but living out here does get awfully lonesome."

She took one last forkful of cake. "So tasty, dear."

Abby gathered her courage. "Begging your pardon, but if a person wished to visit you, which way would they go?"

"Oh, forgive me. I do get off track. Where the trail ends at your wagon path, turn left. Come out on the porch with me, dear." She gestured past Fred, who examined the corn with great care.

"Past that giant sycamore the trail curves, and soon, water flows from the rocks—you can refresh yourself there. Follow the trail to a prospector's shack left to rot."

She scratched her right temple. "Brush may hide the path at times, but our horses graze a little farther on, and then you see our cabin."

"So our places form a triangle with the Rim?"

"I guess you might say so. Travelers sing up there by times, and supply wagons rumble along every few days—I doubt you hear any of that."

Travelers sing... not so far away...

"No." Abby laid a hand on her chest to quiet her heart.

Elda Mae flicked dust off her sleeve. "You certainly have an artistic bent—I suppose a vulture might observe our homesteads as a triangle, but I never thought of it that way. Fred deems those birds so wise. Such awkward flight, wings in that upraised V, wobbling in circles, but they ride the currents like ships in the ocean."

She patted Abby's hand. "I noticed your chicken coop. Do you have a garden?"

"I found squash seeds in the barn and some sprouted turnips. Wild onions grow despite the rocks." Abby led the way around the cabin.

"Gardens take work in this ornery soil. Oh, for Ohio's lush black earth."

Squeaks, gurgles, whines, and a cat's meow issued from a nearby juniper tree. Abby jerked toward Elda Mae. "What makes all that racket?"

"A male cat bird, kin to mid-western mockingbirds." The ruckus broke out again. "A plain grey species, but talented enough to mimic even frogs. No doubt, that one has made acquaintance with our barn cat. The males practice such deception, although the female's song is lovely."

"I see so many unique birds here."

"Fred studies and sketches them."

Abby's fingers ran cold. "He sketches?"

"His employer—I should say, his sponsor—sent him to catalog the great variety of species, so different from the ones back home. Fred cannot say enough good about that man's passion to form a bird society in Cincinnati."

But these details escaped Abby. Elda Mae's wiry, ill-at-ease husband knew how to draw? That meant he must have pencils and paper. Elda Mae went on about Fred's good fortune in meeting a man named Erkenbrecher, but Abby could only wonder how to entice these folks to return? Then she spied her onions and remembered: Mama never let a guest leave empty-handed.

"These onions give stews a special flavor. Let me send a few with you." When she stooped to pull some, her hair slipped from its pins. Elda Mae's sharp gasp reminded Abby of her wound, so she dropped the onions to contain her long curls.

When she recovered and held out the onions, fiery green sparked in Elda Mae's eyes.

"Dear?" Fred's summons startled them both. He peered around the cabin corner like a child.

"Not yet, Fred. Give the horses another drink, why don't you?"

He scampered away, and Elda Mae smoothed Abby's shoulder. "I must ask you something. Please take no offense."

"Yes?"

"Does Ray treat you well?" She groomed her fleshy chin rolls. Abby fingered a few short hairs that finally had spiked through the bump on her head, but no words came.

"How did you suffer such a bad head wound, dear?"

A wave of sickness started low in Abby's gut. "I—I ran into something."

"I hope you will not think me a talebearer, yet you ought to know—" Elda Mae started around the cabin as if she lived here, with Abby close behind.

Near the front porch, Fred met them, horses in tow.

"I watered them."

As if shooing away chickens, Elda Mae pushed out her palms.

"Check their hooves for rocks or sit here on the porch—I shall be along in a minute."

Fred's arms dangled like a slender wooden puppet's. Elda Mae pulled Abby inside, to the table. A shiver slithered Abby's arms, even in the heat.

"Did you know Ray had another wife?"

Another sick onslaught threatened.

"Dear Lord in heaven—he told you nothing." Elda Mae dipped cups of water for them, but the table, the water, this new neighbor sitting here—nothing seemed real.

"I have given you a fright." Strong fingers caressed the back of Abby's hand.

At long last, her whisper erupted. "Did you—meet her?"

Elda Mae pulled her chair close. "Yes, she was young and lovely, like you, but with dark hair and eyes. Indian, I would say."

Abby stared at her ragged nails. Mama would have a fit if she could see them.

"She left some time back, before the conflict ended."

"The conflict?"

"The war. You did know—? Oh, my stars—Ray never told you that the South surrendered?"

"The war is over?"

"Back in '65. Some time before that, perhaps even a few years, Fred met Ray and asked after his wife. Ray said she had left during the night. It was August, I believe. Yes, he said the monsoons blotted out her trail."

She leaned back and scanned the Rim. "I often wonder if that beautiful girl lies up there somewhere."

The cabin walls closed in. Was this what it felt like to faint?

"The poor thing—so thin. Ray kept her so close, we never enjoyed woman talk."

Facts galloped like the wild horses Abby had heard in New Mexico Territory. Ray said he had homesteaded in Kansas and drove his cattle to Missouri in '61 to supply meat for the troops.

Another question crackled from her lips. "What was her...?"

"Maria. I think they lived here for—maybe a year." A tremor entered Elda Mae's voice. "I must tell you something else, Abby. I married someone years before I met Fred."

Verdant emerald glinted through her thick chestnut lashes. "I can take this rocky soil and the challenges here, because with all his peculiarities, Fred loves me. We married eight years ago in April and set out to fulfill his dream."

The lilt returned to her tone. "Even with my shameful past, he chose me. Believe me, one upright man can make all the difference."

Bitter bile rode Abby's throat.

"Like catbirds, men sometimes trick us. A man might look reliable, yet be as ornery and cantankerous as a mule driver."

Elda Mae picked at her sleeve. Outside, Fred scuffed rocky dirt, impatient to leave. But Abby wanted to beg them not to go.

"Can you tell me about your sore now, Abby?"

"I... Ray... he threw me down and pulled—" Betrayal gnawed Abby's soul, so she swallowed the rest. *Love, honor, and obey...* Ray was all she had.

Elda Mae groaned. "You deserve better treatment, dear. For some reason, we tend to believe the worst about ourselves, while making room for the foibles of others. If only we had more time to talk." She drew herself up and her eyes glittered with purpose.

"But you have taken the first step. That begins your journey. Keep in mind, dear, our worth depends on our Creator, not on any human's evaluation. Another person's behavior tells us more about them than it says about us."

The warmth of her hands and her strong opinions ignited Abby's long-buried longing for Mama.

"Life has taught me that we are as sick as our secrets, but now you have shared one of yours. Honesty is the key to becoming strong."

A long-forgotten recollection inserted itself, as clear and rich as Elda Mae's eyes... *strong and full of art.* Yes, from that day picking raspberries with Granny.

"Do you remember how to get to our place?"
"I think so. Past the sycamore and an old building—"
"Yes—keep on the path. If Ray hurts you again, please come to us right away. I will pray for you every day."

Chapter Seven

Terrified squawks resounded over Camp Reno's rugged parade ground as galloping horses spiraled dust over a garrulous crowd of soldiers. Cheers for one side or the other vied for prominence.

"Come on, McHutchins! Swing and grab. That's the way—nothin' to it!"

"Take your swipe now, Ferrell. Waited too long last time—now, git that fowl!"

Martin steered clear of the melee and veered to the mess hall for some coffee. Captain Whitaker and a few other officers had the same idea.

"Not joining the revelry?"

"No, I would have to cheer for the chicken."

"General Crook would abhor such antics." Another officer made a guttural sound.

Captain Whitaker nodded. "They play this deplorable game for the feast of San Juan, so they say. But the feast day was back in June, and I daresay Saint John would be mortified at killing animals for sheer sport."

This disgusting game revolted Martin. Someone buried a live chicken in sand up to its neck. Then from either side, riders attempted to grasp the helpless bird's head. If one succeeded, the next in line chased him to steal the prey. Of course, the bird became a mass of blood and guts.

The other officer turned to Captain Whitaker. "So you are heading out tomorrow to search out cattle thieves?"

"A secret mission, so it seems." He raised an eyebrow at Martin.

"I hear tell of rampant cholera near Wickenburg, the canyons and arroyos crawling with fortune-seekers. Rode Grant's Stage Line from San Bernadino through Prescott to that turn-off back in my youth."

"Hmm, that is not our direction." The Captain offered only that much, so the officer took the hint and joined a card game.

Before the festivities died down, Captain Whitaker left for his tent. "See you at dawn, sergeant."

As always before a mission, Martin had trouble getting to sleep. Captain Whitaker never judged anyone harshly without good reason, so what had he experienced with Colonel Masters? He kept visualizing that circle he drew on the map. No doubt, Captain Whitaker would head directly there once they arrived in the Basin.

In feeble morning light, the two of them rode abreast toward a sheer cliff, with two privates following behind. "Another day of exhilarating sights, sergeant. Tell me, what in this vast territory has impressed you most?"

Amazing natural wonders paraded through Martin's mind. First, Fossil Creek Canyon, two thousand feet deep and within sight of San Francisco Peak. Then Clear Creek Canyon, which they had ascended and descended on their initial search for Camp Verde.

Oh, that cold, pure water at the base, with the smell of wild hops saturating the air in a sweet-citrus lupulin scent. Then Beaver Creek's basalt-walled canyon, where they discovered the wagon road from the Little Colorado to Camp Verde, or— He could reminisce until dawn and still not reach the end.

"A challenging question, but those cliff dwellings at Montezuma's Well still haunt me. To think ancient people labored up and down them each day, toting their children and all their essentials. Can you imagine sleeping up there?"

"Mighty peaceful, I would think, and safe from invaders. Remember the scout trails descending the Rim, the work of Sergeants

Morton and Crawford before our arrival? Say, do you recall General Crook's vegetation list?"

"Spanish bayonet, giant cactus, cedar, hediondillo, madrono, mountain mahogany, mescal, mesquite, mulberry—"

"Ah, the general would be proud of you. Nopal, palo verde, scrub-oak, scrub-pine, and yucca."

"I owe my memorizing ability to Mama, for sure and certain."

"Is that so?"

"She started us young on poetry and Scripture." And, Martin might have added, he attended to his studies to avoid upsetting her after that one awful day. He still shuddered at the sight of Papa, dead in the haymow—try as he might, Martin could never erase that image.

After that, everything changed. His older brothers and sisters helped him with his studies, and he did the same for his little sisters Meta and Lissa. But he had never breathed a word of this awful memory to Captain Whitaker—or to anyone.

"Never met a man like General Crook, so attuned to every small thing. Remember when I suffered that snakebite, and he came to ask after my health? Nothing seemed to distress or annoy him."

"Maybe all those years on the trail taught him how to hide his displeasure."

"Indeed. He is always first awake, even before the cook. The Indians recognized his spirit right off, probably because he learned their uses for each plant."

Afternoon brought relief from the day's heat, and finally, evening stole over the high desert country. Martin ached for sleep, even though bad dreams from the war still stalked him. He repeated the general's vegetation list over and over and when that failed, switched to his catechism. But rest still came hard.

Halfway through that first night, Private Langseth thrashed about and left his bedroll twice. When he sat up the third time, Martin did, too. A low whimper ignited concern.

"Private? What is it?"

"Gut cramps."

Early in the war, loose bowels gained the nickname *quickstep*, and every soldier feared its suitor, dysentery. When the ailment ravaged their camp, the moans of the afflicted equaled or exceeded those of the wounded. Martin ate only hardtack and drank nothing but boiled coffee during those periods. Still, he contracted the scourge—such terrible cramps that he expected to die.

When the camp surgeon announced that the alvine flux was killing more men than the fighting, Captain Whitaker issued new orders. "Move that latrine downstream. Boil the cooking pots and forks before and after each meal." Then he forced remedies down the men's throats, including Martin's. The recollection sickened him even now.

Hearing Private Langseth's groans, Martin sent up a plea. "Oh please, save us from the quickstep." But in the morning, Private Langseth had trouble standing tall. Private Miller, his face the color of bleached sand, showed signs of weakness, too, so Captain Whitaker took things in hand.

"Any symptoms, Private Miller?"

Reluctantly, the young soldier admitted to abdominal pain.

"Blood in your stools?"

A fiery flush told the tale, so Captain Whitaker acted without hesitation. "Your symptoms may subside in a day, or develop into a life-threatening bout. Both of you need some blue mass."

Martin's stomach threatened revolt. The thought of the chalk and mercury mixture revived its gag-inducing, slightly oily smell. The only other medication available, an opium plug, sometimes played with men's minds, so until the devastating outbreak that took down a third of the unit, he had refused both.

But eventually, Captain Whitaker stood over him like a determined matriarch, holding the vile blue mass syrup. Exhibiting the same obedience Martin employed that day, the two privates loaded up and mounted, and Captain Whitaker stood beside Martin to see them off.

"I know how you welcomed this respite from road work, but you must report immediately to the surgeon, Captain Blaine. I am sending a note for him, requesting recuperation days before signing you back into work detail."

His forehead bunched, he kicked at some loose rocks. "Captain Blaine will inform Colonel Masters that we carry on as best we can."

He raised his chin toward Martin, who gave a nod. During the Vicksburg siege, he had helped bury far too many quickstep victims. Once, near the surgical tent, the screams of a man being cauterized brought more terror to his heart than the Rebel yell.

The smells of that day came back—turpentine stupes applied to soldiers with intestinal troubles, blistering and cupping employed to relieve fevers, brandy and wine for terrible pain. Only calomel, a yellowish-white solid mercury compound used to treat typhoid and dysentery, bore no scent.

What a mercy he and Captain Whitaker had survived. Now, the Captain's quick decision might spare the privates' lives.

The privates spurred their horses southward just as the sun made its appearance. Martin murmured, "I hope they get some rest."

"They will. Captain Blaine owes me a few. Colonel Masters has head-butted him more than once, and a well-written report smoothed things over." Captain Whitaker scanned the horizon. No use inquiring further. Martin figured the less he knew about such things, the better.

The Mazatzal Range formed a long crescent to the west and north, and in midmorning light, its wooly lower slopes seemed not so distant. The higher peaks boasting rock cliffs shone red in the sun.

"Looks like a row of men's faces with curly green hair. From the camel humps of the Salt River Valley to this incredible range, this land never disappoints, eh?"

"Sir, I pronounce you the great labeler. Remember those four peaks you called grandfathers looking down on their descendants? A little farther, you said our road looked like a mountain-eating snake. When we felled hundreds of saguaros and mesquite, you said we were shaving the mountain. A couple of months later, we started on the giant's fingers."

A rueful grin punctuated the Captain's reply. "A man has to do something with his mind or lose it out here."

That set Martin to thinking. What did he do with his own mind? Mainly, he followed Captain Whitaker's lead, as he did back in Iowa with his older brothers Friedrich and Henry. Fortunately, when he joined the war effort, Providence placed him under a levelheaded officer.

"Now, to conquer those smooth faces, we need a pass into the Basin instead of hacking through that wooly hair for days on end. Labeling may not be your gift, Martin, but you are a professional pass-finder. I leave that to you."

Not the first time the Captain had looked to him for logistical help. Nooks and crannies known only to the local rebels filled Missouri, Mississippi, and Arkansas, and Martin soon learned the deceptiveness of heights, but his innate sense of direction did him proud. Teamed with Captain Whitaker's genius for outwitting the foe, they often netted their prey.

When an elongated escarpment rose before them in the distance, Captain Whitaker halted. "Your turn, sergeant. How shall we describe that ridge?"

"Could that be what the general called the Rim? We came close to it when we first arrived, before we turned south to Camp Verde."

"Ah, your memory serves you well. Runs two hundred miles, they say, two thousand feet above this basin, a boundary between two distinct worlds—cool high country above and desert below. Right now, that word *cool* tempts me. What say you and I lose our way and never return from this mission?"

His low whistle echoed the vast expanse. "The Verde River runs through here, parallel to the Little Colorado before dropping down to feed the Salt."

"I see it over there—that sparkle of blue."

"Eyes like a cat, sergeant. I guess they named the Rim after a Spanish governor in the last century."

"Say that name again—Magonlian? Mongolian?"

"Mogollon."

"*Mugeeyon.*" The word made an uncomfortable fit, but such protrusions always intrigued Martin—the little hill he and his siblings slid on in winter amounted to nothing at all.

I will lift mine eyes unto the hills... Day by day, this prayer attended him.

Across a gulley-washed miniature prairie, they made camp. They both feared eating too much, and once settled into their bedrolls, the Captain made no move to converse. Such stony ground— Martin closed his eyes and hoped for the best.

The scent of boiling coffee woke him from deep sleep. His face flamed—the captain had already saddled both horses. Before dawn, they headed out and soon found their break in the range. Around noon, Martin squinted and paused. Then he pointed straight ahead to an enormous herd of longhorns.

Captain Whitaker pulled out his field glasses. "You can see them without glasses? Is that what living on a farm does for one?"

"Fresh cow's milk and Iowa corn and beef. Nothing better, sir. Now that you have them in your sights, what do they look like?"

"Sixty-five hundred wind-worn rocks, or that many sheep with horns twice the span of their bodies, spread over Arizona's wrinkled surface like the speckles on my grandfather's arm. No wonder the Spaniards reportedly stayed far south of this wild country, or intermarried in New Mexico." He lowered his glasses. "By tomorrow, we should smell those cattle and see the whites of their eyes."

True enough, morning came, and Martin smelled the herd before he saw them. Approaching these skinny creatures worked its tranquil spell on him.

"Sergeant, how would you describe this massive rim?"

"A giant carved an enormous bowl and decorated the rim with pines and boulders."

"An apt description. Perhaps my ingenuity has affected you?" The Captain chuckled, but then intense concentration lined his face. "Now, to business. Colonel Masters says to ignore what lies beyond the Rim, but what does your gut say?"

"Of course I should like to climb—"

Sharp blue eyes glinted at him. "Talk to the hands first. Then follow your heart. I need to check on something. Meet me here tonight."

Captain Whitaker urged his horse down a path almost obscured by overgrown brambles. After years of unraveling countless puzzles together, his sudden disappearance on a solitary investigation had become routine.

Dark clouds banked to the north, but Martin's spine prickled to know what lay on the other side of that high mass. Men raved of incredible rock formations and tall pine forests beyond the Mogollon Rim. Still, uncertainty niggled as he caught up with one of the cowhands and asked about the herd's losses.

"Lost a few more last night; mighty slippery raiders."

"With such a severe rise on two sides and a creek on the third, that seems strange. How often does this happen?"

"Three times since spring. They time it just right."

"How many have you lost so far?"

A cloud darkened the sun. "Maybe thirty or forty."

A faint light flashed far back in Martin's memory. Somewhere during the war, they had run across a case of cattle theft, too. "Have you run any searches?"

"Nah, the Army shorthanded us. Some of the men already take double watch." A few splashes of rain hit their hats.

"Do the losses increase when you move the herd?"

"'Bout the same, I think."

A shower rained down, yet that towering ridge beckoned—it would never do to offer Captain Whitaker little or no information. Under a rock ledge offering a spacious view of the Rim, something inside Martin whispered, "Go!"

When the rain ceased, he headed his horse, Docker, over a draw and zigzagged up the side. The war had taught him a man could live in any hollow or crevice. On their way South, they discovered men surviving in wild ravines. Some could scarce believe the war had ended eighteen months earlier.

Ragged cliffs outlined the upper Rim, but the lower slopes offered their own challenges. Docker forced his way through wild blackberry hedges, creosote and tangled Manzanita bushes. Finally, over just one more rise, a whole new world opened. A faint whir rose from towering green-black Ponderosa pine. The sky, clear-water blue, bade Martin breathe deep.

About two miles west, a vague glint of silver marked a river or creek. He resolved to return here someday and search out the natural bridge he had heard Indian scouts describe, but now, he must seek evidence. One thing he could already tell for sure—this canyon's lush meadows and water source would supply a good-sized herd.

Once, he could have sworn a wisp of smoke curled near that glint, but his field glasses revealed nothing. With a last look at the beautiful valley, he urged Docker down an elk trail. Back in the basin, a rich bacon scent led him to Captain Whitaker, who offered no information about his findings.

"No sign of a burial ground?"

In the heat of exploration, all thought of that had faded, but tribes marked their burial grounds well—surely he would have noticed. The Captain stared at the darkening Rim.

"You thought you saw smoke?"

"I was sure, but then it disappeared."

The Captain leaned back and slapped his hat over his head. He figured things out piece-by-piece, rarely speaking until he came to conclusions. Anticipating insights from under that shock of thick dark hair made up half the fun.

In the firelight, Martin's sketchy map offered little help. That finger of land he had noticed between the creek and the way to Camp Verde might hold clues, and he wagered the Captain would agree.

But in the morning, new orders surprised him over the strongest coffee the Captain ever produced. "Much as I should like to see what's over the Rim, I need to watch around here for a couple of days. Sergeant, what do you propose to occupy your time?"

A furry dark brown spider the size of Martin's heel crawled toward his boot. He kept his eyes on it.

"Want to spy on that smoke you saw yonder?"

"Sir, maybe my eyes tricked me."

"If you thought it was smoke, it was. And we both know things go better with one rider rather than two at that altitude, since every sound echoes."

As usual, he addressed Martin's discomfort in his straightforward manner. "Despite protocol, traveling alone becomes necessary at times. Remember that night we separated and caught those Rebs smack between us? Where was that, anyway—someplace in Arkansas?"

"West of the White River, sir."

"Ah, yes. Now we must trust our instincts again. Meet me here late on Friday." The rising sun highlighted the tip of his mustache. "And sergeant?"

How many times had Martin received final instructions before they took off in different directions? He braced himself, aware that whatever Captain Whitaker said would come to mind over and over in the next two days.

"If someone finds you, tell a righteous lie, do you hear? Any thief crafty enough to run this operation considers cavalrymen stupid. Save your hide. If that means lying, I command you to lie—you will be in mighty good company."

Chapter Eight

"Scrape out th' pig pen. Fill th' tank, n' don't be slow." Pulling a heavily loaded second mule, Ray gave Abby orders before he disappeared into the brush.

The fierceness in his eyes forbade disobedience. By the time she fed the chickens, gathered eggs, and shoveled foot-deep muck onto the manure pile, the sun blazed. She leaned the shovel against the barn wall and yawned. When she opened her eyes, a ray caught on something shiny stuck in a crevice, so she reached for it on tiptoe.

The silver rectangle fit in her palm, smooth and heavy, like the money cache Papa wore at his waist. Turning it over, she wiped the surface with her sleeve and in the sunny doorway, read:

"C... r... o... n... Crondite. Now where have I heard that name?"

Setting the clasp back just so, her elbow hit the wall and the piece slipped from her fingers. She leaped back as the buckle split in two.

"Oh no! Ray will be furious." With great care, she unfolded a stained paper holding gold pieces—five of them.

In Papa's store, travelers from out West sometimes paid with twenty-dollar double eagles. He tucked these treeasures away for the future.

Crondite—the name danced in Abby's memory. For too long, her thoughts had shunted between fantasy and reality. Now, time seemed to stop as a hog rubbed against a wooden divider. The stash warmed in her hand. Then like a faraway light, a ghostly recollection flickered. That sick man on the trail—he had gone by Crondite!

Stacking the coins inside the paper, she folded and pressed the wad into the buckle. All the while, her pulse thundered in her ears.

"Please, let it slide shut." Her prayer answered, she set the buckle back in its hiding place with a furtive glance.

Hurrying to the creek with two empty pails, she imagined Ray's fury if he learned that she knew about the money. Hearing the soft splash of water, alive with glints and sparkles, brought up another memory—picking raspberries with Granny Ferguson.

What was it she had prophesied—*strong and full of art?* Full of art? Ha! The only thing filling her now was lies.

About ten more trips would fill the tank, but she had all day. Three days, in fact. But as she set herself to the task, this recent discovery haunted her—so much money, and its owner dead. Mr. Crondite's bony visage accompanied her with every trip.

On one struggle up the creek bank, a sound caused her to stare into the bushes until she outwaited some small animal. As it skittered away, the branches swayed a bit.

"Maybe Ray will find that man's widow and return the money."

The pronouncement sat wrong, like a falsehood. With every journey from the creek to the tank, reality gradually overwhelmed Abby, and horror set in. Ray had stolen that money.

"But what can I do?" The call of a wild bird attracted her attention, piquing her desire to climb to the trailhead. No! Ray had forbidden such a venture. She went inside to mix a batch of bread, but the urge increased. What harm could come of it? He would never know.

Soft, pliable dough conformed to her greased rising bowl, and through the window opening, that tall sycamore beckoned her. She rehearsed Elda Mae's directions. To the trailhead, past that tree, and...

Even as she lay on the porch floor with her fresh wound, a murmur had stirred deep within. All this time, she had focused on her foibles and believed Ray would change. But his steamy eyes declared that she would never leave this place.

Her pottery mixing bowl, the rough table, the cool iron of her frying pan, and Ray's rawhide coat hanging on its peg, grounded her. Of course she could walk to the trailhead. And from there, she would see the path leading to Elda Mae and Fred's.

Watering the vegetables took little time since the monsoons had recently infused them with the will to live. While she swung her tin watering can, that raucous catbird made its presence known, and Elda Mae's statement resounded.

Men can deceive us like catbirds.

The mocker switched tactics, exactly what she was doing. Yet how could Ray ever discover her deed? She washed her hands and hurried inside.

"If I use that walking stick in the barn and sing to ward off mountain lions everything will be fine." On a shelf, Mama's little brass bell caught Abby's eye. She used to ring it and place it on the parlor table to announce that someone had come seeking treatment for an ailment.

On this peaceful morning, the bell's smoothness brought strength as she surveyed the cabin. *Love mercy...* Mama loved showing mercy. And then came a whisper.

"Have mercy on *yourself*, dear child."

"On myself—why, I never thought..."

The pine wind enveloped Abby as she set her rising dough under a cloth in the sunshine. Salt-rising dough appreciated a bit of a rest for the ingredients to mellow and work together. Outside, a woodpecker drilled incessant straight lines around a scraggly mountain oak and popped a small acorn into each one for winter food.

Watching this intensive labor calmed her heartbeat. This massive bowl from Aunt Susan's kitchen, a work of art in wide brown and yellow stripes, often brought tears.

"I may have neglected my sketching, but at least I can still bake. Aunt Susan spent so much time teaching me." She shook herself. "No matter what, I am still Abby Ferguson."

"Yeast can fail, so I shall show you how to make salt-rising bread, too. The starter takes three teaspoons of cornmeal, a teaspoon of flour, a dash of baking soda, and half a cup of scalded milk."

"No salt?"

"Odd, isn't it? Last night this dough fermented beside the hearth in the rock salt box. But you must catch it at just the right time. My mother kept her starter warm in the salt barrel above the wagon wheel when they traveled here from Pennsylvania, so thus this recipe acquired its name."

The starter smell, like rotten cheese, told her this batch would work, and a mid-afternoon breeze stoked reassurance. Abby tied her bonnet and set out due east, but part way up the steep terrain, her doubts returned. What if Ray forgot something and turned back?

"No, he left hours ago."

Farther along, the jangly buzz in her ears gave way to lightness. Two-thirds of the way to the trailhead, bright yellow ragweed, lazy Susan, and Indian paintbrush flourished. Tempted to pick some, she quavered. What if Ray noticed them and realized she had strayed? She limited her clutch to a lazy Susan, wild red and white sweet peas and two daisy-like blossoms, a unique violet blue.

When the path met the wagon trail, she spread her arms and turned a circle. From here, the traveled path stretched toward the sycamore sentinel and onward. Down the center, tough wild grass waved a heathery line.

A mourning dove cooed from somewhere. Normally, that cry saddened her, but today, Elda Mae's directions reverberated—*past the tree to a spring. Come across an old shack and continue when the path turns.*

Desire to do just that clogged Abby's throat. She had started too late to attempt the trip today, but determined to travel the distance soon, before winter. But even as she set her mind, trepidation lodged in her chest.

Maybe she ought to pray for Fred and Elda Mae to return instead.

Then she remembered—*Mama said the Almighty viewed our thoughts as prayer.* During these lost years, had all her desperate thoughts risen to heaven? No matter how befuddled she had become, did the Almighty still hear her longings?

Her whisper melded with trees and sky. "Please send what I need."

A sudden recollection arose of the day she and Ray arrived at this trailhead. She only knew the journey had grown unbearable, and Ray said that the Rim would keep people away.

Something stirred the bushes, so Abby poised to swing her stick. But soon a twitching black nose and velvety ears emerged—a half-grown fawn. The creature shied back, then took a tepid step... two more, another. She froze, and it nosed her arm.

At her whisper, the fawn's ears trembled. Then another drew near, perhaps a twin.

A few moments later, they jogged back into the brush, and a vast panorama spread below Abby. Surely, such beauty could soften even the hardest heart.

Far above, the Rim's red crags juxtaposed with late summer greens, and she saw how their farm, situated on a deep ledge between the valley and the Rim, created a perfect hiding place.

What did Ray have to conceal, besides Mr. Crondite's money? A shiver coursed Abby's arms.

"The next time he goes off like this, I *will* visit Elda Mae."

Another dove crooned and a woodpecker drilled into a tree trunk. Branches kept her from sliding, but oozing brown sap stained her fingers. With each step, questions mounted. What was Ray building on the pasture's far side? Where had he stored the wagon they brought from Missouri?

A rabbit startled when she lost her footing for an instant. The furry fellow raced away toward a few elk resting in the shade.

"Would a baby change things?" Mama would have a tea for her barrenness. So would the Indians—and Elda Mae.

Back in the cabin, she divided and shaped the dough into pans, set them near the window again and observed a quarrelsome old hen near the barn.

Why not make chicken stew? The queen of the barnyard squawked, but Abby eyed her butcher knife.

"Enjoy this day, because it will be your last."

Chapter Nine

Oak leaves went belly-up in stifling heat. Since Ray left again yesterday, Abby took to humming a tune Papa used to whistle. Sometimes Mama sang along, about a balm to make the wounded whole.

Ray yelled at her when she sang, "Stop that infernal noise!" But today as she churned on the porch, a few more scattered words returned.

"Sometimes I feel discouraged, and I think my work's in vain—"

Ray's other wife came to mind often, and Abby pictured her living here. Elda Mae had brought such light—now she realized the war was over, too. That fighting had turned her life to ashes. How could Ray have kept this news from her? Just before Elda Mae left, she added another detail almost more shocking.

Someone—an actor—had shot and killed President Lincoln, so Andrew Johnson had taken over as President. By times, these facts seemed a farcical tale—President Lincoln dead? Who could possibly have set his sights on that kind man?

Now she guarded her tongue even closer—what would Ray do if she let on that Fred and Elda Mae had come? A tide of bitterness rose as she churned, and by the time the cream thickened, her wrath was bursting. Leaving the churn, she let out an unearthly scream and pounded a rock with her fist.

"The war ended long ago! A madman killed President Lincoln— why didn't Ray tell me?"

A memory surfaced from when Cactus Joe brought her to meet Ray. At the time, their phrases were muddled, but now, several floated back. "...Gettysburg in June, but they went back and forth all through '64."

"Fools."

"Even after the surrender, the Rebs still fought down Texas way."

Had she been daft? Had the sickness addled her brain? Breezes roused the bushes, accenting that little ticking sound she could never quite place. Time and again, she stooped to stare into the foliage, hoping to catch sight of an insect or small bird.

The steadiness of the sound, like cicadas back in Missouri, calmed her fury. She brushed pebbles from her palms and scrabbled onto the highest rock in sight, where she could see the sycamore tree.

"Now I know the truth. No one can take that from me, and one day I shall pass that tree on the way to Elda Mae's."

A few days after Ray returned, clouds surrounded the valley as she gathered clothes from the line. A tremulous scent, like the earth opening up, called to Abby.

"Oh, please..."

A low growl stretched along the heavens like Grandpa Carmichael's long, low belches after a Sunday feast. Dark and furtive, the rumble grew until it shook the earth. Lightning flashed, and moments after Abby stripped the clothesline, rain struck the parched ground.

The monsoons—she had almost forgotten. This must be August. She held out her arms to the downpour.

The barn door opened and Ray lined up buckets to catch the precious fall. Abby pulled the square tin washtub off the porch and raced inside for her dishpan and every other sizable container.

Barefoot, she pulled her dress up to her knees and swung her legs from the porch. With his hat dripping, Ray leaned on the lower half of the barn door.

"Thank you, thank you!" The humidity widened her breathing, and she slipped off the porch to hold out her dress. Face to the sky, she moaned at being covered, sopped, under a spell.

For a few seconds, Abby imagined Mama and Aunt Susan

swinging her back and forth between them as they scurried from the store to the house. The miserable heat of this lonely place slipped away; and along with it, her rage.

Near the pump, she scooped up a precious bar of lye soap and raced toward the creek. Her dress peeled off like scales, to hang on a low-hanging branch.

Then, as suddenly as they parted, the clouds withheld their bounty. In the fishing hole where the creek turned south, she bathed and washed her hair.

When Ray clambered over the rocks, she pretended not to see him. Then he dropped his drawers and jumped in. When he surfaced, he wore that approachable expression that had tugged at her heart after Aunt Susan's funeral.

Like golden rays through the treetops, long-forgotten words sifted through Abby's consciousness. *For if ye forgive men their trespasses, your heavenly Father will also forgive you.*

She let Ray catch her in the water. Things seemed new, as if the cloudburst had washed away all weariness and anxiety.

For once, his eyes matched the clear blue sky, and the thought of his other wife floated away. Elda Mae must have been mistaken. In that moment, the hunger to be touched and held mattered more than anything else.

He pushed her against a boulder, and she willed a baby to form inside her. If she were with child, surely he would let her visit Elda Mae. Like mother and daughter, they would fashion clothes for the infant. And if she gave him a son, nothing would ever be the same. Hope sprang anew as visions of more sons, blue-eyed, passed before her.

After frying beefsteak for supper, with the air so clean, she longed for fresh wildflowers. "Take a walk with me, Ray?"

"Where to?"

"Oh, maybe up the slope."

"No." His face hardened. "But I kin show y' somethin' else."

She ought to make him a new shirt, blue to match his eyes when the clouds left. If someone ever held a barn dance, she could be proud of how she clothed her husband. They came to a slope and at the bottom he held out his arms.

"Jump!" His tone melded command with dare. Abby set aside her hesitation and let go. The impact of catching her knocked him off balance and he stumbled backward, but managed to stay afoot.

Her giggle, such a foreign sound, surprised him. He blinked as if to say, *You liked that?*

He let her loose, but fished for her hand. Rain-soaked evening warmth seeped into her spirit.

Perhaps he had told her about the war ending, but she forgot. Most likely, the sickness had rendered her dimwitted. What mattered was that right now, he held her hand and walked with her. Maybe he would show her the whole ranch.

Near a snapped tree where broken alligator pine limbs and bristle bushes formed a waist-high refuge, he lowered himself to the earth Indian style. Abby crawled behind him.

In the thicket rested a month-old fawn. Every few seconds, a slight tremor jiggled its spotted sides. After a few minutes, Ray tugged Abby's arm, and she backed away.

Out of earshot, she whispered. "He must have been born very late in the season."

"Umm." He twisted toward the cabin.

"Ray, could we walk farther? Show me where you planted the hay."

"Ain't nothin' t' see."

"Then show me what you're building. I hear you hammering all day long—"

Murky clouds shaded his eyes, and his answer emanated as from a deep cave. "None 'a yer business."

"But I want to know our property."

"What fer?"

"Because we live here. When you marry—"

The last tinge of blue in his eyes leached into grey.

"—you work together. Mama knew all about the store, even though Papa—"

"We ain't your Ma and Pa, woman." His scowl thickened.

"I know, but—"

He withdrew his hand. Why had she let her curiosity show?

East of the barn, Ray spat into the breeze. "Now you see it."

"The alfalfa hay?"

His lips thinned.

"The green is so beautiful, different from anywhere else around here."

His jaw became rigid. "Whaddya mean, anywheres else?"

"Around our place. The last I saw this green was in Harper's Meadow back home, in the springtime."

He snorted and turned away.

"Does our claim end on the other side of this field?"

The little muscle in his cheek danced a jig. His tone set off an alarm. "Why y' wanna know everthin'?"

"Someone might build a store in the valley someday. I might want to go there, or visit some neighbors—"

His retort cut her off. "Ain't nobody comin'." He started walking.

Her mind churned. "Ray?"

He half-turned.

"You never want me to leave here? Ever?"

He spun around. The bristles on his chin shone as he shook her.

"Oughta know yer place b' now." Her teeth clashed. "Oughta had young 'uns long ago, but yer worthless."

Long after he thrashed away, red marks on her wrists mesmerized her. Sudden recollection returned her to Heid's Mill, far away in a Missouri hollow, on the day of the church picnic. When Elwood invited her to skip away from the crowd, she went eagerly.

"You turn fourteen next month, and you trust me, right?"

Of course. At fifteen, he knew his mind—he despised slavery, apprenticed with the local cabinetmaker, and raised sheep to build their future.

Around a long table in the churchyard, women offered luscious pies to raise money for a new belfry. Lizzy and the other girls flocked to the gunnysack race. Smaller children played ring-a-rosy and knurr and spell, the crack of the knurr on the flattened end of a stick lost in the participants' shouts.

"All right, but will we—"

"Be back before the closing? Sure."

Excited to be alone with him, she followed him through a pasture of placid cows, onto the road and down a ravine. Soon they reached the old millwheel poised over a dried-up creek. Elwood left and reappeared with some wildflowers behind his back.

"For you, my lady."

Just then, a male voice broke into slobbery song and Elwood pulled Abby into the shadows. But they turned the wrong way. In the exposed cave-like foundation, someone poured liquid from a complicated contraption and corked his jugs.

Elwood gulped. "A still." The worker leaned their way and listened. People were touchy about their stills—what if he caught them spying?

They were stuck. By the time Elwood guided Abby out, dark clouds threatened, and he noticed marks on her wrists.

"Did I do that? Oh, Abby, I only meant to—"

"I know. Hurry, we need to get back."

When rain deluged them, they took refuge in Elmer Lanabee's shed, and back at the church, the festivities had moved indoors. Papa met them at the door. Mama's eyes sparked fire, and Abby spent the next few days mollifying her.

Now, she stared at these painful red marks, sure to produce bruises by tomorrow. "Oh Mama, I was indeed hasty and given to presumption, and I did love adventure. But that day was so innocent. You knew it—I believe you did. Lizzy was right, you were only worried about me."

She sank onto a rock and cradled her wrists. "Elwood was trying to protect me, but Ray—"

You are not alone... the pine wind brought the message. *The Lord does not willingly afflict the children of men.*

Losing Mama, Papa, and Aunt Susan had not altered God's care. No—but all of those losses did say something about Ray, even if she wasn't sure what.

Blue sky deepened into dusk, stirring the wind. Still, Abby clung to the rock.

"Having a child will change nothing. I must face the truth, or I shall die here—just like Ray's other wife."

Great weariness engulfed her, so she started for the cabin. Likely, Ray would sleep in the barn tonight—good.

A cooling breeze laced the air. Summer's heat might taunt a bit longer, but not for long. Abby raised her chin and studied the Rim top; always steadfast no matter what.

Chapter Ten

Near a shallow cave, Martin warmed beans and coffee over his campfire. The first star appeared, silent and subtle, as he settled back against a crusty boulder. He could scarcely take in all the beauty of this land. Even the sky, so enormous and close, seemed different from what he'd known back at home.

A tell tale trail of smoke rose now, clarified by cool evening air. Yes, exactly where he had spied it before. That whitish whiff against indigo heavens ignited conjecture.

What would prevent someone from sneaking across this massive Rim and pilfering a few head of cattle from the government? All he would have to do is drive them back home. Time to think like a cattle thief, as Captain Whitaker instructed. When he gave those orders, his mustache vibrated with every T.

"Twist your mind into that of a cattle-obsessed scoundrel. What would he sacrifice to build a herd? Keep in mind, this fellow threatens the U.S. Army as much as any Rebel soldier did."

If the war had taught Martin anything, it was to trust Captain Whitaker. As a green private, he soon realized this leader was born to outfox the enemy. Some day he might say, "I once rode with Whitaker," as men bragged of serving under Lee or Grant.

But presently, he might be near enough for the thief to smell him out. Colonel Masters failed to consider one simple fact about this area he circled: a burial ground might stop Apaches, but rustlers would pay it no mind. Besides, not one sign had yet appeared on bushes or paths—Captain Whitaker was probably right again.

A quarter moon found Martin in restless sleep. He saw a burning building—someone might be trapped in there. But he could not rouse himself.

Even under his blanket, he shivered, so he fed the fire. Could the fire in his dream be in that southern Missouri town his unit passed though *en route* from Vicksburg? They had bivouacked a distance away for the night, but as they passed through town the next morning, folks gathered in clumps under lingering smoke.

A sober citizen scraped a shovel through the rubble and relayed dire news. "The general store owner and his wife perished in a fire two nights past. We fought as best we could, but..."

The first time they had camped near Poplar Bluff, headed South to Vicksburg, some locals had approached the captain about their stolen cattle. Captain Whitaker used his wit to play on the area's mix of Union and Confederate sympathies.

"You men for the Union?"

"Yessir." They spat and nodded. "But that don't mean providin' yer meat."

"We have receipts from Ferguson's store, gentlemen." Captain Whitaker drew himself up. "You might consider rounding up the Rebs in the hills instead of fretting over our troops. Governor Jackson's Confederates may well be your thieves."

The accusers left and Captain Whitaker sighed. "Ride into town, sergeant, and find out where Ferguson gets his beef."

As Martin entered, the storeowner climbed down from a ladder. "How may I help you?"

"Some locals have accused us of stealing their stock, so Captain Whitaker desires to know your cattle sources."

"Ah. Not the first time. A man named McHale drives them in from Kansas."

As they talked, a young woman in a bright yellow dress took her place behind the counter. She shared Mr. Ferguson's quiet manner, high forehead and ready smile, but not his height.

"Someone needs you out back, Papa. I shall mind the counter."

Mr. Ferguson excused himself. Words forsook Martin as he faced this girl who had bantered so easily with Captain Whitaker.

"Could I help you, sir?"

"Ah..." His color deepened. "Why, two of those chocolate creams."

She lifted the glass lid, packaged the candy and half-turned. Sunflower flecks laced her dark brown eyes. "Anything else?"

The small bouquets strewn over her pretty dress captured Martin. Finally, he roused appropriate words.

"Maybe a length of twine rope."

"How much, sir?"

"Ten feet should do. No, maybe twelve."

"Give me a few minutes, please."

He tore his eyes away from her small waist, mopped his forehead with his sleeve, and berated himself. Mama said he would outgrow his shyness, but he would never learn to speak with women.

On a deep shelf behind the counter, a wooden coffee box displayed an orange sign, Coffee—*three pounds—one dollar*. A grinder attached to the wall above a glass dish, and nearby, a glass-sided tea container boasting a tin scoop.

Green spice canisters offered cardamom and cinnamon, whole nutmeg and ginger roots near stacks of white granite, woodenware, stoneware, and china. Above the shelves, handcrafted maple chairs hung from spikes pounded into crossbeams.

His sisters Meta and Lissa would like this place, offering far more than their little Mitchell County, Iowa mercantile. Thinking of them usually cheered Martin, but today, nothing could allay his downcast spirit.

Twenty-six years old, and he had missed out. At barn dances in their neighborhood, he had only watched the activity. The few times Meta talked him into going, but bashfulness stifled him. Finally, he gave up the effort.

Another customer asked Mr. Ferguson's daughter about the yard goods, so Martin paced down the other aisle. A sharp lye scent revealed a display of bar soap. Tobacco wafted from packages near the pipes, next to some tonic bottles that bore the name Ferguson, too. Perhaps Mr. Ferguson's wife dealt in medicinals, as did Mama.

Martin touched a candle and eyed some fragile glass lamps. And then the beautiful young clerk returned, his rope in hand. Her warm smile and sparkling eyes wrenched him through, and his fingers trembled when she handed him a packet.

"Be sure to keep the chocolates from melting."

Like a schoolboy with his teacher, Martin nodded and silently slipped the candy into his leather pouch. The captain would josh with her—"A safe place like my mouth?"

"Do you need something else?"

"No, Ma'am."

She figured the total and he set the correct amount on the counter.

"Thank you." She deposited the coins in the till. "Where is your home?"

"Iowa." He swallowed. "On a farm."

He collided with the pickled herring barrel on his way out, set it back in place, and chided himself all the way back to camp. But no matter how he tried, he failed to wipe that girl's image from his mind.

When he learned of the fire some months later, he wished he could ease her distress, for he knew what it felt like to lose a parent. But what could he do?

Now, atop this massive mountain called the Rim, he stared into his campfire. More years had passed—what woman would want a man nearly thirty? Martin reshaped the tattered pillow Mama sent along when he joined the Army, pondering why that little Missouri town had surfaced in his dream. Poplar Bluff, that was its name.

"Everything has a reason, Martin." Mama's sayings often calmed him, but not tonight. When he drifted off, he dreamed again. He and the captain rode into Camp Reno and there stood that lovely Missouri girl, but 'twas Captain Whitaker who leaped down from his horse to embrace her.

Twice, Martin startled awake and added another log to the fire.

When the first ray stole over the Rim, daylight seemed a welcome friend. He ground some coffee beans and set his pot in the fire while he shaved, then poured himself a steaming cup.

But as the coffee awakened his insides, he froze at the sure resonance of pack mules. Yes, headed east up the Rim, only two hundred yards off. He doused the flames and hunkered down—two animals, one rider.

A tuneless whistle marked the traveler's progress, and a sharp slap echoed his garbled shout. Martin held his breath until hooves again clashed on rock. He reached for his field glasses and waited. When movement appeared on the Rim top, he abided another season before kicking soil around the fire.

Someone wound his way to the Rim top. But who? And why?

"Morning, Ma'am."

A heavy-set woman sprang back from her washtub, spraying soapy water down her skirt. She pushed her hair back.

"My goodness, you gave me a start. I must've been singing too loud to hear you."

Martin held out his kerchief. "Sorry to frighten you, Ma'am."

The woman accepted his offer and wiped her temple. "Elda Mae Allen." She returned his kerchief and shook his hand. "My husband should come in soon. He takes his breakfast late, after chores. Sits better with his constitution."

Built against a stand of pine and scrub oak, the barn shrank in comparison to the one back home, but still rose several feet higher than the cabin. The cackle of hens sent forth a welcome that put Martin at ease.

Elda Mae gestured to the trough. "Do water your horse and eat with us. We would be more than pleased."

"Thank you, Ma'am." Martin tipped his hat.

By the time Docker submerged his muzzle, Mrs. Allen had bustled inside, her sturdy build hinting at a German descent. No doubt she enjoyed unexpected company, like Mama, who always produced a hearty feast on short notice.

Near the barn lay a long, heavy iron rod for upending rocks. The last mile, the going had become noticeably easier, and obviously, this solitary settler's labor made the difference.

The barn door swung open, and a tall fellow meager of muscle stepped out holding a frothy milk pail. His long face, dusky brown woolen shirt, and suspenders lent him a schoolmaster's air.

"Why I—good day to you."

"Sergeant Tolzmann, U. S. Cavalry." Martin grasped the man's slender hand.

"Fred Allen." He gave a self-conscious smile and removed his hat, brushing over the thin hair on his scalp. "You spoke with Elda Mae?"

"Yes, and I accepted her kind breakfast invitation."

"We are more than glad for the company."

Fred's delicate frame gave no indication of the fortitude required to manage a place like this. But Captain Whitaker had a slender build too, yet such a powerful constitution and unending stamina.

"How do you make a living out here, Mr. Allen?"

Fred shrugged. "Most people think my occupation strange. Be that as it may, I study birds—ornithology."

"Pleased to meet my first bird scholar."

The cabin's well-scrubbed interior warmed Martin. Elda Mae dished up eggs and pancakes served with hunks of heavy bread, strong black coffee, and thick buttermilk.

After returning thanks, Fred turned to Martin. "And you hail from…?"

"Northern Iowa."

Fred's eyes lighted as he lavished creamy butter and blackberry jam on his bread.

"Anywhere near the little town of Osage, perchance?"

"A little northwest. My family still lives there."

Fred's eyebrows wiggled. "Did you hear that, Mrs. Allen? Our guest knows the maple-lined streets of my younger days."

"Quite the coincidence."

"Indeed. As a child, a man named Bush tutored me. He has now founded a seminary in Osage. He introduced me to the vast and intriguing world of birds. Every man needs a dream, and I knew I had found mine. Did you happen to know a Doctor Chase from Decorah? He plotted the city, named the east-west streets for trees and planted all those lovely maples."

Heaping the platter with more pancakes, Elda Mae gave her husband an attentive smiles. Pride shone in her eyes as Fred continued.

"I plan to publish the first sketches of Southwest breeds." Fred smoothed his fingers over her hand. "With the help of my capable wife, that is."

Elda Mae blushed and turned the talk to Martin. "And how does such a fine soldier find his way out here?"

"The Army keeps thousands of government cattle just over the Rim."

They accepted his reply, and the meal passed all too soon. Elda Mae and Fred assured Martin only two cabins existed on this side of the Rim and directed him to the second.

"Please do us the honor of returning." Fred extended his hand.

"I hope to. Your wife's pancakes rival my mother's."

Continuing his trek, Martin considered Mr. Allen. His diction distinguished him as an educated man, quite out of place in this wilderness—but then, the same could be said of the Captain.

Under a giant sycamore, Docker slowed, and Martin employed his field glasses. Strange, but no sign of the other homestead yet. He rubbed his collarbone, sensing something amiss.

His foreboding increased a few rods farther. At the well-concealed turn-off, a narrow trail thrust downward, so he dismounted. Only rabbit and mule deer scat, along with elk prints—no sign of inhabitants.

The war heightened his awareness of danger—Captain Whitaker's intuition had rubbed off. He must trust this intuition, yet that almost always required conquering the accompanying fear.

Docker nosed a scrub oak as Colonel Masters' instructions replayed, *...upright men must bring these scoundrels to justice.*

This inner niggling swept him back to Vicksburg. Reconnoitering across the river that day, his contingent had discovered nothing, yet anxiety still plagued him. Re-crossing the Mississippi by barge, Captain Whitaker shared his own trepidation.

"You sense trouble here, too, or am I mistaken?"

"Always pay attention to that inner guidance, no matter what anyone says."

Only two days later, their Iowa unit reinforced Louisiana's Ninth and Eleventh infantries against General McCulloch's Texas troops. But the Union supply station at Milliken's Bend swarmed with Confederates, and far too many troops died, many of them freed Negroes.

As they buried the dead, Captain Whitaker summarized the lesson. "Never underestimate McCulloch. He knew Crockett and fought at San Jacinto."

Martin did more reconnaissance while Docker foraged, but found no sign of humans. He brushed away an insect. Nothing to do but proceed with caution.

Mr. Allen reminded him that every man needed a dream. What could motivate the settler living down this path to choose such a remote location? High Ponderosa pines whirred in the wind—the place had its own rugged beauty, that was certain. Then why this sense of impending danger?

Chapter Eleven

"Have I slept the morning away?" Abby clung to the porch rocker until the tingling left her feet. A loud bawl issued from the barn.

"Oh my, the chores." She milked, cleaned and refilled the water pans, scattered grain and gathered eggs. Ray would be gone another day, but somehow, he would know.

The rich aroma of yellow cream reminded her of her churning duties, so she carried a full pail to the porch and set the churn in motion. Its *slap* and *slosh* blocked the pine wind's melody. Soon, her thoughts became as ponderous as the paddle.

Lately, memories of the fire surfaced, and today offered no relief. A persistent iron claw tightened around her—if only she had stayed home from that lecture.

Afterward, tales abounded of all the good her parents had done. People told and retold how Papa gave folks credit to seed their ground, and Mama eased the suffering of so many. How many times did someone lament, "I scarcely can accept their untimely passing, my dear."

Conjectures taunted the faith Abby always took for granted. So many questions—Marshall Tibbets assured her foul play must have played a hand.

In spite of Aunt Susan's attempts at comfort, a vacant space carved itself in Abby. At times, even her aunt's presence irritated her. As if that weren't enough, Marshal Tibbits' inquiries troubled her.

"Who did you see right after the fire?"

"Aunt Susan, and some man who brought us the news."

"Who was he?"

Neither she nor Aunt Susan could recollect.

On this stifling Arizona Territory day, the marshal's accusing face faded even the Rim's glory. Her paddle took on a life of its own, like the flimsy hope that Ray would change. Autumn tinged a mountain oak's leaves with gold. The seasons changed, yes. But not Ray.

Perhaps he had been the one to bring the news to her and Aunt Susan that night. If only she could remember. And then, Aunt Susan perished. Once again, Ray stopped by.

"A kind woman like yer aunt would want a family in her house."

How could he know that many years before, Aunt Susan had closed her heart to romance after her beau died in a hunting accident? Ray had been right—she loved children and often asked them in.

Saying yes when he spoke of Arizona Territory seemed the only thing to do. Why stay in Poplar Bluff, the setting for so much sorrow?

His inherited homestead had piqued her interest—a cabin awaited them with tall pine forest all around, and towering above, the Rim. They would build a cattle herd, he said. Better to leave bygones behind and make a fresh start.

Though the Marshall did his best, he never figured out what started the fire. Everyone had an opinion, but no evidence. But what did that matter now?

Once, early in their trip, she had asked Ray about the night of the fire. He muttered, "Musta been fate."

Mama and Papa would have mentioned Providence rather than fate. When tragedy struck, they often said, "The Lord giveth and the Lord taketh away."

In light of everything that had happened, at least Ray offered marriage, an estate that lasted forever. With each turn of her paddle, the word replayed. *Forever... forever.*

A fly buzzed, and Abby glanced up to see a Union soldier traverse the yard on horseback. A tremor coursed her spine. She rubbed her eyes—she must be dreaming.

Her neck hair bristled, and she chided herself for neglecting her usual watchfulness. Meanwhile, the stranger dismounted and strode close enough for her to recognize his Cavalry unit. She swallowed down her instinctive fear.

Of course, Union—the Confederacy was no more.

Back in Poplar Bluff, stories circulated of soldiers violating young women, and Papa warned her daily. But she had been young and pretty then. Today, only one question flooded her mind. How had this soldier ever found their place?

His warm brown eyes calmed her, even though he studied her a bit longer than polite. But his rawboned face bespoke kindness.

"Sergeant Tolzmann, Ma'am. Sorry to bother you, but I seek a Mr. Ray McHale."

"He has gone off for supplies."

"To Green Valley?"

"I—" Abby shielded her eyes from the sun. She should stand to welcome him, but her legs trembled.

"When will he be home?"

"In two days."

This man looked vaguely familiar, but many soldiers frequented Papa's store. Yet, as this one grappled for words, something from long ago tugged at her.

He hesitated. "Do you mind if I take a look around?"

"Why no. I can show you."

He shoved a mop of sun-bleached hair under his cap. That honest face, a farmer's countenance, tweaked her memory again.

"Help yourself to a drink and water your horse down by the barn."

He dismounted and strode in that direction. Sergeant stripes— what could he want with Ray?

This couldn't be that Missouri girl. Impossible—maybe he had gotten too much sun. But Martin stole another glance.

"There is no harder work than churning," Mama used to say. The way this young woman rubbed her arms, those dark circles under her eyes declared her weariness. The full sun rendered her a phantom. Martin sniffed—cows, pigs, and chickens here. Did she keep up with all this work herself?

Martin filled the dipper and returned. When he held it for her to drink, her deep brown eyes shone with gold flecks, to match her flaxen hair.

Sudden recognition swarmed him. She *was* that girl in Ferguson's store, the one he failed to rescue in his dream. Only once had he seen such eyes, like autumn leaves floating on the dark Mississippi.

How on earth had she come here? As she sipped, more memories surfaced. While a citizen related the details of the fire, a young woman had entered the back porch of the house next door. Woebegone, she stared at the devastation where the store had stood.

That day she looked not much older than he had been when Papa died. Careful to avoid touching her hand, Martin took the dipper after she drank.

The cold water brightened her. She straightened her shoulders and shielded her eyes from the sun. "Thank you."

Heat flooded Martin's face. His good intentions fled, and he stared at his boots.

"Let me show you around." She grasped the churn to move it into the shade, but he leaped onto the porch and grabbed the handles. "Here, let me."

She leaned against the cabin as though her strength failed her. "I appreciate your help. I—"The lights in those brown eyes glistened. Her faded dress blended with wayward strands tucked behind her ear.

"Come along." She limped down the stairs. "Are you stationed at Camp Reno?"

"Yes, your neighbors—"

The sun highlighted her eyes. He stood transfixed as she asked, "Mr. and Mrs. Allen?"

"Why, y-yah. They directed me here. I... ah, come on government business."

"About the cattle, I expect? Ray sells butter to the herders for a good profit."

"I imagine they do hanker for butter." Something about the barn's alleyway, three times smaller as the one back home, eased Martin's tension. Abby opened a side door to a lean-to where some scrawny pigs grunted.

"Soon it will be time to call our milkers. Down there." She waved a hand toward a hardscrabble pasture.

Creamy stock stood out against rusty clay-soil. Exactly like the Army herd over the Rim.

"How many head does he have?"

"Upwards of forty, I believe."

"You husband is doing well, Mrs.—"

"Abby. Please call me Abby."

He must find a way to view those cattle closely, yet another desire overwhelmed him. He wanted to help this young woman.

"You do all these chores yourself?"

"When Ray leaves, yes. Sometimes the dry heifers dally coming up from the pasture. If one of them calved out in the open... We have so many wolves and coyotes here, and fall will soon be here. In winter, they get hungry."

Her shoulders slumped, and she looked so fragile, unlike his Meta, who attended even first-time births in their barn back home. Then there was Mama, with robust German stature. She reared ten children alone on the farm—an iron resolve carried her through.

Still, she had strong sons to help with the fieldwork. Friedrich must have been twenty-five when Papa died; and Henry sixteen.

But this woman did everything alone. Her splendid eyes caught his again, and it was all he could do to recall his mission.

"Ah, Mrs.—Abby, would you mind if..." He scratched the bridge of his nose with his knuckle. "I miss working in a barn. Nothing I would like better than to do your evening chores."

Heat roared up the back of his neck when she glanced away. Had he offended her?

But she turned those intense eyes on him once more. "Are you hungry, sergeant?"

"I will be soon."

"Would you consider exchanging your work for supper?"

"By then, maybe your husband will come."

"No, not until the day after tomorrow. But you can camp right over there." She nodded toward a campfire right between the cabin and barn. "I would be most grateful for your help."

As she left, Martin grabbed the pitchfork and gave himself to the work he knew best. His "Come Bisey!" echoed across the expanse. In Iowa, thirty Holstein-Friesiens would have responded, but only a few Shorthorn milking cows lolled down the path.

Seeing their udders sway, something fell in place inside him. He played with the insides of the animal's ears and soothed them in a low voice.

"Have trouble scrounging enough to eat today?" Nipping corn kernels from his palm, the cows' rough pink tongues tickled his skin.

His efforts at the milking stool produced the steady certainty enveloping every morning and evening of his childhood. Warmth and productivity, safety and security. He carried a pail to the porch, and only one cow remained in the barn when he returned.

"Why does your hair lie smooth one way and rough the other?" The animal's huge brown eyes surveyed him as if she understood. "If only you could tell me where you came from. Over that Rim up there?" Before she headed outdoors, Martin scanned her hide again for markings. None, just like the government herd.

Looking around the place taught him about Ray McHale. A side door badly in need of new hinges declared tidiness and order not his chief concern. Manure had piled up, too.

Cleanliness is next to godliness, children... How many times had

Mama reminded them of this standard? Whatever else folks might say about Germans, no one faulted their hygiene, and *McHale* clearly lacked a German ring.

But where had he heard that name before? He mused as he shoveled, and then it came to him. Abby's father had uttered it. He would bet his paycheck on it, if he ever again received one. Looking for a wagon to hold the manure, Martin noticed Abby on the porch.

She favored her left side, but he recalled no such limp in Missouri when she went to fetch that rope he should never have bought. His face flamed at the distressing recollection and this present odd circumstance. Mama would call entering another man's house and eating with his wife unseemly.

Yet he simply followed orders. Of course, Captain Whitaker had no idea they would include two home-cooked meals in one day while he ate the same old fare.

From the pasture, the cows *mehhed*, and Martin addressed them once more. "If only you could tell me your owner's secrets."

Waning sun provided enough light to clean the chicken coop, so he hauled the debris to the growing manure pile. In Iowa, he would have hitched horses to a wagon and forked this fertilizer over a field.

No sign of a wagon anywhere, so a shovelful at a time, he spread the manure out back. A big bay entered the barn and nickered, so Martin brushed his neglected coat. Nothing like the smell of horseflesh—back home, Friedrich and Henry would be settling the family's big workhorses for the night. Yes, and Lissa's husband.

This would have been a long workday for them, bringing in the harvest. With each brush, this bay's coat shone more—now, why would a man neglect giving his horse a good brushing?

Hopefully, the truth would come forth like the barbs in this bay's hide. But another concern inundated Martin. Now that he had seen her again, could he ever put Abby McHale out of his mind?

Chapter Twelve

Though he acted in the interests of the United States Army, hesitation riddled Martin as evening coolness settled over the land. Abby was right—autumn tinged the air.

Before going inside, he washed his hands at the tank. Crossing the yard, his steps slowed, and with one boot on the first step, his sigh wafted toward the Rim top. There, shadows vied with patches of remaining sunlight, even as tightness threatened his chest.

"Please help me now."

Abby's quiet voice startled him. "Thank you, sergeant. You have done far more than necessary."

"Would you like me to carry the butter inside?"

"I need to tote it to the creek, but it can wait." A tantalizing ham and biscuit aroma floated from the cabin. "Supper's all ready."

"Pardon me, but I—"

"Ray won't be riding in tonight, honestly. I expect him Thursday night at the earliest."

His stomach a jumble, Martin followed her inside, realizing that she understood his quandary. The cabin's bare walls surrounded a lopsided table and two chairs. Compared to the Allen's home, this might be a miner's shack, but Abby gave him the slightest smile.

"Please, do have a seat."

He set his cap near a jar of wildflowers on the table. "Something sure smells good in here, Mrs. McHale."

"I would so appreciate you calling me Abby." She transferred ham onto a platter. Her hair looked different, and she'd washed her face, but best of all, she smiled.

"Then you must call me Martin."

The lantern light made her eyes flash. She must be exhausted, but her deft movements put him in mind of Mama after a hard day's work

Savory steam ascended from the gravy, and Abby served biscuits as high as Mama's. When she took her seat, Martin folded his hands as he would at the long trestle table in the Tolzmann kitchen.

"For this Thy bounty, heavenly Father, make us truly grateful. Amen."

Abby raised her eyebrows. Did this signal surprise or distaste?

"Serg— I mean, Martin, thank you. Papa used to…" She dipped her knife into a bowl of lush yellow butter. "At every meal, he held my hand and Mama's to say grace. I had almost forgotten."

"Is your…" Martin halted. Though he knew the answer, something urged him to confirm his conviction.

"Is my father alive?"

He nodded.

"No. He and Mama married late, and I was their only child. I lost them both back in Missouri, during the war."

She attended to her meat, so Martin took knife and fork in hand. Quiet filled the cabin, except for the sound of pine wind in the treetops. Seconds passed as the quiet shushing almost formed another presence.

He ought to relay condolences, but something stopped him. If only he could converse like Captain Whitaker. Then he realized he could ask Abby about the pine wind.

"That blowing in the treetops, do you hear it all the time?"

Her face came alive. "Almost. Sometimes I feel certain the wind speaks to me."

"You remind me of my sister Meta. She attunes herself to the outdoors, but I doubt she sees tall pines where she lives now."

"Meta? I like that name. Where does she live?"

"Wyoming Territory, up in high plains country. She married and left with her first husband after I went off to the war."

"Do they have a family?"

"Ah... no. Er... yes." It might have been recitation time in the country schoolhouse back home. Martin's memory never failed him, but with the whole class listening, his voice often did. He cleared his throat and started over.

"Her first husband died early on, so Meta married a Texas cowhand. The last I heard, an old trapper was helping them set up their horse ranch, and she was with child—their second."

"And I remind you of her?"

He chewed a delectable bite of buttered biscuit. "Mrs—ah... Abby, may I say these biscuits rival my mother's? And you stand the same height as Meta. She has dark eyes, too, and curls, though hers are dark as an Indian's."

Finding a topic he knew so well loosed Martin's tongue as Abby began eating. "Meta does whatever she puts her mind to, and with all the work here, you must be... like her."

The comparison sounded lame. He stabbed another piece of meat and reached for a second biscuit. The pine wind filled the cabin, lessening his agitation. Maybe, like Meta, Abby allowed for silence.

When their plates were nearly empty, she flattened her hands against the table. "Would you like more? I made plenty." Before he could answer, she refilled his plate.

Martin patted his midsection. "I may have to enlarge my uniform."

Flickering shadows highlighted her eyes even more, and resting her elbow on the table with her chin in her palm, she made a winsome picture.

Oh, my. Remember, you are nothing more than an old, fumbling farmer, Tolzmann. Besides, she already belongs to someone.

"What you said earlier, about your sister..." Abby's gaze found the rafters, and a curl slipped to her shoulders. "That she can do whatever is needful... I used to be like that, but now I barely finish my day's work. You cannot imagine how thankful I am for all your labor."

Her sigh reached a spot under Martin's ribs.

"You even cleaned out the chicken coop. I have let it go far too long."

He wished he could offer to camp up the slope and ride down to help her when her husband took his trips. The very idea heated his neck.

"You have a lot of work here." Martin searched for something else to say. "Mr. and Mrs. Allen—do you know them well?"

"They stopped by once, but I have yet to visit their place. I want to go in the worst way." Her fingers smoothed the rim of her cup.

The silence grew long. "Do you ride? Your fine horse could make the trip in about half an hour."

"Half an hour?" Her eyes sparked. "I do ride. Papa made sure of that. Maybe some day..."

Martin buttered one last biscuit. "Who would ever have thought that way out here, beyond the Mogollon Rim, a man would study birds?"

"What did you call the Rim?"

"Mug—cc—yun. Took me several tries to get it right."

Puzzlement filled her brow, and she played with the name. "Mogollon—Mogollon. I was surprised to learn Fred's occupation, too." Her smile accented her dimples, so Martin concentrated on dabbing his biscuit in gravy.

"He said he patterns his work after a Dr. Kirtland. Have you heard of him?"

"No, but Mama kept *Birds of America* in our parlor, and I studied Audubon's paintings as a girl. I have her to thank for my interest in nature. She wanted me to become an artist or teacher."

"Why, my Mama did the same thing—not the sketching, but the book. She made us practice our English, and *Birds of America* interested me more than anything else. She determined we would all talk like Americans—made us say *yes* instead of *yah*."

"Did you say ten children? Yours must have been a busy

household." Abby gathered the plates, so Martin carried their glasses to the dishpan.

"Could I help wash? Mama taught me well."

"Thank you, but..." She glanced out the window. "If you want to see the back pasture, we ought not dawdle."

"Shall we take the butter to the creek?"

"Yes, that would be good." On the porch, Abby scooped the butter into a pan and draped a cloth over the top. "I can clean the paddle later."

Martin hefted the load and followed her toward the creek. She stopped where the channel turned and pointed. "Down there you will find a canvas—you can slip the pan inside."

Not so different from Mama's stash, but with her limp, how would Abby have lowered this pan, pulled the string tight, and retraced the incline? And how did she manage everything else around here?

Slivers of waving grass showed beyond the barn's lengthening shadow, and Captain Whitaker's orders stood front and center: *find evidence.* Martin ignored his anxiety and fell in step with Abby.

Evening birdsong brought a peculiar quietude, as if he had walked with a woman hundreds of times. The sun slid lower, rendering the sky as rosy as Manzanita bark.

Before he knew it, Martin blurted, "I never tire of this time of day, when everything seems at peace."

A sigh escaped Abby's lips. "My aunt called sunset *the day's reward*, and through New Mexico Territory, I agreed. That incredible beauty each evening made all the hard travel fade. I ought to have counted each sunset twice."

"What do you mean?"

"If I had known Strawberry Mountain would hide the sunsets here..." Her sigh rent Martin's heart, but she changed the subject. "Did you always want to come west?"

"I probably never would have, except for the war. Did you?"

"Oh, yes. The talk in Papa's store stirred my restless side, always somebody striking gold or families from St. Louis traveling through. Oh, the tales Papa told Mama and me at suppertime. My—my betrothed felt the same way."

Her voice floundered, so Martin jumped in. "Three of my sisters married men like that, and two of them homesteaded in Nebraska."

"And now you have your own adventures."

"If you call road-building an adventure. Most folks picture cavalrymen fighting Indians and naming new territory, but our exploits involve a pick and shovel these days." He paused as three elk startled and loped away.

"But what would the travelers do without your roads? When Fred and Elda Mae came westward, they had even worse ones, yet somehow they managed."

"Some day, we might read a book about birds by Fred Allen, ornithologist."

The first steer came into sight. "They always come up from this direction, but I have never..." Her face flushed. "I am unsure where our land ends. Maybe you can get a better look tomorrow."

The sudden dullness in her eyes sent a pang through Martin. She stumbled on a rock, and he caught her elbow. The strength of his urge to scoop her up and carry her to the cabin rendered him speechless.

"I think I will camp here tonight, if you are certain." He pivoted toward the porch as the last light danced on the railing.

"Oh, please go ahead."

"With your permission, then, I can take care of the morning chores."

"Oh, that would be... I cannot thank you..." Her tone rang of exhaustion.

"You already have. Your barn takes me right back home, and that dinner you cooked was thanks enough for any man."

Starlight carved a path toward Abby's bed. Normally, she

stretched the canvas window covering taut, but after she shut the cabin door, she dropped her shawl on the table and eased onto the feather tick.

If Ray were here, he would have driven Martin off. She shuddered at the thought of missing their supper conversation. Martin seemed so familiar, like someone from her class at school. The thought that he pored over *Birds of America* endeared him, and she imagined his rough features in a child's face.

Now she had walked all the way to the pasture. Ray would not countenance such a simple joy. That placid stroll helped her sore muscles and paved the way for the pleasant sleepiness that wooed her.

She wiggled her toes and stretched her arms to touch the coarse log wall. Moonlight rippled across her quilt, reminding her of the unbarred door, but someone strong and caring camped nearby.

Careful with her sore hip, she rehearsed the clean-swept chicken coop and barn floor, the manure pile several feet higher without effort on her part, and best of all, Martin's enthusiasm. While she prepared supper, she heard him whistling—a tune Papa often hummed in the store.

What was that melody? Partial phrases flitted, something about an old man coming to town and getting home too late to eat his supper.

All those sisters and brothers—what would it be like to grow up in a family like Martin's? During last night's meal, light from the window had accented his brow when he described how he once pored over Audubon. Just the sort of detail Mama taught her to attend to. "One small shadow or bit of light can make all the difference, dear."

His carefulness with words when she asked about his family tickled her fancy. Like a lullaby, the wind had risen, and Martin noticed it too. What delight, to share such a simple thing.

She squeezed her eyes shut. "I do so want to sketch him. Such foolishness, leaving behind my sketchbook and pencils."

No use pining lost opportunities. With uncommon gratitude, she fell asleep humming Martin's tune.

Under a starry cavalcade, Martin burrowed in his bedroll. After years of living outdoors, the heavens still drew him. Why would the Creator arrange the stars into constellations rather than fling them thither and yon?

Friedrich always sowed seed and transplanted only with a waxing, never a waning moon. He and other farmers discussed how a heavy rain often fell immediately after a new or full moon. Perhaps some book had been written about these correlations.

But this evening, questions he had entertained since afternoon took precedence over such thoughts. How was it that he came across Abby out here in the wilderness? Life played such strange tricks.

Although he knew so little about her, her resemblance to her father marked her as his child. And somehow, conversation with her had become possible tonight. He shook himself. Should he have told her he remembered her from Poplar Bluff?

So many questions remained, but one stood out. Why had she married McHale? Maybe loneliness drove her to him. After all, her papa did business with Ray. That must be the answer, but this fellow made a poor match for a girl like her.

Ah, but judging him too swiftly would never do. Captain Whitaker often warned against hasty conclusions.

Things did seem mighty odd, though. How could Ray amass a herd this size with income from selling butter? He grew no crops to sell here, and no self-respecting homesteader could do without a wagon.

Like a nagging horsefly, curiosity kept him awake. What would make Abby so hesitant to go into her own pasture, and why so many half-finished statements? She wanted to visit Elda Mae and Fred, but what was stopping her?

Even during his short visit, it was clear that Elda Mae understood their homestead. Mama, too, kept track of each field and took part in the farm's workings. In long-ago evenings, his parents' voices wafted from the parlor each evening. Should they clear more land down by the creek? Should they hire a man to help with the haying? Mama and Papa shared their thoughts on everything.

The instinctive warning that plagued him earlier this afternoon dissipated against the tall pines' stirring under a starlit sky. Back and forth they swayed, like the wooden metronome atop Mama's parlor organ.

Martin laced his fingers under his head. Of course, women had to work hard in a place like this. He imagined Meta and his older sisters doing the same. But to leave Abby here all alone for days at a time...

"If I had such a beautiful wife, I would—" He punched his pillow. What utter foolhardiness! "Wife, my foot! For me, such a thing shall never be."

He turned on his side, but the thoughts persisted. He failed to comprehend this man Ray McHale, and all his tossing and turning brought him no closer to understanding.

Chapter Thirteen

Pails clinked in the milk house. Abby almost rushed out of bed, but then she remembered Martin. Picturing him milking the cows, she relaxed. When she stretched her arms in a lazy arc, the stitch in her side refocused her thoughts.

Even if she never saw this farmer-turned sergeant again, she would never forget the reprieve he gave her. She visualized him meeting Ray. A head taller, gaze steady, he would hold out his hand, but Ray would avoid Martin's eyes and shift his feet.

"I must remember Ray's past, his parents dead of cholera, and that awful orphanage."

Brushing her fingers on her mending pile, she maneuvered from bed. The touch reminded her of what she had found the day Elda Mae visited. She rummaged around and finally unearthed the envelope and the woman's hankie. With the hem of her nightgown, she brushed dust off the address.

Lola McHale
Abilene, Kansas

Smudges obscured the rest of the inked letters. The stiff parchment crackled in her hand. Faint humming began low in her chest and reached her eardrums as she focused on the embroidered blue letters *L. M.* against a pale peach background.

The chicken coop door squeaked. Martin, doing more than she expected. His name slipped over her tongue like a prayer.

She ought to get dressed and make breakfast, but these objects riveted her. Carefully, she pulled herself up on the bed to open the envelope and peruse the contents.

Bill of Sale:
Property rights due east of Pine Creek and northeast
of Strawberry Mountain to Lola McHale.
One mile north of Indian trail descending from
the Mogollon Rim. Sixty acres, sole proprietorship.
Signed this twelfth day of May, 1858.
Abilene, Kansas Territory.
Witnesses: Alonzo Fairbreth
Millard Truman

"This must be our land. 1858. Of course. Kansas became a state in January of '61. Maybe Ray came down here back then."

But Elda Mae's message about his first wife swam in Abby's ears. She had stuffed that away, but in her mind's eye, a dark-skinned wife named Maria came to life. A squaw who died somewhere under the very Rim that surrounded this ranch—Elda Mae had even met her.

Discomfort tightened Abby's throat, and her voice issued raspy. "Dear Lord God, Thou knowest all. Please show me more about this Lola McHale." Something about her utterance spread quietude through her. At the same time, she wished she had never discovered this envelope.

Stashing the items beneath her mending pile, she scurried into her dress and tied on her apron. With an extra log in the stove and coffee boiling, she raced outside to fetch water, but a pail on the porch stopped her short.

A full pail shimmering in the morning sun, fetched and delivered for her, like the milk Martin toted here last night. She skimmed the cool rim with her finger. This luxury seemed too vast, like Papa noticing the empty potato bin and digging some for Mama, or harvesting a clutch of parsley when he knew she had invited someone for supper.

"Little things make a marriage." Mama shared her sentiments more than once. "Many poor women go through life without this extra thoughtfulness."

When had Ray paid her a single unexpected kindness?

Cackles came from the fence around the coop. Thanks to Martin, she wouldn't even have to check on her hens until evening. That thought rendered the water pail light. Soon, a slab of bacon sizzled in the skillet and cracked eggs filled her mixing bowl. She fetched the milk pitcher from the counter.

"Oh my, how could I have forgotten?" Then she grinned. "But sour milk makes even better griddle cakes."

Near the barn, Martin called to his horse. *Docker—such an interesting name.* As he saddled up, Abby realized no shod horse had entered in this yard for months. How could she possibly cover these new tracks before Ray returned?

The cabin filled with the coffee's aroma. Batter sizzled on the hot skillet, and bacon grease formed variegated patterns around the edges. By the time Abby stepped out to fetch fresh milk, a pile of cakes lay stacked on Mama's china platter.

Whistling, Martin approached. A length of rope flung around his shoulder aroused an abrupt recollection. The breath caught in Abby's throat.

"Good morning. I hope you won't mind if I gather the eggs? Mama ruled our chicken house, so I never got to do that job." He smiled, and an image clarified. That shy soldier speaking to Papa in the middle of the day...*Two butter creams and a length of rope....*

Martin's forehead bunched. "Are you all right, Ma... Abby?"

"I... why, you came to Papa's store during the war. Ferguson's General Store. Do you remember?"

Martin colored as he croaked, "Yah."

"Papa knew your captain, I believe."

"I… yes. Captain Whitaker. Our unit bought beef from him." His pained expression touched her.

Another memory rushed in, and she blurted, "Vicksburg! You were going to Vicksburg, weren't you?"

"Yah, and the Captain and I saw out the rest of the war together. Afterward, we both joined the cavalry."

A morning breeze ruffled hair across his eyes. He set the milk down and bit his lip.

"I never thought to meet anyone again who knew my hometown, but when you first rode up, you looked so… Did you recognize me?"

"You looked familiar, but meeting you out here seemed so unlikely, I never—"

"Yes. But I must tell you, that day after you and your Captain bought the shovels, I sketched you. Remember the puppy you petted outside the store? I sketched him, too."

Martin scratched his head. "The war has dissolved many of my recollections."

"That day marked the first time I had the desire to sketch again after my betrothed—after Elwood's death." Abby rubbed the back of her neck. "Have you met Ray, then? He supplied beef for my father's store."

"No."

"He brought in a herd from Kansas." The statement seemed unimportant, but the wind was picking up. Soon, all chance of speaking with Martin would flee.

Docker stamped a fretful hoof, and Martin surveyed the gathering clouds.

"Do you still want to walk back to the pasture?"

Papa supplied Martin's unit with beef. So many puzzle pieces. Still, she ought not disobey Ray. But why should a complete stranger walk there without her?

"Yes."

She gathered her skirt and maneuvered the steps. "Ray has been clearing brush back there ever since we came, but I have only gone as far as those bushes."

Down a mild slope, Martin turned to her. "Do you know those bushes over there?"

She shook her head.

"Wild blackberries." He strode ahead. "Whoa—quite a crop here. Smell them?"

"Oh!" Abby skipped ahead. "We can top our griddlecakes with these."

"Watch out for thorns."

But she already had charged into the patch.

Such a small thing, but finding those berries flushed Abby's cheeks and enervated her. Martin thought to help her, but those clouds—better take this chance to explore.

At the far end of the pasture, twisted brambles and unruly Manzanita created perfect cover for a wagon outfitted with new wheels. The tongue straddled a rugged but serviceable path. Toward Camp Reno—two hours to the Verde's East fork and down toward Green Valley.

Deep wagon tracks revealed that McHale hauled heavy loads here at regular intervals. Martin propped his foot on the wooden tongue. The trip from Camp Reno would take three days at the least, but McHale could afford the time, with Abby shouldering the farm work.

Under a tucked-in canvas, the wagon box stood empty, but a sideboard housed a harness set. Tall dry grass scraped Martin's boots, while an increasing whoosh flattened the grassy meadow in the quickening wind. Fierce brittlebush spattered the way back to the blackberries, where he offered his kerchief to carry Abby's harvest.

Twenty minutes later, they savored their last bites. When Abby again refused his help with the dishes, he took his leave.

The picture of her standing on the porch, shading her eyes, stayed with him long afterward. "Pemberton," she said suddenly. "Wasn't he the Confederate general at Vicksburg?"

Martin nodded.

"And the Union defeated him." It was as though she had just now recollected the details. A moment passed and Docker whinnied.

"I… I thought I had forgotten everything about the war, but…"

Martin patted Docker, and Abby's voice quavered. "Will you come back?"

His chest pinched. Better to avoid a promise he couldn't keep, although surely Captain Whitaker would want to explore further. The quirk of Abby's left eyebrow ignited Martin's desire to comfort her as he would his sisters.

"Perhaps—everything depends on my orders." He clicked his tongue to Docker and gave Abby a salute. She grasped the porch pole, and her forlorn expression ignited a swarm of bees in his stomach. A moment later, the longing to turn back nearly suffocated him. *Keep your wits about you, Tolzmann.*

Before he even spied the trail leading south and east, a gale whipped at his back. He might get drenched, but at least he had not disappointed Abby. How could he say no, when she had breakfast all ready? A deep rumble rolled from behind the Rim, followed by a rising mass of heavy red dust.

"Glad we found this lower trail, Dock. Now, here is our riddle. McHale hides a serviceable wagon from his wife and labors over a road she has never seen. In fact, she had never been within sniffing distance of those blackberries. What do you make of that?"

Docker shied at a snake slithering across the trail.

"Just an old grass snake, boy. What do you think McHale hauls, and where? Has to be more than butter." Martin clicked his tongue as an ominous thundercloud created deeper shadows. "Come on, maybe we can outrun this storm."

Twice during breakfast, he had almost shared what he discovered in the pasture, but to what end? The last thing Abby needed was more worry. Besides, she carried the conversation with talk about Poplar Bluff.

Soon a punishing rain pummeled the land, so Martin made

for the first rock outcropping. In its shelter, he whispered, "The heavens are on our side, boy. This downpour should erase every trace of our visit."

Tiny, intricate insect designs covered the boulder, exactly the sort of thing that would interest Abby. Most likely, she would sketch this rock's underside. After all, she said she sketched a puppy, and even his own likeness. The thought made his face burn.

When the deluge subsided, he urged Docker in an arc around the looming Rim, but distance failed to shake Abby from his thoughts. Ray must have some eerie hold over her.

Mama's cousin Greta came to mind. What had Mama said?

"Some men possess an uncanny ability to control others." Greta lived in a far corner of Mitchell County, where her husband Karl ruled with an iron hand—or fist. Mama tried to help, but Karl always succeeded in keeping Greta bruised and miserable. Worked to an early death with a brood of nine, she never had a chance to relish her grandchildren.

On one of their visits, something happened with Meta, and Mama sent Martin out early to harness Karl's team. Then she throttled Karl out in the yard.

"Ach! I'll not mention this to Greta, but keep your distance from my girls."

The next year, news came that Greta had caught a violent cold that turned into pneumonia. When it took her from this earth, Mama wept.

"I ought to have gone to her. He would have stormed at me, but I should have visited her."

When Mama and Friedrich returned from Greta's funeral, Mama sat at the kitchen table with the girls when Martin entered the back porch. The regret in Mama's voice stayed with him for months.

"God forgive me—mine was the sin of omission. But Greta's pastor could not have chosen a better verse—*I will restore to you the years the locusts have eaten.*"

"But how can Greta's years be restored?"

"Only in eternity. But I think he meant those words for Greta's children."

Docker shook off a wayward fly, and in the east, a small rainbow danced in sudden sun. Could things ever be made right *before* eternity? Captain Whitaker could outsmart McHale, though he often fled from recognition. Still, justice prevailed once, when he received his promotion.

"If not for him, Dock, where would I be right now? Back in Iowa, and this country would be a far-off mystery." *And Abby lost in my hazy war memories.*

But now, she traveled with him—and after these two days, how could he dissuade her presence in his thoughts? In an attempt to control them, Martin called up more recollections of Captain Whitaker.

After the armistice, he took on yet another mission. The night before most Union soldiers boarded troop trains for home found the two of them beside a Virginia campfire.

"Remember that nurse, Miss Barton, at the Cedar Mountain aid station? She has created a refuge for missing soldiers, and needs seasoned men to search them out and get them back to their homes. My training makes me a perfect candidate—nothing bothers me anymore—sleeplessness, heat, cold, danger."

"You won't be returning home?"

"Not yet. I could easily be one of those men lost to an abominable camp like Andersonville. Families as far away as Minnesota or Maine wait for their sons to come home, but many prisoners lack strength for the journey."

Through the night, his idea tugged at Martin. Somehow he had come through the fighting unscathed, save for one small wound, when so many lost limbs or eyes.

By morning, he volunteered with Captain Whitaker, and instead of boarding a train for Keokuk, accompanied him to the Capitol. They spent the next year ferreting out lost soldiers and chaperoning them home, or discovering that some listed as missing had already died. Mission after mission led either to heartening results or to reporting a Union soldier's demise.

Too many times, a wife or mother collapsed in their arms at the news of their loved one's death. But the reunions encouraged Martin and the Captain to continue until Miss Barton's long list had shriveled.

After they delivered the last veteran to a small town near Pittsburgh, a tattered letter from Friedrich caught up with Martin. Carefully written lines declared Lissa married, and reported that Mama had passed back in August, even before his decision to work for Miss Barton.

After he and the Captain parted, Martin hesitated on the railroad platform. Until then, he had thought to board a westbound train.

Most soldiers already took up their pre-war lives, and a lawyer from Cerro Gordo County awaited the train, too. They might have traveled together, but in the end, Martin lingered after bidding the Iowan Godspeed.

With Lissa's new husband on the farm, his brothers no longer needed him. The two people he most desired to see, Mama and Meta, he would never see again. Things would never be the same. He sank on a bench and pondered.

The gait of a man strolling toward him caught his eye. Martin looked again.

"You seem lost, Sergeant Tolzmann."

"All these years I have pined to go home, but now a part of me—"

"Misses the Army?"

"Maybe so, strange as that may seem."

"One good thing, if you joined up again, they would issue you a new uniform." The Captain eyed Martin's frayed coat, long ago altered from blue to dismal gray.

Martin shied away from his decision. Family always centered his life, so this urge to strike out on his own seemed peculiar.

Captain Whitaker came to his rescue. "Get a room for the night. A good dinner might help, and I shall buy."

River traffic on the bustling wharf only deepened Martin's struggle. The Monongahela, Allegheny, and Ohio converged here. Sighting the Captain's new charcoal roan, uncertainty nearly strangled him. He missed the faithful mount that saw him through their work for Miss Barton.

Captain Whitaker flicked his fresh-trimmed mustache. The glint in his eyes bespoke adventure, and his suggestion made sense.

"All right, Sir."

"Leave off with the saluting. You and I can be officially normal citizens for a while."

Martin shook his head. "You will always be Captain to me."

"Then I shall continue to withhold my given name." Captain Whitaker led the way to his hotel. Throughout the war, he offered high stakes for the man who could guess his name, but no one ever did.

Five minutes later, a hotel clerk offered, "For a nickel extra, we draw your bath." Martin fished out the coin.

"A nickel more for washing your uniform." The clerk's red beard shook with each statement. Martin complied.

"Be up in ten minutes." The clerk barked orders into the back room. Captain Whitaker retired to his room, and Martin fetched his belongings.

The promise of a real dinner set well. Down the street, people assembled, and laughter filled the city air. The war had been over for months, but today its finality seeped into Martin's consciousness.

A steaming copper tub, lie soap, and a towel awaited him. He set his long johns and uniform outside and sank into the steamy water. When he opened his eyes, daylight waned. He blinked at his hands, wrinkled and pink. Scalp to toes, he lathered in the cool water. Sure enough, his neatly folded long johns and uniform waited outside his door.

The brush of clean fabric against his skin and the soft welcome of a real bed called up images of home, but a pile of letters and coins dumped from his pockets onto his bedside table evoked fresh sorrow. In one, Lissa described Mama's passing, and the loss loomed insurmountable.

He nodded off, but started at a rap on his door. Captain Whitaker entered, laughing out loud. "Your hair has changed color. I thought 'twas black all this time."

His never-faltering humor helped troops through more than one rough encounter, and listening to him describe Arizona Territory over a thick beefsteak, Martin debated. Could he—should he—sign onto the cavalry?

In the end, he followed Captain Whitaker, and by noon the next day, had purchased a beautiful American Saddlebred horse. The Captain pointed him out at the stables.

"That one looks to offer a smooth stride. Why not try him out?" Martin did, and the deed was done.

Ten minutes later, walking along the docks, the perfect name occurred—Docker. He and the Captain bought some supplies and headed back to Washington, D.C.

Now, Docker's nicker returned Martin to this lonely Indian trail in the middle of nowhere. Yet this particular *nowhere* already had a hold on him. Some wet-backed elk raised their heads when Docker whinnied.

"All right, boy. We camp alone tonight. I have given little thought to Captain Whitaker's first name for a long time—maybe tonight, I can figure it out."

Chapter Fourteen

Cold salted water soaked the sinewy hen overnight. In the morning Abby rubbed its pimply flesh with bacon leavings and browned pieces in her iron skillet. *Roast an old hen a full day in a Dutch oven if you want the meat tender*—Mama's advice to a young bride at a "blessing" held in their parlor instructed her.

The recollection brought a smile as Abby basked in freedom from her usual morning chores. She meandered within sight of the blackberry tangle that had produced such a lush harvest earlier.

Now dear, let the berries tell you when they are ready—if they resist at all, their sweetness has yet to come in. Leave them until the morrow, when they fall into your hand. But if you wait longer, the picnic bugs will devour the fruit. This voice belonged to Grandma Carmichael, who lived in the downstairs bedroom until Abby turned five.

"I have only one more day, though—then I must wait until Ray leaves again."

Dark purple stain outlined the lines of her palms—best scrub them again, lest he notice. At noon, a hunk of bread dripping with butter and honey satisfied her hunger, and then, like a cloud-shadow on the Rim, great weariness descended. She meant to rest only a few minutes, but wakened in late afternoon.

Time to check on the chickens and milk the cows. Abundant heady cream in the can stored in the barn's coolest corner foretold more churning tomorrow. But at least she only had to milk once today.

Like thunderclouds sweeping over the Rim, an unruly idea rose.

How would Ray ever know if I dug a hole and poured out this portion of cream? But one of Mama's injunctions contained her rebellion—*Always do your best, no matter what the circumstances. Then you can enjoy a clear conscience, daughter.*

The wooden churn fought her as she dragged it out for the morning. A southeast breeze wisped the back of her neck in late afternoon heat, and Ray's rocker proved too inviting. Aunt Susan's thick crocheted handiwork cushioned her shoulders as Abby let go her cares.

Any minute now, the mules would crunch down the path, but she had plenty of time before Ray would expect supper. Back and forth, creak, creak...

A flapping noise startled her awake, and the crick in Abby's neck testified to her negligence. Pale pink light bathed the barn as though a huge celestial lantern beamed at the ranch.

Long ago, Ray squashed her longing for glorious Ozark sunsets. "Pshaw! Not till you move old Strawberry Mountain, woman."

But now, reflected radiance held her rapt. The sun dipped, bringing low, red-tinged clouds to envelope the ranch.

"Oh, I do hope Elda Mae and Fred are witnessing this—and Martin."

Pink became flaming orange and receded into a dusky rose. Then the shades gradually melded into lavender, deep violet, purple, and gray. The first evening star winked like a firefly, and the heavens moved closer. Ray must not be coming until tomorrow—yet another gift.

God still watches over you. The whisper belonged to Papa, from the day of Elwood's funeral. This unique firmament enlivened a long-denied hunger.

You bear life's sorrow so young, daughter, but one day, you will experience joy again. Papa might have been standing here in this outrageous twilight spectacle with her.

"I made a dreadful mistake in believing Ray. But now I see the error of my ways, and this glorious color still regales me. I give Thee thanks."

Time stalled. It seemed Providence had designed this show just for her.

At full dark, she spooned tender chicken onto her plate—what would Ray think of her eating this late, by lantern-light? Yet the old hen had cooked up succulent and tasty. Abby set her mind on churning at dawn, but at the same time, visions of pouring that cream into a dry hole still tempted her. Could wasting food ever come to a good end?

Waste not, want not.

At dawn, she tackled the churning. Stringing along six new cattle, Ray returned at noon. Abby was relieved to see no new heifers in the bunch.

That night, Ray scratched away in his record book while she wandered the yard and visited the cows. Those blackberry branches would provide another hefty haul by tomorrow, if only she might pick them.

When she finally plopped on the top porch step, her hunger for talk got the better of her. "What did you do this afternoon, Ray?"

When she asked him again, he swatted her. Then he hit her again, knocking her down the steps. Hard stones grazed her head, and something popped in her side.

Mercifully, he rushed past her to the barn. Abby's ribs caught at every deep breath, but she made her way to bed. In the morning, chores waited like always, and manning the churn proved daunting. All day long, the future hung like a pall over her.

Three days later, Ray harnessed the mules again, and yelled, "Bring me the butter." The pan suspended in the creek produced hard, golden mounds to wrap in an old canvas tarp he loaded into a grass-lined crate for the mule to carry. She averted her eyes, lest he read her thoughts.

He toted the crate past the barn. "Be back tomorrow."

Tomorrow? He had never left for just one night. Once the forest swallowed him and the mule, his rocker beckoned again—anything to lessen this dull throb in her side. A strange birdcall filtered through the forest, perhaps from the big sycamore.

You played the fool. A wheedling voice incited a sickening sensation. *You lost your inheritance.*

So true. Out in the pasture, the proceeds from Papa and Mama's house meandered the meadow. Aunt Susan's house sale outfitted their wagon, yet the contraption had disappeared. What had Ray done with it?

This morning, his elbow showed through a hole in his shirtsleeve. She ought to sew him another, but ice encased her heart. *Let him wear rags.* The thought careened like a vulture in flight.

Six pounds of butter at forty cents a pound. The rocker creaked back and forth. Two dollars and forty cents a week for butter. Like the pain in her head, Ray's constant figuring pulsed inside her.

Mama or Elda Mae would brew sassafras or willow-bark tea for this headache, and apply an herbal tincture for her hurting ribs. But how to locate the right plants? Her thoughts suspended between the porch and the lost world of Poplar Bluff.

"Slice a potato, Abby. Hurry, Mrs. Penney's headache has come back." Mama sprinkled black pepper on the slices layered in a hand towel to tie around the visitor's forehead. "Pepper side down. Your great-grandmother's recipe rarely fails."

Even Poplar Bluff's educated doctor sometimes consulted Ma Ferguson. Once, Abby had known her remedies. Would the recipes return if she tried to concoct?

A streak of sunlight found her, so she sat and watched for turkey vultures. Ray scoffed at them and sometimes brought one down for sport. "Injun portent—ha!"

The only portent in her life had been Granny Ferguson. But at the same time, her blessing sounded. *A thinking mind, a ready heart...strong and full of art.*

Oh, for those days when she and Lizzy sketched down by the river, but that was in another world. If only Elda Mae and Fred would ride into the yard—but they might not come again until spring. Or never.

Thoughts of Martin, she shooed away—having him here only

exaggerated the loneliness that stalked her now. The rocker's creak wooed her to sleep. Weariness was all she knew for sure.

Beside his fire, Martin drank scorching coffee. With the Rim backed by a gorgeous sunset, he relished this time to study the heavens. Captain Whitaker said the ancients understood that the moon and sun caused the tides, but a thousand years later, Galileo thought differently—'twas the earth rotating instead.

But Pa and Friedrich planted their fields by the moon, with good success. Martin set down his cup and mused on the Captain's wide knowledge of history. Then something flashed near a large fallen log.

A burnished hump undulated along the far side. He fixed his eyes on where it might next appear, and the patch of bronze skin shone as purplish-gray shadows lengthened.

With one wary eye, he hunkered under his blanket. Later, under a flood of stars, he did some tracking. A distance away, the odor of bear grease indicated a native, but Martin found no one and wound back to camp.

After that, only high desert animal sounds disturbed the stillness—jackrabbits, Martin guessed, followed by a coyote's yip. Something about counting the stars went through his mind, probably from his confirmation lessons. An impossible task even in a Midwest sky, but this dense mass of heavenly bodies covered horizon to horizon.

Through long wakeful hours, the tantalizing flecks in Abby's eyes appeared before him, along with her dimple. If Indians roamed here, what prevented them from nearing her cabin?

The vault of heaven hovered so close. In every breath, Martin sensed the Creator. Thousands of stars—millions; and on this earth, millions of people. Tonight, though, alone in this vast universe, he might easily be forgotten. Yet the war had convinced him of all those lessons he had learned in his little Iowa church.

The One who saw a single sparrow fall knew where he camped tonight. Knew who skulked around his camp, and for what purpose.

On a similar night a few years back, a peaceful evening when all had seemed secure, Confederate troops moved in on his contingent. Unnoticed by the guards, they set up, and by dawn, amidst gunfire, terrified Union troops rummaged for their guns.

He might easily have joined the six good soldiers that fell in that skirmish. That was one time he counted sleeplessness a blessing.

No sound anywhere the rest of the night. No movement. Finally, Martin dozed. Then not far from his ear, dry grass quivered. He dared not breathe. In slow, calculated moves, someone was crawling closer and closer. Should he rise up shooting or allow the stalker the first move? It seemed that Captain Whitaker always knew what to do without parsing his options.

The horizon lightened a smidgeon, fading the stars. In minutes, night would remove its cloak. Martin peered into the darkness until a waft of dawn air brought the musky grease scent he had detected earlier.

A moment later, a heavy tallow odor overwhelmed him. For a moment, the smell took him back to Iowa, with Henry, slaughtering geese for Christmas dinner.

Next, a faint pecking sound ensued—an early-rising bird working a rocky area for errant bugs and grass. Then from his left, very near, came a metallic glint.

Thwak! A blade whizzed too close to his ear. Martin started whacking blindly with his gun butt. A resounding *thud*, a low groan—something sprawled against his boot.

Aware that his assailant might rise up as quickly as he fell, Martin sought a look. Panting, he knelt on the rocky earth

Any second now, light would graze the east, but no man could hurry sunrise. Nothing to do but wait—as Mama always said, time would tell. Then came the almost imperceptible alteration, and a spark of sunrise that clarified his stalker, only one in a long list of felled bodies Martin had witnessed.

But this morning afforded him leisure to study his enemy. What tribe did he represent? If a burial ground lay nearby, why had this native passed this way? Perhaps his presence verified Captain Whitaker's instinct that no such thing existed.

Already the night air warmed and yesterday's rain had deepened the intense pine scent. The dew set sparkles in each intricate bunch of pine needles. Such a shame this Indian would greet the day with a lump on his head.

Water gurgled a few feet away, so Martin refilled his canteen and determined to stay until the brave regained consciousness. After he ate and doused the fire, the brave's eyelids fluttered. When they opened fully, black eyes fixed on Martin. The Indian's lips twitched, so Martin poured a trickle into his mouth and made the sign of peace. Those onyx eyes blinked in now-brilliant sun.

"Better get you into the shade before I leave." Martin half-carried, half dragged him a few feet closer to the pines and water.

"Apache? Tonto?"

No response.

"Yavapai? Hopi?"

From the shadows, the eyes glittered recognition. At least, it seemed so. Martin dug in his pack for the bread Abby sent with him and set a chunk on a rock. Farther away on a mid-sized boulder, he left the brave's knife. It would take some time for him to edge that far.

When he mounted, the Indian raised his palm.

Martin patted Docker. "We did our best, boy." Docker gave an understanding nicker and trotted off.

A late September palette of indigo and reds charmed Abby. A cool breeze staved off the day's heat, though yesterday had remained hot. She never knew which to expect.

So it seemed with her life. Once, love enveloped her, but the war reversed everything.

The brutal journey from Missouri plagued her thoughts. Why had she not run away when Ray visited a settlement? Those men and women holding an evening prayer service—she might have sneaked to their campsite in the night, or begged Cactus Joe to leave her with the Indians.

"But I was afraid of everything—Indians and wild animals, and that trail of graves along from Texas through Oklahoma. And that sickness..."

So many times, she might have died. This reality underscored a painful truth—at least now she could put words to it.

"Had it been up to Ray, I would have. He expected that when he left me with the Indians."

Yet thanks to their remedies and the prayers of the Spanish priest, here she stood on the cabin porch. She had gained enough strength to keep up with her work. Today's task, washing clothes, brought relief from churning. But another force burgeoned in her, as sure as the rising sun.

As pinkish-blue sky lent rocky outgrowths a rosy cast, a brilliant golden-rose filled the east. Sudden light created a jagged shadow over the Rim's western hulk, and she anticipated its gradual descent until daylight wakened the entire valley. Immersed in the transformation of pre-dawn to daylight, she failed to notice Ray approach.

"Whaddya see?"

"The sunrise." She lowered her eyes. It would never do for him to notice her expectation.

"Ain'tcha figured they ain't no sunrise here, jest like they ain't no sunset?"

Ah, but the sun comes down the western slope of Strawberry Mountain every morning. The light climbs down instead of up—this has become my sunrise.

He kicked her feet out from under her and left her in the dust. She picked herself up as he headed for the pasture. Inside the barn, baby owls flitted among the rafters.

If they could speak, they would proclaim that Martin pitched hay here one day not long ago. Leaning against a stall, Abby breathed deep. Ray had no idea anyone had come, no idea at all.

The thought warmed her through—she knew something he could never discover. And she also knew about the money he had stolen.

For a few minutes, scenes flooded her mind. The morning Martin rode off was etched there, but after he left, anxiety had overcome her. Even one of Docker's tracks would alert Ray.

With his fading hoof beats, she scuffed hay into the barn floor in case any boot prints remained. Wind moaned through the building like a woman in labor, and when she opened the door, dust dervishes whisked through the yard. She checked the chicken coop and found it cleaner than ever before.

"But Ray never looks in here, anyway." The hens clucked in consternation as a gust snatched her skirt. She hastened to the cabin and from the porch, watched the heavens gush forth. Small oaks that had looked dead now showed signs of life.

As she lifted her eyes to the Rim, her fears calmed. This rain and wind would cover everything. Ray would have no way of knowing that she and Martin walked the pasture, that she picked blackberries, or that Martin had camped here. Like a benediction, the realization washed away the tightness in her throat.

When the downpour quieted, she returned to the barn, where the elfin owls darted at will. *Things can change*, they seemed to say. The day after Martin left, Ray returned to a yard full of red clay, with all traces of her visitor washed away. He still had no idea anyone visited, much less that an Army sergeant was searching for him.

And she had kept this secret—maybe, after all, he had no power to read her mind. Besides that, she had these memories to cherish. Strength grew inside her—the quiet expansion brought satisfaction as she pulled down a wooden crate from the lean-to and crossed the yard.

"From now on, I need to be watchful, and I must learn to pretend even more. God *does* care for me. That rain told me so."

On this quiet morning, an image rose of a baby owl finding safety under its mother's wing. At the same time, an idea occurred. She could fight back— perhaps not when Ray hit her, but in other ways.

Thankfully, no churning beckoned, so she would replenish the kindling this morning. With pounding echoing from the pasture, she might just spread her wings a bit farther than last time.

Turning north, she swung the crate from side to side. "And who knows what else I might find?"

This side of the ranch bordered the forbidden path leading to the sycamore. She settled the crate between Manzanita bushes and pulled out thick dead branches from under the plants. Most of them broke over her knee, and the crate filled quickly. She refilled her arms, but at one point, whirled around to see no crate.

Manzanita, from three to fifteen feet high, massed everywhere, and the more she searched, the more lost she felt. Even the sycamore hid from her sight, and she had set it as her North Star. A panicky tide threatened as she backed against a tall pine.

"Stay calm. Think. That crate simply could not have disappeared. Why, it was right over there..."

But *over there* had dissolved into alpine air. This close to midday, a glance at the sun's position helped little. Eventually, Ray would come home, follow her tracks, and be furious that she strayed this far.

But just then a racket started, wild thrashing and thumping accompanied by an odd groaning. Moving closer, she grabbed a walking stick, for this could be wild pigs—javelina—and they might turn vicious.

The next instant she giggled out loud. Not twenty feet away, a young elk rubbed its antler velvet on the crate. But one of the points had gotten stuck between the slats, and he suffered his own panic trying to shed the ungainly box.

Crash...thud! The crate landed in a Manzanita as if it had sprouted there, and the elk snorted his indignation. After he ran off, Abby retrieved the scattered contents. Soon, she recognized her whereabouts and made her way back to the cabin. Visualizing the scene again, another giggle escaped. The unfamiliar sound struck her as odd.

And then, only a few feet away, a poison sumac bush caught her eye. Ray had warned her to keep her distance from these plants, for the slightest touch might cause a miserable itchy rash.

Ruing the pain in her leg where he kicked her, she set down the crate and lifted her skirt. A bruise had already formed. His sneer had revealed delight in seeing her grovel on the earth.

Her next thought brought a gasp. Tomorrow she would do the washing—oh, what she might do with a few of these sumac leaves! Her next thought came straight from Mama—*Do no evil.*

But the throb in her leg raised its voice too, and careful to shield her fingers with her skirt hem, she gathered some leaves. Lying atop the Manzanita branches, they looked so harmless.

Toting the crate to the cabin, she chuckled again, and the pleasant sensation created a stronger outburst. How good to know she still remembered how to laugh.

Chapter Fifteen

Tough old turnips threatened to bend Abby's knife, but she still added them to chopped onions and a wad of soaked dried beef. With autumn's cooler air, stew would taste good. Already, Ray donned his heavy coat in the mornings and told her to pile the wood higher around the shed.

When the mixture bubbled, she restocked the wood box and pulled out her mending. Something fell to the floor—the letter and hankie from that day Elda Mae and Fred visited. Reading the notice again, she turned her thoughts to this woman named Lola.

"Must be Ray's mother or sister, or an aunt." But cold fingers down her spine reminded her of his orphan childhood—no brothers or sisters, and his mother died in childbirth. Suddenly an idea occurred—*Elda Mae must read this letter.*

If only the Allens would come again.

The cloudy afternoon gave way to darkness as Ray tromped in. "How did your work go today?"

He slung his coat on a hook. "Why y' wanna know?"

With a shrug, she filled his plate. "Supper's ready."

He dropped into his chair and began wolfing down her creation. When she glanced up, his chin ran with gravy. He squinted and drew his sleeve across his mouth.

"Man oughta be able t' eat in peace."

When she retreated to the back corner and lit the lamp to mend, he followed, kicking her shoes across the floor. His loud mockery carried a whiskey odor.

"Miss High n' Mighty, there y' sit, all dried up. Yer an old woman, worse'n th' cheapest Injun squaw." He raised his arm and she shrank back.

His nose blue-red in the dim light, Ray reconsidered. "Yer not worth m' pains."

He spat and turned on his heel. The slammed door reverberated, and Abby leaned against the wall—at least he had changed his mind. But she had a mind, too. A plan had been maturing. Tomorrow, she would wash clothes, and her secret weapon lay close at hand.

A glorious sunshiny day—Abby hurried to tend the chickens when Ray reached for his long johns that morning. After breakfast, he crossed the yard toward the barn, pausing to scratch his nether parts.

Biting her bottom lip did nothing to stop the laughter from bubbling up. Near the tank, he wriggled around, attempting to stop his itching. At that point, she bent double and heehawed until she cried. The whole time, she kept one eye on him, and fortune smiled upon her. He entered the barn.

Oh what a day! He spent most of it pounding and sawing in the pasture, but every time he came into the yard for something, he was still scratching. Best of all, she pretended not to notice.

After supper, he retired to his rocker and notebook, but she stayed inside, wrapped in the star quilt Grandma Carmichael had stitched for her a lifetime ago. A vague memory tugged, something Mama said about Grandpa Carmichael.

"Your grandmother used to sneak out to the shed and loosen the corks in Pa's stash or set the bottles in the sun to weaken the brew. She always held out hope that he'd come to his senses. He never did, but at least she outlived him to enjoy her final years."

The manure odor on Ray's boots still lingered in the cabin. "But he has such a strong constitution, I cannot hope to outlive him. I can only use the sumac once. Dear God, show me what to do."

A tall, kind cavalryman's face appeared. "I could pray for Martin to return, but Ray might kill him. No, Elda Mae is my best hope."

After Ray went to the barn, a full moon drew her to the porch. Something banged against a wall in the barn. A few minutes later, a sudden clank followed by a heavy thud aroused her curiosity. When all was quiet, she tiptoed across the yard and skulked through the side entrance. Through deep purple shadows, a moan led her to the back stall.

Step by step, she neared a figure twisting in pain on the dirt floor. "Ray?"

Another moan. Through cracks in the wall, moonlight glistened on a glass bottle.

"Ray?"

"Unnhh…"

A stain ran the length of his trouser leg. Abby fingered the dark glass with its woody peat odor and an illegible label. One touch revealed how much blood Ray had lost.

In a moment of reckoning, Abby shook her head. No. To let him bleed to death would be to kill. That, she could not do.

She rolled up his trouser leg and dashed the remaining liquor over the wound. He jerked when she tore his shirttail for a bandage and laid cold eyes on her, but fell back on the hay without a word.

When he snored, Mama's story about Grandma Carmichael urged her to search. *Where would he hide his bottles?*

In the milk house, she scraped away a pile of empty gunnysacks and uncovered a ramshackle trapdoor. Groping across hand-hewn planks in moonlight from the door, she grasped iron—some sort of latch. Inside, smooth glass met her touch.

The ice in Ray's look bore into her as she retreated to the cabin for a few hours of sleep. At first light, he still hadn't moved. Her heartbeat pounded in her ears. What if she found him dead, like Mr. Crondite?

But when she set foot in the stall, he lifted his head. "Wha…?"

"You hurt your leg. I can ride up to the Allen's place. Elda Mae knows the Indian remedies—"

Cruel fingers crushed her ankle. "Wha...?"

"I can fetch help."

"Who y' talkin' 'bout?"

"Elda Mae and Fred, our neighbors. They stopped by one day. She studies the herbs—"

Ray shot up, his eyes venomous. "Woman—" He pulled her into his filthy breath. "Y' ain't goin' nowheres. Now git out."

Out in the light, Abby dunked her hands in the tank and splashed water on her face. From the bushes came a loud "Meow." That catbird had learned a new sound... exactly what she must do. She could go right now and risk Ray's wrath, or wait until his next selling trip.

Later, a cold mist fell, and he still snored in the same position. Henrietta gave more milk than usual, and the other cows seemed far too productive, too. With the cream can full and not enough pails, Abby fetched another container.

Halfway to the cabin, an enormous bird spanned the yard. Its regular *flap, flap, flap* took her back to the night Ray pulled out her hair. Was this the same vulture?

"Now I am all right," she called. "And I shan't be fooled any longer." She peeked to make sure Ray still slept before lugging two full milk pails toward the blackberry bushes.

Rich milk gurgled into thirsty soil. After every drop soaked in, Abby tipped the second pail.

Before she returned the pails, the sky brightened. Sudden sunshine radiated through her shawl and resolve braced her. "I am not Ray's slave," she whispered.

Half-expecting to find him standing outside the barn watching, she turned. But only a half-grown owl regarded her from the roof. Inside, Ray's snore still echoed.

At dusk, he stumbled from the barn. Through the cabin window, Abby watched him call a mule and struggle onto its back. He rode around the yard twice, slid off with a curse, but kept his balance and headed toward the cabin.

"Goin' t' Reno tomorra." Not even a look her way. "Whatcha hidin'?"

"Nothing, Ray." She despised the quiver in her voice and the tremor that coursed her backbone. But if he struck her, so be it.

"Musta been rum-headed, bringin' y' here." A mule brayed and batted against the water tank. Animal-like, Ray growled. "So now y' know we got some uppity neighbors."

The window showed autumn's deep buttercup yellow gracing the Rim as he walloped her with his hand. She staggered, concentrating on how one splash of color radiated all the way to the top of the Rim.

Full of art... strong.

He clomped out, and she stood. That lone sycamore steadied her. Even as her skin burned, Elda Mae's directions sashayed. *Continue up to the road, past the sycamore...*

Strong enough to leave. But before she did, those corks in Ray's bottles would sit loose for a day, and for good measure she would pour a little from each one and add some water. And every time she recalled how terribly he had itched for two days straight, she would smile.

Docker relished a drink at the mouth of a narrow gorge while Martin studied enormous rock escarpments extending into thin air.

"Dock, what do you think? Could heaven be more beautiful?"

Men raved about a huge canyon farther northwest, but how could anything be more striking than this? He almost lost track of time, until a scuffling sound alerted him.

Then a dusty cavalry hat bobbed along the trail. Soon, Captain Whitaker reined in his horse as if they had deigned to meet at this exact spot. He swung his arm wide.

"Quite the phenomenon, wouldn't you say?"

"This must be what they call the natural bridge?"

"Umm. I have attended your progress for some time. Had I known 'twas you, I would have explored while I waited." Captain Whitaker gestured toward cave-like entrances in massive boulders. "What did you discover?"

"Two settlers live over there, one named Ray McHale. He has a secret road that leads here and has outfitted a wagon for load bearing. Captain, do you recollect Poplar Bluff, Missouri?"

"Was that the little town where the general store burned?"

"Right. You sent me to speak with the owner about cattle thievery, and McHale supplied that store's beef. He may be continuing his underhanded dealings out here."

Captain Whitaker slapped his thigh. "Good work, sergeant. Glad you found his trail. Maybe he met Masters and two scouts the other night an hour southeast of here."

"The Colonel?"

"Masters gave a man a pair of Army field glasses and a spyglass. Looks as if they plan to exchange torchlight messages."

"The scouts know about this?"

"Perhaps Masters pays them to cover for him." Captain Whitaker's forehead formed a wrinkled map. "This outlaw delivers his goods, and Masters divvies payment to him a few cattle at a time. My guess is the Apaches exempt McHale's ranch from raids in return, but what do they get from the deal?"

"Always new questions."

"True. By the way, did you spy a burial ground?"

"Not a sign."

"As we surmised."

"As *you* did. But I did meet up with an Indian. He spent a whole night sneaking up on me and reaped a bad headache."

"Hmm. No scars, I see?"

"Not for lack of trying."

"Is that how you got the slash in your sleeve?"

Martin twisted his elbow to look. "Guess so."

"Remember when our quartermaster fitted us with those woolen goods they called *shoddy*?"

"My uniform fell apart the first month."

"Before Montgomery Meigs became quartermaster general, scoundrels made a killing buying surplus muskets for three dollars apiece and selling them back to the army for twenty. Even spavined mounts brought absurd prices. It seems that some people choose to profit no matter what the situation.

"Meigs stopped all that, and finally we rated decent uniforms. Who knows how much the Union owes that officer?"

"Did he get some glory?"

"Not that I know of. But see how far the war brought us? We have standardized uniform measurements, manufacturers have adopted Army sizing charts, and if you stitch that tear, your uniform will last another ten years. We travel the road of progress!"

Some mule deer meandered by, and Docker snorted. "There, boy. Just some of our friendly neighbors."

"What Meigs did gives us an example of what the Army needs right now. Someone like him, honest and fair-minded, must investigate McHale's deeds."

"I would say so."

"That, my friend, falls to you and me."

They made camp, and over beans and the rest of Abby's bread, watched the sun set. The whole time, Captain Whitaker analyzed the situation.

"Masters uses McHale to supply the Yavapai and Apache. I would bet six month's pay he distributes guns and ammunition to them." A minute later, he burst out in a less controlled tone. "And *wampum*."

"Don't forget fire water."

"Right you are. Think of all the good men we lose building the road, from gunshot wounds, snatched mail dispatches and raids. And all this time, we assumed the Indians acquired their guns and ammunition from the northern Hopi and Navajo."

Martin stirred the fire. He still hated to think of Colonel Masters being this deceitful.

"Masters' trickery galls me."

"You believe he helps himself to the supplies intended for the new forts?"

"Channeled from New Mexico Territory, right under General Crooks' eye, and also from our own cache at Reno. Who would guess the Indians' ammunition originated in our own stores? What better ploy, though, for a commander going up in the ranks?"

"Sir?"

"Masters' weekly report to Washington numbers the losses and the dead." Captain Whitaker emptied the coffee pot. "Those numbers make all the difference in the value placed on the Colonel's services. They proclaim his worth to the United States government."

"How could he think to carry out such a scheme?"

"No one devises a plan like this unless he worships power and prestige, and that describes more than one officer. As long as Indian skirmishes continue, Camp Reno will prosper, because Washington will continue to send supplies and fortify the outskirts. I wouldn't be surprised if Masters maneuvers his congressional contacts into renaming the miserable place after him."

The fire sputtered and belched. Pine bark and pitch exploded into flame as Martin rinsed plates and forks. "But he already has been promoted to colonel, and generalship usually follows. Why would he go to all this effort?"

"Impatience, don't you see? The glory train travels the same rails as our paychecks—a ponderous journey. And now that the war has ended, promotions are less frequent. But as long as the tribes have access to firepower, raids will persist. In that case, Reno stands a better chance of becoming a bona fide fort equal to Donelson and Apache. Does that make sense?"

Martin nodded—so much to ponder.

"The more Masters provokes the Indians, the greater his promotion when we finally quell them. Nothing must stand between him and personal gratification, and there's not much we can do about it. Yet."

Dark half-moons sagged under Captain Whitaker's eyes as Martin shored up the fire. One last time, the captain peered from under his cap.

"Do you understand why we needed to reconnoiter separately? We must be quick about this, and if even one lowly private gets wind of our findings, word will drift to Masters, giving him time to cover his tracks. Worse yet, he passes the buck to us."

Knowing how Colonel Masters liked his poker games, Martin had to chuckle at "pass the buck." But Captain Whitaker always stood for the right. These accusations would risk him discharge, court martial, a lengthy imprisonment, or even execution.

By the time a snore issued from the other bedroll, Martin's stomach settled. One thing was sure. If worse came to worse, the two of them would go down together.

About an hour later, he startled awake. Ah—the captain was astir, muttering something about a girl. Martin hovered in his bedroll, waiting for a sign. His comrade wrestled up and walked through some bushes. About twenty minutes later, he returned, fed the fire, and slipped under his blanket again.

He would say, "Another leg cramp—confounded things, anyway."

But Martin experienced his own persistent war visions. One in particular, of a skeletal Andersonville prisoner who died before they could reach his home, occurred often. He forced the apparition back into the darkness, but the ghostly visitor persevered.

Finally, sleep came. At dawn, he took on breakfast chores, so steamy coffee waited for Captain Whitaker when he wakened later than usual.

"Sergeant, today we explore, though I cannot rightly say quite how this will inform our mission."

Chapter Sixteen

All day, snow dusted the Rim top. Patches of white grew while Abby caught up on her duties. When Ray retired to the barn, as he did most nights now, she locked the cabin. She used to wonder what he did out there. Every time she stood on the porch to listen, she heard scraping, pounding, sometimes even shouts.

But now, the relief of having him gone outweighed her curiosity. After washing dishes, she pulled Mama's Bible from the trunk Papa built for her long ago. Could ten years have passed since then? It seemed impossible that she was almost twenty-three, yet at times, her feet dragged like Grandma Carmichael's.

Papa's handiwork grew more beautiful with age. He let her choose the ash tree from river-bottom land, even took her to watch the sawmill produce wide planks. Then, they spent winter evenings together sanding and polishing. The work took four months, but those hours with Papa would remain with her forever.

What was it Aunt Susan used to say? *Golden hours ... our reward.*

The lovely wood grain caressed her touch. With no chance for good-byes, the trunk and the dress shoes Mama ordered for her only weeks before she died meant so much—more than they should, according to Ray.

Her raging sickness and the winter with the Indians shoved the memories even farther down. After the descent to their place, the months stretched into years, as if she sleepwalked through that passage of time.

When longings for her family surfaced, she always tamped

them down. But since Martin had come, an even deeper loneliness stalked her. And lately, little by little, recollections crept back, pieced together like a quilt.

"Martin walked our streets. He knew about the fire. Sometimes it seems impossible that he came here."

Seeing him with the rope over his shoulder had brought it all back. Even the way his captain introduced Martin; "Sergeant Tolzmann at your service," rang in her ears.

Not so long ago she had forgotten her own name, but at this moment, that day in the store might have been yesterday. The sudden influx of memories quickened her heartbeat. Did this mean other lost memories would return? As if to prove they would, a passage from the second chapter of *Oliver Twist* interrupted her thoughts.

"How comes he to have any name at all, then?"

The beadle drew himself up with great pride, and said, "I inwented it."

"You, Mr. Bumble!"

"I, Mrs. Mann. We name our foundlin's in alphabetical order. The last was a S,—

Swubble: I named him. This was a T,—Twist: I named him."

"Oh my—Oliver lost himself, too. I never really thought about that. And surely that girl Cactus Joe told me about experienced the same thing when the Indians took her."

Setting the Bible on the table, she paced the cabin. Mr. Bumble's made-up name for Oliver had sufficed for his selfish purposes—for a time. But he failed to take into account one important fact. Oliver's likeness to his mother and father eventually saw him through.

Hadn't Martin said she resembled Papa? Family traits showed, no matter what.

Oh, what was that Psalm Mama used to quote? Abby concentrated with all her might, and some of the words returned:

"...searched me and known me...my downsitting and mine uprising. Thou understandest my thought afar off. Thou compassest my path and my lying down..."

Perhaps Elda Mae had been right—the Almighty understood

her troubles and sent help just in time. Surely she and Fred had not simply happened to ride down the trail that day they visited. And how could it be that the one other woman in this wilderness had experienced living with a man like Ray?

"I took it all for granted—our home, our little sanctuary's beauty. I thought they would always be there; those solid oak pews, the stained glass window of Saint Peter walking on the water and Jesus with the children, the pump organ Mrs. Owen taught me to play."

Often when she entered the building during her childhood, light enhanced that scene with Peter about to drown. Done in browns and dark greens, it revealed hope in the very worst situation—right in the midst of danger.

Yet after Aunt Susan died, she had rejected it all. Oh, how she longed to hear just one of those old hymns. Would she ever?

At least Ray had gone outside so she could read.

"Blessed be the Lord my strength, which teacheth my hands to war, and my fingers to fight." Wasn't this the passage Pastor Fox preached on when the war broke out? Yes, just before Elwood and the other boys left to fight—they felt so honorable as they left on their mission.

But with the slaves now free and the country expanding west, peace reigned.

Yet you are still at war. Abby held up her scratched hand mirror. Weariness, loneliness, despair and even hatred—the emotions of war—framed her features.

Aunt Susan lost her beau, but she never drank the wine of bitterness. Mama said that the morning after Elwood and Anthony's burial, but tonight her words resounded with deeper meaning.

The quiet cabin attended to Abby's whisper. "Grandma Car-michael suffered and so did Elda Mae. Yet they came through it all, and I will, too. I will see Elda Mae, and soon." A restless sleep came until a shadowy dream woke her.

A dark-haired man riding a fiery steed drew near, while a

redheaded woman drove a buckboard in the opposite direction. Granny Ferguson would say the dark-haired man meant good luck, since he approached. But the woman foretold misfortune.

Mama would say, "None of those Highlander legends of evil minions or even the Sith, the good folk, hold water."

"But she said a woman with red hair—"

"Fairies do not haunt people or places, either here or in the old world."

"But Mrs. O'Halley—"

Mama jerked up from her sewing that day, her voice uncharacteristically sharp. "She suffered terribly after her husband left her, but that silly tale about red hair hails back to when the Vikings terrorized Scotland. Why should we heed such things?"

She held out her hands. "Come here, Abigail Belinda. Your Aunt Susan once had bright red hair. Does that make her wicked?"

Aunt Susan, the kindest woman on earth?

"Put your faith in God's promises, not in Granny's feeble tales. Now think. Which of the promises fits this situation?"

"God hath not given us the spirit of fear, but of power, and of love, and of a sound mind?"

Mama brandished her needle again. "Very good. Remember, sometimes old folk can lose their way, too."

A sound mind. Power. Love.

Now, she dozed again and woke thinking, "Today is the day."

After eating his pancakes and ham, Ray lingered while she cleared the table. He normally left earlier for Camp Reno.

"I fetched the butter for you."

He rose and opened the door as if she had said nothing. By the time she finished the dishes, he had loaded the mule and left.

The sensation of Elda Mae's hug returned full force, and Abby might have taken off running toward her cabin. "No. Take your time. Check the barn. Then wait a bit, just in case."

For an instant, the Rim loomed menacing, and the forbidden journey struck fear despite her long-held desire. She fed and watered the chickens, checked the pigs, and stored the milk and cream. Then she lifted the heavy saddle from a stall divider.

The bay exhibited patience when she dragged a milking stool over. With the last strap cinched, she wiped her forehead and glanced around the barn. Not a sound in the rafters. The owls must be asleep or off on their own adventures.

Sunshine filtered through the cracks as if to impart a blessing, and her apron pocket bulged with the letter and gloves. The hunger to sketch urged her, too. Perhaps she might exchange a sketchbook for... ah—some blackberry jam. She ran to the cabin and wrapped a jar in a cloth.

Near the break in the bushes leading to the path, apparitions appeared. "Only deer or javelina out scavenging." But she gave another long look.

Three long years—could she truly take leave of this place, even for a few hours? Ambivalent voices joined in. How could she leave the chickens, her mending pile?

But she persevered, and gaining the path, calmness settled in. Full sunlight proclaimed this a good day. Things had changed—Ray realized she knew about the Allens, but had still gone away.

The distance sped by as the sun's warmth cheered her. Animal skitterings accompanied the bay's steady trot, and soon the massive sycamore with its vast canopy welcomed her.

"At last I see you close-up." Plate-sized leaves dried on pale, shiny branches, and in the distance, several javelina crossed the path.

The bay slowed as the babies trekked up the slope. The mama groused for tiny acorns and insects with her snout. The papa brought up the rear.

The little ones, perfect caricatures of their parents, reminded Abby that her trek took her uphill, as their tiny back hooves pierced crusted snow a few yards higher. Near the final turn gurgled the clear spring where Elda Mae had said to stop for a drink. Though she longed to get to the cabin, Abby stopped, and the freezing water brought a gasp.

The woods brought memories of days at the river with her child-hood friends. They built tree forts and ate a picnic when the noon whistle blew. Their mothers trusted them to return after Poplar Bluff's evening whistle. Only once, engrossed in digging a pirate cave in the creek bank, did they forget.

Lizzie had stayed over that day, and Papa came searching for them. Elwood heard his voice first. "Oh no, girls, we must've missed the whistle."

Covered with mud from head to toe, Abby emerged from the cave. "Papa?"

"Why, who are these strange girls?" He touched her slimy shoulder. "I recognize this one's voice, but not her face."

"Look at the tip of my nose."

"I thought 'twas a muskrat, but that nose does indeed resemble Mrs. Ferguson's. Maybe I have found our daughter after all!" Papa's incredulous tone brought giggles.

He sniffed. "Indeed, I do believe this muddy mess to be my child."

Behind the store, he helped them wash up to spare them punishment. This fresh spring water brought back the sacred moment when Papa tucked her in that night.

"No matter how dirty you get, I will always find you, dear daughter."

Papa could not find her now, but Elda Mae and Fred had, and Martin too. The bay picked up his pace as if he knew something good lay ahead.

Throughout the day, Martin and the captain traced the crevasses of this remarkable natural bridge. When they made camp, Captain Whitaker informed him of their next step.

"In the morning, I will make Camp Verde my destination. General Crook will recall me from his first Ohio volunteers. That was before the war, when they transferred me to guide you greenhorns."

"The general commanded volunteers?"

"In California with the Fourteenth, before Manassas. A considerable number of officers left the regular army to command state volunteers. The general rose through the ranks before Antietam and Chickamauga won him his promotion. I chafed at being transferred, but the army made a good decision—for once."

He surveyed the horizon as he groomed his horse. "The Indians call him *Nantan Lupan*—Grey Wolf—to show their respect. He cares about justice, even for them."

Captain Whitaker always produced a new story, and tonight was no exception.

"Know who I thought about last night, sergeant?"

"Someone of interest, no doubt."

"None other than General Stonewall Jackson during the Mexican War. Although General Lee gave the command, Jackson refused to obey a withdrawal order. He recognized that turning back would cause more deaths than continuing his assault on Chapultepec Castle. Far outmatched in artillery, he disobeyed orders anyway, and because he persevered, the next brigade succeeded. The army promoted him to major.

"Some called him *Tom Fool*, others *Old Blue Light*. Depends how you looked at him, but though he fought for the Confederacy, I respect his tenacity. He mastered the art of surprise, used to great advantage against us at Chancellorsville."

He downed the last of his supper. "Tragic to die of a bullet wound at the hands of one's own soldiers."

"Is that what happened to him?"

"True as time. You never heard that some Rebel mistook Old Blue Eyes and his men for Union troops? He lost an arm before dying of pneumonia."

Their fire cracked and popped against the night sky. "I regale you with this story because I fancy you believe me impetuous at times."

Martin emptied the coffee pot into Captain Whitaker's cup. "Never, sir. You think everything through, forward and backward, or as my school teacher would say, around the county line and back."

"Hmm. I hope to return by Wednesday midday. Keep watch on McHale. The ranch lies a quarter mile from where Pine Creek widens, looking toward High Point, is that correct?"

"Yes, that broad neck would make a good meeting place."

They slipped into silence until Captain Whitaker mentioned the unique brightness of the North Star this evening.

"Who was that ancient writer that knew about the moon affecting the tides?"

"Pliny the elder. From his Natural History, written in 77 A.D."

"So he was a researcher, like Fred with birds?"

"You might say so. He compiled scholars' writings for the common man in thirty-seven volumes, always careful to state his sources. But his primary occupation might surprise you."

"No doubt."

"He was a cavalry commander in the Roman army. Began his service in Germany and wrote his first book about the use of spears in warfare. Before writing *Natural History*, he wrote twenty volumes about the wars in Germany and served as a governor in France."

"Tell me more."

"Ah, you want a bedtime story, sergeant, but I need my sleep."

After a scanty night's rest, the Captain mounted. "Discover all you can. Hopefully, General Crook will send some men back with me to deal with Masters."

He extended his hand. "Sergeant Tolzmann, you are one reason I know the army sent me in the right direction. Be careful. I do wish you had given that Indian more than a headache the other day."

As he rode away, Martin stroked Docker. "It's you and me again, boy. First off, we figure out how to keep track of McHale."

Chapter Seventeen

A whiff of some plant reminded Abby of Mama's salve, so she glanced around to check.

"I thought sure I smelled—" A ground squirrel skirted a six-foot pine sapling and stopped to regard her.

"This meadow would be perfect for herb-hunting. Maybe Elda Mae will have some liniment like Mama's."

Passing the tumbledown prospector's shack, she hurried the bay along, and around a bend, came in sight of a cabin. A few strides forward and Elda Mae hurried toward her.

"Oh, my dear girl, you came all by yourself. I admire your spirit." Abby slid down into the older woman's arms. "Every day I think maybe you will come, and here you are!"

Holding her at arms' length, Elda Mae sighed. "Still so pale, and all alone on that steep trail—"

"Our bay is sure-footed, and I rode astride, like you."

Elda Mae grabbed at her waist and grinned. "With my size, that is my only choice. But Ray...?"

"He left this morning." Abby patted the bay. "I ought to—"

"Fred will take care of her."

The porch floor creaked under Elda Mae's step. The cabin issued a cheery welcome. A small round table with a flowered cotton cloth graced the far corner of the porch. Opposite, on the shady side, a wooden cooler bespoke abundance.

"Do come in for tea, dear."

More pleasant surprises waited. Six matching chairs circled

a large table, a vase of wildflowers on the windowsill brought a snow-patched meadow right into the cabin, and pine shutters framed several windows.

Abby had longed for a cup of tea, but Ray spat when she mentioned it. "Think we got money t' waste?" She had brewed some from herbs, but smelling Elda Mae's was intoxicating.

"I might be back in Poplar Bluff with Mama's morning circle." Sunlight filled the space, and Abby imagined the lavender scent belonged to Mama, welcoming her guests.

"She liked to entertain?"

"Oh yes, she knew everyone in town and rarely met someone that raised her ire. The women discussed the day's events: would that tall, gangly Illinois lawyer indeed run for president? His newspaper caricatures did him no favors—surely he could never be elected. Then he won, and they turned to the question of secession."

"Mm…" Elda Mae, busy with her preparations, reminisced. "Missouri's status bounced back and forth after the 1820 Compromise, if I recall. People from Ohio thought it dreadful that she allowed slavery."

"Yes, but most folks in Poplar Bluff abhorred the practice. Some of the women feared this war would tear our state asunder. I remember one woman saying, 'Mark my words, town will fight town.' Oh my! Her name was Mrs. Abernathy—I have not thought of her in years. Her frightening prediction rang true. After the women left that day, Mama had me sketch the state map, using my imagination. Missouri turned out to be a caricature of a frazzled woman."

"How creative—your mother sounds wonderful."

"Yes, she was. But now, all of the fears of those women have receded, and that lawyer-turned-president had gone on to his eternal repose. I cannot express how grateful I am that you caught me up on the state of our nation."

As Elda Mae sliced some shortbread, her shiny poplin curtain formed a backdrop. Patterns of pears, apples, and grapes on the fabric brought such lovely color to the room. The fragile-looking teacup set before Abby brought consternation.

"Such dainty handles. I fear I might—"

"Pshaw." Elda Mae's full neck folds shook in her good-natured chuckle. "I held my breath when the men dropped our wagon off Nash Point, I admit. Somehow, our window glass survived, along with my china."

Sitting down, she urged Abby to eat, but kept on describing their trip out West. "I took myself in hand that day, for along the way, a woman in our wagon train died when she climbed down from her wagon. Her skirt caught on the break rod and threw her under a wheel. I fancy her scream never even reached her husband, who was driving the team. Someone else had to alert him to her death.

"That day, we all learned never to leave a moving wagon, and after that, I figured nothing we had brought made much difference. Arriving here alive was all that mattered."

Her down-to-earth attitude settled Abby's nerves, and so did a squeeze on her hand. "People are what matter, and I must say, I wanted to visit you again, but a few days after we returned home, Fred came down with a case of the grippe. His weak lungs have taken such a long while to recover, but we think of you every day."

Delicate flavor trickled a healing stream down Abby's throat, while Elda Mae's friendly manner loosened her tongue. "I hope he has healed."

"Yes. Later, you shall see where he watches the birds."

"Oh, I would like that. I miss sketching."

"You have stopped?" Elda Mae gestured at a corner cupboard laden with pencils and brushes, so many that Abby gasped.

"Is something wrong?"

"All those brushes take my breath away. I left all my tools in Missouri." She swiped at her eyes. "I must have been daft, and so short-sighted that I neglected to bring any paper at all."

"Here, use this." Elda Mae handed her a cloth.

"Oh my, it has been so long since—"

Elda Mae crossed the room like a lynx and fetched Fred's tools. "Look closer."

One stubby pencil was the kind Mama had kept for her in the store. She had used it to sketch Martin and that puppy. She longed to touch it, hold it in her hand, but…

"Which one do you like best? By all means, take it home with you."

An avalanche of tears threatened as Abby reached out and picked the pencil from its jar. "Oh, you cannot know how…"

Sipping her tea and taking a bite of shortbread, Elda Mae remained quiet. After Abby set the pencil down, she smiled.

"You have had a long, lonely siege." The kindness in her voice seemed almost too much to bear, so Abby concentrated on her tea. Somewhere, a clock ticked, reminding her of the large wooden one she had left in Poplar Bluff. So many memories coming to life in such a short time, far too many to put into words. But Elda Mae seemed not to mind sitting together in silence.

When they both emptied their cups, she said, "Come with me on a tour before we have another cup."

The cabin boasted a separate bedroom and sitting space near the fire. Here and there, scatter rugs and pillows added brightness. At a high narrow desk, more pencils caught Abby's eye, the brand Mama gave her for Christmas every year.

"Everything looks so fine."

"Fred told me we would live way out in the wilderness, so I planned ahead. Pretty linens help when the seclusion troubles me."

A lump formed in Abby's throat—planning ahead—just what she had failed to do.

Fred says, "The morning begins with beauty in the sunrise, and ends with beauty. The Navahos understood this, so the prayer song of Dawn Boy in the Mountain Chant focuses on beauty.

Beauty before me, I return.
Beauty above me, I return.
Beauty below me, I return.
Beauty all around me, with it I return.
Now on the trail of beauty, I return.

"You learned that from the Indians?"

"No, Fred taught it to me. Often in the mornings, I think of dawn as a boy, chanting this song. Sunrise comes to us second hand here, but still brings such beauty."

So, Elda Mae saw this, too. Something let loose inside Abby, and a sense of belonging settled over her.

"One more thing I must show you. Fred's pride and joy. See here?"

In a far corner, Elda Mae moved aside a beautiful hand-woven screen and Abby gasped. "You brought this organ?"

"Fred learned to play when he was young, and the music calms him. He renders the old hymns from time to time—singing benefits the lungs, also."

"Just the other night, I recalled our church in Poplar Bluff, and it seemed as though I might never hear those songs again."

"Ah—do you play?"

"I used to. I would need to practice."

Elda Mae beckoned her back to the table and poured more tea. "And Ray. How are things going with him?"

Fumbling for a reply, Abby remembered the letter and pulled it from her pocket. "I thought—" But her throat closed up.

Elda Mae reached for her hand. "Talking about one's private life can be so vexing. Yet there came a point when I had to, for my own sanity."

"Sanity?" The word burst out like spittle. "How could I have married Ray if I were sane? After Mama and Papa died—" Abby bit her lip. "And then Aunt Susan, too—Staying in Poplar Bluff seemed impossible. Everyone was so…"

"Sympathetic?"

"Yes. How did you know? And Ray's talk about the West enticed me."

Elda Mae held one hand to her chest. "My dear, my first husband deceived me—I lost my sanity, too. I believed everything he told me, but it was all lies."

The letter fell from Abby's hand onto the table. "You did?"

"Yes, and I must ask one thing. Are you in danger?"

"Sometimes Ray hits me. But, Mama always said, *for better or for worse.*"

Elda Mae's brow wrinkled. "Would your mother countenance someone hurting you?"

"Oh, no, never." A few moments of quiet underlined this truth—Mama would be so upset if she knew. "She…she never liked Ray. She told Papa she could not trust his shifty eyes, but I…"

Abby thrust the letter toward Elda Mae. "One day, I found this. I brought it for you to read. Would you please?" She handed over the letter.

After perusing the deed, Elda Mae's wide emerald eyes met Abby's. "It appears that Ray has bamboozled more than two wives." She turned the hankie over. Watching her sniff its embroidered fabric, Abby's chest tightened.

"Store-bought, not homespun. And starched. Whoever Lola McHale might be, she has money." Elda Mae grasped Abby's hand.

"You may have made a bad choice, but so did Maria, and this Lola." She bit her lip. "Long ago, William Ainsley courted me, a perfect gentleman. His manners misled me, and my parents, too. I think they wondered if anyone would ever propose to such a daughter as I, and Will charmed them.

"I had set my sights on teaching. Of course, most eligible men sought a wife who would be satisfied with a home and children." She covered Abby's hand again. "I wanted children, too, but the desire to teach came to me as a little girl."

Her eyes took on a faraway look. "I met William when I was in training. How could I have guessed his violent nature? Was it the same for you?"

"Yes. But I had lost everyone. I was bedeviled."

"And with your thinking in disarray, Ray appeared stable and wise. Overwhelming sorrow plays with our minds, dear. You have survived so much, and I wager Ray accuses you of all sorts of things, but your sanity is not in question. These men say *you, you, you,* as if Providence assigned them to define us."

Ray's pronouncements rang in Abby's mind. *"Yer worthless. Yer never satisfied."* A carved, carefully lettered plaque above the bedroom doorway caught her eye. *Fortitudine vincimus.*

"What does that sign mean?"

"By endurance we conquer—Fred spent hours notching it in Latin, and it fits our situations quite well. You and I may have made serious errors in judgment, but we see the error of our ways."

She pressed her fist to her forehead. "William said he wanted me all for himself, so we moved to another town—its name was so unfitting for my time there—Mount Pleasant. Then his ravings began, and continued until a man of the cloth found me almost dead.

"He took me to his wife, who cared for me and taught me so much. When I had nearly healed, she said God endows us with innate human dignity, and we must act on our own behalf at times." Elda Mae peered at Abby. "Even if that requires leaving someone who hurts us."

"Leaving?"

"Yes. I doubted at first, because I had *made my bed*. But I came to see that certain men would strike out at any woman. After I left, William continued his vile deeds, showing me I had done the right thing."

"But I always speak out of turn or ask a question to rile Ray."

"A proper helpmeet must ask questions. I thought I caused William's fits, too, but if I had stayed, he would have made short work of me. That last time, I would have died if the pastor hadn't found me."

"I keep thinking if I could only give Ray children..."

"Mm—I thought that would change William too." Elda Mae leaned closer, her tone earnest. "My new friends reminded me that children are the Almighty's gift, and I could not produce them of my own will."

Outside, pine boughs swayed against a crystalline sky. At footsteps on the porch, Elda Mae set aside the letter and hankie. "Shall I keep these for you?"

"Yes, thank you. Ray has no idea I found them, and he went into a state when I mentioned your visit."

"Before the worst storms arrive, I hope to come again—if only I could know when he takes his trips."

"I have no way of telling. This time, he said he would come home tomorrow—he has never done that before." Abby leaned against a doorframe. "I must confess I have been mischievous. One day I saw some poison sumac, and—it sounds so childish, but I... I rubbed some of the leaves on Ray's long Johns when I did the washing."

Elda Mae's hoot filled the cabin, and Abby joined in as Fred entered. When Elda Mae recovered enough to speak, she panted, "Goodness child, we do think alike—I used poison ivy from the woods behind our house in Ohio. Seeing Will itching to distraction did me a world of good."

Fred took his place, and Elda Mae fetched him some tea and refilled Abby's cup and the shortbread plate. "These days, Fred pays special attention to his birds."

"Oh, I watch them, too, and a turkey vulture visits me."

Fred blinked, but said nothing before diving into his shortbread.

"Have another helping, Abby—take strength for the ride home. Then you must see the arbor." Elda Mae patted Fred's hand. "Dear, Abby likes to sketch, too."

"Wonderful! Perhaps you can sketch that vulture you mentioned."

Later, his eyes sparkled as he pointed out his sketching table in a lovely arbor. Here and there, small piles of peelings and seeds lured winged visitors.

"Fred has arranged everything here for viewing."

He rocked back on his heels. "A soldier stopped in a while back, and showed great interest in my work."

"I meant to ask you about him, Abby. Sergeant Tolzmann was seeking Ray. Did he find your place?"

"Yes, but Ray was gone."

"That sergeant had such clear eyes."

"He did. Could you two tell me what happened at Vicksburg? I believe he fought there."

Fred leaped in. "Surely. Such an important conflict—I thought perhaps the war would end sooner once General Pemberton was routed by the Union there. Did you know this occurred at the same time General Lee lost a battle in Pennsylvania, at a place called Gettysburg?"

"No, I… I missed out on so much during those years."

"President Lincoln said of the victory at Vicksburg, which put the whole course of the Mississippi in Federal hands, 'The great Father of Waters again goes unvexed to the sea.'

"Such a severe blow to the South, that defeat, but politics and common sense often fail to mix. Those Confederates in places of power could not countenance losing their precious states' rights, so the dreadful killing went on for two more years.

"The battle at Chickamauga, alone, cost our troops 16,000 men and the Confederates over 20,000. Such frightful carnage."

Fred gave a woeful wag of his head and changed the subject. "Would you like to see some sketches?"

"I would, so very much, but the sun is waning. I must get home to do the chores. Perhaps next time?" Abby hugged Elda Mae while Fred fetched the bay. He helped her mount, and Elda Mae's parting words saw her off.

"Keep your wits about you, and flee to us if necessary."

Martin hated to see Captain Whitaker ride away. He studied the Rim's craggy outgrowths before turning Docker onto yesterday's route.

"This is how it is, Dock. The Captain was born to lead, and I was born to follow. But here we are, all alone again."

That put him in mind of Friedrich, who became more father than brother to him after Pa died. That horrible day, Martin had shinnied up the ladder after Friedrich and Henry after Mama discovered Pa's body. The image of the hay rope cinching Pa's neck still lurked as fresh as morning dew.

But Friedrich took things in hand and set him and Henry to work. It was spring, after all, and the planting must continue.

During the year since his little sister Imelda's accident, Mama had kept the Tolzmann household stable. But the guilt that descended on Pa must have proven too much to bear.

Not once did Mama allow her tears for her youngest child to show, but then came Pa's death. The way he died hurt almost more than losing him. Finally, after a special meeting, the church council agreed to bury Pa in the cemetery, and Mama found her way again.

Following the funeral, she gathered the family. "We do not discuss this, children. Not in this house, and nowhere else. Never. Do you understand?"

With Friedrich taking over the farm work, Martin slipped into Henry's shadow. When schoolmates whispered about Pa's sinful choice, Henry ignored them. Martin tried to, but when they eyed him askance, something inside turned to stone.

He relegated his questions to a secret inner niche. Now, he attempted to force Abby's image into another far corner.

Even in full sunshine, winter tinged the air. Pale blue berry clusters decorated the uppermost juniper branches and pin oaks dripped acorns for the woodpeckers. A downed pine boasted thousands of their evenly drilled holes, each holding a single nut. The sight brought a grin—a veritable corn crib in a fallen tree.

In all of Martin's travels, nothing rivaled this distinctive Rim. And that natural bridge they had stumbled upon—no matter why Colonel Masters chose him for this duty, he lifted his eyes and gave thanks.

Chapter Eighteen

From the fresh perspective of the Allen's cabin, the eastern Rim presented such an array for the eye. Dappled with white, distinctive boulders appeared even larger, and Strawberry Mountain revealed slopes hidden from the ranch far below.

New energy filled Abby, yet Elda Mae's message replayed like Granny Ferguson's premonitions. *You made a bad choice, but so did I.* Halfway down the Allen's path, she remembered the jam and her desire for a sketchbook.

Too late to go back, but at least she had gained a pencil. Once again, she must bide her time. Still, even the shrubs and grasses seemed brighter, as if the world had transformed during her short visit. Mourning doves cooed their sweet, sentimental call foretelling evening tide, but she refused the melancholy their song often brought. Everything would change now—she felt it in her bones.

She bent to the bay. "You are such a good horse. What if I call you Sergeant?"

Some men control everything and everyone—they believe this shows their strength, but truly, it reveals their fear. Elda Mae's perspective had opened her eyes. What secret fears might Ray harbor?

"You must accept Ray for who he is and face the truth. We rarely do that all at once."

Sergeant juddered at something, so Abby gripped the reins tighter. A peculiar resonance in the bushes spiraled an alarm, but nothing could lessen the joy of this day.

"Elda Mae is right. I can never please Ray, but I can take back my life a little at a time."

Interspersed with these thoughts, a timeline of the war began to form in Abby's consciousness. She must find out more the next time she saw her new friends.

Then, with no warning, something crashed into her left arm. Sergeant's shrill whinny startled her, and she reeled backward. Then another blow struck the small of her back, sending her floating, falling, falling...

Rocks scraped her chin, and boots ground on red rock near her head. The thick soles carried an unmistakable manure smell as pain ricocheted through her inward parts. Abby squeezed her eyes shut.

A familiar sour odor pervaded as Ray hissed, "Why'dja make me do it?"

You, you, you...

He kicked her abdomen then, and administered a blow to the back of her head. Fire exploded through her body. Far, far away she slipped, above the highest pines, beyond the top of the Rim, past the meaning of sunrise and sunset, into an endless grey territory.

Late afternoon light spangled Ponderosa pine, sycamore, and juniper. Martin raised his glasses to scan Ray's wagon path. Could he have widened it even more in this short time?

Opposite the ranch, a spot offered a view of the ridge, the cabin, and the wagon road—a perfect observation post. Ample Manzanita on a substantial outcropping between two massive boulders would obscure him completely. Martin turned Docker into scraggly underbrush to settle in before late afternoon shadows invited snakes.

He urged Docker up the incline paralleling the Allen's turn-off for one more look. Just then, an odd flash of color halted him. He refocused the lenses and a speck waved in the breeze, like clothing on Mama's line.

The cloth was tinged blue and flapped to the side, exposing

something small and brown. Martin cleared his eyes—must be seeing things. But no—unmistakable tanned leather with buttons formed a shoe—a woman's shoe. His pulse careened as he tied Docker to a branch and scrambled down the hill.

Twenty yards from the trail, he lifted the glasses again, his pulse now a loud staccato. *Oh, dear God!* Abby had worn that shawl when they walked the pasture after supper. Dust swirled around him as he slid to a stop.

There she lay, like the lifeless rag doll Lissa used to rock. Blood spattered the rocks, and a cut extended from Abby's cheek into her lips. Blood mixed with something blue smeared down her torso. It took a moment to realize it was jam—blackberry jam. She must have been taking some to the Allens and suffered a terrible fall.

Afraid to touch her, he bent close and detected faint breathing. He glanced around. *No help for her at the ranch.* On closer inspection, traces of straw stood out in some boot prints beside her head, along with unmistakable shreds of manure.

The tracks led into the brush, where a shiny object reflected light. Martin leaned over to retrieve a whiskey flask initialed R.M., and stilled the impulse to grind the thing under his heel.

Preserve the evidence. Plenty of time to deal with McHale later.

Aware of pine boughs swishing high above, he scrabbled up the slope for his poncho, led Docker down and wrapped Abby with care. As he tucked her limp arms inside the canvas, heat sparked behind his eyes. Time stood still, but his thoughts raced. What if she died in his arms? "Mercy, grant us mercy."

Steadily upward he trod, cautious on the rocky path. Past the sycamore, the cold spring made music over rocks. Then came the fallen-down shack, and with every step, one plea beat a consistent rhythm. "Keep her alive. Keep her alive."

Not a flutter from Abby's eyelids. Life could take its leave in an instant. Could his pitiful prayers make a difference, as Mama believed?

Elda Mae came running from the cabin, and though her face

crumbled, she whisked into action. "Fred, hurry! Fetch clean cloths. Throw another log on the fire, and get my medical supplies." She ushered Martin into the bedroom.

"Put her in here. Where did you find her?"

Martin nudged Abby onto the quilt, his throat so swollen he could barely reply. "On the wagon path. Not far from the sycamore."

"She was fine an hour ago—such a good horse, that bay—would never have thrown her." Elda Mae ran for water and took a pile of cloths from Fred. His arms hung like pendulums, and he shook his head back and forth.

"No, not that horse."

"From the prints, I would say her husband..." The accusation stopped Martin mid-sentence. "He attacked her." He sank into a chair.

Elda Mae's face turned a violent red. "I could kill that man myself." Her breath came in spurts, and she leaned over Abby's still form.

Fred hovered outside the room like a native bird, circling and tentative.

When Elda Mae glanced up, she gestured toward the kitchen, "Martin, go out on the porch for some fresh air. Fred, fetch Martin something to eat."

Could he trust his legs? He had often carried heavier loads far greater distances—why should he be so spent?

Hot coffee and leftover venison stew revived him. Fred, in his shy way, ventured some questions.

"You think the horse startled at something?" He fidgeted. "Such a fine animal. I fail to understand—"

"Someone attacked her."

"That beautiful girl?" Fred's Adam's apple worked with emotion. "Oh, but evil men do walk this earth. I recall hearing President Lincoln say much the same years ago. I happened to be passing through Alton, Illinois when he engaged in a debate."

"You saw him face-to-face?"

"Indeed, but it was his words that impressed me. It was something like, 'The Bible says somewhere that we are desperately selfish. I think we would have discovered that without the Bible.'"

"In this case, *wicked* fits better."

"Do you think Miss Abby will recover?"

Fred's lip trembled, so Martin continued. "If your wife has anything to say, she will regain her strength. Shall we go out and finish your chores?"

Fred lost no time grabbing his straw hat. When Martin peeked in to check on Abby, Elda Mae tiptoed over. "She needs prayer, and you need sleep. Surely you will stay the night?"

Martin nodded, but after doing the chores he paced up and down the path, formulating feeble prayers. Then he ventured to the back room, where Elda Mae met his eyes over Abby's still frame. Her mouth contorted, so he backed away and bedded down in a corner of the porch

The next thing he knew, someone shook his shoulder. He started up expecting the Captain, but Elda Mae stood over him.

"Do you mind watching Abby? I can serve her better tomorrow with a little sleep." She handed him a fresh cup of coffee. Inside, Fred snored near the fireplace.

"She has an enormous bruise low on her back. He walloped her several times." A tear slipped down her cheek.

"You are doing your best."

"But only Providence can heal her. What would I have done without you here?" Her solemn eyes gleamed in the firelight. "What would have happened to her if you had not come along?"

To Martin's shrug, she added. "The Lord guides the right people to care for his children." She patted his sleeve. "Call me if anything changes, and above all, keep praying."

Seeing Abby like this sent Martin back to the times he helped surgeons tie down victims of exploding minie balls. Once positioned on makeshift platforms, they were administered chloroform and whiskey. Putrid odors enveloped the temporary surgeries where harassed medical personnel snatched any soldier they could find for an assistant.

This deathly stillness unnerved him even more than that wartime chaos. For some time, he wavered near the end of the bed, but finally pulled a wooden chair near Abby's head. A snuffle issued from the next room, but minutes later, regular breathing told him Elda Mae had fallen asleep.

The right people...

Had he ignored his impulse to take one more look, no one would have found her. This, he knew. Her face was swelled now, and purple. McHale must have hit her awfully hard—or kicked her.

No doubt, the intention was to kill. If time had allowed, he might have found whatever knocked her to the ground. Most likely a shotgun's blunt end—a blow like that had felled many a soldier. The thought produced a sick sensation.

A coyote's yelp pierced the darkness, but Abby made no move. Martin leaned his head into his hands.

"We offer ourselves as instruments into Thy hands..." During his youth, these words always preceded Pastor Schultz's final Sunday prayer, and they expressed Martin's desire. Whatever it took, he would see McHale punished. But the longer he kept vigil, an even deeper urge enveloped him.

Before the first paper-thin lines foretelling dawn, he bent toward Abby's still form. Her shallow breathing razed his soul.

He blinked as if someone turned on a bright light and whispered something he never dreamed possible. "If it be Thy will, this—this desire in me... I accept it."

The profile of Abby's face, though bruised and swollen, sent a thrill through him. Helpless against the tide, he could only own what eddied up in his heart.

He dared not consider what this fresh emotion meant. Perhaps, were Captain Whitaker here, he would quote that fellow Pliny and remind him of the moon's pull on the earth.

Until dawn broke and Elda Mae stirred, Martin begged the Almighty to spare Abby Ferguson's precious life.

Barred doors blocked her way, so Abby sank back. Fire consumed her, a Titian inferno, a fist inside her head, squeezing, squeezing.

A man's mellow voice recited something over and over. Hard-drawn breaths—a door creaked and a soft lavender scent wafted. Coolness bathed Abby's forehead and face. She slept and wakened.

"Come back to us, Abby."

The absence of pain wooed her to stay, riding a large horse on a steep path. Under heavy shade, dewy spider webs laced glowing grass stalks and flower stems. Sun on her hands, breeze massaging her face—how she had craved this freedom.

Graceful yellow roses and black-eyed Susans surrounded her, azaleas, purple verbena and catmint, bellflowers, clumps of day lilies. Even painted ladies raised their heads.

Then Mama and Papa appeared through walls of flame. Mama's delicate glass vial of healing oil enticed her. Abby tried to call her, but suddenly, Papa hovered near, his hearty proclamation strong and sure.

"Your life is not over, Abby Ferguson."

Clay dust stifled her breathing. Nancy, held captive by Fagin in his ring of thieves, cried out about her wretched state.

'I am chained to my old life. I loathe and hate it now, but I cannot leave it. I must have gone too far to turn back, and yet I don't know.'

The wind swirled her away with Fagin in pursuit while Oliver Twist watched. When the scene changed the scent of lye soap and horseflesh reigned. A rough hand stroked Abby's, and a voice, low like Papa's, quieted her. Step by step, that resonance wooed her back into this world.

By midmorning, Martin manned his surveillance spot with his field glasses. Not long afterward, Ray entered the barn. For hours, nothing changed. Finally, Docker nickered, and Martin crept over to check on him.

Some time after he settled in his niche again, Ray circled behind the barn. When he disappeared around the bramble thicket, Martin focused on the pasture. In a few minutes, the canvas tarp slid off the wagon like a shed snakeskin, exposing piled wooden crates.

McHale lifted something sparkly—most likely a bottle—and tipped back his head. Martin gritted his teeth as a band of natives approached on horseback. Each animal pulled a travois, or as the Plains Indians called them, a *parfleche* of stiffened, stretched buffalo hides.

Details from his third grade history lesson were still vivid. Miss Anderson described the boiled beaver tail glue used to bind tanned hides to logs for carrying heavy loads. During recess, the older boys fashioned a replica.

Echoes floated from the valley floor as several braves struggled with the obviously heavy crates. The wind picked up, and soon the Indian band dispersed. A few headed down Ray's secret road, and others faded into a bank of trees. Then Ray fished something from the bushes at the clearing's edge.

No. *Someone.* Martin stared dumbfounded as Ray jerked the arm of a black-haired squaw. Dressed in rawhide, she offered no resistance. Knowing how that wretch treated his own wife, would Captain Whitaker move in right now, or wait?

Think like a cattle thief—only one thing matters. Cattle.

But what about this woman? McHale shoved her into the barn, and Martin wanted to race down the incline and burst into the building. He took a few deep breaths and lifted his canteen to wash away the ugly taste in his mouth.

How did Abby end up with this reprobate? What power did Ray possess to beguile her? These questions gripped him as Docker foraged for wild grass.

After an uneventful hour, daylight waned, so he returned to the

Allen's, where Fred met him in the yard. He grabbed the reins as Martin shinnied down.

"Is she—?"

"Still alive." He gestured Martin inside and took Docker to the barn. In the cabin, Elda Mae hurried from the back room and pointed toward bread and bacon still warm on the back of the stove. Her earnest words gave him hope.

"Not a movement yet, but these things take time."

After a massive slab slathered with butter and honey, Martin allowed Fred to refill his plate and recount the day in a hushed voice.

"Elda Mae never leaves her side." He stretched his fingers every which way as he spoke. "And that vulture flew over again, several times. Such a mystery. Abby said one visited her down below."

Finishing his meal, Martin rubbed his middle. "How about finding some work for me in the barn? Waiting and watching all day leaves a man in need."

Fred leaped at the suggestion, and the quiet building seemed to calm Martin. An hour later, having scooped and raked and shoveled, they returned to the cabin. Fred bedded down near the fire, and Martin peeked into the bedroom.

Elda Mae turned, her face an anxious kaleidoscope. "Never saw anyone stay like this for so long."

"You need some rest. Let me take first watch."

She touched Abby's hand and gave him directions. "Hold her hand and tell her we want her to come back. She may be able to hear us." She wiped her eyes. "Once today, I thought her lashes flickered, but my imagination must have deceived me."

Martin pulled up the chair and waited until Elda Mae's snores melded with Fred's. Even then, his first words sounded like a bugle call in the night.

"You have a whole life ahead of you, Abby."

He ran his fingertips over the back of her hand. So soft; so febrile. Three hours later, he bent forward again and repeated the same words for the hundredth time.

Her fingers moved!

Or did he imagine it, as Elda Mae had earlier?

"Abby, come back."

Nothing.

"This is Martin. Please, please come back to us."

Was that a movement under her eyelids? Yes—minute, but definite. He launched his message over and over. The ripple recurred, and then he could have sworn her fingers moved under his.

He raised his voice. "Elda Mae, come quick."

In a flash, the older woman stood beside him.

"Watch her eyes, and just now, she moved her fingers. There—she squeezed my hand!"

Elda Mae's hip met his shoulder as she bustled closer. Martin almost fell off the chair.

With all her might, Abby pushed against a large hand.

A man's voice echoed. "Come quick..."

She fell back against the clouds, but now, a woman pleaded. "Squeeze my hand, Abby. I know you can do it."

Weariness enveloped her, but the urgent plaint continued. She exerted all her strength and someone gasped.

"Yes, I felt it!"

A vulture swept close—the same one she heard long ago on a porch, in the moonlight. Such a clear recollection—pain seared her scalp, but the great bird left her a feather.

Next, an elk trapped in a wooden crate thrashed about. A dark-haired man approached on a steed — "More sorrow, I fain would tell."

Granny's reached her bent hands forth, and she cackled, "Strong, full of art..."

In a twinkling, everything changed. Serene light enveloped a room in soft violet shades, and a woman with pine green eyes pronounced, "By endurance we conquer."

Those mighty wings flapped again. Nearby, someone let out a sigh as Abby rested back on the turkey vulture's mighty wings.

Brisk cold energized Martin when he wakened. He washed his face and wolfed down bread and eggs before tiptoeing to the bedroom doorway. Abby's pale skin shone almost translucent in dawn light, but Elda Mae's eyes gleamed.

"She squeezed my finger again. I'm thinking to bathe her this morning. If ever in your life you prayed, Martin, pray now."

After another scalding cup of coffee, he accepted a packet of food from Fred and entered a crisp white world. Silent snow sifted down, and the pines marching along the Rim top resembled chalky limestone cliffs.

Docker's mane received his grateful tears.

"She's able to move." He leaned his head back. "Heal her, I beseech Thee." A barn cat poked around the haymow opening, and Docker's soft nicker broke the ethereal quiet.

"All right. Time to find out what McHale is up to." Along the path, purple shadows aided night animals hurrying home while the giant sycamore extended massive white-laced branches in the prequel to full daylight.

Hunched under his poncho, Martin clenched the fingers that so recently touched Abby's hand. All those hours beside her. He would never be the same.

A wolf's howl sailed high and lazily descended the scale. Day animals scuttled from their dens into fresh snow. As dawn faded the stars, the pine wind narrowed to a mere tinge in the very tallest treetops. The snowy quilt heightened every sound as Martin stationed himself on the lookout—best take care, for the slightest resonance might alert McHale.

Seconds after sunrise, Ray left the barn, washed his hands at the tank, and entered the cabin. A few minutes later, he dropped some gunnysacks near the barn. From this distance, he appeared short and wide-shouldered, with heavily muscled arms.

A woodpecker drummed its steady beat. Fred had mentioned several species in the area; clown, ladder-back, hairy—which one was this? Soon Ray led a saddled horse outside, stuffed the sacks into his saddlebag, and rode toward the back pasture. Over the next fifteen minutes, the glasses revealed his progress down the secret road.

Long after his tuneless whistle receded, Martin mounted Docker and descended the trail. On level ground, he skulked past the cabin, wishing in vain for Captain Whitaker to appear. If no storms assailed, he might have reached Camp Verde by now.

The sun encased the Rim in glitter, transforming rows of pines into majestic ivory sentinels. Fresh hoof prints led east, but otherwise, the pasture lay deserted. A jagged piece of wood torn from a crate poked awkwardly from the snow.

Stamped on the back with U.S. Army weapon identification numbers, this evidence substantiated their suspicions. Nearby, a small brown object sparkled in the snow—a cork smelling of whiskey. No wonder those crates were so bunglesome. Martin turned the cork over in his palm and searched for anything else Ray might have tossed aside.

Finding nothing, he followed his trail back to the barn through knee-high drifts. Despite his desire to avoid anything McHale touched, the barn might contain more proof.

Certain the Indian woman had disappeared into the forest, Martin slipped through the side door. Soured milk, well-worn leather, and the dense aroma of moldy hay permeated the ghostly atmosphere.

Outside, the cows foraged despite the snow. Ray must have undertaken another three or four-day journey—in this weather, his trek might take even longer.

From the matted straw, Martin retrieved a crinkled square of paper and read what he could. There it was—Colonel Master's signature followed a list of crate numbers and a date—September 16, 1867. Captain Whitaker's reliable intuition once again proved accurate.

The barn's recesses beckoned, so he lighted the lantern hanging at the entrance, and tremulous auras lighted his way. In the months following Pa's death, these ominous shadows would have sent Martin into retreat—back then, entering the barn required all the courage he possessed.

Only Henry's consistent understanding conquered that fear. "I don't like going in there, either, but we mustn't let the stock starve." Even years later, though, that grisly image of Pa taunted Martin.

A metallic odor and a faint hiss drew him. Battles had produced that same ominous ebb far too many times. A primal chill coursed his spine as he came upon what he dreaded. In the far corner, rugged gasps cast an eerie spell over the dim space. He edged toward a misshapen lump in a pile of straw.

Slim light revealed a woman's bruised face, an arm wrenched from its socket, blood pooled on a buckskin dress. Abby's countenance and that of another girl—a war memory—flashed before him.

So recently, he had listened for Abby's breath, the breath of life, but this squaw evidenced only a death rattle. Martin's fingers curled—he would relish beating McHale senseless. But right now, his victim deserved full attention.

Through a thicket of dark lashes, the woman's black eyes stared without sight. With the barest touch, Martin closed her still-warm eyelids. A battle memory buried deep inside nearly wriggled free, but he shoved down the vivid recollection.

This tawny-skinned beauty now lay lifeless; fingers dangling like shriveled leaves. One of her arms twisted at an unnatural angle to match her broken neck.

Had this same sensation overwhelmed Pa when he backed the wagon over little Imelda? That shy little sister with long dark pigtails and an infectious laugh had become a tiny speck in Martin's memory, but Pa could never get her out of his mind. Had she become more real than ever to him after the accident? Right after it occurred, did he kneel beside her like this, searching for a heartbeat? Then, aware that all hope was lost, what could he do?

His flesh and blood had perished at his own hand—an accident, but he bore the responsibility. Fresh understanding flooded Martin. Surely Pa had suffered sleepless nights and relentless inner accusations. The brokenness of Imelda's body must have replayed in his mind until he crumbled under the weight.

Tears traced Martin's cheek, and impetuous words flowed. "Pa, no one blames you. If only you could have seen how much we..." Whether his words reached Pa or not, they seemed fitting.

In this smelly stall, more questions rose. Had this woman tried to escape and hit her head on the post? Or did Ray wrench her neck out of sheer malice?

He ought to hightail it out of here with the evidence and not look back. But compassion flooded him, and something he read long ago came to mind—Mama had him commit to memory the passage from Hawthorne's *American Note-Books*. But it had been years since he had thought of its meaning.

There is so much wretchedness in the world, that we may safely take the word of any mortal professing to need our assistance; and, even should we be deceived, still the good to ourselves resulting from a kind act is worth more than the trifle by which we purchase it.

The girl's forehead felt cool—her time for seeking assistance was past. But what kind act could ever right this wrong?

Though his whisper would go unheard, Martin still offered her his regrets.

"This evil white man had no right to hurt you."

Chapter Nineteen

*S*omeone massaged her hand, then her forearm. Mama's face floated so close the wrinkle lines around her eyes showed. Then gentle hands eased Abby onto her side, and a feather pillow nestled her in a lavender scent. She must move her arms, but they had grown so ponderous.

Someone bustled about. A chair moved here, a pillow plumped there, a window opened—everyday movements mixed with a soothing tick-tock. Abby desired to see that clock, but her eyelids refused to open. She had struggled like this before, after a bad dream.

A murmur began, a familiar vibration. Then something clinked. A waft of cold air reached her, and a door tightened against its frame. Again, she struggled to open her eyes. Then suddenly, dark log walls surrounded her. Light filtered through an open window onto a pine floor.

Outside that window, snow-covered branches swayed against a glassy blue sky. Why, it must be winter. She longed to hail whoever moved about, but cotton coated her tongue. She managed to clear her throat and instantly, skirts swished, launching a swift shadow over the bed.

A plump female face appeared, and extra chins trembled when the woman drew a deep breath.

"I knew you would wake up today! Do you remember me? You rode the big bay over to visit us, and we drank Ohio tea."

Ah yes, heartening tea in fragile china cups—and Fred's wondrous drawing pencils. Later, he showed her an arbor and said perhaps she would be first to sketch the turkey vulture in flight.

When she chuckled, his countenance remained somber. "Maybe you will, Miss Abby, if you set your mind to it."

Above her, this kindly woman's great green eyes demanded a response, but Abby's attempt resulted in a hoarse moan. "Wa…"

"Of course, and anything else your heart desires."

Nothing ever tasted so delightful as that cool splash down her throat. She swallowed another spoonful, then another. But soon, weariness draped her back into sleep, where a horse named Sergeant flew free as a valley bird, almost to the sycamore, halfway home.

A pot lid clanged somewhere, and something plopped into water. Potatoes? Oh, yes—these people brought seed potatoes from Ohio where Elda Mae lived in her youth. She met Fred in her thirties, years after her first marriage to a man who—

Fortitudine vincimus. The words had been carved somewhere. Now, knitting needles clicked against each other, and a rocker creaked over floorboards. A *rat-a-tat* sounded from beyond the window to Abby's right, and she spied a woodpecker. Such consistent industry! This was no dream.

When she braced on her elbow to rise, the room swirled, so she fell back on her pillow. Instantly someone appeared in the doorway and a woman called.

"Oh my dear girl, how are you feeling?" Such rich green eyes, like a velvet settee in a parlor somewhere long ago.

"Feeling—yes." Abby blinked. "Quite well, thank you."

Martin forked hay and milked for Fred, but questions troubled him the whole time. McHale valued the butter his cows produced, so would he let them agonize until he came home? Surely, he would not risk them dying from hardened or burst udders. Or would he?

Suddenly, Fred's head showed over the ladder. "You work too hard, son." With stems of dry hay shooting from his hair and clothes, he climbed into the mow.

"This is my way of taking out my wrath on a man who kills in cold blood, out of pure malice."

Baby birds still partially covered with white fluff stirred in their nest near the cupola as Fred took his time. "I only know the Almighty declares, 'Vengeance is mine. I will repay.'"

A sudden loud *char, char, char* echoed from the rafters, and he cranked his neck for a look at a small brown bird.

"How peculiar—a cactus wren way up here." He addressed the mother. "Your brood ought to have been out on their own weeks ago." The tiny creature chittered as though she understood.

"Raucous little one, your bravery exceeds that of your northern cousins." Fred shook his head as the wren flew off.

"This species normally inhabits the desert and is much friendlier than its northern cousins. Have you seen any *cholla* cactus on your travels, my friend?"

"Thousands to the south. The officers warned us about their spines."

"Normally, this mama would make her nest in a deadly *cholla*. What a mystery she found us here, where none grow. This must be her second brood of the season. At such times, I find it helpful to ask *how* rather than *why*."

Fred continued to puzzle on the way to the cabin. "So peculiar, like discovering a rabbit nesting in a tree. The local creatures must feel the same about us, after having this territory to themselves for centuries."

"When did you decide to study birds?"

"William Gambel preceded me, and his work provided guidance. Have you heard of him?" Fred beckoned Martin to the arbor and opened his sketchbook and pointed to a bird. "In all your travels, have you seen this amazing creature?"

"I think so—yes, I remember that topknot and the red patch. What is it?"

"Gambel's Quail was named after William, a young student of nature who followed the Santa Fe Trail and traveled on to California back in the '40s. At only fifteen, he collected specimens in North Carolina with Thomas Nuttall, a Harvard botanist."

"You met Gambel?"

"Unfortunately, no. Typhoid took William's life in '49, but in his short twenty-five years, he contributed much to our body of knowledge. When I first noted his research, I knew exactly what I wanted to do."

As they headed to the creek, Martin voiced the question uppermost in his mind. "How do you think McHale wooed Abby here?"

"Impossible to know—we must leave room for things beyond our understanding." Fred's mischievous grin peeked out. "Human behavior defies logic at times. After all, Mrs. Allen allowed me to woo *her* here." He caught himself after stumbling on a rock.

"No doubt this question disturbs Abby, as well. I would never make certain choices again, but at the time, only a portion of the truth was available. Have you found this to be true, young man?"

Young? Today, Martin felt quite old. "Perhaps, but my wild imaginings held me back from making choices altogether. When others launched out, I hemmed and hawed. That tendency troubled Mama, so I learned to hide my misgivings.

"When I let something slip, she would say, '*Achh Mein*! What has troubled your head?' I regretted causing her distress, but my fears seemed larger than reality."

"Yet you went to war; a decisive action."

"Albeit with trepidation." How could he explain what appeared to him in force in the night hours? Such complicated inquiries niggled him every time he climbed the haymow ladder back home.

Where were God's angels when Pa cinched that rope around his neck? And when Imelda died, where were they?

Like persistent sunlight through shadowy pines, Pastor Schultz's sermons eased his quandaries at least temporarily. These basic truths, Mama believed with all her heart.

God created earth and heaven, yet still observed even an insignificant sparrow's fall and shed sunlight on both the righteous and the wicked. The Creator combined justice and love, while still allowing for humans to make choices.

On the snow-speckled path back to the tank, Fred turned quiet, and Martin's questions tumbled forth. "Why is there so much injustice? Why did our country's founders allow slavery? And how could men like Thomas Jefferson keep slaves, yet write *all men are created equal?*"

Fred pondered aloud with him. "I would guess the war only multiplied your wonderings. So much lost on the part of the Union to ensure final victory, and even more for the South. Both sides believed they died for the right—what a dreadful thing for our nation to endure. Even now, I scarce can fathom the numbers who perished."

"Yah. Some of their faces still come to me." Along with Pa's. Martin might have added that when he left for the war, people still whispered about his father. They pronounced that taking one's own life ranked worse than any other sin. In a rare moment years after Pa's death, Mama allowed that if Pastor Schultz and the deacons had not held a special meeting, she and Friedrich would have had to bury Pa at the farm.

But her injunction from long years past still rang in Martin's consciousness. These things must not be spoken aloud.

At least, as time progressed, the ghastly scene in the haymow lost its terrifying hold. How strange that now, a barn's shadowy recesses offered serenity. But as Martin filled a pail with grain, another question birthed yesterday bothered him. Could he have done more for that Indian woman?

After wrestling a trench from belligerent soil, he gave her the best burial he could. With the last shovelful of red soil, a turkey vulture circled and landed on a fallen log. Perhaps the creature did have a special relationship with the tribes, as General Crook believed.

Maybe it would lead the squaw's people to her. But just in case the vulture had a meal in mind, Martin placed five large rocks upon the grave.

Now, he poured smelly swill into the trough. Food scraps and sour milk tickled his nose as squealing pigs made for the slop.

At the squaw's grave, he ought to have recited a fitting Psalm or a prayer. Instead, he had merely murmured, "I commend her soul to Thy care. Ashes to ashes, dust to dust..."

Chapter Twenty

After another day of observation, Martin headed to the Allen's. Their friendliness told him he was as welcome as family.

All this waiting and watching gave his thoughts far too much leisure to wander. They traveled from childhood scenes to the shallow grave near McHale's barn, but always ended with Abby, still lying in Elda Mae's bed.

Long legs sprawled out from the porch corner. *Fred must be reading.* Such a peculiar fellow, but anyone could sense his benevolence. As Docker drew near, and Martin dismounted, Fred set down a thick volume and rose to greet him.

"Welcome back. Not much change here, I'm afraid, but Elda Mae holds out hope. As for me, that cactus wren has me thinking, and this morning, a turkey vulture flew over the yard so low its wings whistled. Never saw one this close before." He studied the sky.

"Abby told me a big vulture often visited her at the ranch, but I scarce believed. Now I wonder if it might be checking on her."

"Could that be true?"

"Suddenly, a cactus wren appears in the haymow to birth its young out of season, far from its normal home and with no *chollas* for miles. And just after Abby suffers her injuries, a turkey vulture pays us a call. I have no answers, only questions, which fits my field of study. Few absolutes and much conjecture—but then, my teacher once said I thought more than any rightful boy ought."

Fred gestured to the far end of the porch. "Do have a seat—you look weary. Let me fetch you something to drink."

The welcome shade invited Martin to a chair. Fred's offering of a sarsaparilla quenched the thirst that had plagued him on the path, and he exclaimed over its effects.

"Elda Mae brews this from the sassafras root." Fred tapped his fingers on his own glass. As for thinking too much, you and I have that in common. I go from question to question, sergeant. As soon as I write *always,* a new discovery produces more inquiries." Fred's sideways grin charmed Martin. "You see, I must learn constantly, which makes for a delightful vocation."

"It seems to agree with you. What are you reading?"

"Victor Hugo—what joy to take in his entire work in one volume. Such an insightful, caring soul. Did I tell you I received word from a guard in the prison camp at Johnson's Island that men incarcerated there bantered about Cosette's fate?"

"No, but Captain Whitaker took to Hugo's story, too. Maybe I ought to read it."

"Such a gift from France—testifies to the power of one man's efforts. You may borrow it at any time." Fred tapped his fingers on the volume. "And you—did you learn anything about that—that merciless McHalc fellow today?"

"Plenty enough, but my mind traveled far and wide while I waited—too far and wide. I am more suited to hard labor."

"Ah... with that I can oblige you." Fred made no move to the barn, but eyed another book lying open on the table.

"You have been reading something else?"

"The diary of one of our first presidents, John Adams. His outlook calms my soul. Did you know the existence of evil greatly troubled him?"

"No—my knowledge is limited."

"He decided that God permits wickedness," Fred leafed a few pages back, "because not to do so would destroy the liberty without which there could be no moral good or evil in the universe. Without human choice, life would be 'a mere chemical process, a mere mechanical engine to produce nothing but pleasure.'"

"Hmm."

"Adams maintained such objectivity, sergeant. He says about his mind: 'I can as easily still the tempest or stop the rapid thunderbolt as command the motions and operations of my own mind. My brain seems constantly in as great confusion and wild disorder as Milton's chaos... I never have any bright, refulgent ideas. Everything appears in my mind dim and obscure, like objects seen through a dirty glass or roiled water.'"

"My sentiments exactly—perhaps I might borrow that volume, too?"

"Indeed. After we do the chores."

Cows milked, manure in the wagon, water tank full; Martin felt better already. He and Fred labored in silence, with that cactus wren and her babies for company. And then Fred leaped to attention at the sound of a cowbell.

"Mustn't be late. Elda Mae will have our hides."

A few minutes later, skillet in one hand and spatula in the other, she gestured them toward the laden table. "Cause for celebration, gentlemen—Abby awakened again an hour ago. This evening, I think she might be able to sit up for a few minutes." She carried a bowl of porridge into the bedroom, and her prophecy wafted back.

"Tomorrow you might even eat with us."

"Thanks to you."

Abby's voice, though weak, sent a thrill through Martin.

A few minutes later, Elda Mae returned with an empty dish. "She has her appetite back."

"Will she—will she return to the cabin?"

"Over my dead body." Elda Mae glowered like a mother mountain lion.

After their meal, Fred gathered his drawing pencils and eased outside. "Still enough daylight for visions to appear."

Martin informed Elda Mae about the squaw as they dumped

scraps for the elk and deer. "Yesterday I buried an Indian woman I found in the barn. McHale broke her neck."

"Merciful heavens!"

"I dug a grave for her, but—"

"As if finding Abby weren't enough." Elda Mae gritted her teeth. "That man is evil, pure and simple. But you gave that poor girl a decent burial. Everyone deserves that."

She straightened. "Except Ray. Not worth the square feet to lay that scoundrel out."

"Soon, Abby need never worry about him again." Aware of her eyes fixed on him, Martin paused. "But I do wonder what will become of her."

"She has a home here, if she desires. In her delirium, she called out for someone named Oliver, though, and a girl named Nancy—someone called Stipes, too. Or Skites? Did she mention any of her family to you?"

"She said she lost all of her people in Missouri."

"That was my impression, too. Poor child—grief and injury can certainly warp a person's thinking." Elda Mae's voice broke, but she took herself in hand. "Once we know that blackguard sits in jail, or worse, we can fetch her things."

"I promise to let you know when we arrest McHale."

"Surely you will bid Abby farewell?"

"I... yes."

But when he went inside, their patient slept, her bruises already turning the yellow-green of an Iowa summer sky before a tornado. He memorized her peaceful expression. But what if he never saw her again?

Elda Mae peered around his shoulder. "Sleep will heal her, and chicken broth."

"I must leave early in the morning. Will you tell her good-bye for me?"

"Of course. Fred and I think to build a lean-to for her off the west side, if she agrees to stay."

"She could never have found finer folks." The gloom he had felt bidding farewell to Mama descended, but duty called. After saying goodnight to Fred, Martin brushed Docker and bedded down.

The sun reached its zenith as four riders trotted along the path with Captain Whitaker. Tending a fishing line, Martin scrambled to his feet and saluted.

"Good day, sergeant. Have you caught us lunch?"

"The fish shy away today, but I do have extra jerky and hardtack."

Captain Whitaker dismounted. "At ease. Private Reser packed us ample provisions." The others led their horses to the creek and, he introduced Colonel Simms and Sergeant Bowman.

"Tell us about your discoveries."

Pulling the wooden slat and cork from his bag, Martin handed over the list with Colonel Masters' signature. Then he described the exchange he had witnessed.

Colonel Simms pocketed the items. "Where is McHale now?"

"He left yesterday morning. Normally he spends two or three nights away."

"Is anyone at the ranch?"

"No. He beat his wife almost to death, so a neighbor took her in."

"A real prince of a man, eh?"

"He also murdered an Indian woman the night of the exchange."

"Where is she now?"

"Buried on McHale's land."

The colonel exchanged a look with Captain Whitaker. "Captain, you certainly left this man with plenty to do." Then he focused on Martin again. "What do you propose?"

Colonels and captains were the ones to make proposals, and sergeants merely did their bidding. But everyone awaited Martin's response.

"McHale generally comes back from these trips with a few new steers. It may be possible to catch him red-handed."

"They pay him in cattle?"

"It looks that way. I wager most of his longhorns originated in the government herd, but they have no markings."

Captain Whitaker jumped in. "They run the animals like wild buffalo for the Indians to kill, so no one bothers to brand them."

"Hmm. Any witnesses besides yourself?"

"One, sir. McHale's wife."

"Would she make a statement?"

"Right now, her severe injuries would prevent her." He paused, recalling how light Abby had felt in his arms. "She has been fighting for her life after the bludgeoning McHale gave her."

"Umm. Unfortunately, the general wants him brought in alive."

In a ravine near Martin's original lookout, they set up camp, and Private Reser produced biscuits and gravy to rival Elda Mae's. But the bawling of Ray's cows destroyed the evening's peacefulness. When darkness fell, Martin climbed the ravine where a private kept watch.

"Might we put them animals out of their misery, sergeant?"

The field glasses revealed the outline of miserable creatures rubbing their sides against the barn. "I hope so, Private. Wait here."

Back at the campfire, he found Captain Whitaker. "Those cows need to be milked in the worst way. McHale must not have made it home tonight."

"You feel certain of this?"

"I walked a ways down the slope. The animals are waiting to be let in like they do every evening."

"You have expertise with cows?" Colonel Simms leaned forward.

Captain Whitaker answered for Martin. "Born and bred on an Iowa farm. Knows a whole lot else, too."

The pitiful lowing turned Martin's stomach. "Private Reser and I could relieve them in less than an hour."

"What do you think, Colonel?"

"The blamed things will bellow all night otherwise. Go on, and take Reser. We shall cover you in case McHale rides in late."

Stopping often to listen, Martin led the way around gangly Manzanita and bristle bush. Private Reser copied his Indian crawl through large vine-covered rocks behind Abby's chicken coop. A cool night breeze brought familiar barnyard odors.

"Smells like home, eh, private?"

Urgent bawls filled the night, so they led the swollen animals inside, causing them even more discomfort. Once-docile cows pawed the earth and snapped their heads.

When Martin rubbed Henrietta's hot sides, the cow cricked her neck. What a sparkle had filled Abby's eyes when she introduced this creature to him.

"I named her after my cousin on Papa's side, a tomboy who did everything Mama refused to let me do. She taught me to ride. Of course, Papa knew what we were up to."

What were those names Elda Mae said Abby had whispered in her delirium? Nancy and Oliver? Maybe Oliver had been her betrothed.

At first, Henrietta's hard teats squirted warm oily liquid, but Martin persevered, and soon smaller portions entered the pail. Menacing shadows reminded him of the squaw, but he steeled himself. What was it Fred said about turning one's questions around?

Instead of asking the *why* that haunted him, he focused on how these cows survived until now, and the slight alteration produced a better perspective. Private Reser milked a second one as Henrietta wandered off, and Martin tackled another painful udder.

"These girls would have spent a miserable night. A man would have to be daft to leave 'em like this."

"Or just plain cruel."

They drank their fill and dumped full pails into a milk can that Private Reser hefted. "Bet the Colonel will be happy to partake."

Making their way single-file, Martin took the rear. Back at camp, everyone made short work of the milk, and Martin offered to return the can. "I can run it back to the barn in five minutes and maybe find us some eggs for breakfast, too."

"Private Reser, accompany Sergeant Tolzmann."

Captain Whitaker exchanged a quiet look with Martin. This time, Army rules mattered. The Private and Martin slipped into a haze of semi-darkness enveloping the valley. Above them, a quarter moon showcased Orion, and the private reminisced.

"Oma called Orion the storm bringer."

"Your grandmother? Hope she's right—a rainstorm would do us good."

They shinnied down the incline, deposited the milk can and started for the chicken coop. But a noise sounded, and Martin held Private Reser back.

"Maybe in the morning, we can—"

Sudden scuffling broke out behind them. Before Martin could draw his weapon, a stringy rope lashed his mouth and hands.

Iron arms wedged him against the building. Then another set threw him bareback onto a horse. Smooth chests and a ubiquitous greasy smell identified the attackers, but what had become of Private Reser?

The paint plunged into the night, and galloping hooves blocked all other noises. Four or five riders surrounded him now.

The last thing Captain Whitaker needed was to organize a search party. Martin recalled a jog in the wagon road where for a few seconds he would be out of sight from the brave behind him. If he leaped at just the right time, he could make for the campsite.

But how could he leave Private Reser? Oh, for Captain Whitaker's presence of mind.

Halfway across the pasture, the braves halted. One of them grabbed Martin's hat while another pulled his horse so close, his heavy breath razed Martin's cheek.

"McHale?"

Martin shook his head and touched his shoulder patch to indicate his army connection. Glimmering black eyes set on him like beacons—something about this Indian seemed mighty familiar.

"You kill squaw?" The Indian loosened his gag.

"No. McHale."

"Where?"

Martin raised his arm toward the east. "Cattle."

"Army kill McHale?"

"Yes, we kill."

The two braves conferred. Then the one clutching Martin's hat plopped it back on his head and whacked him on the shoulder.

"Go. Kill McHale." One of them pushed him into an ocean of grass that swayed around his thighs—already the snow had melted. The Indians untied his wrists and sped toward the road.

Perspiration poured down Martin's face. Oh, for Mama's jar of burn salve, buds of the Balm of Gilead plant with mutton suet boiled down from sheep's stomach fat. The smell alone would force your ailment to leave, Pa used to say.

As Martin headed back to search for Private Reser, a horse galloped close.

"Had enough adventure for the night, sergeant?"

"Colonel, Sir. Private Reser. I think—"

The hard lines of Simms' face broke. "Your Captain has him in hand, nursing a wicked bump on his head." He offered a hand up, and Martin slid behind him.

Around the campfire, Captain Whitaker tried to make sense of the evening's events. "The Indians want McHale dead?"

"They asked who killed the squaw. They already knew it was McHale, I think, and I told them the Army would take care of him.

"They believe we can handle things, eh? You know, this may be the first time we fight *with* the Indians."

"And if they find McHale and scalp him before he gets home?" Private Bowman asked his question around a slender pipe clenched between his teeth.

"They would torch his homestead. Maybe he has double-crossed them before."

Colonel Simms leaned over Private Reser. "After our evening's diversion, who wants first watch?"

"I do."

The others found their bedrolls while Martin fed the fire, secured the horses, and paced the perimeter. He and Captain Whitaker may have survived the war, but life could still end without warning.

That reminded him of Meta's husband dying so soon after they reached Wyoming Territory. He must write her soon. She might share some Indian encounters of her own.

Tonight, those two braves communicated with almost no English. *McHale* and *kill* made all the difference. That one might be paying him back for letting him go the other day—he could not be sure.

A low shelf extended from a boulder, perfect for propping his boot. Orion twinkled at him, and Martin whispered, "You brought us a storm tonight, but this valley lies so serene."

The night wind answered, and Abby's face formed against the stars. What would it be like to walk through this earthly life with someone like her?

But she was not the same girl he had met in Missouri. Even if Ray soon met his Maker, she might never consider marriage again, and who could blame her?

A coyote yelped and received a reply. As happened often, Martin's family came to mind. Friedrich, always so responsible, and Henry. Alma and Greta, the older sisters he scarcely remembered, probably had grandchildren by now. Margita's gaggle of little ones must be nearly grown up, too. And Meta and Lissa, both married now.

Under this lush quarter moon, a sense of peace replaced the restless sensation that often plagued him at twilight. In the utter quiet, his path became clear, though he could never have explained how. He wanted to plant crops and harvest. He wanted a yard with apple trees.

An image rose of the time Pa took him along to tend the orchard, where slugs threatened some young trees. Pa taught him how to wrap the trunks with strands of horsehair because "The broken points of the hair will wound and kill snails and slugs."

Not long after that, the infestation came to an end. One simple solution to a myriad of challenges around the farm.

Captain Whitaker would probably call this his *farming knowledge,* and rightly so. As a shooting star found its rest somewhere over Strawberry Mountain, the deep desire of Martin's heart flooded him—he longed to establish a homestead.

Sons and daughters would grow there, and he would teach them everything Pa had taught him. Here in this wild country, they would learn so much more, as would he. These children would visit Fred, read books like he did, and find their way in this world.

A breeze trembled in the treetops, and Docker nickered in the distance. Such a faithful friend.

The pines soughed a new theme tonight—*Home.*

Chapter Twenty-one

Abilene, Kansas

A well-dressed stranger scanned the smoky saloon as he curved his long physique into a chair. The players shared pleasantries before commencing an evening game.

From his velvet vest, the outsider removed a cigar and a gold matchbox. He struck a match on the sole of his boot and lingered over his first puff.

Hazy smoke could not hide his trimmed fingernails and crème-colored silk shirt collar folded into a black cravat. The arched line of his nose carried an aristocratic air that caused a flurry in Lola's pulse. As the proprietor of this saloon, she kept a sharp eye on newcomers.

The town banker took the lead. "Joseph A. Carter, here. How's the weather out East?"

Instead of reciprocating with his name, the new arrival posed a question. "What portion holds your interest?"

"Boston, if you please."

"I hail from New York, where the new Steinway Hall hosts such celebrities as Charles Dickens, but I do follow the Boston's Harvard Baseball Nine. They still fare well after their spectacular 6-0 season in '65."

"Everybody in?"

Lola slapped down the cards, and Joseph split the deck. Heads bobbed to survey the hands she dealt. That is, except the pompous stranger's. She fought to keep her gaze low, but his steely surveillance burned her cheeks.

He focused somewhere between her forehead and the glazed beauty mark painted on her cheekbone, but his steely gaze would not shake her. Truth be told, the uneasy ripple in her midriff thrilled her—nothing better than a lively poker game.

Before making a risky decision, she strung out the highfalutin' maverick to the very end. She might live to regret losing this round, but in the long run, such a minor loss could well net a far greater pot. A lady must use strategy to her advantage.

Two hours and several wins later, the stranger collected his earnings and donned his hat. "So, Mr. Carter, how has business been in this fair town of late?" Ignoring Lola, he followed the banker out.

That told her exactly what she wanted to know. She'd hooked him like a catfish in the riverbed outside of town.

"Leave the door unlocked, Lenny. We both know he'll be back. I shall ready my gun."

Lenny's brown eyes signaled obedience. Lola smoothed her revolver, a gift of sorts from a former Confederate officer. She would never forget that exhausted man's mutton chop whiskers or the new word he taught her.

"Them there, they call sideburns." He made the remark when she stroked his facial hair. "After Gen'l Burnside, that is. Grew 'em a purpose t' honor 'im. Most a' th' troops did."

Considering all the drifters she had met over the years, why should she remember that weary renegade right now? Maybe it was the utter neediness in his tender brown eyes. But that had been before Ray McHale came along with his lies. Lola's jaw tightened at the mere thought.

Lenny grabbed the broom. "What do you want me to tell him, Miss Lola?"

"The truth if you know it, or make up a good story. Say anything you can think of to find out what he wants."

Leaving the door to the back room ajar, she made a pretense

of retiring for the night. After the harrowing game, sleep would ignore her, anyway—losing at poker got on her nerves.

But this Eastern fellow intrigued her—hopefully he would join the game again. Then, if things worked out, she might have some work for him to do.

Out in the main room, Lenny swished his broom in strokes too regular for her style. Then, measured steps echoed on the boardwalk. A pause, and the outer door squeaked open.

"Evening, sir. Can I get you something?"

A barstool creaked. "Whiskey."

Liquid splashed into a glass.

"Thought you'd be shut down for the night."

"Always happy to serve a customer." Glasses sloshed in the dishpan.

"Lola gone to bed?"

"Um hmm." Lola pictured Lenny's earnest expression. He would never disclose her whereabouts—men you could trust were few and far between. Good thing he came along in the aftermath of Ray's stinging betrayal.

"She hinted about some land she owns down in Arizona Territory. Do you know the original owner?"

"Nope. Even if I did, she might not like me telling you."

"How would she find out?"

Lola imagined Lenny's shrug. "Your name, sir?"

Scuffling and a sharp gasp tightened her fingers around the cold steel of her double-action Starr Revolver. Sputtering and hacking ensued, so she peered out to see the stranger with Lenny in a chokehold.

"Get my message?"

"Yes, sir." Lenny gulped water, and the glass jiggled onto the bar.

"Now then." The stranger straightened his collar. "Albert Aldrich, lately of New York City. Pleased to make your acquaintance. Provide me with the information I require, so that we may remain friends."

"Uh, the Arizona Territory property. Fella by the name of Layton owned it. Bradley Layton, I recollect."

"Thank you kindly. That is, if you have indeed spoken the truth." Metal coins fell onto the polished bar, and Mr. Aldrich's boots hit the floor. "Keep the change."

Lola stayed put until Lenny bolted the outer door. Then she emerged with her best smile. "Thank you, Lenny. Some name you thought up."

He pawed at the red finger marks on his neck. "An old schoolmate, Ma'am. That Aldrich fella ain't trustworthy, 'pears to me."

"Wait and see. Go on to bed now."

Lola leaned her elbow on the counter. The city man knew his business, and she bet it had to do with land. The enticing tidbit she let slip clearly had garnered his attention. From now on, she would have to play her cards with even greater care.

Still, Aldrich was the sort of fellow to get things done—just the kind she needed. Trust him? Not from here to the mirror, but she might still make use of him. She patted the back of her hair. Time to redo the black lacquer.

The door opened, and Lenny's shiny head appeared once more. "Need anything else?"

"No, everything is just fine. You deserve a raise, Lenny, starting tomorrow."

He shuffled back into his room. He did what she asked—more than she could say for her husband. She ought to have been smarter in the first place.

The trouble was, McHale's shy demeanor had played on her sympathies. When he told her his wife and child died on a Nebraska Territory dirt farm, harassed by pro-slavery immigrants, his sappy story had hooked her.

She kicked a chair and sent it spinning.

"Shan't be long before I get my revenge on that low-down, thieving liar, and when I do, Arizona Territory will never know what hit it." She ground her fist into the table until her knuckles hurt.

The porch door opened and closed. A few seconds later, Abby looked up from sketching in the arbor with Fred as Elda Mae carried them a tray of hot tea and toast.

"You must keep up your strength." She brushed Abby's shoulder with her hand.

"Smells wonderful." Abby patted the end of her log seat. "Will you join us?"

"I need to keep working. Good weather doesn't always last, even though we haven't had snow in so long." Elda Mae pointed to the cabin. "If I get those rocks all out today, tomorrow we can wet down the clay and start laying a foundation. Then—"

"Such hard work. Are you sure—?"

"Absolutely certain. We want you here and have long spoken of enlarging the cabin."

"It has been so many weeks already—"

"Shush, dear. We love having you with us." Elda Mae sank beside Abby and took her hand. "You are helping so much. Besides, creating a useful room with my own hands gives me pleasure. Everyone has their gifts, and construction suits me."

At first Abby could not believe the Allens' invitation. But a few weeks back, she had played along with their conversation at supper one night.

"Mischief's afloat. I can see it in your eyes, Fred."

"Even sparrows have nests, Miss Abby. Elda Mae and I have decided to build a room for you off the kitchen. 'Twill be no palace, but every inch will be yours." He touched his thumbs and forefingers together. "With a window looking out on the arbor, you can study our feathered visitors, and we might even fashion your own door to the arbor."

By meal's end they convinced her, and Elda Mae set to work leveling the ground and measuring. Straight through each day she labored; digging holes, adjusting posts, and laying rocks. Fred toted and sawed, fetched and chinked, happy to be of help.

Over the cold months, Abby's walk increased in length each

day, and little by little, her strength returned. With full access to Fred's pencils and chalks, she spent hours in the arbor. Sometimes a longing for a certain brush or pencil of her own overcame her—whatever had become of all those she left in Poplar Grove?

Maybe the marshal had held an auction, once he realized she had gone away for good. Perhaps Lizzy attended, and bid on those brushes. She might be teaching her daughters to sketch with them.

No use distressing over the matter—she already had wasted more than enough time looking back. As Elda Mae spouted, "Regret offers nothing for today and nothing for tomorrow."

Now a real future stretched ahead for Abby—no more remorse. As Granny Ferguson predicted, hers had become a quiet life brimming with art.

After another hour of sketching, she prepared supper, and over the meal, Fred launched his latest query about the turkey vulture. Before clearing the table, he read the evening Scriptures.

Make a joyful noise unto the Lord, all ye lands.

Serve the Lord with gladness: come before his presence with singing.

Know ye that the Lord he is God: it is he that hath made us, and not we ourselves; we are his people, and the sheep of his pasture.

Enter into his gates with thanksgiving, and into his courts with praise: be thankful unto him, and bless his name.

For the Lord is good; his mercy is everlasting; and his truth endureth to all generations.

Elda Mae's sigh closed out the reading. "I may be His sheep, but it certainly took me some time to find the right pasture."

"I could say the same, but here we are, dear."

Elda Mae patted Abby's hand. "And now you have come to us."

"I can never thank you enough for taking me in."

"Your smile is all we need." Fred's eyes moistened. Elda Mae reached for his hand and addressed Abby.

"Are you ready to fetch your things, dear?"

"Perhaps not just yet." Even the mention of the ranch repulsed her—she shoved down every thought of those squandered years and kept to herself her intention never to marry again. Fred earnestly believed that one day she would see her name under sketches in a book like John Jay Audubon's and had written to his sponsor in Cincinnati about her. Such meaningful work would suffice.

Elda Mae went back to fitting wood for a window, and the simple task of washing dishes provided a sense of security. This safety surrounded her like Mama's quilt. She still took great care venturing out, since official word of Ray's capture had not yet arrived. What could have taken so long? Perhaps the Army had sent Martin far away, so he was unable to send word.

On cold winter mornings, Fred compared and edited his sketches inside while Abby helped with household chores. By afternoon, comfortable temperatures returned, so unless a storm blew in over the Rim, they kept to their outdoor schedule.

Sitting in direct sunshine, Fred even took off his scarf some days, always with a grin. "Back in Ohio, I dared not step foot outdoors in winter with my constitution. But here, one would think spring had come. I judge this the best possible location for our work, because turkey buzzards and woodpeckers never migrate south. They still must eat, and we can aid their search."

Each morning, Abby scattered seed in the arbor to the tune of ever-present woodpeckers drilling the side of the cabin, oblivious to the enormous pine forest all around. The comical expressions of the clown variety intrigued her most.

One day, Fred's excitement made his voice quiver at the noon meal. "A ladder-back woodpecker flew in recently." He showed one of his sketches to Elda Mae. "See the variegated white and black on its back and the muted red of its head, compared with the acorn woodpecker?"

"Mmm. So many species here, and endless work for you." She turned to Abby. "I do hope you see how much Fred needs your help?"

"Especially with the turkey vultures, but so far, they keep their distance."

Elda Mae made a distasteful scowl. "Birds of prey come far down on my list."

"Ugly they may be, but they have their usefulness. Who knows how much disease they prevent simply by following their diet?" Fred twitched his nose. "I have yet to spy a nest, but hope one day to sketch their offspring. Remember, my dear, if handsomeness determined worth, you would have found me an unsuitable husband."

"Likewise. Still, I would rather watch those vultures from afar."

"If I ever have a chance to see one up close, I hope I shan't forget the glory of their flight, lacking grace, but still so efficient." Fred addressed Abby. "Did I ever tell you how one flew over the yard for several days when you first came to us?"

"I daresay it was the one that watched over me last year."

"Perhaps." In the arbor again, he opened his sketchbook. "Let us review our recent work."

They compared sketches—both kinds of woodpeckers and a beautiful, nameless bluebird. A bevy of shiny black ravens flew into the arbor, their scraping calls insistent.

"I get the feeling they would rather we leave."

Fred eyed the birds askance. "Such an aggressive sort. Observe the length of their beaks, perhaps one-sixth of their bodies. Maybe their presence has kept the vultures away. It might be months before one of them lands here again."

Riled about something, the contentious ravens flew off. Abby focused on her drawings, but a while later, glanced up and gasped. With the toe of her shoe, she prodded Fred's leg and gestured toward a visitor not twenty feet away, clutching dinner in its claws. The sparkle in Fred's eyes animated his long, thin face.

This vulture must have been there some time. How had they missed its landing? Now, the giant bird ripped into a meal, and the arbor's normal birdsong ceased. The massive raptor's wings rotated up and down, out and in as it ate.

Every once in a while, the creature stretched its head to scour for enemies. Then, like a pump handle, it lowered its neck again. At one point, Abby wrote Fred a note.

"From the sky, how could he possibly see prey in this shade?"

Fred pointed to his eyes, then his nose. He already had shared his belief that vultures can focus at the same time on both close and distant objects, and could hone in on the scent of flesh from far, far away.

The shoulder connection and curve of the wing entranced Abby. Oblivious to their pencil scratches, the vulture plunged its head again and again. Its distinctive white beak extended more than a full inch, and a black rim similar to a raccoon's partially circled the eyes.

This specimen seemed different from the *Birds Of America* sketch. Would its beak feel like wood to the touch, or more like ivory? She jotted a few notes; "Some mottling on the frayed wing tips."

In Audubon's sketches, the bird's skeletal nasal passages, visible to the naked eye, resembled delicate twin cave openings. The raw bone had no covering, and formed an obvious passageway. Without these unique nostrils, the vulture would suffocate while gorging on carrion.

Their unlikely visitor craned its neck backward. Short black hairs stood up through wrinkled red skin on top of its head, and black ruff feathers framed what Elda Mae labeled an ugly face.

Fred handed over his spyglasses and shared with Abby. The glasses highlighted an unblinking gray eye. The coloring contributed to an impression of age, but how could one tell? What did the gigantic creature see as it cranked its head toward the barn?

The vulture's head dipped out of sight, giving another perfect view of its shoulder dimensions, out of proportion compared with the rest of its body. A minute later, it stirred, its beak dripping blood. Sourness razed Abby's throat—a good time for a happy memory, like the afternoon Elda Mae finished sewing the dress she wore today.

"Stand extra still." Elda Mae took a tuck here, placed a pin there.

"Breathe in. Soon you can throw away that old rag you've outgrown. Then we'll start another frock."

The recollection did nothing to reduce the roiling in Abby's stomach. Just when she thought she would have to leave, the vulture raised its head and flapped its vast wings.

Pushing off required determination, but in a gradual ascent, the mighty bird cleared the trees. A whirr sounded as their visitor swooped westward.

"Sometimes they eat so much they must wait for their food to digest before flying. You can see why they have no head plumage." Fred tracked the flight with his glasses. "Headed to Pine Creek. The Lord knows he needs a bath."

He picked up his pencil. "Probably a good thing these big fellows don't fly at night, so they leave some food from other carnivores."

Abby took a deep breath. "I need a little walk."

"Not too far?" Fatherly concern hunched Fred's eyebrows.

"No." She turned back. "Are you certain vultures fly only in the daytime?"

"Yes, but I always stand to be corrected, and only patience brings truth to light. However, our observations today do confirm one fact. With their small weak feet, these birds never kill with their talons. Perhaps that is why the Cherokee call them the Peace Eagle."

Had she imagined the lone turkey vulture swooping so near the porch on that miserable night at the ranch? A lizard scampered over a rock as sickness threatened Abby again, and flaming rust sumac wooed her down the path.

"But that stippled feather may have fallen from this very vulture's wing."

Years ago, that lecturer from the East said, "Patience served our ancestors well and still leads to success. Our inventors fail often, but their inquisitive natures continue to drive them."

At a disturbance from the wagon road, mule deer stalled their chomping. Everything turned silent as a wagon lurched into sight and the driver pulled two scraggly mules to a halt. Then a shout rolled down the steep slope.

"Help! My boy's been snake-bit!"

A man's voice—a child's whimper in the background . . .

"Wait. I will fetch help." Abby took off for the cabin, yelling all the way. Elda Mae raced from her work on the new lean-to.

"What is it?"

"On the road—somebody is calling for help, says his son's been bitten."

"Get ready. We may need some live poultry flesh." Fred eyed the chickens scratching near the barn as she dashed toward the wagon road.

It was all Abby could do to keep up with her as the shouts grew closer. Then she saw the traveler, a big-boned fellow with a child in his arms. When he spied Elda Mae, he loped faster.

"Rattlesnake—playin' in th' rocks—his ankle—"

Elda Mae took one look and jerked her head toward the cabin. "We shall do all we can. Hurry."

When Fred came into view, she spat, "Rattlesnake bite."

He hurried off toward the barn, and Abby raced to boil water. The man refused to come in, but laid his son on the porch. Maybe eight or ten years old, Abby guessed, and so pale his freckles seemed to hover above his cheeks. His lower leg bled from two ragged cuts above the bite wound.

Elda Mae ran to wash her hands, and as she burst through the door again, Fred approached, gripping a hen. She gathered her tools while Abby brought a dishpan and towel and fetched the water.

Fred braced the chicken on the floor as Elda Mae slashed it from neck to entrails and thrust its ragged body onto the bite. Fred produced a length of rope, and they wrapped the hen around the boy's ankle.

She caught Abby's eye and mouthed, "Pray."

Chapter Twenty-two

Private Reser took first watch. Captain Whitaker and Colonel Simms still talked beside the fire, and their exchange carried to Martin in his bedroll.

"Three years with the Cavalry? By now I would think... Does Fort McDonnell have an over-abundance of majors?"

"No. Masters took a disliking to me during the war. I expected to serve under General Crook, but you know Army paperwork—I ended up under Masters.

"One night, I covered the guard tower and observed the colonel on a solitary midnight outing. I volunteered to cover the watch often after that, and his outings became habitual. Later, he discovered I knew about his philandering."

"Why did you stay in after the war?"

"Good men—steady, solid fellows like Sergeant Tolzmann."

"Few officers would even consider the risk you are taking right now."

"Duty, honor, country. Ousting a reprobate like Masters brings me more satisfaction than a promotion."

Finally Martin dozed, and a few hours later they broke camp. After the sun peaked over the Rim, a whistle echoed. Then discordant moos swept up from the ranch.

At least Henrietta and the other cows would soon find relief. This morning, Colonel Simms had refused to allow another milking, though he openly grieved the loss of eggs for breakfast. Captain Whitaker added a comment.

"We are about to capture a man guilty of crimes against the

United States Army, mankind, and Heaven itself, yet your sole concern remains those cows, sergeant. I'd say you have missed your calling."

Captain Whitaker and Colonel Simms focused field glasses on the ranch.

While he waited, Martin turned over a red clod. Could a man actually coax crops from this unruly soil?

"Sergeant Tolzmann, lead us in, before McHale gets those cows milked."

Captain Whitaker drew Martin aside as the Colonel alerted Sergeant Bowman and the privates. "I know you would rather stand watch, but duty calls."

Martin waited for the others at the trailhead. At the bottom, Colonel Simms gathered the men. "Remember, the general wants him alive."

If only McHale would put up a fight and force us to kill him. The thought jolted Martin. Even with Rebel prisoners, he had often found a spark of compassion.

"If he makes a dash, Captain Whitaker and Private Reser, on the perimeter, will capture him. Sergeant Bowman, take charge outside the barn."

Martin sucked in his breath. He would sooner be dragged by wild horses than face this reprobate who almost killed Abby. But in an odd way, Papa's death grounded him. Having survived that, he could overcome anything.

Captain Whitaker and Private Reser faded into the brush, and Colonel Simms repeated his orders. "No firing unless he shoots first."

An awareness enveloped Martin, similar to what he experienced before battle. What he once thought to be cowardice squeezed him like a vice. Docker's muscles tightened too, so Martin stroked his mane. As Colonel Simms approached the barn, Martin fingered his Remington New Army six-shooter.

Colonel Simms scanned one last time for Private Reser and

Captain Whitaker. A flash showed in the trees, and then the door squeaked open.

Cold sweat broke on Martin's neck. Within minutes, the Colonel exited with the scoundrel, hands held high. His soulless glare magnetized Martin. Sergeant Bowman bound his hands as McHale spat at Simms.

Spittle ran down his chin, but the Colonel only stiffened. Sergeant Bowman cinched a rope around McHale's waist, pulled him to a scraggly juniper and secured him.

Already, Colonel Simms was devising a plan. "Perhaps Sergeant Bowman and I ought to proceed to Camp Reno while you escort Colonel Masters back to Camp Verde. Who knows what he might try if you were to confront him, Captain."

"Nothing would bring him more pleasure than to kill me."

Colonel Simms tapped his gloves on his saddlebag. "We have no orders to inform him of the charges, so the reason for the journey to Camp Verde will remain a secret. This way, General Crook can enjoy all the thunder."

"Perfect! Masters will think the general has summoned him for a promotion."

"You will accompany the prisoner, then. We shall follow you in a few days, but you must remain at Verde as witnesses."

The Colonel glanced at Sergeant Bowman. "Who rides west with them?"

"Sir, Sergeant Tolzmann and Private Reser already have some history of success."

Colonel Simms chuckled. "Indeed." Martin figured his own countenance probably matched Private Reser's florid coloring.

And so it was. After the Colonel's party rode east, Captain Whitaker took over. "Sergeant, saddle the prisoner's mule. Best get this over with while the weather's good."

Sick at the thought of guarding McHale all the way to Camp Verde, Martin made quick work of it. Then he ordered Private Reser to prod Ray forward.

When he struggled, Captain Whitaker barked, "The sooner you cooperate, the better." This produced a low growl, and Private Reser shoved McHale into the saddle.

With every mile, regret tinged Martin. Now he would have no opportunity to relay the good news to Abby. By nightfall, they straggled to the top of the Rim, where he looked toward the Allens' place. If only—

But this mission waited for no man. On the second afternoon, huge snowflakes turned red clay into a soggy mess. New lines decorated Captain Whitaker's forehead when they made camp.

"T'would be easier for the prisoner to escape in this cold," he declared. "Never leave the prisoner alone, not even to relieve himself," he commanded.

Martin accompanied McHale and Private Reser to a secluded spot, with McHale sputtering the whole time.

"Private, assist the prisoner."

Private Reser sucked in his breath. What worse duty than unbuttoning a dangerous man's trousers? Stark hatred coursed Ray's eyes—he looked as though he would slay a man for breathing. If only General Crook had asked for him alive or dead.

On the third night, Private Reser tethered McHale to a tree a distance from the crackling fire and whispered, "Sir, could we untie the prisoner, just while he does his business?"

"If a chase ensued, we might be forced to shoot him, but I promise to report your faithfulness to duty." Any other time, Martin might have exchanged places, but his skin crawled at the thought.

Private Reser swallowed his objections as recollections swamped Martin. If McHale should escape, he would stalk Abby and finish the job.

Her bruised face rode Martin's memory, along with the sensation of holding her in his arms. To make up for Private Reser's abominable task, he took cooking duty and made conversation with him once McHale was tethered for the night.

"You come from Kentucky, private? What led you here?"

"Wanderlust. Joined up with a buddy after the war."

"Sounds familiar. And now we're freezing to death guarding a miserable criminal."

Private Reser took first watch, but sleep evaded Martin. McHale had gotten under his skin. What a riddle—meeting Abby in Missouri, being reunited here, and now this.

Pastor Schultz said the Almighty ruled over all, and Mama found unique comfort in believing. But why did He allow men like McHale to live, and an innocent young woman to fall under his wicked spell?

Chapter Twenty-three

"The lad looks so wan. I surely hope he pulls through." Elda Mae's tone revealed such concern that Fred looked up from his reading.

"Mr. Fuller tells me the poor child lost his mother just a few weeks ago on the trail."

"And they had just this one—David?"

"No, they started out with another boy and an infant. Buried both somewhere in New Mexico Territory, along with his wife."

"These folks come ill-prepared, with no idea about the rigors of the journey."

"Yes. They possess abundant hope, but far too little preparation."

As she listened, Abby mopped David's forehead with a wet cloth. Elda Mae had nursed the boy all night and finally allowed her to take over this morning.

After refusing Fred's offer of the warm barn, the child's father had fallen asleep over in the corner.

"With his fever, the cool air actually proved a blessing."

Before Elda Mae went inside, Abby offered, "Fred and I filled the tub for you to bathe."

"Oh my, how thoughtful. But I may fall asleep and drown."

Soon a splash carried to the porch. So intent on nursing David, Elda Mae had no idea how she looked. Working all day yesterday on the lean-to, she'd been covered with red mud when David arrived, and sacrificing the old hen had spattered her with blood.

Meanwhile, David still thrashed with fever. Fortunately, his father slept on after Elda Mae entered the cabin. Losing two of his children and his wife had to take its toll—most likely typhoid, Fred said.

But somehow David had survived, only to meet with a rattler. His fair eyelids shuttered—could he be waking? No more sounds from inside. Perhaps Elda Mae had fallen asleep with her head propped against the edge of the copper tub.

Over and over, she freshened the cool cloth and applied it to David's skin, and gradually, his fever decreased.

Engrossed in watching him, she barely noticed when Fred went inside, and heard no movement when his father suddenly appeared at David's other side. "Yer an angel 'a mercy, ma'am."

Abby doused her cloth again. If only he knew how far she fell short.

"Thet yer Ma n' Pa?" He gestured to the door with his head.

"No, but they are my family."

"Hain't got one a' yer own?"

"Mister... What was your last name?"

"Kett'rin'."

"Mr. Kettering, would you please get me some more cold water from the tank?"

He eyed her askance but did her bidding, and she had half a notion to summon Fred from the house. But just then, David let out a moan and twisted on the quilt Elda Mae had folded under him.

"There, now. There—"

"He done waked up? He'll be all right then, I wager." Water sloshed, and Mr. Kettering's trousers brushed Abby's arm. A shudder took her as David lifted his head a bit. With no warning, vile green liquid projected from his mouth, straight at his father's face.

He leaped back. "Upchuckin', n' right on yer Pa, eh?"

Just then, Fred stepped out with a bucket of hot water. "Go right on down to the tank and wash up."

His expression a mixture of chagrin and disgust, Mr. Kettering obeyed. Clearly, his wife had handled the sickness in their family.

"Miss Abby, are you all right?" Fred helped her slip David's foul-smelling shirt over his head. "You look awful pale."

"You brought the water just in time. Thank you."

"One of my old shirts might fit the lad." He glanced toward the tank. "It will only take a minute for me to fetch one."

His eyes revealed his concern. He had taken in the scene and understood. But even she could not have predicted the upset in her stomach when Mr. Kettering had come so near.

"Elda Mae, come quick! Never saw such a sight in all my born days!"

Abby bumped into Fred as he raced up the porch stairs with straw clinging to his shirt. What could be stranger than a man toting his son from the wagon road with a rattlesnake bite?

Two weeks had passed since Mr. Kettering and his son went on their way. Elda Mae warned that David was not ready to travel, but the man set his mind on leaving.

"Oh my heavens." Fred's eyes popped as Elda Mae joined him on the porch.

"Well, knock me over with a feather. How is that contraption holding together? Such a light frame—even Dougherty wagons have trouble out here."

A dandy in a gray flannel frock coat pulled a rickety buckboard to a stop. From his blue silk brocade waistcoat and neckerchief to the contrasting cuffs and collar, he painted quite the picture. His left hip showcased an engraved leather gun belt.

Beside him, shaded by a delicate red silk parasol embroidered in lavish black scrollwork, sat a shapely woman. As they neared, she could not hide evidence of her rouge running in the heat.

Elda Mae planted Fred against the porch pole and hissed, "Stay right here, or go in and heat the coffee. Let me handle them."

Fred's shoulder trembled against Abby's, and she recalled his agitation when he and Elda Mae first visited her. Meeting new folks must distress him.

"Go on, then. You can watch from inside."

Dust whipped a whirlwind around the lurching vehicle as the

lady fanned her face with her gloves. She half-stood. "Is this the McHale ranch?" Her coarse voice matched her dress, a brilliant scarlet hue.

Her coiffure, a harsh blend of blue and black, blazed in the sun. Her shoulders and chin jutted forward so that her bust, already notable in the low cut of her dress, became even more so. She might be an exotic bird torn from its natural environs.

Could this be one of those *saloon women* Mama's friends used to describe at tea? Mama never allowed Abby to walk to the end of Main Street, where the saloon sent forth music and laughter and an abundance of smoke.

Fred wheezed, so Elda Mae shoved him toward the door. He hurried in as she addressed the visitor.

"No, but I can give you directions. The McHale place lies about a half hour south of here." She drew herself up. "But you must park at a trailhead and descend on foot."

The tall fellow's face turned stony as he faced the woman. "See? I told you so."

"What better idea did you have?" His companion slapped at a gadfly and muttered under her breath.

"Would you like to refresh yourselves?"

"Very kind of you, madame." The stranger's handlebar mustache bounced when he moved his lips, reminding Abby of dashing male heroes in theater productions that once passed through Poplar Bluff.

"Abby, please bring the coffee." Elda Mae descended a step and held out her hand. "Elda Mae Allen. Good to meet you, Mrs.—"

"McHale. Lola McHale."

Elda Mae never flinched, but Abby staggered back against the cabin.

"Help yourself to some water at the pump. It always helps to wash off the dust of travel." Elda Mae turned. "Dear, would you please fetch a clean towel for our guests?"

Like a wooden puppet, Abby did her bidding and returned to the stove.

Lola McHale...

Would her heart ever resume its normal beat? But Elda Mae's steady green eyes infused her with strength as she peered in through the door. Was that a glint of humor, too?

"Slice that bread we baked yesterday and bring out a pot of honey while we get better acquainted."

Fred grabbed Abby's arm as if he were sinking in a stormy sea. "That woman, she—" His breath came hard. "Would you mind if I—" He gestured toward Abby's room and the arbor, his voice a conspiratorial whisper.

"Of course not. What a good idea you had to build a second door back there."

He slipped out while she corralled her thoughts. Then she carried the bread and honey to the porch and retreated as the visitors seated themselves.

While the tea steeped, she peeked out her bedroom window to the arbor, where Fred shifted from tree to tree like a hummingbird. With every round, his forehead furrows eased a bit. He paused to study a grey squirrel scrabbling up a tall pine, peeling off bits of bark in its wake.

"For whatever reason, he knows what he cannot manage—" Her whisper settled over the small homey room like a prayer. Yellow curtains and a quilt cheered her simple furnishings—bed, table, wardrobe, and chair.

Today, Elda Mae's work on the door proved mighty handy. Fred made regular trips around the yard until his lowered brows declared him almost back to normal. Finally, he sat at the arbor table, as was his custom.

If he could calm himself, so could she. The teapot whistled, and Abby returned to the kitchen.

"Stop shaking!" She commanded her fingers to cooperate, and teapot in hand, stepped onto the porch. Elda Mae gestured her to a chair across from Lola and poured the tea.

"What brings you to Arizona Territory?"

Mr. Aldrich twirled his mustache. Abby and Lizzy used to wager whether the actors glued on their mustaches, but this one seemed unmistakably real.

"Business." His tone matched the ice in his eyes.

"Miss McHale, you must be Ray's sister?"

Lola brushed her lace-lined bosom on the table's edge as Mr. Aldrich tightened his hand around her elbow.

"I seek my ranch. Mind you, I am *Mrs.* McHale." Her tinted fingernails scratched against the table.

Few women in Poplar Bluff buffed their nails with scented red oils until they shone, and Mama always frowned on such frivolity. "Who has time to shape their fingernails and shine them with a chamois cloth? Rubbing in a little sweet oil gives the same effect."

Lola bared her teeth like a rabid dog, revealing harsh lines around her mouth through her applied veneer. "I have the great misfortune of having *married* Ray McHale."

Abby massaged the base of her neck, wishing Elda Mae kept smelling salts in the house. But she was not one to believe in fainting. Now, she played the grand hostess, and her smile ruled over all.

"Oh, really? How long have you been married, dear?"

"Far too long, curse his rotten soul."

Mr. Aldrich's long fingers tightened again, and Lola fidgeted. "You have met Mr. McHale?"

"We spoke with him years ago."

"You have visited his ranch?"

"Oh, yes. At that time, Mr. McHale had a—" Elda Mae angled her head. "He seemed to have a different wife."

Tea spewed across the table and dripped from Lola's chin. Aldrich reached for the towel while Elda Mae mopped a puddle from the bread platter.

"Why, that no good for nothing—" Lola snarled, but controlled her outburst after another hearty squeeze on her shoulder.

"I married Ray in '57, proper-like, in Kansas Territory. Brought the certificate along to prove it. That ranch belongs to me, and I'll be hanged before some other woman steals it. I won that land in a poker game, won my saloon too, fair and square. That low-down thief stole my deed when he lit out—"

Abby's ears rang. Ray had married a saloon owner and stole her ranch? At that wagon encampment on the way, he condemned those travelers for taking more than one wife. But he—

That deed Elda Mae kept for her—she tore her eyes away from Lola and sought Elda Mae, who anticipated her unspoken question. With a flick of her fingers, she dismissed the idea.

Mr. Aldrich slid his hand down Lola's arm. "Mrs. McHale has been wronged, and now has suffered a shock. She followed this rapscallion from Kansas Territory to a paltry Missouri town where Ray practiced even more deception. For the sake of justice, I accompanied her to this godforsaken wilderness."

The Rim's eastern side, gorgeous in full sun, caught Abby's eye. How could anyone call this sprawling creation godforsaken?

A paltry Missouri town? Practiced more deception? He must mean Poplar Bluff!

Elda Mae swept her hand over her brow. "Why, I *never*! I am so sorry for your misfortune."

Lola dabbed her eyes with her hanky, and Elda Mae murmured, "My, my." Then she addressed Aldrich. "You are a lawyer, sir?"

"Mm." He slid his hand over Lola's. "Would you be so kind as to direct us to the McHale ranch?"

"Certainly, but I just recalled. A cavalryman stopped by a few weeks ago, also looking for Mr. McHale." Elda Mae leaned back to observe the effect of her words.

Mr. Aldrich paled, and Lola's tone spiked into staccato. "Cattle thieving. That fool could steal cattle from heaven's gates." She flashed a venomous look at Aldrich. "Hurry! We must find him before the Army does."

"Oh, my. I never would have surmised—" Elda Mae led the way down the steps.

Lola followed her, creating an upsurge of perfume. Abby's

head swam, but the tightness in her chest slackened as the couple climbed aboard. They followed Elda Mae's pointed finger.

"Past that tall sycamore, the path leads to a hidden trailhead. Watch for a sparkle from a tin roof down below. To take that trailhead down to Ray's place, off on your right, you must abandon your contrivance. The climb down the rest of the way forms a mighty steep drop. Do be careful."

"If—ah, if we find no one, where might we locate that cavalryman?"

Elda Mae squinted as if calling up special insight. "The soldiers are building Camp Reno southeast of Green Valley, across the Rim."

"Are we likely to meet his so-called wife at the ranch?"

"I am afraid not, sir. She passed from this earth years ago."

"At his hand, I expect." Lola flung aside her partner's arm as he urged the horse down the path.

Abby finally managed something besides a shallow breath as Elda Mae clomped up the porch steps.

"You look white as hominy." Fire sparked her eyes. "Those folks brought good news, don't you see? Your marriage never was legal. Ray must have pulled the wool over some judge's eyes."

Abby dropped her head into her hands, but Elda Mae pulled her up.

"This is cause for rejoicing. If the Cavalry fails to squelch Ray, Lola will. You shall never lay eyes on him again."

The rest of the day passed in a fog and led to a fitful night. In a full moon, Abby sat on her bed trying to make sense of everything.

In winter, the oiled canvas window in their old cabin let in almost no light, but now, she could look out any time. How had this glass remained secure through that inconceivable drop over the Rim?

Something clattered in the kitchen, and she smelled milk warming. Then Elda Mae stood near. "This will help you sleep, dear."

"You really think Ray is gone forever?"

"I feel it in my bones. Lola and Aldrich will never rest until they see him dead."

"But the deed—are we not being deceptive?"

"Ha! Lola would never settle on the ranch. She wants revenge, plain and simple. You earned every inch of that place. You may rest easy—all is well."

"Learning to trust again can be so hard."

"But it can be done. Remember my journey, child." A smile toyed with Elda Mae's lips. "I would say the good Lord has sent you a special sign today."

"I wish I could see it the way you do."

"Ach! Things like this take time." She slipped off her shawl and wrapped it around Abby's shoulders. "Let this warm you, and you can borrow my faith, too."

After she left, Abby sank into her rocker facing the moonlit arbor. Once again, she leaned on someone else's faith. Yet the image of Ray's face persisted. A parade of events filled her mind, beginning with Martin's arrival at the ranch.

From the moment he rode into the yard, his kindness touched her. The seed nestled into her heart when he cleaned the outbuildings and fetched water, and took root when he showed her the blackberries. And now, he had rescued her from certain death.

"He called you back, Abby. It was his hand you squeezed."

It seemed so easy for Elda Mae to believe, but what if Martin never came back? How could she be sure Ray had met his demise?

Loneliness clutched at her. Even now, the pine wind soughed high above.

She had vowed never to remarry, but a stark question prevailed. How could she bear never seeing Martin again?

Chapter Twenty-four

Mercifully, the snow stopped and temperatures mellowed. Mile by mile, tall pines gave way to juniper, scraggly mesquite, prickly pear, yucca, and century plants. Finally, Captain Whitaker's small contingent trotted down the trail toward Camp Verde.

The dusky green and brown Verde Valley spread before them like a blanket. A mild downward grade peppered with jutting rocks followed the Verde River, a silver thread extending to the horizon.

A day's travel down the graduated slope transformed winter to full spring, and Martin shed his poncho. Captain Whitaker's outlook took a jovial turn. Along the way, he drew out Private Reser's life story from three generations back.

"Private, it sounds as if your grandmother might have a lot in common with Fantine. You have read her story, I assume?"

"Yes, during the war. Our captain passed the translation among us men."

"Good for him—I heard the volume sold by the hundreds of thousands. My father sent me a boxful to share with my men, as well. He only paid a nickel or dime each for them, but they certainly provided a distraction during the worst of it. Did you hear what happened concerning them amongst the Rebs?"

"Not that I recall."

"The translator, Charles Wilbour, printed *Les Miserables* on the back of each colorful broadside. In the South, a publisher called West and Johnston decided to forego the copyright law, since we were at war. They released the five parts, censored for the Rebs.

"Of course, the tale became popular among them. But as time passed, the Confederates took to thinking the title of the original French writing was *Lee's Miserables*. A fitting misconception, eh?"

Private Reser's chuckle produced a grin. Riding along, Martin took in the humor—why should their prisoner's state cast such a pall over his outlook? That night, Private Reser rummaged through his rucksack and pulled out one of the *Les Miserable* pamphlets before he settled in near the fire.

The next morning, Captain Whitaker turned to whistling *The Ship That Never Returns* until Martin hung behind to clear his head. When they camped, he rubbed down the horses before supper, and the evening silence embraced him like a gift.

Every day, Ray's belligerence intensified, so one-by-one, Captain Whitaker decreased his sparse comforts. He and Martin discussed what pleasure Ray derived from hurting himself, but came up short.

Often during his watch under a starry show, thoughts of Abby surfaced. Martin pictured her asleep by now. Elda Mae and Fred would surely provide her a happy Christmastide.

He kicked himself for failing to notify her of Ray's capture. Captain Whitaker might have considered his request, but he had failed to ask. As it was, she had no idea whether McHale still skulked around the Allens' property.

Cottonwoods surrounded the camp. By day, their light-colored branches glistened in the sun, but starlight turned them into beautiful frosty arms.

With a blanket thrown around his shoulders like an Indian scout, Private Reser approached to take the watch. He also brought news. "The Captain tried to make conversation with the prisoner when he offered him a blanket. McHale lashed out with his handcuffs." Private Reser produced a small round ointment can from his pocket. "This might help his wound, sergeant."

When Martin neared the fire, even the shadows of Captain Whitaker's hat could not hide the deep red gash edging his jawbone. A rod away, McHale slumped against the base of a mesquite, blanketless.

Martin swallowed down the urge to shoot him on the spot. Instead, he neared Captain Whitaker. "Sir, are you awake?"

Silence. Martin pulled his bedroll to the fire and laced his blanket around his face. He felt more than saw the prisoner's stare, as raw as the Captain's wound. He thought to crash his rifle butt into McHale's skull and end his pathetic life. How could Abby have endured this hateful soul?

One scene recurred through the coming hours—her slender figure on the ramshackle porch, bent over the churn. Why had she never left, with the Allens close by? In the next second, the answer came. McHale had threatened her, and his attack only proved why Abby took so long to risk the short trip to see her neighbors.

Something Elda Mae said kept coming to mind—Abby cried out some names. What were they? Oh, yes—Nancy. And Oliver. Who could they be? Finally, in the depths of the night, restless slumber attended Martin.

"Sergeant."

In the darkness, Captain Whitaker leaned over him, his order abrupt. "Get up. We make Verde today if it kills us."

Martin crawled out and reached for the coffee pot. Now the captain's bone-deep scar shone in the firelight.

"Only coffee this morning, sergeant."

"Sir, let me dress that gash."

Captain Whitaker never winced at the cold salve, but in the background Ray watched like a bobcat. Martin alerted Private Reser, grabbed a handful of jerky, and saddled Docker.

"Hope you got some rest, boy. A long day lies ahead." The horse whinnied as if he recognized their mission, and Martin went to untie McHale for his time in the woods.

But the Captain thrust out a thick horsehair rope. "Let the prisoner dirty himself. Double-tie him to the saddle horn—time he gets some exercise."

Private Reser perked up when he heard there would be no latrine duty today, and they started off. At the six-mile signpost, Captain Whitaker's wound still flamed and oozed.

"Sir, more liniment?"

"Sure, but out of McHale's sight."

"Mama used this same Stramonium Ointment for sores."

"It's definitely sore, all right. A genuine battle scar to impress the ladies, eh?"

"I would say so, sir."

"Tighten the prisoner's handcuff ratchets." The Captain sought Martin's eyes. "You think me cruel, sergeant?"

"Not at all. The scandal is letting him live at all."

Captain Whitaker kicked at some rocks. "Hatred can eat you alive, but by tonight this wretch will be out of our hands."

Fred brought the wagon to a halt with such gusto, Abby expected exciting news. Five days' absence revealed how much this quiet man brightened her days.

Elda Mae gushed as they loosened the wagon canvas and carried parcels into the cabin. "So glad those miners set up shop in Green Valley. Before that, we had to do without unless the stage happened through."

Fred's eyebrows danced. "You ought to see the Tonto Basin. The gama grass will grow wagon top high by full summer."

He waved a swatch in the wagon three feet tall. "Green Valley will surely become a rightful town one day. Since our last trip, another new homestead has sprung up."

"The tribes have farmed there for centuries—of course, settlers will steal their land. Didn't you tell me how several tribes merged along the Salt River to form the Salado people?"

Puffing under a heavy load, Fred nodded. Abby helped Elda Mae haul two large crates, a twine-bound mail packet, burlap sacks of Apache corn and beans, a few shriveled pumpkins, and some gourd-like vegetable, maybe a variety of squash.

"I saved the mail-reading for you, Mama." Fred loosed the letters from their string.

"Oh, my goodness, so many!"

"I did open the package from Mr. B already, and guess what?"

"Tell us."

"He approved my sketches, sent more supplies, and..." He made a flourish in the air, "also paid ample for our needs."

Caught breathless in Elda Mae's embrace, Fred peered over her shoulder at Abby.

Releasing him, Elda Mae plopped into the rocker with the mail.

"You never know, Abby. There might be something here for you."

"No one even knows where I am."

After an awkward pause, Elda Mae and Fred began discussing who had written. Her chest burning, Abby detoured to the arbor.

"How could I have let Ray deceive me so?" She kicked the table leg and moaned. "So dim-witted—he even told me the Rim would keep everyone out." Her second kick toppled a chair.

Tight-fisted, she raised her eyes to the treetops. "Help me— please help me! I mustn't deluge Elda Mae with these awful feelings."

Wait.

"But I have already wasted *years!*" Kicking rocks and growling, she circled the space. A javelina family crossed on the far side, but fled when they caught her scent.

"You are wise, you stinky creatures, to get away from me." Maybe Ray was right about them being destructive and good for nothing. But at the end of the line, one baby about the size of a housecat turned its long snout in an endearing glance. Abby's fury abated, and a chuckle came forth.

"You are so ugly, but you do have a certain charm." With a lighter heart, she rearranged the chairs. "If I can see something good in a javelina, maybe there is still hope."

Mama had been wise to send her to her room after an angry childhood outburst, though her ragdoll usually suffered the consequences. But now, she must master her emotions.

For supper, they feasted on cooked pumpkin, and Elda Mae read some letters aloud. "The people who helped me rescued another woman this winter. My friend writes, 'a long road ahead, but she is learning to open her heart.' This surely takes me back."

Every few minutes, she burst forth with news that incited Abby's curiosity about Poplar Bluff. Surely Lola's visit had sent a buzz through the populace—it wasn't every day that such a woman came to town. What was it Mama called them? Maybe the word was *floozy*.

"Oh my, who would ever have thought…" Elda Mae kept reading to herself until Fred cleared his throat with gusto.

"Sorry. I can hardly fathom this bit of information. Mount Pleasant became a refuge from the cholera during and after the war, and now…" She paused again and Fred gave Abby his best raised-eyebrow look.

"There is talk of changing the town's name to Mount Healthy now. Why, forevermore! Have you ever heard of such a thing?"

Neither of them had, and after discussing this, they listened to a few more interesting bits of news. Oh, how much a letter from far away could mean. Abby could hardly imagine what it would be like to hear from Lizzy or Annabelle.

By now, Lizzy probably nurtured a passel of her own children in addition to her inherited family. Lying in bed brought even more inquiries to mind. What if, after all this time, she and Lizzy could correspond? Did Marshal Tibbits still investigate the fire? What if he had discovered some new evidence?

She tossed and turned until sleep finally came before dawn. Then Elda Mae's exclamation woke her. "Look out your window. If Fred had gone to Green Valley one day later, this storm would have mired down the wagon."

Snowdrifts decorated the yard, so after a hearty breakfast, they shoveled while Fred tended the stock. Physical labor invigorated Abby, though Elda Mae punctuated the time with warnings not to overdo. With paths cleared to the barn and milk house, the roof already dripped, and every time someone opened the door, the freshness of new fallen snow wafted in.

After washing the breakfast dishes, Abby could wait no longer. "Would you mind if I went for a walk?"

"I thought you would never ask—surprised you held out this long."

Glossy branches drenched in sunlight framed the cabin. Nearby, several small brown birds pecked on a wooden fence near a scalloped bush where more twittered.

Leaning close, Abby whispered, "Even now, you persist." Farther down the trail, mule deer peered through the brush.

Seconds later, a muffled thud startled her. Then a second echoed, and a third resounded. Suddenly, snow cascaded from towering Ponderosa branches, sparkling and cold, causing her to jump back. But sunlight still warmed her toes through the fur-lined leather boots Fred had made her.

Pulling off the thick mittens Elda Mae knitted, Abby held out her hands. Such pristine white wilderness, such joy to breathe the cold, clean air.

Pines bowed low with wet snow formed giant rainbows with the earth. With the melt, they sprang back landing spray on her nose and hair like stardust. She tipped her head back to let the downfall dance on her tongue. Other than these showers, quiet shrouded the forest.

Bough after bough relinquished a thick blanket as the sun's rays penetrated deeper. Free of their heavy loads, saplings bounced and swayed. The scene brought back winter in Poplar Bluff, filled with sledding, making snow forts, and sleigh rides through the countryside. Afterward, hot cider warmed her through and through.

Even now, these memories blessed her. Maybe Elda Mae was right about healing—in due time, she would experience its balm. *Memories... our reward.* The burdened trees breaking free from their loads wooed Abby to let go of all but the good.

Right now, she wagered that Elda Mae observed her from the window. Soon her call would float up the hill, so like Mama's when she loitered. So much had happened since those old days, but had come to a good place.

A sudden avalanche from a high branch sent snow everywhere. Shaking the fall from her hair and coat, a giggle escaped. Just then, a *whirr, whirr, whirr* sounded overhead, and a turkey vulture flew over, searching for food. How would he ever find enough?

"If I ever return to the ranch, I must search for that feather you left me." With the toe of her boot, Abby forged a circle in the snow. "Help me to keep searching for good things."

Reminding herself for the hundredth time that something unexpected must have waylaid Martin, she turned back toward the cabin. Fred's whistle from the barn guided her and she hurried in to help Elda Mae with supper.

Chapter Twenty-five

A swarthy sergeant wiped spit from his coat and scanned Captain Whitaker's face. "That fool's gotta learn not to spit. Did he give you that scar?"

The Captain grimaced. "He's a mean one."

"Leg irons and cuffs, and no meals for him today."

The punishment provided some satisfaction as Martin accompanied Captain Whitaker to General Crook's anteroom, where the captain motioned him to a seat.

"That's one sorry job finished." He propped one of his boots on the other. "I wager we all sleep better tonight."

"What will happen to McHale?"

"General Crook will give him more justice than anyone else.. He'd be hanging from a tree if those cowhands had found him. What do you think he deserves?"

"Whatever the law says."

Captain Whitaker stared out at the parade grounds. "Stealing Army cattle, weapons, and liquor; supplying the enemy; killing a squaw; leaving his wife for dead—"

"Plus assaulting an officer."

The captain started to answer when a messenger gestured them down a short hallway. Martin had the sensation of being a little boy again, entering Pastor Schultz's study at Mama's side.

Maps covered an enormous table engulfing half of the office. Tall and tanned, General Crook's full beard parted at the chin. Close-cropped hair framed his thin visage, and a frayed canvas hunting outfit the shade of rebel uniforms hung on his spare frame. A trapper or scout might sport such stained cuffs.

"At ease, men. This must be the Sergeant Tolzmann you have mentioned, captain." The general leafed through a sheaf of papers. "I have here your report and the evidence." He pointed toward the crate slat and whiskey cork from McHale's pasture. "You found these on Ray McHale's property?"

"Yes, Sir."

"Ever meet the man before this investigation?"

"I had no idea who he was. I found the items under the captain's orders. He, ah—"

"Yes?"

Martin squirmed. "He had an intuition to explore the canyon beyond the Rim."

General Crook rubbed his beard. "An intuition, captain?"

"Colonel Masters forbade searching there because of an Indian burial ground, he said, but we found none."

"And your fresh injury?"

"The down side of the prisoner's handcuffs. I ought to have known better than to get so close."

"Our surgeon employs some herbal Indian remedies. Stop in there for one of his plant concoctions." The general ran his fore-finger along his own jaw. "Stay here until that wound heals over, captain. Anything else to add?"

"My misgivings run stronger than ever after the past week."

"And you, sergeant? Feel free to speak."

Martin glanced toward Captain Whitaker, who urged, "Tell him everything."

"I found an Indian woman dying in McHale's barn. He broke her neck after he delivered the goods to the natives."

General Crook squeezed his eyes shut, but motioned for Martin to continue.

"A day earlier, I discovered McHale's wife on the trail, barely alive. A whiskey flask lay nearby. Here it is." He handed over the flask.

"R. M." The general massaged his forehead. "This brings my Mary to mind. If anyone were to— Begging your pardon, but sometimes I wonder why certain people carry on, while innocents die." He lifted a paper.

"Perhaps you have not heard that within the past week, Apache warriors have again raided Camp Reno. If only Chief Del-che-ae's brother had not been killed three years ago. But that was before your time, Captain?"

"True, but I believe Del-che-ae's people might have supported our work on the Green Valley road. Unfortunately, his death confused the other Indians. The command kept changing—who they could trust?"

"Indeed. Things took a bad turn after the commander imprisoned the chief's brother and killed him when he tried to escape." The general's sigh filled the room. "Was that about the time you two reached your unit?"

"We came just in time for the Fort McDowell supply train attacks."

"We have nearly finished the road, but paid for it in blood." General Crook winced and grabbed his side.

"One of your mementos from the second Pit River expedition, Sir?"

"Humph. Not everyone can say a poison arrow resides on their person—just last week our surgeon had to forcibly remove an arrowhead embedded in a soldier's leg bone. Infection set in, but at present, he shows signs of improvement." The general rubbed his hip. "But back to Camp Reno. I hoped November's natural phenomenon over the Tonto Basin would quiet things down. Did you witness it?"

"Yes, from east of the Mazatzal Range—like flaming rain sent straight from heaven. The sight brought us to attention, Sir."

"Others have compared it to battle. The earth heaved and the skies thundered, they say. The vision scared the Indians for a time, but now they've become so hungry—" General Crook's shoulders sagged. "I see no way around more bloodshed. But I digress. Captain, visit the surgeon immediately—that's an order."

"Colonel Simms asked us to wait here until he arrives. Do you agree?"

"Yes." The general's tone hardened. "For your ears only—Colonel Masters faces court martial. His replacement has already been summoned." He drummed his fingertips on his desk. "Sergeant, I want you available as a witness."

They took their leave, and at the bottom of the steps, Martin asked his burning question. "He has a poison arrow in his hip?"

"From California gold country. His bravery resulted in his commander naming a fort after him. Impressive, eh? Let's eat and do some exploring."

"Sir, what about the surgeon?"

"Ah, yes. But first, we eat."

Over hot biscuits and beef drowning in thick gravy, all conversation ceased. Finally, Captain Whitaker quipped, "Behold the fruits of justice. As we feast, McHale's stomach growls with no relief."

From the mess hall, a private led Martin to their quarters while Captain Whitaker saw the surgeon. In evening light, he entered their room with his jaw bandaged.

"Creosote leaf poultice from the Pima." With that, he collapsed on his bunk and fell asleep in an instant. Martin nodded off, wondering when the other contingent would arrive. The sooner he could tell Abby about Ray's imprisonment, the better.

The next thing he knew, a woman's voice grated outside. Across the room, the captain still slept. Martin stretched toward the window opening, where she verbally accosted a guard.

"I demand to see Ray McHale. That no-good, filthy cheat belongs to me, his rightful wife."

Martin shook away his lethargy. Wife—McHale?

"State your name, ma'am."

"I told you, Lola McHale. Now, let me in!"

A man spoke with a genteel accent. "Begging your pardon, sir, Albert Aldrich lately of Abilene. Mrs. McHale is most... ahem... indisposed, since we have traveled far and wide in search of your prisoner. A Camp Reno detachment sent us here, and we would be most gratified for your help."

"Past the parade ground, third building on your left."

Martin pulled back the shutter, and the scene almost hurt his eyes. With a tattered dress, hat askew, and dull hair flying loose from its pins, a worn-out matron sat atop a dilapidated rig.

McHale's wife? His heart did a flip.

Immovable as a post, Captain Whitaker still snored. The surgeon must have drugged him with sleeping powders. Silently, Martin pulled on his boots.

With a deep sigh, Elda Mae looked up from her chair beside the bed. Deep crevasses lined her brow at Fred's tortured rasp. Abby slipped out to the porch, and her own breath, visible in the cold air, rose to the sky.

"Oh God, please protect Fred." During the night, he coughed even harder than Papa when he had pneumonia.

From the cooler, she removed the wet burlap cover from a bowl of cream. Screens let air circulate throughout the cooler's three slatted shelves to keep perishables safe. Another loud spasm issued from the bedroom as she ladled out some cream and replaced the bowl.

The strong onion poultice drew her back inside, where Elda Mae fetched more hot water. Amidst more dreadful hacking, her voice remained calm.

"Dear, please prepare the sumac."

Pouring boiling water over some dried berries, Abby awaited the resulting faint lemon scent. Elda Mae, pale and disheveled from her nursing duties, welcomed the brew.

"Would you let me watch him for a while?"

"Maybe later, if he sleeps."

Fred's form, a mere bony rise under the blanket, sent a shudder through Abby. Back on the porch, she set her hand to his handmade wooden plunger. Nine carved potato-sized openings he had crafted forced cream up into the churn.

"Such a brilliant invention—the texture stays consistent as the butter forms." Elda Mae had praised his ingenuity the first time she showed Abby the plunger. "Makes the job far easier and saves time."

Long after sun splayed the east window, the up and down motion centered Abby, until Elda Mae sent her scurrying to the barn for more onions. The difficult descent from the mow had her grappling with her skirts.

"I should make myself some bloomers. If Mama could see the conditions here, even she might approve."

With the Huckaback towels already warming, she and Elda Mae sliced onions until one towel overflowed and wrapped two more around the mass. Together, they pressed the healing poultice over Fred's chest and piled on blankets.

Elda Mae was right—their patient was completely dependent on Providence. Elda Mae possessed no power to save Fred, and in the same way, she could have done nothing to change Ray's behavior. Was it Pastor Fox who said, "Trouble and despair drive us to prayer?"

Her plea for Fred rose once again.

By the time the butter formed, the poultice and tea had quieted Fred's cough. Abby removed the plunger and spooned fragrant yellow mounds into a granite bowl to set in the cooler. Then she peeked into the bedroom.

With her forehead against Fred's chest, her torso rising and falling in rhythm with his, Elda Mae rested. Her chins trembled against her bodice with each breath, and her plump fingers splayed in exhaustion.

"He means so much to her, and to me, too. Please let him live." Sending up her faltering prayers seemed far too little. There must be something more she could do.

Meat still clung to a chicken carcass they roasted yesterday, so she could make soup, Mama's all-purpose healer. And fresh corn bread—ah, yes. The scent might pique Fred's appetite.

When the bread had baked and the soup simmered, Elda Mae finally emerged with good news. "At last, his fever broke."

"I have supper in hand and can do the chores. Please rest a few hours."

That evening, Fred drank chicken broth. Two days later, even skinnier than before, he walked out to the porch. The next day, the barn became his target. When he resumed his sketching, his grin widened like normal.

One afternoon the next week, when most of the snow had melted away, Elda Mae led Abby far afield to hunt for herbs. "The Indians gave me creosote powder for foot fungus and taught me to put heated branches directly on Fred's chest. You can gather them all year long, even in the cold, but they only grow down this slope."

Being outdoors spurred her tongue. "I ran out a few days back, but the next time he suffers, we can boil these leaves and have him breathe the steam. I add some to my bath water, too, for aches and pains."

They topped a ridge overlooking a meadow alive with small plants, despite the temperature.

"The Indians led you here?"

"Yes." On a large flat rock, Elda Mae pressed a reddish substance from a creosote branch into a small glass vial before turning the branch to press the other end.

"This gum makes a sore throat wash and an ointment for cuts and scrapes."

Around them, green-black Ponderosa pine and blue-tinted juniper joined light green bristle bushes. Here and there, yellowed leaves added light strokes. Undulating along the Rim, shadows darkened the palate.

"My drawings could never do this country justice."

"How long have you sketched?"

"When I was little, Mama gave me a canvas and brushes and taught me the essentials. My teacher encouraged me, but then I let everything go."

Elda Mae unwrapped a packet from her coat pocket. "But now, you are busy once again. Have a biscuit. I imagine our place gives you a different perspective of the Rim. Surely you sketched from the ranch?"

"I longed to, and just before I rode to your house, I considered stealing a page from Ray's record book."

From the west, a large bird sailed their way—a turkey vulture?

"Oh, a golden eagle." Elda Mae shaded her eyes. "I do hope Fred sees it."

"The wingspan must be seven feet."

"More will come some day. Fred means to catalog every species."

"But what if a golden eagle never lands near the cabin?"

"One will. The White Mountain Chief told us about the Thunderbird and honored us by fanning its feathers over us in the Thunderbird ceremony to bless Fred's work. Of course, we don't believe the eagle's eyes issue lightning or that it portends victory in battle. But Providence created all things, and the Indians chose this eagle as their symbol for power and protection."

"Like an idol?"

"So some folks assume, but the tribe also acknowledges the eagle's creator. The Thunderbird ceremony resembled our church's farewell service for our wagon train."

The eagle swooped and ascended, clutching some unfortunate animal in its beak.

Elda Mae touched Abby's shoulder. "Have you ever read God's promise to renew our strength?"

"My memory fails me."

"We must remedy that. Some passages were meant for claiming."

Back at home, she fetched her Bible and read. "*They that wait upon the Lord shall renew their strength, they shall rise up with wings as eagles .*"

"The other day I asked how long I needed to wait. Perhaps this is my answer—until my strength is equal to facing the future."

Chapter Twenty-six

Loud banging, grunts, groans, and exclamations came from the stockade, so Martin skulked behind the buildings in that direction. He had missed some sleep last night after the stockade guard had told Lola to return in the morning.

"You will let me in, or—" Someone rattled the latch.

"Who goes there?"

"Lola McHale. Confound you, let me in. And hurry."

Putrid latrine odor assailed Martin, who froze against the back of the frame structure. His heart beat a crazed staccato, for if this woman—Lola—had really married McHale, that meant Abby...

"What goes on here?" General Crook's voice—the noise must have drawn him, too.

"Sir, we seek entrance." Lola's male friend made the request.

"On what pretext?"

"Legal right. Ray McHale is this wronged woman's lawful husband. We attempted to prove this last night, but were thwarted."

"What evidence have you?"

Dry paper crinkled as a forlorn birdcall issued from patch of bushes.

"You see, general? I married Ray years ago, in the Territory of Kansas."

The tips of Martin's ears burned as he peered around the corner. Slinking along like a criminal to eavesdrop—but the scene magnetized him.

In the same canvas as yesterday, but wearing a shabby pith helmet,

General Crook studied a wrinkled document. "Indeed, it seems the law binds you to this man."

"For better or worse. And he owes me." Lola's flimsy hat teetered when she tossed her head.

"Is that so?"

"Blamed thief stole my—"

General Crook cut her off. "You wish to speak with him now?"

"He took the deed for a ranch I won fair and square in a poker game. I mean to get it back."

The man at her side nipped her waist, so she quieted down.

"But I heard in good faith that Mr. McHale beat his wife nearly to death."

"Who knows how many women he so-called married?"

"I grant you five minutes." The general turned toward his mule, and a guard drew out his key. Martin side-winded to the back. Seconds later, Lola's cursing at McHale would have put the toughest soldier to shame.

Even from this distance Martin reeled at her screeching. Then someone muttered. "If only all men could be like Padre Kino, taking nothing for himself. He gave his all, and left this world a better place."

A mule's muzzle showed around the stockade corner, and its rider continued. "Quite the pair, selfish as this land in a downpour." He stopped short when he saw Martin.

"Enjoying yourself, soldier?" The sparkle in General Crook's eyes called Martin to attention.

"At ease, Sergeant Tolzmann." A smile pulled at the general's lips. "Most excitement here since the last Apache raid. I presume you have reason for spending your leisure in this muck?"

"Hearing Mrs. McHale's voice whetted my curiosity."

"How so?"

"She maintains to be the prisoner's wife, yet—"

"You carried that other wife to safety?"

"Yes, sir."

"Sometimes the look of things falls far from reality. That other wife the prisoner nearly killed—how far did you carry her?"

"Perhaps a half hour to the neighbor's cabin."

General Crook's mule stamped a hoof. "Apache. Patience." He patted her neck. "My apologies. Apache loves her morning promenade and shows little tolerance for changes in routine."

For a moment, he seemed to have forgotten the subject. Martin wished he could quietly disappear, but General Crook dismounted and advanced.

"Interesting things happen to a man's heart when he totes an injured woman that far, sergeant. Her name?"

"Abby, Sir."

"Will she be all right?"

"She had regained her senses before I left."

"Good. You will check on her again?"

"I promised to let her know when McHale could no longer hurt her."

"And well you should, after all her suffering." A howl from within the stockade made the general grimace. "If McHale's true wife has any say, our prisoner may perish before his hanging. Your Abby can rest easy now."

Your Abby. The phrase skipped through Martin's consciousness like a rabbit on the run.

"Perhaps you think me meddling, but have you feelings for her?"

"Sir, I thought I had no hope—"

"No such thing while we live and breathe, sergeant. That's what the Spanish explorers thought about this country—hopeless. Wasteland. Why would anyone settle here when New Mexico Territory offers one great verdant canyon with the Rio Grande's lazy gradient, suitable for sustaining life?

"Possibilities abound here, but require men of foresight and character, like George Cooke. Think of his fortitude in leading the Mormon Brigade all the way to California. After Gadsden's Purchase, Lieutenant Cooke's labor along the southern border set the stage for everything we attempt today.

"Can you imagine what those troops suffered back in the winter of '46? Desert, mountains, Indian attacks, and deprivation of every sort. But nothing stymied Cooke in blazing the Gila Trail, known more properly as Cooke's Trail."

"Cooke's and Crook's—you continue his work, sir. You spoke of a padre earlier. Was he like Colonel Cooke?"

"Indeed. Almost two centuries ago, an Italian Jesuit trained in Austria set his sights on missionizing the Orient. You have heard of him?"

Martin shook his head.

"History often fails in awarding its prizes. In 1687, when Padre Kino's community drew lots, he lost the Orient to another brother. He was sent here and embraced this land instead. For a quarter century, he explored her rivers and worked in the northern Sonora.

"He introduced grain farming and livestock, founded Indian missions, and left a legacy as a cartographer and astronomer. I aim for his endurance. He rode on horseback from the San Pedro to the Colorado, from the Concepcion to the Gila. He mapped the Sea of Cortez and discovered Baja was a peninsula instead of an island."

"I wonder why I have never heard of him. Coronado, of course, and—"

"Very perceptive, sergeant. Coronado quested for gold, so we recall his feats. But Padre Kino, Eusebio Chini by birth, sought only to know God and help the natives. What a model of humility and strength he left us."

Sunlight created an aura around the general's helmet. "Now you may search out more information about him. But back to this Miss Abby. Mind your emotions. Soldiering befits me, but my Mary's devotion is what makes life worth living."

Heat flooded Martin's face as Apache pawed the ground.

"There, girl." The mule snorted, but General Crook lingered. "That Indian woman—tell me more about her."

"She looked young and healthy, but McHale wrenched her arm and neck. He left her to die in a back stall."

General Crook groaned. "Oh, that our government punished such deeds, but the Indians are viewed as less than human. Some evils find retribution only in eternity." He scuffed the rocks with his toe. "I trust you provided her a decent burial?"

"The best I could, sir."

"Some things rank worse than battle. Speaking of that, how fares Captain Whitaker?"

"He was sleeping soundly when I left, with a fine poultice on his wound."

"Hmm..." General Crook mounted. His cork helmet's oval shape defined his high forehead and probably worsened the heat, but Martin swallowed his opinion. A few curly dark strands fringed the general's face as he tightened the reins.

"Tell him to stop in my office for fresh orders before you leave." The mule trotted ahead a few steps and he twisted. "That is an order, sergeant."

Captain Whitaker had not exaggerated this leader's intuition. It seemed the general read his very thoughts.

Interesting things happen to a man's heart. Mind your emotions.

That awful day he found Abby roared back—she might easily have died. Martin shook his head against the possibility—she had a strong constitution. But now, it appeared she and Ray had never legally married.

The emotions he had shunted down ignited, but did they signify the marrying kind of love? How could one know for sure?

One thing was certain. The general had succeeded in fishing out the truth. Longing to gather Abby in his arms again, Martin gazed northeast. *I will lift my eyes unto the hills, whence cometh my help...*

The copper laundry tub squeaked into place, and Abby fetched boiling water. Elda Mae dropped a load of dirty clothes and snatched two clean towels.

"Let me help you with that heavy pot."

They dumped the water, shaved in waxy lye soap curls, and swished them around with a stick. Then Abby added cool water from the tank.

"At the ranch, washing clothes took me all day."

"You had plenty of soap?"

"Mama used to make her own, but when Papa ordered bars at the store, she moved ahead with the times. At least I had the sense to pack every one I could find, plus Aunt Susan's reserve."

"See, you did have some foresight! Before you came, Fred always lent a hand on wash day, but now I think he might be too weak."

"He should market his creative plunger, and the one he fashioned for the churn."

Elda Mae left, but reappeared in a pair of men's trousers, definitely not Fred's. Her profile resembled President Lincoln's predecessor, the rather portly President Buchanan.

"I should be back by supper time. Binding the rest of the hay won't take me long."

Abby rolled up her sleeves. How anyone could like that miserable, itchy task baffled her, but Elda Mae was one-of-a-kind. By ten o'clock, most of the clothes swung from the line, and the wash water moistened the purslane plants transplanted near the cabin.

On closer look, tiny buds with light centers covered what had been straggly starts a few weeks earlier. Elda Mae's prophesy echoed.

"Soon, delicate yellow flowers will flourish under the west window. Purslane does best in bright sun."

"Just like her to see potential in something and make the most of it."

In the cabin, Fred prepared one of his sketches for mailing. Abby leaned back into the deep front step and watched a gray squirrel arch his tail and body into two perfect rainbow shapes. On closer inspection, they formed the letter *M*.

"M for Martin." The Rim, steady and sure, beckoned her. "Elda Mae says we must admit our powerlessness, and I can do nothing to hurry him. But oh, this weak heart of mine. Oh, to be more like her, seeing the potential rather than the problems."

She stood and squared her shoulders. "I *shall* climb you, old Rim, when my strength comes full. One day, I shall—just you wait and see."

Suddenly, fulfilling that vow seemed possible, like the eagle visit Elda Mae anticipated. At first, her confidence had seemed like putting the Almighty to the test. But she believed if a certain task were assigned a person, He would provide what was needed to carry it out. The concept sounded simple, but the waiting proved anything but easy.

The squirrel scurried off, and Abby went inside. She had peeled half the potatoes when voices rose from the arbor.

"Been trappin' since I's a young'un. Pap heered of a notice in th' St. Louis 'publican. Henry n' Ashley, Jedediah Smith, James Clyman, n' a feller named Fitzpatrick set up th' Rocky Mountain Fur Comp'ny. Pap married a squaw up in Ideeho and bush loped till the beaver done played out."

"He knew Jim Bridger and Etienne Provost?"

"Sure 'nuff. Had me memberize them names." The voice sounded familiar, so Abby ran to her bedroom window.

"What do you trap?"

"Most-wise coon, n' some snarin'."

"You hunt birds?" The question barely squeaked past Fred's lips.

"Feisty creatures. Feller jest gets ever'thin' set, n' somethin' wrecks th' trap. Sech a lot a' watchin' and waitin', all fer some fancy women's hats.

"But feathers pays right fine—cain't hardly give it up. Fix them branches jest right, loop the lasso, tie up a stick and angle th' noose t' snap at th' first pull. Gotta lure 'em like y' wuz fam'bly. Oftimes, I hold a pile a' sod up to m' lips to mask m' breath."

Fred turned pale, but the trapper paid no mind. "Bait 'em with baubles, berries, seeds. Oft as not, they set off th' snare, so y' start all over."

"How do you ah... How do you take the feathers?"

The trapper's cackle mimicked a raven's shrill cries. "If they cor-perate, I pull 'em out n' let 'em go. If'n they fight like Hades, waal…"

The clear picture he painted of a bird in a fowler's snare created another image that brought Ray to mind. Before and after the fire, Ray had plotted, set his snare, and left the tiniest bit of bait. He made himself known to Papa, but no one else. After the fire, he managed to appear often enough to pique her interest.

For two years he circled, waiting and watching. Then he pulled the noose. Sickness washed her throat. Why hadn't she realized he only wanted to use her?

Nobody's 'roun' here, nobody a'tall. The Rim'll keep ever'body else out.

"But I failed to comprehend. What a fool I was."

"Come here mos'ly on account a' curiousness. A few years back, a feller left his fevered wife nigh death's door up near Sante Fe. Come spring, th' Injuns roused 'er passable, so I brung 'er t' Green Valley. Alus wondert how that brown-eyed gal fared—thin as water, she was—too weared out even t' parley."

Could this be Cactus Joe? Only the stranger's eyes and nose showed above his beard, but her heart raced at his scratchy tenor, and she leaned closer when Fred asked him a question.

"Do you recall that man's name?"

"McHale. Never forgot 'im—had eyes thet passed from blue t' gray. Never saw such, 'ceptin in wolves."

"Wolves?"

"Gotta git mighty close t' see it."

"Indeed." Fred cleared his throat. "I can tell you that woman survived."

"'Y don' say?"

"She's a strong one."

"That so? Back then, she could barely sit a mule. Thought fer sure she woulda past by now. That feller left 'er fer dead, n' never give me no pelts fer m' trouble."

Fred gestured toward the cabin. "You will take a meal with us, Mr.—?"

"Joe. Cactus Joe. Thank'ee, but bein' cooped up discombobulates me mighty—got m' campsite a ways down thar." He gestured west and made to mount his mule.

Fred ran in for a loaf of bread and a jar of honey. He caught up with him and issued another invitation. "Do stop in again if you return this way."

The wayfarer leaned into his reins. "Thank'ee kindly."

"What has you thinking so hard, dear?" Elda Mae scrubbed a frying pan with sand as Abby hung out the dishtowels, wet from supper dishes.

"I should have gone out and thanked that trapper for his kindness, but his story shocked me so."

"Hearing you survived was thanks enough. Clearly, the Almighty sent him to preserve your life."

"To Ray I wasn't even worth a few animal pelts."

"Yet you conquered that terrible sickness, and we have come to know you. I could never calculate your worth to Fred and me."

Distasteful memories flooded Abby. "I spent so many years—"

"You saw no other alternative, dear. But Providence kept you in life."

A young mule deer nipped at sparse grass near the cabin, and another nosed the turnip peelings. With white tails high, others followed.

They darted into the brush when pails clanked in the barn, but the first one merely lowered its head. After one more *clank*, it startled and fled, too.

"They have no idea Fred's pails can do them no harm. Just like them, I once gave fear too much power. Being thought imprudent frightened me more than anything. Now, I realize William saw that tendency before he picked me. He sensed I would never leave him, would never want to disappoint my parents by failing."

"*Imprudent.* That fits me, except I stopped caring what anybody thought."

"Losing your parents altered your whole world. In such dire times, trepidation clutches us, and anything seems better than the unknown."

Elda Mae fiddled with her shawl fringe. "But you have healed so much in body and spirit, and you are waiting. Remember the promise about that? You will rise up with wings like eagles."

"I cannot even imagine."

"Of course not. I recall that same feeling, but during my waiting time, I finally understood what I really wanted. Do you know what you want most, deep down inside?"

A blush forced its way up Abby's cheeks. Speech failed her.

"You have yet to give a worthy man your love." Elda Mae looked off where the plantana imbibed sunshine, though the day was late. "I once vowed never to marry again, but in my heart, I still longed to give and receive love."

Flecked with straw, Fred traipsed from the barn to the milk house. This evening, he said he had something to finish out there.

"Fred seemed an unlikely sort, but little by little, my path became clear. My new friends talked about God making me to know wisdom, and opening myself to joy and gladness.

"I recall thinking they must be daft, but did what they said— prayed over and over, *make me to know wisdom.* Gradually, I understood my worth, exactly as I was. Just because one person failed to count me worthy did not alter my value. My faith grew ever so slowly, but our heavenly Father never gave up on me."

She circled Abby's shoulders with her arm. "To Him, we are worth whatever it takes to bring us back. No matter what we have endured, He sees us as fresh as sun-drenched blossoms, and meant to hear joy and gladness."

"But how can that be with no church in this whole territory."

"I shan't give up on having one here, but the sounds of joy and gladness begin to dwell within as our strength grows. Then our hearts become a sanctuary of our own."

A woodpecker flew over the clothesline, leaving a white, runny trail. Elda Mae leaped up and flung her arms in the air. "Shoo!" She wrenched the towels from the line. "That little marauder hit not just one, but all three."

Fred raced up, arms akimbo. "Scaring my woodpecker off?"

She shook the smelly stain under his nose. "Observe this mess your subject made on our kitchen towels!"

Her glare would have scared off an intruder. Then her face crinkled and she let go a laugh. Abby joined in, but Fred, bemused, only raised his brows.

Finally, Elda Mae nudged him. "Fear not, dear. Your hairy friend always returns. Our cabin has become his private granary."

Chapter Twenty-seven

"I trust you found some relief, Captain Whitaker?"

"Thank you, general. The poultices relieved the pain."

"Ready for new orders?" General Crook's eyes flashed the same mischievous glint they had shown behind the stockade.

"I have a brief mission for you and Sergeant Tolzmann, since your new commander will be *en route* to Camp Reno for some time. I have often hankered to send someone to survey the Jerome area, where copper mines are being dug. Perhaps you realize it lies on the north route, through beautiful red rock country."

"We spotted the rocks, and straight ahead, that massive peak."

"Squaw Peak. Half a day's ride north sits Cleopatra Hill. When the Yavapai settle down, a town will no doubt rise, but presently, the miners have cut off their food supply, and Indian raids have increased. I want you to spy and report back to me.

"Have the post store outfit you as trail hands, so no one in Jerome will suspect your military connections. The more fair play from the mine owners, the better things will turn out for the Yavapai.

"One of our scouts will await your report below the hill. Then I want you to return to Camp Reno by the Northern route as soldiers again, via Oak Creek to the Rim trail. Take your time. You both deserve a rest."

"Yes, Sir."

"Captain, the paperwork for your promotion has been sent, and Sergeant Tolzmann merits compensation for his detective work as well."

"No one more deserving."

"One more thing." That twinkle played in General Crook's eyes again. "Sergeant Tolzmann must keep his promise."

"Promise?" Captain Whitaker eyed Martin. This would be the time to confess, but Martin put it off.

"Forgive me, General Crook, but I made another vow to commend Private Reser, who rides with Colonel Simms. He endured the worst duties with our prisoner on our trip."

"I shall see to it." General Crook retrieved a thick envelope from his desk and walked them to the door. There, he handed the envelope to Captain Whitaker. "Both of you read this now, but deliver it to that young woman named Abby. She deserves to know the truth.

"By the way, McHale received a mortal wound in an escape attempt last night. His wife and that fancy fellow judged the U.S. Army incapable of doing away with him. I had hoped to pair him with Colonel Masters to see justice done completely." He kicked at some sand on the boardwalk. "Ah well. I turned them loose for Kansas, on their word never to return to this territory."

The general rocked back on his heels. "Captain Whitaker, do you think it wrong to hang a woman?"

"Justice is justice."

"Thankfully, McHale has received his. Now, stop in at the cook's—he has orders to outfit you for a week's journey."

On the way, a contingent of privates hefting shovels passed them, and the captain questioned the officer in charge. "Burial detail?"

The leader nodded. "That cantankerous new prisoner."

"Sooner than we thought, eh, Martin?"

"And you have earned a promotion."

"If it ever materializes. But I fail to understand how General Crook read my mind about going back the north way."

Martin shrugged. "He sees things others miss."

"It appears he can read your mind, as well?"

Under the mess sergeant's welcome, Martin ducked the question.

Then they visited the post, and outfitted like kings, folded their uniforms into their saddlebags. Captain Whitaker revisited the surgeon before opening the envelope from General Crook.

Sitting on his bunk, he read the information aloud.

"The Poplar Bluff Marshal has found new evidence concerning the deaths of Loyal Ferguson and his wife. Someone reported seeing Ray McHale behind the store minutes before the fire, and another witnessed him leave the Ferguson house an hour later.

"A third witness observed McHale at the stables early the morning of Susan Carmichael's accident. Do you know who this is?"

"That must be Abby's aunt. She said she died in a buggy accident."

The Captain shuffled the papers. "A Justice in Doniphan performed a marriage for one Ray McHale in March, '64 with an underage woman, one Abigail Ferguson. No consent form and no bonds published. Seems that Justice only wanted to collect his fee.

"Hmm '...however, Mr. McHale's lawful wife, Lola, recently visited our town in search of her husband, now wanted for kidnapping Abby Ferguson. Also sought for Miss Ferguson's murder. Said fugitive is wanted for previous cattle thieving in Kansas, as well.'"

"A five hundred dollar reward overriding all other previous warrants. So, this is the same Abigail whom McHale nearly killed?"

Martin nodded. "I could hardly believe it when I saw her."

"You remembered her from our time in southern Missouri?"

Another nod. "And I—I promised to let her know when Ray could no longer hurt her." Martin released a long breath. There, he had finally said it.

"Well, what do you know? A true outlaw, and punished accordingly. My father used to quote Seneca, who said *Injustice never rules forever?*"

"Sir, do you happen to recognize the names *Oliver* and *Nancy* from your reading?"

"Hmm; let me think on that overnight. Better bunk down early."

Before dawn, they rode a steady line north until sunset flamed over a spectacular formation of red rocks. Oak Creek's placid surface reflected the outcropping in misty orange detail.

In the water near the bank, a distinct black line accentuated variations in stone and soil. Did a daguerreotype work this way to re-create reality? Was that why Papa's picture in the upstairs hallway always seemed so real under its thick glass?

The evening spectacle highlighted obscure tunnels and caves in the rocks. Captain Whitaker twisted in his saddle. "How about camping here?"

"No better spot, Sir."

He scouted firewood while Captain Whitaker brushed the horses. Oak created the hottest fire, but dried Manzanita and Pinon pine gave off a captivating scent.

Later, sparks met the Milky Way as the truth from the Poplar Bluff marshal settled in. A murdering thief devoid of conscience had deceived Abby, but despite his wiles, she survived. A sudden recollection jolted Martin in a visible shudder.

And you held her in your arms.

"Sergeant?"

"Sir?"

"I asked you a question."

"I must have been dreaming."

"Ever have a sweetheart?"

"Far too shy, but I expect you have had several."

The captain snorted. "Only one, with hair soft as down and eyes to break your heart. We talked of marriage. Such a quiet, loyal girl—or so I thought."

Something wrangled in Martin's gut. This story would take a bad turn.

"During the early days of the war, her letters got waylaid, but one finally found me toward the end of the Vicksburg siege. The day it arrived forms my clearest memory of that time." Captain Whitaker poked the fire.

"She wrote me that she had married another man. Before I left, my uniform impressed her, but that fellow never even signed up."

Now and then a flame reached for air. What sounded like a whole elk herd tramped through Oak Creek.

"What was her name, sir?"

"Roseanna."

Scenes rose from Vicksburg, where Captain Whitaker's unrivaled bravery cemented the troops' respect, but through it all, he nursed a broken heart. Someone might be suffering right beside you without you knowing it.

How could this Roseanna have betrayed him? So many of Martin's questions revolved around that one small word—*how.*

"Her letter soured me on romance, but there must be more to life than the cavalry. Do you want to build roads for the rest of your life?"

A perfect time to mention Abby, but Martin hesitated. "I do ponder settling down." The somberness of his own voice scared him, so he added a light touch. "Sure would hate to end up like Ray and Lola, though."

That re-routed his thoughts to Abby, and he sifted through all he had learned about her from Elda Mae. But what caused her to cry out for a man named *Oliver?*

"I never thought about it—too busy farming. But what a climb to get up here. I felt sympathy for our horses during that hard scrabble."

"What is your first impression of this place, sergeant?"

"Not that different from an army camp at the outset of battle. Everyone seeks their place and wonders what will happen next."

Even though the hill offered incredible views, and they met men from all over, some of them former soldiers who had come to work the mine, Martin's impatience increased. That night at their camp outside of Jerome, Captain Whitaker scrawled their findings by lantern light, to deliver to a scout the next day.

"So you think the general can rest secure about this mine's construction?"

"We may have met some scoundrels in disguise, but by and large, the owners seem fair-minded."

"What about those fellows we saw skulking from the entrance last night?"

"Smugglers, maybe. Always a possibility."

"Have you always been able to sniff out that kind of thing?"

Bent over his report, Captain Whitaker gave no answer. The fire highlighted his profile as Martin got to his feet.

"Time to check on the horses."

A few rods away at the stables, Docker whinnied at him, and earthy smells soothed him. Enough of this mining town—it was high time he got back inside a barn.

After a dusty climb the next day, Martin found a flat ledge affording an astounding view. Black hills sided the Verde River like guardian bears, and far away Mazatzal peaks peeked through a southeast morning haze.

Scraping and clawing on the next cliff produced a familiar blue cap. "How'd you get up there so fast, sergeant?"

"You climbed the wrong pillar."

Captain Whitaker inched abreast the precipice and swung his legs over the side. "Nothing east of the Mississippi compares with this. Does Iowa offer anything close?"

"Only limestone cliffs along the Mississippi."

"The government has decided to hire California express riders now—we could see more of the country that way. But at least in the cavalry, we own our own horses. Such vast territory—we could pick our place out here, but how would we make a living?"

He gestured toward Jerome, now a day's ride west. "Never had much desire to mine or prospect, though they say gold lines the Salt River heights. We would only need a pick and shovel, and most likely have to build an *arrastra*. But I wager the Indians would still trouble us."

His deep sigh stirred something in Martin. Settling down appealed to him, but how could a man establish a home without a wife?

"The Army will stay here for a good long time—must be something we could do to support them. General Crook will soon devise another project, most likely widening the trail across the Rim to Camp Verde."

"You think so?"

"Ten years ago, who would have thought anyone could carve a way through the Mazatzals? Yet at the general's behest, we have accomplished that feat. Some men see the impossible and forge ahead, like that Swedish chemist who created dynamite—his name was Nobel, I believe? His invention will expedite road building from now on."

"If anyone ever builds a road over the Rim, I sure hope they leave that natural bridge alone."

They made camp, and an evening breeze fanned the fire. Somewhere a coyote yipped, awaiting a response. Meanwhile, the creek's low gurgle backed twilight's descent.

"A man could always sell butter, milk and meat to hungry workers." The captain closed his eyes. "You could raise a herd and do that. But what would I do?"

"Settlers mean towns, and you know what every town needs."

"What?"

"A sheriff."

A guffaw bounced off the rocks. "Sergeant, you outdo yourself."

"No one concerns himself more with justice than you."

After a while, Captain Whitaker leaned forward, eyes flashing. "What if we built an outpost? You supply the farm goods, and I stock the store from the Salt Valley. We would have to make regular runs down there."

Martin mulled his words.

"We could man a mail and telegraph station, add a stable out behind, build a sleeping room or two, even provide meals. I can cook steak, beans, and biscuits."

"You would forsake the cavalry to become a businessman?"

"We can only fight Indians so long. Besides, I could never get used to being a Major. Might as well get out before those new orders come through."

They bedded down, but under a masterpiece of stars, Martin remained alert. "Captain, are you asleep yet?"

Captain Whitaker shifted his hat brim ever so slightly.

"Have you recalled an Oliver or a Nancy from anything you read when you were young?"

"That would be Oliver Twist and a beggar girl in his gang of thieves. Charles Dickens—surely you have read that book about the underbelly of London?"

"No, Mama must not have known that one."

Sleep came a bit easier this night. At least no one named Oliver would be coming to seek Abby in this vast wilderness.

Soon they would reach Abby's valley. A lone vulture, majestic wings spread wide, curved up to their right, and majestic pine tops punctuated the horizon.

The powerful bird swooped closer, rendering a peculiar inner stillness, the same sensation Martin had when nearing the farm after a time away. Captain Whitaker noticed how quiet he had become.

"Everything all right?"

"Sir, I have neglected to tell you something." On a nearby pine, a woodpecker jiggled its head in a pecking frenzy. The pure air carried the barrage like a drummer's call.

Captain Whitaker shaded his eyes.

"I…that is…" Martin cleared his throat. "When I found Abby at the ranch… I…" The words simply refused to flow.

"What is it?"

If only he could hide his burning countenance. "Remember when I rode north in March of '64?"

"On your veteran's furlough, before we all met again in the Tennessee hills, bound for Atlanta."

"Some officers from the Thirteenth Infantry rode through Missouri with me to catch the train at Saint Louis. When we passed through Poplar Bluff, Ferguson's store had burned down."

"Right. And?"

"Then, when you first sent me over the Rim, I—I camped at the ranch, and Abby was so worn out and melancholy. She had a limp and… We—Abby and I—we talked."

"Why, sergeant!" Captain Whitaker shook his head. "According to what we have learned, her marriage to Ray was never binding. Once she learns that, she can admit how she has pined for you, so our visit will be well received on two counts."

"I doubt she pines for me."

"What makes you think so lowly of your chances?"

The turkey vulture and his mate veered close before plunging back over the valley, riding air currents as men rode horses. *Maybe romance is like that.* The idea startled Martin—could good actually come of a bungling cavalryman and a woman betrayed?

The next moment, he scoffed. Soon, he would be an old man. What could he possibly offer her?

"Matters of the heart require concentration—tomorrow might be your big day." Captain Whitaker eyed him askance. "I must say, sergeant, you look as though the war has begun again."

"I will keep my promise, of course, but harbor no hope for Abby and me."

"Duty calls, eh? Well, we shall see."

Chapter Twenty-eight

Flames reflected on the hearth as Elda Mae munched some pinon nuts. "We can never gather too many of these. One winter, with the elk up on the Rim longer than usual, our meat supply dwindled, and these little delicacies saw us through."

While Abby put the finishing touches on a sketch, Elda Mae knitted. Now and then she replenished the bowl from a seemingly endless tin.

"How do you gather them?"

"Fred drops the cones onto a tarp to drag home. We sort and scoop them into burlap bags, and turn them every other day to dry. When we pour the nuts into one of those wicker trays from Haas Tin Nez's people, the broken scales and bracts blow away."

"What does his name mean?"

"Tall Thin Man. We can never forget his people's kindness."

"When Grandma Carmichael first came to Missouri, Indian women showed her herbs in the hills, too. She taught Mama all she knew."

"The same with my grandmother back in Ohio. Fred and I brought along plenty of seeds and staples, but we would have run out eventually. Fortunately, when cold weather set in, one of the braves showed us how he unrolled a dried animal skin under a pinon, climbed up and tapped on the cones.

"I still remember the tinkle as thousands of seeds rained down. The Indian's hair ran with pitch, but he dipped into a greasy pouch and combed it with his fingers. The gum came off in his hands, and he stored it in a different pouch."

"For ointment?"

"Pinon resin dries harder than creosote gum, perfect for water-proofing baskets and water bottles. The Nez Perce concoct black pinon dye too, and call the seeds Manna of the Mountains." A shadow crossed Elda Mae's face. "No natives have visited this area for such a long time."

Abby took up her knitting. "Elda Mae, you said that your... William hurt you. Could you tell me more?"

"He gave me a broken arm and some lacerations, but the worst injuries were inside. The local doctor and my new friends tended me, but I could never bear a child, and my heart took even longer to heal."

"I have a question about Fred, too. Yesterday, a black ruffed male bird with red eyes and a stiff collar landed in a nest left from last year. His mate had a long dark tail, and clipped brown feathers framed her eyes and beak.

"The cowbird."

"Yes. Fred called it a brood parasite that plants its eggs in other birds' nests and lets them care for the babies. The pair eyed a western bluebird's nest, and Fred called them the oddest species he knew. He seemed ill at ease the whole time."

"Let me guess. He closed one eye? That's his habit when he's disturbed."

"But why?

"The mother cowbird sneaks to another bird's nest early one morning and deposits an egg. Young cowbirds grow fast, so sometimes the host parents unknowingly delay their own fledglings' growth by feeding the orphans more.

"The mother has nothing to do with her offspring—I expect that's what was troubling Fred. His mother fled after his birth—she never even held him. Then the cholera swept New York, and passing through several orphanages left him anxious, especially around women."

"No wonder Lola drove him to the arbor. But his father must have fetched him at some point?"

"Times grew lean, and one of his brothers died. His father eventually tried to make up for those early years. He noticed Fred's scholarly bent and sent him to his uncle in Iowa. When Fred returned to Cincinnati, he became acquainted with Mr. Erkenbrecher, long before he met me."

Before bedtime, Abby walked in the sunset. As often happened, the eastern Rim's reflection beckoned her. So many sunsets missed since the New Mexico trail, yet all this beauty surrounded her, and her strength had returned.

Tonight, she had knitted for over an hour without pain—perhaps her healing time drew to a close. A blend of yellows, reds, and purples enveloped a few clouds against a dusky blue sky, and something Elda Mae once said resounded.

We make allowances for others, but tend to believe the worst about ourselves. Our worth depends on our Creator, not on anyone's evaluation. Another's behavior tells us more about them than about us."

Suddenly, light spangled the heavens, as if to show that sunshine still reigned. Abby sank to a fallen log—the glow rimmed the clouds in an ethereal aura. Crimson became rose, yellows transformed to gold, and periwinkle caressed deep purple.

"Could I have been befuddled all this time?"

The scripture Fred read at supper filtered back—*The Lord hath appeared of old unto me, saying, Yea, I have loved thee with an everlasting love: therefore with loving kindness have I drawn thee."*

The day's warmth still hovered, and with it, a sense that all was well. The sky flamed for several more minutes. *This beauty and my love for you are one.* She hugged the message close. "Perhaps, after all, I am loved."

Twilight shifted into dusk, fading the colors, yet not the glory. Even in the near-darkness, this golden moment lingered. Elda Mae called, so Abby turned back to the cabin with wonderment floating along.

The next morning, Elda Mae handed Abby a woven basket for herb hunting. "A Haas Tin Nez woman gave me this burden basket. At the time, I could only bow and say thank you."

Along the path, willows tinged with pale yellow-green, while Manzanita bushes already dropped their delicate pink blossoms. Elda Mae had shown her how to rub the ends of Manzanita twigs into bristles to clean her teeth.

"I met the women right here that first spring, and wish I could relive that time. Do you ever feel that way?"

"Oh yes. If I had begged Elwood not to go to war, he might have listened. If I had stayed home the night of the fire, or gone with Aunt Susan the day of her accident—"

"That lecture may have saved your life, and your aunt's accident might have taken your life too." Elda Mae leaned on a misshapen tree. "But I know what you mean. I still think, 'if only I had asked for help earlier.' But I thought I knew what was best."

"If you could relive the day you met the Indian women, what would you change?"

"I would give them something. They showed me horehound to boil for Fred's cough, mountain sorrel for salad, the mesquite flower and pod, Manzanita leaves for flour, and berries for cider. Of course, I could never repay them, but I would try.

"When I told Fred about my newfound wisdom, he ordered a book on herbal medicines. The author confirmed the Indians' tips, but no one has recorded their concoctions."

"Someone ought to write down everything they taught you and illustrate the plants."

"A wonderful idea—you could be that someone."

Suddenly, the terrain looked familiar. "Are we about halfway to the ranch?"

"I expect. Would you like to fetch your things soon?"

"Maybe my trunk and Mama's platter—" *And that vulture feather.* "By rights, the first fifteen cattle belong to me."

"You had money when you married?"

"I sold the store property, our house, and Aunt Susan's house, too."

Elda Mae clucked. "You paid dearly for that ranch."

At the final curve before home, they could already hear Fred in the barn. Once again, the arbor welcomed Abby, and today she had no urge to kick chairs.

An acorn woodpecker spattered a pin oak with yet more holes as Elda Mae patted Abbie's hand. "Fred and I had our troubles, and so did you. Still, we all survived, and here we are together."

Wild imaginings beset Martin. Maybe if he concentrated on figuring out Captain Whitaker's name, his fears about seeing Abby would subside.

"Sir, give me a clue about your name."

"I have never known you to cheat."

"After all this time, you think I deserve no special consideration?"

A few rods farther, a burst of butter-colored fluff exploded in the junipers. Soft yellow down covered every inch of the land.

"Seems they all released their pollen at the same time."

"Remember when Major Lewiston puzzled over his wife's illness? He called it a bad case of catarrh or cold plague, but the surgeon connected her condition to the change of seasons. He mentioned the juniper in particular."

Beside the fire that night, the captain made his offer. "If you still want that hint, my given name has something to do with my mother and with searching for things."

"Ah. How about Cain?"

"What does Cain have to do with my mother?"

"She gave you your name."

Captain Whitaker snorted. "This puzzle requires far more thought."

The mystery finally carried Martin into slumber. Perhaps the name had something to do with Orion, the hunter. When pre-dawn coolness wakened him, the same curiosity reigned. *What was that tune the captain sometimes whistled?*

By midmorning, inspiration struck. Captain Whitaker spoke of the surgeon as a friend. Back at Camp Reno, Captain Blaine might provide some insight.

Chapter Twenty-nine

Against the porch wall, the churn languished on its side. Inside the cabin, the table had been overturned, baskets and tins tossed every which way, and the cupboard ransacked. Abby's mending and knitting littered the cabin like fallen leaves.

"Someone let go their rage here." Elda Mae scowled. "But at least Ray will never be back."

But dark thoughts assaulted Abby. What if he broke free from the cavalrymen? Through the torn window canvas, the back pasture loomed—what if he hid out there even now?

Scrapes on the stove revealed where Mama's china platter met its demise, and shards created fine white powder with every step. The grinding set her teeth on edge.

Elda Mae produced a gunnysack. "We may as well take what we can salvage."

In this cabin, Abby had boiled coffee every morning, fried eggs and ham in this iron skillet, baked bread and mended Ray's trousers. She stacked wood, churned, and watched for her vulture friend. But right now, none of that seemed real.

Hushed, Fred and Elda Mae bagged clothing and small objects. Fred's face contorted, and something constricted Abby's throat.

Sitting outside on the top step, she looked to the Rim. The rocker lurched on the earth like a cow on ice. Across the yard, a javelina family carved a wavering path toward the creek, and the barn lurked silent and ominous. The side door dragged like a broken wing. Months ago, Fred rescued the animals, but something drew her, still.

The pigpen floor, dried and flaky, swarmed with flies. Light through a hole in the roof created phantom diamonds on the walls. Moldy hay assaulted her senses, and above, some small rodent skittered across the haymow.

Then a glint caught her attention. On tiptoe, she touched something smooth and shiny. Memories spiraled like dust motes—Mr. Crondite's body near their camp, smoke rising from Ferguson's Store, the Marshal holding that sawn-through buggy axle...

Surely Papa could have gotten Mama out of the store that night.

Unless someone locked them in.

They's both gone now.

Suddenly, she knew it was Ray who bore the news that night. The disgusting odor of his breath swept over her as if he stood here now.

He locked the doors. He set the fire. The realization brought her to her knees on the hard earth floor. "He killed them, and Mr. Crondite, too."

The barn walls encroached, and a long-denied sob wrenched free.

"Abby?" In an instant, Fred knelt and held her like a child.

Gasping, she pointed to the buckle. "Ray killed a man. My parents, too. And my aunt. Now I see it all."

His bony shoulder muffled her wail. When her sobbing abated, she whispered, "How could I have been so ignorant?"

His tender eyes took her in. "Ignorance only means you dwelt in the dark. No shame in that, child." He reached for the coins.

"Now you have strength to reckon with the darkness."

Again, she sobbed while he held her. The old structure creaked in a strong pine wind, and somewhere, relentless woodpeckers bent to their endless task.

"But I have been so—so dim-witted."

"Once, I felt bedeviled, as though no good could ever come to me again. But Father found me and sent me to study with my uncle. Then God gave me Elda Mae. Ever so slowly, I came into my own."

They heard Elda Mae at the wagon, so he fitted the coins into the buckle and drew Abby outside. The Rim's sure presence proclaimed hope—she need never return here again.

In the arbor, peace descended, sending the shadows away. A clown woodpecker's familiar *rat-tat-tat* made Abby smile.

These simple surroundings sustained her until Elda Mae called supper—fresh cornbread, milk, and honey. Afterward, Fred produced Mr. Crondite's money.

"Some day you may need this, Abby."

"You said you still spy Cactus Joe's campfire at night. He deserves this."

"A good idea. I shall search him out tomorrow."

Imagining the trapper's surprise lulled Abby to sleep. Maybe now, he would stop seeking beautiful feathers.

The next morning Elda Mae sought a suitable recipe for two quails Fred brought home. "Ah yes; soak in salt brine—I already have. And use an abundance of herbs to mellow the wild taste and bring out the flavor. I have sent Fred to gather mushrooms—what a feast we will prepare!"

She lifted out one bird from her enamel pot, and with a *craaack*, sawed through the backbone. "I hid away a sack of rice he bartered for in Green Valley. Why not eat it today? Would you cut up this other quail while I brown these pieces?"

Sunshine glimmered through the foliage, and a morning breeze buoyed Abby. With each chop, she reminded herself how things had changed. The morning promised summery warmth, the garden was growing, and—

Chut chut—her turkey vulture nearly grazed her shoulder.

"Good morning to you, too."

Somehow, this vulture knew how to find her. She had been so distressed at the cabin, she had neglected to search for the feather, but Elda Mae threw her apron in the wash pile. She could still check.

Or perhaps she would let it go, along with her recollections of that awful night. "No more clinging to bad thoughts—I am strong and full of art."

A year had passed since Elda Mae and Fred made their way down the steep trail to the ranch. Not long afterward, Martin rode down that same path, and yesterday Abby had faced that cabin, that barn.

As she slashed away at the quail, Elda Mae's off-tune singing wafted. "I dream of Jeanie..."

Soon, heat would swell the afternoons, but one day, clouds would bring the monsoons. Rain would descend like Union troops reaching Poplar Bluff years ago.

"And with them came Martin. Meeting him again seems like a story Mr. Dickens would write." Two squirrels squabbled about something, drawing Abby's eyes upward.

"Surely he meant to return, but was ordered somewhere else. No more silly schoolgirl pining—dreaming of him was only a fiction. I have Elda Mae, Fred, and my sketching, and the Almighty to tend my heart."

A half-pail of water drenched the cutting board and darkened the wood grain. Soon it would dry, tempered that much more. The same applied to her—storms had toughened her until she stood strong.

Just last week, Fred sent one of her sketches to Mr. B, as she had taken to calling him, seeking remuneration for her work. Every successful sketch proved she could earn her own way. Astir with shadows and sunlight, the Rim summoned her once more.

"One of these days, I will indeed climb you, old Rim."

Less clean cut than Elda Mae's, her pieces of meat would taste the same. That was the secret—focus on the bright side.

"Maybe faith has finally found a foothold in me." The high pines soughed a benediction as Abby took the bowl inside.

Captain Whitaker and Martin devoured their beans and bacon. "Be careful, sergeant. You might break Abby's heart."

"But I have nothing to offer her."

A smack on the shoulder surprised him. "Just look at our fire. Air must flow for the kindling to catch, correct?"

"Sir?"

"We possess a God-given need for a mate. Present yourself, and if a fire kindles, so be it. We men fear rejection almost more than death, but such blows can be survived. I ought to know."

He settled beside the fire. "Do you know what ails you? You think too much."

"Right as always."

Murmuring pines breathed tranquility over their campsite. Captain Whitaker merely described what a grown man does when he loves someone—instead of running away like a scared farm boy, he faces her.

But contemplating the actual deed incited terror. *Present yourself.* Precisely the problem.

The captain tapped his pipe on a log. "You trust in divine guidance, sergeant. Even I find it difficult to believe no coincidence occurred when you found Abby here."

The fire sputtered and popped, and though Captain Whitaker finally held his peace, Martin knew he awaited a reply.

"Sir, I believe I have changed my mind about your job."

Captain Whitaker broke into a curious scowl.

"Instead of the sheriff, you ought to be the preacher."

"That deserves no reply at all. But changing the topic will do you no good." He pulled his hat over his face.

Musings inundated Martin. One moment, Abby rejoiced to see him, but the next, she turned away. Even first light brought no relief.

By midmorning, a gangly rider jockeyed their way. Martin recognized Fred and gave a shrill whistle.

"Why, sergeant, you gave me a start. You have come back not a moment too soon. Our Abby has watched and watched for you."

"She has recovered?"

"One would never know how much she suffered."

A relieved sigh escaped Martin's lips as the captain caught up. Good thing he hadn't heard what Fred said. Maybe Abby did watch for him, but only because this news would change her life.

"Ray is buried at Camp Verde."

Fred's eyes lit up. "Then we have reason to celebrate."

"How close are we to your place?"

The captain rode up and jostled Martin's elbow to remind him of his manners. "Fred, meet Captain Whitaker, my mainstay throughout the war."

Captain Whitaker saluted. "Pleased to make your acquaintance, Mr. Allen. What have you slung over your shoulder?"

"Mushrooms to accompany some quail the women are baking. You might think they knew company would arrive today."

"Lead the way." The Captain fell in beside Fred, leaving Martin to ponder his fate.

"Now, add greens, a handful of wild mustard and those winter onions."

Abby sprinkled chia seeds into the rice too, and awaited Elda Mae's reaction.

"Heavenly—try some."

Hooves throbbed in the distance, and the dust revealed more than one rider.

"Looks as though Fred came upon some visitors."

At the sight of cavalry blue, Abby's heart lurched. But a dashing officer with fine-boned features rode beside Fred, who spread his arms with a flourish.

"Ladies, meet Captain Whitaker, U.S. Cavalry. Sir, let me introduce my wife Elda Mae and Abby, our dear friend."

Elda Mae darted forward. "Welcome."

Just then a third rider, heavy-boned and sitting taller in the saddle, entered the yard. Abby's vision swirled and she grasped for the porch pole.

"Abby, look! Martin!"

Martin braced for Elda Mae's hug, but a *swoosh* refocused her attention.

"Oh my goodness, Abby must have fainted. Please carry her inside, Martin."

She turned to Captain Whitaker. "Such a shock—Martin saved her life, you know."

"Not at all surprising, ma'am."

Martin's heart rode his throat—had the mere sight of him distressed Abby? Captain Whitaker's teasing energized him. "Hang onto your heartstrings, sergeant."

"Fred, take the captain to wash up for dinner?"

Abby's flowered skirt fluttered in the breeze, just as it had months ago. Martin lowered his trembling arms and took in her soft lavender scent.

Chapter Thirty

"Delicious, ladies. A far cry from Army chow, I must say." Captain Whitaker puffed out his cheeks.

"Thank you. We might have baked a cake, had we known you were near."

"An impossibility to eat at this moment, madam." He gave a mischievous grin. "But perhaps a bit later."

Chagrined by her fainting spell, Abby hung back. Thankfully Elda Mae directed the conversation.

"Martin, tell us about your journeys."

"Captain Whitaker and I delivered the prisoner," he shifted toward Abby, "to General Crook at Camp Verde. You never need trouble yourself about him again, ma'am."

Abby's heart plummeted. He called her *ma'am*, as if they had just met.

"The Army holds him in custody?" Elda Mae covered Abby's hand with hers.

Seeing Abby's reaction, Martin stalled, so the Captain continued. "Mr. McHale suffered a mortal wound in an escape attempt." He raised his brows at Martin. "Sergeant Tolzmann aided greatly in the investigation, and General Crook himself insisted we bring you word."

Fred piped up. "So we can rest assured?"

Captain Whitaker washed his hands in the air. "We witnessed the burial party ourselves." He glanced at Martin. "And, I might say, McHale's wife Lola hastened his demise—saved the army the trouble of hanging him."

The pine wind picked up as a knot in Abby's midsection dissolved. Ray could never come near her again. But the mention of Lola made her cheeks burn. Martin knew about her—what must he think?

Meanwhile, Elda Mae demanded details. "She and that high-falutin' fellow made it all the way to Camp Verde in that slipshod buckboard?"

Captain Whitaker drank a large draught of milk. "Money lust can accomplish great feats. You have made Lola's acquaintance, then?"

"They rode in here one day—" Fred stopped midsentence at Elda Mae's terse look. "Please continue, Captain."

"Lola and her consort tried to help Ray escape, but a guard shot him. We also offer further evidence of the prisoner's lawlessness, Miss Abby." He handed her the envelope. "Having heard you were bound for this territory, your local marshal relayed this to General Crook, who entrusted it to us."

"Finally dear, word from your hometown. Gentlemen, thank you." Elda Mae reached for the empty platter. "Would anyone care for more?" Groans provided her answer.

"Then we shall take our coffee on the porch." She half-stood, then sat again. "Surely you will spend the night?"

Captain Whitaker shrugged, passing the decision to Martin.

"Be assured of our welcome." Elda Mae caught Abby's eye. "We can promise leftovers and maybe even a cake for supper."

Captain Whitaker chuckled. "That settles it."

"Why don't you show the captain around, Fred? Our coffee can wait."

"Come along, sir." Fred charged outside with Captain Whitaker close behind.

"Abby, would you see Martin to the porch? I will be out soon." But Abby bent her head and busied herself clearing the table.

"I ought to work off some of your fine meal, Mrs. Allen."

The haymow called to Martin. He had been right. Abby only wanted to know for sure that Ray would never bother her again, and had no interest in him otherwise. He kicked at some straw. "If only I could have told her sooner."

The dusty hay scent relieved the tightness compressing his chest. Plenty of work beckoned, and Fred looked even thinner than before. The pitchfork handle fit Martin's hand like an old work glove. He forked hay, shoveled the stalls, and distributed clean bedding. Then he carried several loads of water to the tank, but kept an eye out for Abby.

If she came, he would... what? Confess how much he had thought of her these past weeks? Hardly.

Back in the mow, he leaned against a post. The door hung open, giving a bird's eye view of Pine Creek. The familiar landscape brought a lump to his throat. So much had taken place here. If only... But that could never be. Abby fainted at the sight of him, and now seemed distant. He had presented himself, but no flame kindled. He chewed a dry stem and firmed his will to accept the truth.

But corralling his anxious thoughts might not be so easy. When he placed her on Elda Mae's bed this afternoon, her eyes had shuttered open. As she regained her senses, a light burned there. Did she recognize him?

"Ach—I must forget my selfish dreams."

But what would Abby do if he strode into the cabin and invited her for a walk? No, she probably pored over the contents of the Poplar Bluff marshal's letter right now—yet more disconcerting news.

Fleeing to Wyoming Territory might make more sense than going into business with Captain Whitaker. At least there, he could help Meta and her new husband with their ranch. Lost in conjecture, he hardly heard the door creak open.

"Martin?"

He peered down. Elda Mae, her face flushed with afternoon heat. "Ma'am?"

"Thank you for helping Fred, Martin. His lungs have suffered another bout since you left, but Abby has been such a comfort to us."

Martin descended the ladder.

"You saved her life. Even her limp has disappeared now. Your prayers helped as much as my ministrations." Elda Mae flopped on a hay bale and clasped her hands. "I do hope you will visit us again?"

"Depends on my orders. The army will soon be sending troops north to the Powder River. But Captain Whitaker and I might not stay in the cavalry."

"When does your commitment end?"

"In late winter."

Elda Mae pursed her lips. "Would you return to Iowa, then?"

"No, but the captain has the idea of starting a trading post in these parts."

Her eyes popped.

"He thinks we could succeed, if I supplied meat and produce—"

"Oh my—what a joy to contemplate a dream."

"I wish I knew how all the pieces fit together."

"In Green Valley last fall, we met a man desiring to homestead on this side of the Rim. What about building a trading post here?" Her earnest eyes glimmered in the dim light. "Such rocky soil, but some meadows look promising."

He remained quiet. No use voicing his constant questions about the future. "Martin, I must ask you something." She lowered her voice. "Do you hope for a family some day?"

His shirt neck felt far too tight. "I have little to offer a wife. Army pay is mighty slim."

"But if your plans work out," she touched his sleeve, "your labor would provide. And living out here, you would certainly need a wife."

Could she read his mind like General Crook? Her visage revealed only concern, and her quiet tone bade him lean closer.

"A young woman would be fortunate to find a husband like you. I doubt you see your own strengths."

After waiting in vain for his reply, she went on. "You possess two important qualities. A man is known by his kindness and honesty. When these are present, a woman needs no fortune in silver or material goods."

Something niggled at Martin's chest. He reckoned Mama would say the same.

Elda Mae fluted her apron between two fingers. "Abby thinks the world of you."

The space between them suddenly shrank, and sweat coursed Martin's neck. He tried to clear his throat.

"Did you want to say something?"

He did—would Abby consider him a proper suitor? But he could scarcely form the thought, much less voice the words.

His hostess waited. Straw dust sifted onto her dress from above.

"You have done so much for Abby, and for us." She laced her fingers. "We would be thrilled to have you settle nearby."

The moments dragged, and she brushed her skirt. Phrases formed and reformed, but turned to ashes in Martin's throat.

Elda Mae sighed. At last, she stood. "A woman who sees hard times begins to doubt that honorable men still exist. I experienced that years and years ago." She paused, but his throat constricted. "Whatever happens, you have given Abby hope."

The swish of her skirt muffled other sounds, and the door creaked as his stammer broke loose. "Would she—?"

But she heard nothing, and left Martin alone with the animals. He tilted his head toward the rafters, where captured prey filled cobwebbed corners—flies, moths, bees, and wasps. He banged his fist on his knee.

"I might as well be one of those bugs up there."

You have done so much . You have given Abby hope.

Light slanted from the peak. Confound it all. What he had done could never be enough.

Abby slid a pan of buttermilk-colored dough into the oven and wandered to her bedroom. Marshal Tibbets' envelope waited on her bed, but she wavered.

On any other afternoon, she would be peeking at Fred's woodpecker sketch. He called this species "Hairy," with puffy feathers covering its slightly elongated head. He had such a great capacity for simple joys.

To think, I have the privilege of cataloguing the winged creatures, even naming some of them!

In the arbor, their prime hairy specimen extracted insects, but her desire to sketch had fled. Besides, her stomach bothered her— maybe a walk would help. Halfway across the yard, she nearly crashed into Elda Mae.

"You have the cake in the oven already?" Elda Mae eyed her askance. "What troubles you, dear?"

"My digestion—often, a walk helps."

"You can go about freely now—what a relief. If you don't mind, we could use some fresh salad greens." She fetched a basket from the porch, but stalled in handing it over. "Dear, I must ask you something very personal. Please take no offense."

"After all you have done for me?"

"But this is—quite private. Sit down with me."

Porch steps warmed by the sun welcomed them, and Elda Mae lost no time. "Captain Whitaker and Martin might settle down here and start a trading post."

"They would leave the army?"

"So it seems. Has it occurred to you that... Oh, I might as well spit it out. Could Providence have a plan for you and Martin—that is, more than friendship?"

"How can I ever be sure? Besides, Martin only carries out his duty."

Elda Mae angled her head, and Abby pecked her on the cheek. "Mama always told me to trust."

Going down the path, Abby chuckled. "Here I am, advising Elda Mae. My, how things do turn around!" She stooped to pick an early daisy.

Around the bend, a patch of dandelion and plantain relished afternoon sun, even though a few days ago, snow covered this terrain. *Such a glorious afternoon—if only Martin...* She gritted her teeth. Just last night, she determined to be done with him.

"I can hardly believe he came, but if we cannot talk to each other —" She stamped her foot. "And that silly fainting spell. I have never fainted. What came over me?"

A sudden breeze loosed a willful curl from its pins. *Let this go— stop trying to understand. Thinking does no good, so why not enjoy the sunshine?* A distance from the cabin, she settled on a rock. The pine wind offered its gentle presence, but soon, clouds enveloped the Rim.

In spite of the news about Ray, thoughts of a hopeless future beset her. Leaning back, she squeezed her eyes against haunting recollections of her folly.

"I ought to rejoice and celebrate." The sun found her again, and she drifted until a distressed cry floated from somewhere. She wielded her basket as if woven grass could protect her.

Then a patch of blue appeared over the rise, and she shaded her eyes to see Captain Whitaker racing her way, red-faced. He was yelling something. A moment passed before Abby understood.

"Bees!" But no swarm pursued him. When he paused near her, panting, she grinned.

"I believe you lost them."

He stared at her wide-eyed and glanced back.

"Maybe you ought to sit down for a while."

He wiped his dripping forehead with his sleeve. "Fighting Indians did nothing to prepare me for this."

"Where is Fred?"

"He seems fearless with those bees."

"He has a way with them."

"We trekked all the way to your... Ah, to the ranch. Did you know Martin sneaked down to milk your cows when we stalked your... ah, *our* prisoner?"

"Really?"

"Their bellowing troubled him, but when he and a private relieved them, they found more than they bargained for." A storytelling glint filled his eyes.

"What happened?"

"Some Indian warriors clubbed his partner and captured Martin. But he escaped, using his wits and ingenuity."

"I never knew Indians to cross the ranch."

He changed the subject. "I take it bees like the color blue."

Picturing the scene with him and Fred, she giggled.

"After embarrassing myself, I should regale you with my exploits."

"You survived the war."

"Yes, Martin and I pulled through together. On another tack, I imagine fresh honey and cream will taste good with that cake? Can we hold Elda Mae to her word?

"She is watching it right now." Two young mule deer sauntered up the slope. "I love their big ears."

"They sometimes snoop around our campfire." Captain Whitaker bit his lip. "Pardon my presumption, but the streaks on your face speak of tears. Might I help?"

Abby brushed her hot cheekbones. "Right now, my worst trouble lurks within."

"Ma'am?"

Her groan erupted unbidden.

"Perhaps I can relate, since I once lost my beloved to another man. Even though that time is long past, I always wonder if I had been more attentive..." His voice drifted off.

"Surely, you will find another."

"God willing. Martin and I talk of establishing a business. With him for a partner, we would succeed—he is one of the finest soldiers I know."

Abby's heart beat faster.

"In grave danger, he proves utterly courageous—I could relate plenty of stories. But when it comes to—shall we say, *etiquette,* he never learned that side of things, especially with women."

"You mean dancing and such?"

"That, and even how to make conversation. None of his battlefield bravery attends him in social situations." The captain rubbed his chin. "Like me with those bees, I guess."

Yes, Martin was an awkward sort—who could forget those shovels clattering back in Papa's store? Yet he did her chores and stayed by her bedside, calling her from the brink of death.

"The question is not what you look at, but what you see."

"Why, that is from Thoreau—Papa used to read his work."

"Yes, his journal of August, 1851."

When she was about to ask his exact meaning, Fred's floppy straw hat bobbed into sight. He toted a heavy pine knot dripping with honey, and the captain hurried to heft the load. With a lighter heart, Abby began her search for greens.

Chapter Thirty-one

"**W**hy does General Crook insist on sending the clans to reservations?" With the cake, Elda Mae served whipped cream and her candid opinions.

Throughout the meal, Abby willed Martin to look her way. When he finally did, the tops of his ears flamed.

Aha—just as Captain Whitaker said—he is bashful. When she sent him an encouraging smile, he wrinkled his brow. Just then, a hairy woodpecker assaulted a pine outside the window, and he glanced out.

She tucked this away for later, to bring up if she had a chance. No—she would *create* a chance.

"The general believes in wearing down the tribes little by little. His men spend whole nights on narrow ledges to catch them cooking their mescal in long narrow pits lined with rocks. In high desert country, they eat some of this agave cactus and dry the rest, like we do with our jerky."

Elda Mae beamed as Martin massed another huge scoop of cream on his cake. She produced seconds for both soldiers, but stuck to her viewpoint.

"That sounds unkind to me."

"Try to put yourself in his place, ma'am. No matter how he sympathizes with the natives, history has him trapped. Settlers will only increase here, but the tribes will never stop fighting for their homelands. Better to nip their heels and drive them away than endure continuing bloodshed."

"Maybe at least some will survive." Elda Mae slid another piece of cake onto Fred's plate, and he broke into the conversation.

"Dear, this cake is by far your finest."

"Abby baked it for us."

"You did?" Martin's contribution deepened his violent blush.

"Yes, I used Mama's recipe." Speechlessness overtook him again, so Captain Whitaker leaped in.

"After this fine fare, we had better run up and down the Rim. Martin, what say we do the dishes before we make camp?"

"Oh no, my job."

Fred joined in with Elda Mae. "And we insist you sleep in the haymow tonight. The air gets so chilly nowadays."

"We can all sit on the porch later, but Fred, why not show Captain Whitaker your latest work? And Abby, would you mind fetching more water?"

"I can do that." Martin jumped to his feet and left without a word.

"He was such a help to us when Abby was ill, Captain." Elda Mae turned to Abby. "We also need to turn the herb bags in the side yard, dear. Would you mind?"

Rounding the porch corner, Abby crossed paths with Martin. He met her eyes, so she shored up her courage.

"Such a beautiful evening. Would you like to stroll down the path?"

Without a word, he hurried to take the water inside and fell in step with her. Around them, rustlings hinted of nocturnal animals waking, and after a few moments, Abby broke the silence.

"Did you notice those woodpeckers making all that racket during supper?"

Martin nodded.

"They make regular rows along the back of the cabin, too. To them, wood is wood, I presume."

He cleared his throat, but made no reply.

"Do you recall seeing them in *Birds of America?*"

"My recollection fails me, but I do recollect that you read it, too."

"Yes. Now Fred lets me sketch them, and the turkey vulture, as well. My mother started me sketching when I was young, but I gave it up when…" Abby's voice trailed off, and silence accompanied them until Martin gathered his courage.

"On the Rim path yesterday, a turkey vulture swooped low, like an escort. I knew we must be almost here—they sure seem to like this valley."

"One night last summer when I felt so melancholy, a vulture grazed the porch and left me a feather. Does that sound far-fetched?"

"Why no, a feather is a feather."

Such a simple, comforting answer—maybe she hadn't imagined what happened, after all. At the wagon path, they turned back.

Halfway to the cabin, Martin offered, "Thank heaven you can live at peace now. What Ray did to you—" He cleared his throat again. "I never met such a man—he even attacked Captain Whitaker."

"That scar along his jaw?"

"Right. The Captain took him a blanket, and Ray struck him with his handcuffs. The whole way to Camp Verde, he kept making things worse for himself—I never could understand him."

"You tried?"

"A snowstorm hit us on the trail. He was suffering, but showed his cussedness over and over. Then, when he attacked Captain Whitaker, I—" Martin's voice trembled. "The Captain and I—he saw me through so much during the war—saw all of us through."

"It must have been so difficult for you to see him hurting like that."

"Yeah. McHale's—Ray's attack made me want to kill him, when a short time before, his condition had touched me."

"Oh, I understand! All these years, I kept thinking something would change him and expected to see some spark of goodness."

Martin took a deep breath. "I—regret how long it took to bring you word."

"I felt certain the army must have prevented you, and had given up. So it was a shock to see you." Chuckling, Abby paused in the path. "And you had to carry me all over again. Honestly, I have never fainted before."

The last daylight shards lit Martin's soft smile. "It was my pleasure. At least this time, I had no fear for your life."

"Elda Mae told me how you brought me here and prayed for me. How can I ever repay you?" A bit of straw fell when she touched his sleeve.

"I was so afraid you—" His voice broke. "But you survived." In encroaching twilight, he croaked. "You are happy here?"

"I keep busy sketching. Fred and Elda Mae treat me like a daughter, and now I know Ray will never return."

Longing swept through her as she touched Martin's hand, and suddenly, the evening seemed cool. But he kept his arms tight at his sides.

"Thank you for this walk. I have missed you, Martin." In the last of daylight his lips twitched, but he only nodded. Abby started up the cabin steps. "Good night, then."

He murmured something, but made no move as she slipped inside.

"What do you mean, Abby has no interest in you?" At their campsite *en route* to Camp Reno, Captain Whitaker scrutinized Martin. Beside them, the Maztazals ranged over a natural spring flowing from sheer red rock.

"I stuttered the whole time. She could never be—"

"Hogwash, to borrow one of your terms. Didn't you say she asked you to walk? And I witnessed her tears when she said good-bye. They meant nothing to you?"

Muteness overtook Martin as Captain Whitaker gave a great sigh. "What did you talk about?"

"She thanked me for finding her, and I tried to think of something to say."

The Captain drummed on his boot with a stick. "You absented yourselves from our company for quite some time."

"She told me about her new life—sketching with Fred keeps her happy."

"Slim companionship on cold nights, I reckon." Captain Whitaker spat into the fire. "But what matters is how you felt."

"Why, I wanted to—hold her hand and tell her..." Martin would gladly forfeit a month's pay to end this discussion.

"She loves you. I see it as clearly as this campfire, but only you can declare yourself." The captain pulled on his ear lobe. "You must not feel lonely enough yet."

Martin's ears rang. They both jumped when an elk trumpeted nearby, although mating season passed long ago.

Captain Whitaker guffawed. "Sergeant, maybe there's hope for you yet."

Martin sought his bedroll, but it brought little solace.

A horrific Rebel yell surged through the Tennessee woods, and Martin fired in tandem with the private next to him. One Confederate soldier fell, but his comrade, a slender young man, propelled forward like a cannon ball.

The private whacked the soldier in the temple, and blood flowed from the wounded man's ear. But he still managed three final words.

"Maudie... oh... no."

Another bevy of shots peppered them as more Rebels exploded through the woods. Finally the noise subsided into tenuous silence, and Captain Whitaker broke through the line.

"Cease fire, men. Take prisoners." He drew Martin aside. "Our troops secured the wagon bridge over the Appomattox, and the fight has moved to Virginia, a place called Farmville. The sooner we get out of here, the better."

The sprawled Reb bodies were mostly young men who ought to be home planting crops. In waning light, two privates helped Martin check the fallen. This appalling task never changed, but some wounded soldier might still be breathing.

Something drew him to the ones he and the private had felled an hour earlier. His heart wrenched at the delicate stature of one—not much more than a boy. Then the soldier's cap slipped, a swatch of light brown hair swarmed out, and eyes as brown as Meta's fixed on him. A girl.

With her last breath, her voice trickled out. "Samuel. My brother."

Under Martin's grimy fingers, her pulse ceased. In that moment, the sorrows of the last months amassed beneath his collarbone. This girl might be Meta or Lissa—and he had killed her.

Through a blur, he gathered her hair under her cap. He felt those silky tresses even now. Her narrow arched nose matched that of the young Confederate nearby. Brother and sister, their futures dashed into this verdant Tennessee soil.

Too weary to rise, Martin bowed his head.

"Sergeant, Private Kelly needs you over there." Martin gathered his senses and followed the messenger across the knoll—nothing to do but continue on.

But tonight under the starry Arizona Territory sky, that girl's face emerged and he woke gasping. The pressure of Captain Whitaker's hand warmed his shoulder.

"Martin?"

Freed from a cloud, the moon revealed the mountains' massive black bulk as Martin fought for control.

"Tell me your torment." Captain Whitaker pulled up a log and fed the fire.

"Sir—"

"Could we do away with the *sir*?" Dark color creased the captain's eyes.

"Yes, sir. Oh. Sorry."

"Does your night terror concern that Tennessee skirmish near the end of the campaign?"

"Why—how did you know?"

"The engagement still haunts me, too. That one soldier I shot..." He stared into the fire. "Why is it so much harder to accept a dead woman than a man?"

Martin's head spun. "That girl—?"

"Yes. I shot her."

"No." Martin found his voice. "I did, and I closed her eyes, so like my sister Meta's." Captain Whitaker's jaw dropped as a torrent gushed from his stalwart sergeant. Finally, the storm subsided in the questions that taunted Martin by night.

"I took that girl's life. She can never be a wife or mother." He despised this blubbering, but could not cease. "How can I ever take a wife?"

"This must be some vile comedy, sergeant. All this time I have regretted pulling the trigger. That particular soldier seemed hell-bent, I got a bead on him, and—"

"Begging your pardon, but so did I. Private Lumley killed her brother with his rifle butt. He called out *Maudie* as he fell."

Setting the coffee pot in the fire, Captain Whitaker replied. "Only Solomon's wisdom will do tonight, Martin. You and I must split the guilt. Otherwise, you call me a liar, and I you."

Though the Captain was not one to spout Scripture, the story of King Solomon's advice to two women fighting over a child rang in Martin's head. The king instructed his men to cut the child in half to satisfy both women. Of course, the true mother's refusal revealed the other's deception.

Share the guilt—how could that be? As Martin pondered, a horse's hooves pounded and someone yelled, "Whoa!" before leaping to the earth just outside the circle of light from their fire.

"Our Abby is gone."

Fred—what was he doing here?

Captain Whitaker took charge, as usual. "What do you mean, gone?"

White-faced, Fred stumbled toward him. "We searched the cabin, the barn, and down the road. Oh, thank God I found you." He bent over to catch his breath, and

Martin grasped his thin shoulder.

"Take a minute. You have been riding hard."

Gradually, Fred's wheezing came under control, and his hands ceased twitching.

Captain Whitaker's voice turned business-like. "Have some coffee and tell us what happened."

"I worked out in the arbor last evening while Elda Mae busied herself with her herbs. We thought Abby was sketching in the cabin, but when Elda Mae went in, we—"

"Any tracks?"

"Only one set. Maybe someone stole through the trees and sneaked in when... I will never forgive myself if—" Fred's eyes flooded. "Please, please help us find her."

Ray's angry visage hovered before Martin as if he had risen from the dead. Emotions swirled. General Crook sent Lola and her partner to Kansas, but what if...?

Captain Whitaker fastened on his gun belt and strode beyond the campsite. His head drooped as always when he contemplated a plan, and he rubbed his left ear.

Fred's thin fingers flew in a nervous dance. "Do you believe—?"

"Captain Whitaker needs time to think." Martin poured Fred some more coffee. "Drink this while I take care of your horse. By then, the captain will have devised a strategy."

Fred obeyed. Faces passed before him—that slain Tennessee girl, the Indian woman he found dying, and Abby. Then Lola's appeared, and he felt certain of her kidnappers.

He packed up their bedrolls and saddled Docker. Soon, Fred had caught his breath.

As always, Captain Whitaker's policy issued clear and crisp. "You must ride home the way you came, Fred. Be prepared to use your gun. These scoundrels are spitting on the mercy General Crook showed them."

Fred fingered his weapon.

"Martin and I will search the trails, but you and Elda Mae must still keep close watch."

"You—you will find her?"

Martin replied for them both. "We will."

As soon as Fred took off, the Captain saddled up. "What do

you say we follow the escarpments back toward that hidden trail McHale built?"

"Makes sense to me."

Hours later, a line of sumac in full autumn brilliance fringed the Rim's folds. Captain Whitaker halted and gestured at some fresh tracks.

"McHale must have told Lola and Aldrich about the wagon road. Foolhardy to traverse with less than a heavy wagon, but their money lust is driving them."

The path revealed fresh indentations, careening imprints showing only two mules pulling a light vehicle. Lightning zigzagged Martin's temple—these fools could easily crash down the Rim side.

"Chances are, McHale told Lola some half-baked story about a money stash, and said Abby knows the location. Maybe Lola told him about meeting her at the Allens', and this represents one final stab at her. Otherwise, why would they bother with her?"

Martin heaved a sigh. It was all about money.

"Did you ride this path when you crossed the Rim from the cattle camp?"

"No, farther north, near those bighorn sheep." Martin pointed to patches of white in the distance. "Why would they come this far south?"

"Maybe they mixed up the directions, but more likely, Ray led them astray on purpose. Even dying men cling to their gold."

"Believe me, the girl knows where he hid the money."

The sizzling fire covered much of Aldrich and Lola's conversation, but Abby strained her ears. In the end, she made out enough to guess her fate.

"Tell me Ray's precise words."

"I told you six times." Lola's voice ground in the thin night air. *"Take the wagon path beyond the pasture to where some large boulders form a cross. Turn due south, and you'll find the stash off to the left, in a cave-like depression."*

"If she holds till noon tomorrow and no cross shows up, I say we shoot her and hightail it out of this hellhole."

Abby gritted her teeth—a wagon path right in their pasture?

"Leave this damnable place without Ray's stash? Over my dead body!"

Lola looked half the woman who had held Elda Mae's fragile teacup a few weeks back. But even with her black hair now washed-out orange and her bustle ripped off, the fire in her eyes remained the same.

Sympathy stole over Abby. Ray had cheated and betrayed her, too. Under different circumstances, she might ask how he managed to hoodwink her.

Granny Ferguson's tone, grainy as a hen's cackle, floated through the mist. "A red-haired woman brings bad luck, child." Her notions may have contained some truth, after all.

Strong and full of art.

Ever since Mr. Aldrich sneaked behind her on the porch two evenings back, a odd, serene sensation had claimed Abby. Even though her heart went wild at first, she realized that her hope lay in compliance.

"Grab some food. Hurry. If you scream—" He prodded her with his gun, so she took bread and ham from the side cooler, grabbed blankets and followed him. Elda Mae might appear any moment and point the shotgun in his face, but he timed his visit just right.

Up on the road, Lola gave her a royal welcome. "You little hussy—married to my husband, ha! You will regret it, I swear."

Under her breath, Abby sputtered. "I have been sorry for a long time."

Aldrich tied her in the back and drove east. The rough wagon side reminded Abby of the porch wall at the ranch. How many times had she leaned there as the sun's reflection turned the world rosy gold while Ray worked with his figures?

Peculiar, the tranquility that attended her as the wagon jolted back and forth. Her only concern was for Elda Mae and Fred when they discovered her missing. *Don't let them follow us. Please keep them safe.*

As she prayed, yet another view of the Rim opened up. Maybe Fred was right. "Mr. Emerson says, *Every artist was once an amateur. But you have been given special sight, Miss Abby.*"

If only she had thought to grab the sketchbook he supplied her. Straying through this land like a mighty river, the Rim defined everything in sight. Now, she finally saw the jutting crag mimicked on the west side each morning as sunshine shooed shadows down over the valley.

With a more complete view of Strawberry Mountain from this vantage point, the whole picture clarified, and Fred's latest Scripture reading instructed her.

Now we see through a glass, darkly, but then face to face: now I know in part; but then shall I know even as also I am known.

As twilight thickened the shadows, she assured herself. "Surely Fred will fetch Martin and Captain Whitaker."

After a day of her captors demanding answers, they finally left her alone. Forest bordered their camp on all sides. Once Aldrich and Lola slept, she could roll a distance away, then a little farther. But mountain lions hunted these slopes at night, and wolves.

Best to bide her time and rest for tomorrow. Perhaps Martin and the Captain already had sniffed out their slipshod trail. Martin's countenance hovered near when Abby closed her eyes. He rescued her before, when she had even less control over her fate. In that assurance, a mellow pine wind wooed her to sleep.

Chapter Thirty-two

Late the next day, with little progress before making camp again, a couple of cowpokes approached Aldrich and Lola. "What you folks doin' out here?"

"Joy riding, whadd'ya think?" Lola lanced her reply as an older fellow straggled into camp.

"Ma'am." The younger one raised his hat to reveal coal black hair. "There's somethin' you oughta know. Old Sam here busted broncs down at Fort Grant before General Crook's time." He kicked at the red dirt.

"We jest crossed from Fort Craig on the *Journada del Muerto—the day's journey of the dead man*. Quicksand claimed our other partner, but we passed on through Fort McRae's ruins to the Mimbres Mountains to Cow Springs and Fort Cummings.

"At the Apache Pass in the Chiracahuas, Injuns attacked. That was only the first two hundred miles. Old Sam here needs a few minutes' rest while I scout out a campsite. By times, he thinks hisself back on a bronc, and might be prone to do some bustin'. *Comprende?*"

Aldrich answered. "Do share our humble meal, sir."

"Thank you kindly." The cowpoke disappeared, and his white-haired partner neared the fire. His brittle knees creaked as he sank onto a log. Aldrich hastened to fill a coffee mug.

"Never dreamed to meet a real bronco buster. My wife will fetch you some food, and I would be delighted to hear tales of your work, Mister Sam."

From the shadows, Lola launched Aldrich a malicious scowl.

Old Sam spat into the fire before testing his voice. "Waall, m' rowels was wide as m' hand. Had a mesquite club fit t' fell a ox."

Lola hissed at Abby. "Get that mangy old scum some supper."

"Broncs look up atcha first, with their feet bunched up like they's yer pal. Oncet, one shnookered me into thinkin' them Californee sellers tricked us with a dowcile horse. But once m' rowels spurred 'im in th' flank, thet mane and tail flew. Et' sand ever single time—cain't bust a bronc 'thout fallin' off at least oncet."

He lunged into the meager food Abby set before him. Under a haze of whiskers, his fine-boned features and the musical rhythm of his speech intrigued her, but Lola retired to her bedroll.

Old Sam's images of life on the San Pedro came alive, and once again, Abby longed for her sketching tools. When the scraggly fellow's comrade returned, and they took their leave, she paid attention to their direction. Aldrich claimed his bedroll, so did she.

A full moon lent a mystical aura to the night. Old Sam had brought Cactus Joe to mind. She sat up, and the glint of a campfire in the distance fueled her hopes.

The moonlight made it possible to walk tonight. Without a sound, she gathered her blanket around her, and with every step, her resolve steeled. Why wait for someone to save her?

"Hey Missy, where do you think you're going?" Lola had stalked her.

"To relieve myself." She pretended to do so and headed back toward camp with the best of Granny Ferguson's predictions keeping her company.

Strong and full of art.

A cool night breeze belied this present danger, and confidence settled down inside. This attempt may have failed, but Lola could not stay awake all night.

An abandoned buckboard, its tongue tangled hopelessly with torn harness, claimed Martin and Captain Whitaker's consideration. Ranging beyond, hoof prints squiggled a wary line up the Rim side.

"Two mules, three riders. At least they let Abby ride—shows they see her value."

"But she knows nothing."

"McHale must have convinced them that she does."

Fear ricocheted through Martin. His desire to wrench the outlaws' necks sweltered as he followed his partner. But at least last night's fireside conversation had somewhat freed his mind.

For years, the two of them had suffered the same terrifying memory. Captain Whitaker would never deceive him about this, not even to relieve his anguish. In spite of Martin's intense apprehension concerning Abby, a massive weight had lifted. What an idea—sharing the guilt for killing that girl who had followed her brother to war.

About half an hour later, they froze behind a boulder at sounds wafting down the trail. More than one traveler, one of them telling singsong tales.

"Make it halfway t' Verde by tomorra night, I s'peculate. Last time we went thataway, we give them Injuns the slip—"

"Mem'ry serves y' well, Sam. Confusin' them Injuns musta been our best trick ever."

"Jest like we done with that fancified feller yesterdee. Now, we jest gotta figger how t' gitcha where youse goin', Miss—"

"What in thunder?" Captain Whitaker bounded into the path. "Who goes there?"

A wizened man came into view, with legs so bowed he had trouble walking. His comrade, half his age, held a shotgun at the ready. Between them, Abby picked her way down the incline. Martin's heart nearly bolted the confines of his shirt.

The men failed to hear the captain, but Abby did. Her expression—what was written there? Something different from the last time Martin saw her. When she spotted him, her countenance fairly glowed.

On the path atop the Rim, Martin dared a glance down at Abby's fingers, tight around his waist. He imagined delight on her features at all of this beauty.

"Whoa, Docker." He twisted back. "We should stop here a while to spell Docker." Careful not to disrupt her skirts, he slid off and held out his hand. His pulse catapulted at her touch.

Abby's eyes met his. "Thank you. Here I am, causing you trouble again."

"Trouble?" He must look daft, but bumbled on. "No trouble at all."

"You could never imagine how I have longed to climb up here and see what's on the other side. Every day at the ranch, I watched the sun rise on the western rim, right over there. About an hour later, the light finally traveled down to the cabin. When Ray was gone, I would sit on the porch and study how the two sides worked together.

"Then with a whole new view at Elda Mae and Fred's—" She touched his sleeve. "Thanks to you—my curiosity grew even more. Now, you have rescued me once more, and here I am on the Rim."

Her smile nearly broke his heart.

"This reminds me of the kaleidoscopes Papa used to order at the store. So many possibilities in such a small contrivance. Up here, all I see are possibilities, too, but in such a grand space."

The sparkle in her eyes mesmerized Martin. If only he could think what to say, but Abby seemed not to mind. She skirted some Manzanita bushes and disappeared, so he turned his attention to Docker.

"Hey, boy. Still finding some good grass up here, eh?" A yearling elk stuck its nose through some Manzanita bushes, reminding him of Captain Whitaker's prodding.

"Bugling for a mate this late in the season—maybe there's still hope for you."

Could that be true? The gurgling stream calmed Martin's

impossible heartbeat. With ten shades of green carpeting the valley, this day was made for an artist like Abby. She returned with lightness in her step, and more of Captain Whitaker's joshing came to mind.

"Don't be Miles Standish, too timid to say what you feel. Remember, this second chance might not allow for a third."

A few minutes later, Abby slipped beside him. "Oh, Martin. How could anything ever be more lovely?"

Words tumbled forth. "Something could be."

Her brow puckered—too late to retreat.

"I mean some*one*."

Her stare did nothing to ease his angst.

"I—I mean you."

A flush crept over her cheeks as a territorial-sized lump lodged in Martin's throat. But it was now or never. Before him stretched endless lonely years.

Another sharp declaration roared in his soul, *You must not be lonely enough yet.*

But I am. I *am!* Still, Abby's closeness struck terror in his heart. Finding her had already made this day momentous, but then the captain ordered him to return her home.

"Listen to Dr. Samuel Johnson, children. 'To improve the golden moment of opportunity, and catch the good that is within our reach, is the great art of life.'"

So Mama was whispering to him at such a momentous time—*to catch the good within our reach.* Well, now he'd plunged in, and there was only one way to know if this great good truly lay within his reach. Abby stood absolutely still, her eyes wide and dark. If only he possessed Captain Whitaker's way with words.

"What I mean is, nothing could be lovelier than you." Martin breathed again, and waved his arm over the scene below. "Not even—" Sweltering heat overtook him as Abby stepped closer.

"Not even?"

"Not anything in this whole wide world."

Chapter Thirty-three

Just after Martin declared her lovely, Abby's stomach growled, and her giggle lightened the moment. "Sounds like a bear on the prowl."

"Not so long ago, we were hoping and praying you would feel hungry again."

"Elda Mae said you prayed for me."

Martin held up his hands. "What man could disobey her?"

Abby's laugh embraced the expanse around them. "She said you and the captain talk of building a trading post? Of course, Elda Mae could never keep a secret."

Ideas spun in Martin's head, and before he knew it, he had shared everything, even his fears. "Neither of us has experience in that sort of work." He shrugged. "But with Captain Whitaker at the helm, we might find success."

"He told me he feels the same about you. You could use all you learned on the farm. Mule trains bring the Allens' mail to Green Valley, but Fred has to fetch it. Having a closer trading post would mean so much."

"I expect so, but getting supplies would be the challenge. Your father surely counted on better roads for his deliveries, and trains from out East?"

Perched on a rock, Abby took a bite of Martin's hardtack. "Usually they came from St. Louis, but late arrivals frustrated him, and sometimes companies sent the wrong items." She searched the area as a gigantic bird swooped low.

"Life has taught me that nothing this side of heaven can be

totally reliable. But if we demanded a guarantee, we would never try anything new."

All the things Martin wanted to say melded in his throat. He wanted to declare, *Oh Abby, I would never fail you if it were in my power.* "You have endured such guile and unfaithfulness, but still show such spirit.

His clamped lips ignited a fire in his gut, and Abby's sigh wrenched him through.

"How can I ever thank you for this time up here, Martin?"

If only he could speak, he would declare, *I know a way, if you could think to marry me.*

But he sat there mute. With a rhythmic *whirr,* the vulture took flight. That wild creature did with ease what nature intended—why could he not do the same?

A late butterfly drew Abby to her feet. "See over there? Elda Mae took me to that meadow the other day, where Indian women used to hunt herbs. I simply must come up here again."

He almost said, *No—not alone.* But she had no need for a man to set her boundaries even out of love. Yes, *love.* The word echoed through the far reaches of Martin's being.

Suddenly she flitted to a boulder at the Rim's far edge, where tall pines appeared twenty feet lower because of the steep angle. "Martin, come here! Why, I believe this area ought to be called a canyon instead of a valley. What do you think?"

He scratched his head. "Strawberry Mountain on one side, the Rim on the other, and no outlet."

"I had no idea that several canyons funnel up to the Verde from the south. Those peaks beyond must be the Maztazals?"

"Yes. Did you come here that way?"

"Cactus Joe wasn't much for explaining, but I believe so." She fluttered in the other direction. "Everything between Strawberry Mountain and the Rim forms Pine Creek Canyon. How do you like the sound of that?"

"Fred's penchant for naming has worn off on you."

"Maybe so. It will take weeks to believe I didn't dream this."

The redness of her lips against teeth so white—Martin held himself together, but barely. When a sudden shadow fell over them, Abby glanced around.

"Every afternoon I watch these shadows announce the beginning of evening, starting here and working down."

Again, Martin's tongue and throat united against him.

"This Rim is like my life, what folks call a hardscrabble journey, with the sun rising in the west and setting in the east. But maybe after all, there has been a purpose."

She clapped her hand over her mouth and her eyebrows rose. Had something frightened her?

"What is it?"

"After Mama, Papa, and Aunt Susan died, a preacher once told me Providence still had a purpose for me. But I threw a teacup at the door after he left. I was still dreadfully impatient. Now I would beg Pastor Fox's pardon if I could."

The shadow encroached even more, but sunshine still lent gold to her hair. "I never imagined the Rim top being so wide. I pictured it narrow and steep, but there's plenty of room, and now I see how the path runs."

Martin followed her gaze. Fortunately, no ambulances or supply trains interrupted them.

"We could watch the sunset from here—another time, of course. Oh, I would so like to see the sun rise and set again!"

The longing in her eyes wooed him. He breathed in a hint of lavender, even after these days out in the wild. Possibilities beckoned—picnics in this place, sunsets to watch, and an even closer view of the stars.

But the shadows nipped their feet now. Abby cinched her brows. "I suppose we ought to start down?"

"Probably so."

With every step of the descent, Martin chided himself for his slowness of tongue. *Captain Whitaker will have my neck if I say nothing.* Halfway down, he halted Docker in hazy violet shadows, and Abby went off the trail for a moment.

She had walked away from her captors in the wee hours before dawn, and conquered her memories of the fateful horse ride when Ray almost ended her life. Her spirit put him to shame. In spite of her pale thinness when he rode into the ranch almost a year ago, she had become vibrant—her strength rivaled Mama's.

Near the trail's end, a sudden recollection gripped him of soldiers playing "correo el gallo" or *run the chicken*, torturing the helpless creature to a gruesome death. In much the same way, McHale had trapped Abby.

And Captain Whitaker had insisted on him doing reconnaissance over the Rim. It was almost as if he knew something important awaited them. And that dream he had about Poplar Bluff the night before he found Abby—how could all of this have been mere happenstance?

Besides those signs, Elda Mae said the Almighty must have deigned for the two of them to meet. *"Good comes to us when we are ready to accept it."*

A yearning twisted his insides as he helped Abby up on Docker before the final descent to the Allens'. As their hands touched, her eyes shone. He looked away, spied something along the path, and squatted to inspect.

"Look here, a gift for you."

"Black walnuts! They smell like Missouri. I never knew they grew around here."

Abby squeezed his arm as she scrambled down. "You always lead me to good things. Luscious berries, the Rim top, and now, black walnuts."

Fire raged under his ribs, but his throat scratched like dry hay. "What is it, Martin?"

"I—here, we can fill my hat." He searched for another container while she gathered. Gigantic sycamore leaves littered the path, as wide as both his hands.

With their smooth gray-white bark and leathery leaves, sycamores prospered in this pungent pine forest. Wind and rain mottled their bark, but they stood firm, arms twisting every which way toward the sun. Like a big old farmer, they might look awkward, yet hope flamed again as late afternoon coolness swept the land.

"Elda Mae will be thrilled, but it will take a week to get the odor off our hands." Abby poured a final handful onto the poncho. Her nearness scalded Martin.

He held out a leaf. "You deserve flowers or a fine necklace, Abby. I have pondered and pondered how I might ask you—"

"What is it you want to say, Martin?"

Darkness and light played over the path, reflecting summer and winter, morning and night, justice and oppression. Fred and Elda Mae still had no idea that Abby was safe. If they knew how close he and Abby lingered, Fred might understand, but Elda Mae would end his life faster than a poison arrow to the heart.

"Pardon my slowness with words. You—" He looked to the Rim as if for instructions. "If you would consider me a... a suitor—" He almost spit out the last word, hardly daring to look up, but when he did, tears washed those incredible gold flecks. Had he somehow managed to bring her even more pain?

But Abby stepped closer, her cheeks moist as a dewy sunrise. Martin raised a trembling finger to quell the flow.

"Dear Martin, you are the very best."

Despite his quaking, he reached for her. "Do you—do you mean—?"

"I mean *yes*, Martin. Yes, I will consider you a suitor—my one and only."

Under a starry showcase, a campfire beckoned. Fred and Elda Mae stayed for some time, and a shooting star inspired Fred to share a story.

"Ancient scholars saw shooting stars as lightning bolts streaking the sky while the gods battled. When they crashed, people took them as signs of divine wisdom."

"Where did you learn that?"

"Somewhere or other." He turned to Elda Mae with a yawn. "Come along now, dear. The birds will be calling me early in the morning."

"Good night to you both." Elda Mae's knee popped as she rose, and they headed toward the cabin.

"Fred led the way tonight—a rare occurrence. Those two are such opposites." Abby snuggled against Martin.

"But they seem so happy together."

"Yes. Sometimes I look back and wish—"

If her wish were in his power, he would surely find a way to grant it.

"When my beau died in the war, I had a prideful way of thinking. I assumed if I could understand why things happened, I could better endure the consequences."

"I always thought the same about Pa's death, so I kept expecting answers. But then Mama's cousin Greta perished in a sorry state. Her husband never treated her well, and after her funeral, Mama came home with a message from the sermon. *"I will restore to you the years the locusts have eaten."*

"She said finally Greta was free from the lies and pain that ate her up like locusts. But later, my sister Meta and I agreed that her freedom came too late. Why did her deliverance have to come in death? I guess we were impatient too."

Martin took Abby's hand. "But you are restored now, here on earth. You have your strength back and can start all over again."

Chapter Thirty-four

"How soon will you build your trading post?" Elda Mae made no attempt to hide the impatience in her tone.

Over a heaping bowl of elk stew, Captain Whitaker considered. He and Martin had worked for Fred all day. Now, after a late afternoon walk together, sitting beside Martin at the table made Abby's heart skip a beat.

"Umm." Captain Whitaker smiled with delight. "Mrs. Allen. How do you flavor your wonderful stew?"

"With native plants." Elda Mae maintained her focus. "And your trading post?"

"First, Martin and I must weigh possible sites, but this visit has supplied much-needed clarity. Dealing with Lola vexed me no end, so to maintain a calm exterior, I put my mind to the challenges at hand."

A visible shudder preceded Fred's comment. "How did you manage with her, and so quickly?"

"Lady Luck aided me. Who would have dreamed that as I moseyed down the mountain with Aldrich and Lola, along would come an army ambulance loaded for Fort Brevard, New Mexico? You cannot imagine my delight."

Elda Mae failed to contain herself. "You sent them on the ambulance?"

"Indeed. The major in charge willingly accommodated them. I might have gone on to Camp Reno then, but—"

Elda Mae leaned forward. "Something drew you here?"

With a bemused glance, Captain Whitaker referred her unspoken question to Martin. "My future entangles with yours, sergeant—how are we to answer?"

Martin reached for his milk glass as if he hadn't heard.

More agitated by the second, Elda Mae fidgeted and let go a sigh. Fred reached for her hand, but she drew it away.

Underneath the table, Abby touched Martin's hand. Declaring his intentions before a crowd would scarcely be easy. But he surprised her, squeezing her fingers the whole time.

"I had little hope that... ah... Miss Abby would have me for a suitor. But—" The lines in his forehead relaxed. "The Rim top inspired her to accept me, such as I am."

Elda Mae clutched her throat. "Then, you—you are betrothed?"

Martin gave Abby a long look. "You may consider it so."

"Oh my goodness." Elda Mae's sputter almost blotted out Captain Whitaker's statement.

"Thus our planning had become a bit more... er, complex."

"How so?"

Elda Mae had never seemed so impatient. Abby had to bite her tongue.

"In order to provide for the store, our location must be suitable." A faint twinkle entered Captain Whitaker's eyes. "Suitable to all of us—Martin, Abby, and me. And we hope it will prove convenient for you, as well. After all, are we not all family?"

Fred spoke up. "Absolutely, and the finest I can imagine."

Captain Whitaker allowed for a pause before commandeering the conversation once again. "First, we must conjure a name. We could combine our surnames and call the post Tolzaker's Exchange or perhaps Whitman Trading. What do you think, Martin?"

Martin reached for the biscuits. "I think another helping is in order."

"Oh, come now. This will be our first big important decision."

An idea occurred to Abby. "What about the Pine Creek Canyon Trading Post? Our trip to the Rim top convinced me this area is more canyon than valley."

"That has a pleasant ring. PCCTP—the letters even rhyme. We must decide soon and start building, for the Army will relieve us of our duties in the fall. In the meantime, though, I believe we both have leave time coming." He slid back his chair and draped his arm over the slats. "Martin, do you like the name? Of course, it would mean we must locate somewhere in these environs."

"Yes, but one other occurs to me. We could call it Rigel's Post."

Captain Whitaker gaped. "Why you old wizard—you figured out my name!"

While Martin grinned, he explained to the others. "At the war's outset, I challenged my men to guess my given name. No one ever did, though many attempted. But somehow, Martin has finally discerned it.

"Thanks to you, Miss Abby, we have also located some willing workers. Those men you accompanied down the trail are familiar with others who seek work. They happened on Lola, Aldrich, and me again during my exchange with the army ambulance.

"Sometimes things do work out as though planned in advance. Old Sam and his sidekick continued on to Camp Verde, but promised to return with able workers weary of the terrible disease outbreaks farther west. Though old Sam is past his building days, I can picture him and his sidekick making supply runs to the Salt Valley for us.

"I imagine they have faced every possible danger—nothing would waylay them." He mused some more. "Personally, I like the sound of Pine Creek Trading Post, but there is the matter of location. Meeting that ambulance opened my eyes."

"Sir?"

"I had no idea of the travel on that road. The surface is quite paved from all of the wagons. Considering the distance from New Mexico, voyagers might make good use of a rest stop around here."

Fred chimed in. "I have become expert at leveling rocky areas and would be delighted to offer my services."

"Offer accepted. We would need all possible help. And did I

hear that someone has single-handedly added a sturdy lean-to to this fine cabin?"

"Nothing I like better than a construction project, captain."

"It behooves us to explore some more, then. How about tomorrow, sergeant?"

"Yes. But I would like to know my reward for guessing your name."

"That may take some time. After all, many men have sought this prize through the years. Probably upwards of one hundred, so it seems to me that the original treasure must be multiplied. Perhaps—"

"Humph!" Elda Mae broke in. Turning to Martin and Abby, she blazed her question. "Have you chosen the date for your vows?"

Martin's cheeks flamed. "Not in detail, ma'am."

Captain Whitaker interjected, "It might take some time to find a preacher. I will check with the new colonel when we get back to camp—perhaps a chaplain is expected in the near future."

Fred folded a huge mound of blackberry jam into another slice of bread and made to bite into it. But Elda Mae growled his name through clenched teeth.

His amused smile matched the twinkle in his eyes. "Oh, yes—how could I forget? Dear friends, this seems an apt time for an announcement."

He rose and pulled a yellowed envelope from the bookcase across the room. "I may hold the answer in my hands." He pulled out a set of papers and thrust the top one toward Captain Whitaker. "Would you do me the honor of reading this?"

"As duly appointed chancellor of the Ohio Presbytery, I hereby pronounce one Frederick C. Allen ordained before God and man. As a preacher of the Gospel, he fulfills all responsibilities and privileges thereof."

He stared at Fred. Abby held her breath as the Captain continued.

"May the ministry of Frederick Charles Allen bring guidance to those who seek, succor to the oppressed, comfort to the dying, and hope to all who wait upon the Lord. Duly installed at Mount Abrams Presbyterian Parish, April 17, 1856."

Jaws dropped all around, and Captain Whitaker began, "But you—"

Fred chirped, "'Do not go where the path may lead, go instead where there is no path and leave a trail.' Ralph Waldo Emerson makes a living with his words; I make one with my birds."

Elda Mae burst out, "Fred and I humbly propose a wedding right here in our home."

Fred set two large gold coins on the table. "Miss Abby, I must share a providential provision. Maybe this windfall is meant to help you and Martin build your cabin and the trading post."

"I thought you gave those coins to Cactus Joe?"

"I attempted to, but he had already taken his leave of our fair territory. In my opinion, this circumstance gives justice its final say."

The warmth of Martin's hand calmed her, as it had earlier on their walk. Along the path, he explained his search for Captain Whitaker's name.

"A couple of nights ago, I recalled the names of the brightest stars. Rigel, in Orion, satisfied the captain's hints about hunting." Martin chuckled. "And now, you can help me guess what he named his horse. That may take us years."

Outside the cabin, sunlight stroked a clown woodpecker's comical head as he raised a ruckus. In this circle of friends, one final knot in Abby's stomach gave way. Not all of her questions had found answers, but the present moment held such promise, she could scarcely take it in.

The woodpecker paused its mad attack on the pine and suddenly, she realized all eyes were on her. Elda Mae and Fred still awaited an answer.

"Why, thank you. Martin and I..." Her voice broke at the inconceivable love that surrounded her. The emotion in Martin's eyes, Fred's beneficent grin, and Elda Mae's nurturing spirit declared that love. Even Captain Whitaker's disarming grin proclaimed commitment for the future. For a moment, she imagined several Tolzmann children calling him Uncle Rigel.

Surely all of this, along with the grace that had kept her through all her trials, would suffice for whatever lay ahead.

"We say yes."

"You will stand up for me, Captain, even though I guessed your name?"

"Indeed. Nothing could make me more proud."

"Then I would say we have all we need."

Just then an untimely elk bugled, and Captain Whitaker raised his milk glass. "Sergeant; Miss Abby—shall we drink to your new-found happiness?"

Epilogue

December, 1868

The delicate pale yellow—almost ivory—silk bodice boasted tiny pearl buttons Abby had re-sewn in a careful row. Roses Elda Mae embroidered around the hem made this a fitting garment for such an auspicious day.

Touching the fabric after bathing on the morning of the ceremony brought back a bevy of memories. Mama would approve of this simple but lovely dress, and she and Papa would be so pleased with Martin. Elda Mae did her best to provide a fitting connection with the past.

"You are like my daughter," she had replied when Abby objected to her offer to cut into her own nuptial gown. "Oh pshaw! When will I ever wear it again? Besides that, I have put on weight since Fred and I said our vows—how would I ever wiggle into it?" Her pretend movement brought forth a chuckle.

"This will be your special day, so you must have a beautiful dress. I can hardly wait to watch Martin's face when he sees you in it."

"Oh, but you are kind!"

"Not too many have called me that."

"Then they must not have known you well."

"You are the best gift Fred and I have ever been given, and to think of you and Martin living so close makes me smile. Fred has been beside himself with delight to think you will be sketching with him for some time to come."

"I am so happy about that, too—and my earnings will help us during this first year. I can hardly believe Mr. B agreed to Fred's proposal. To think of being paid anything at all, much less a full quarter per sketch!"

"You deserve every penny, my dear. And the men decided so quickly where to build the trading post. Captain Whitaker seems pleased to have his quarters in the back, and your new home lies just around the bend.

"Just in time, it now boasts a roof."

Carefully fitted floors and a window in each room—three in all. Abby could scarcely believe the men's handiwork. What joy to fashion curtains, a tablecloth, and spreads for the beds, with Elda Mae's supervision. Aunt Susan would be so proud.

Now, the men had laid the stone foundation for the trading post and had begun framing the walls. Once they left Camp Reno, the work began immediately. Those two went at it like beavers fashioning a dam.

"Abby, you had best get started." Elda Mae bustled in and pulled the drapes. "The men have come into the arbor, and Martin looks so…so fine. And nervous, I might add."

"Of course. He would rather have the attention on someone else."

"Yes. I would venture that Captain Whitaker oversaw his preparations today. I have never seen him so—clean-shaven."

That brought a chuckle. "No doubt."

"I would bet he suffered a mighty cold bath in the creek. But he would do anything for you."

"Hmm—I cannot believe my good fortune." Abby rose from her rocker. "All right, I will need your help with the buttons."

"Call me—I shall wait right outside your door."

Half an hour later, a radiant sun sparkled through the tall pines, making every single Manzanita leaf shine. Fred stood in the arbor, dignified and proper, while Captain Whitaker held out his elbow for Abby. In the dress re-fitted from her dear friend's wedding gown, she stepped from her room.

The look in Martin's eyes, filled with utmost devotion, defied description. Captain Whitaker made a pert stop and relinquished Abby's arm to her betrothed, Elda Mae positioned herself next to Abby, and the service began.

"*Even the darkest night will end, and the sun will rise.* Victor Hugo leaves us this summary concerning the difficulties his characters face, and Holy Writ substantiates the concept. Our mourning can be turned into dancing. Light conquers darkness, and ashes transform into beauty through the compassion of our gracious God.

"In one way or another, our lives all attest to this truth. Though this life includes suffering, the human spirit eternally hopes for better days."

As Fred paused for a moment to turn a page in his book, the deep breath Martin took matched the strength of his grip on Abby's hand. She leaned against his arm, so steady, so strong, and the image of her second journey to the Rim top passed before her.

He had planned everything, and their picnic had been even more perfect than she could have imagined. He had come back to see her again in November—caught the stagecoach on the way and the Army ambulance on the way back. Such a long, dusty trip, and all for her.

That day together had given her so many moments to recall in the past weeks and much to treasure as she looked forward to their life together. It was as if the intimacies of a long courtship had been magically rolled into that one unique outing. Martin stayed in the barn that night, and precious hours beside the campfire had only heightened her longing to spend the rest of their lives together.

"Dearly beloved, we gather here today in the sight of God and of this company to unite this man and this woman in holy matrimony..."

The Rim smiled down on them, a woodpecker made new holes in the barn over yonder, and the future shown as bright as the cheery yellow checked curtains that adorned the kitchen window in their freshly hewn cabin. In one finishing flourish, a turkey vulture floated overhead—a good omen, Elda Mae maintained.

Tears filled Abby's eyes as Fred continued. In that moment, Mama and Papa seemed near—always near at heart here in Arizona Territory.

Thanks

With grateful thanks to Lynn, Leslie, Ellen, Machelle, Jane, and others who have read this manuscript over its twelve years of development.

Thank you also to J. D. Winninger, who offered wisdom concerning the bovine species, and to Holly Schimmelpfennig for pertinent information about Poplar Bluff, Missouri. Finally, a hearty thank-you to Louis Kutcher, Associate Professor at University of Cincinnati Blue Ash College. What a joy to discover significant facts through individuals living in a portion of my setting!

About the Author

Words have always been comfort food for Gail Kittleson. After instructing expository writing and English as a Second Language, she began writing seriously. Intrigued by the World War II era, Gail creates women's historical fiction from her northern Iowa home and also facilitates writing workshops/retreats.

She and her husband, a retired Army chaplain, enjoy grandchildren and in winter, Arizona's Mogollon Rim Country. You can count on Gail's heroines to ask honest questions, act with integrity, grow in faith, and face hardships with spunk.

Visit Gail online at www.GailKittleson.com

Also available from

WordCrafts Press

The Pruning
  by Jan Cline

Angela's Treasures
  by Marian Rizzo

Pipe Dream
  by K.L. Collins

Katie's Plain Regret
  by Sara Harris

Grace Extended
  by Paula K. Parker

www.WordCrafts.net